BOOK 3 – HEAT & HORIZON

TEMPEST WICK

Hot Behind

www.TempestWick.com

First edition.
ISBN: 979-8-218-91051-8

Published by Tempest Wick
United States of America
Cover design by Evgeniia Gurcheva
Interior formatting by Lorna Reid
Manuscript editing by Sarah Waterman

Important Note For Readers

Hot Behind is part of an interconnected standalone contemporary romance series. While this novel can be read on its own, it **contains spoilers for the first two books in the Heat & Horizon collection. The Heat & Horizon Series:**

At Boiling Point
Salt & Smoke
Hot Behind
More stories to come.

Each book follows a new couple navigating love, longing, and the places that shape us, from kitchens simmering with spice to salt-kissed shores. These stories stand alone, but for readers who journey through them all, familiar faces return and deeper connections emerge.

An interconnected series spanning coasts, continents, and kitchens, where heat lingers, hearts are tested, and love rises like steam.

For the ones who kept asking for his story.
This one is for you.

Chapter 1

I JUST WANT IN

Have they even looked at my fucking résumé?

I skid my skateboard to a stop outside Le Début, the top French spot on this side of San Francisco. My knife roll's cinched tight across my back, the blades inside worth more than everything in my shitty apartment combined.

White tablecloths. Wine glasses. Silver set in military precision for tonight's guests.

Dark. Quiet. Untouchable.

You need to work French if you're going to move up, Kyle, Ritchie tells me—weekly.

Get the fuck out of this shithole seafood house, Ritchie tells me, also weekly.

So, I wrote the résumé. Sent the email. Now, I wait.

"I need four swordfish, three crab—all day!" Vic yells, slapping the ticket into the rail.

"Heard," I call, sliding the pan off the flame to check the temp on my fish.

"Chef, make that five sword, all day."

"Heard."

Plate. Garnish. Wipe.

"Order up." I slide the plates into the pass, wrist flicking with muscle memory.

"Thank you, Kyle." Macy sing-songs through the expo window. *That smile.*

No, Kyle. Don't even...

Ritchie nudges my elbow. "You heard anything yet?"

"What?" I blink, still plating my crab.

"Le Début. They call?"

I shake my head and stab the ticket through the spindle. "Order up." Heat sticks to my skin as I step off the line and into the walk-in.

The cold air bites at my lungs, but it's not enough to kill the fire screaming in my head.

Butter... butter... where the fuck is the—

"Incompetence!" I bark, spotting it shoved behind a crate of wilted lettuce. The lid is cracked and barely on.

"Fucking stoners," I mutter, slamming the door open into the heat and noise. Back to the line. Same chaos. Same lazy hands.

I yank out the empty Cambro of butter and drop the full one in its place. Same shit, different shift.

Ritchie leans close. "Listing still up?"

"Yeah," I snap.

"Kyle, we need two Rockefeller, one scampi!" Vic calls.

I drop a pan on the burner, toss in a slab of butter. It hisses. So do I.

"Maybe it's me," I mutter. *Maybe I'm too scared to admit it.*

Ritchie slides the oysters under the salamander, jaw tight, eyes steady on the broiling mollusks.

He smirks my way. "No fucking way."

~~~

The street's mostly empty when I skate past Le Début on my way home. No guests now. Just shadows moving behind those spotless windows—folding napkins, breaking down stations, checking lists. The low light inside glows gold and soft, spilling onto the sidewalk like butter from a hot pan.

I slow down. I always do. The clink of glassware, a burst of laughter, the faint scrape of metal on metal—closing sounds. Another perfect service wrapped.
~~~

It pulls at me every time: the hum of their night settling, the quiet pride in it.

I hover at the edge of that glow, close enough to feel the warmth but never close enough to belong.

Their laughter fades, but I'm still standing there, one foot on the board, one foot off, staring through the glass like it's a portal between two worlds.

I picture myself at station six. Chef Henri Vallois calling orders down the line with that sharp, quiet voice that's already in my head from watching his cooking shorts on YouTube.

I'd kill it. I'd work like my life depended on it. Because it kind of fucking does.

But I don't go in. I just stand there, arms crossed over my knife roll, until the cold starts to creep in under my hoodie. Then I push off again, wheels humming over cracks in the pavement, headlights washing over my shadow as I head back to my shitty-ass apartment.

When I get home, my fingers still smell like garlic, and there are two new burns on my forearm.

Still, I grab my phone.

Le Début posted twenty minutes ago.

A close-up of tonight's amuse-bouche—a single seared scallop on parsnip purée, topped with something shaved and stupidly delicate.

I zoom in and study it like it's porn. The sauce is clean, not a drop out of place. *Chef Theo plated that. I know it.*

Next photo. Two cooks tagged in a back-of-house selfie. Wine in hand, linen aprons streaked with sauce, hair tied back, grins loose and proud.

I stare too long. I know their names. I know their fucking *stations.*

God—who does this? Who memorizes a restaurant's staff lineup like it's a goddamn band? What the fuck is wrong with me?

I toss the phone across the bed and it bounces, screen up, glowing in the dark. It's open to a photo of the duck confit from last weekend. The one I could taste in my sleep.

I fall asleep faster than usual. Maybe it was the two glasses of box wine, maybe skipping dinner again, but the dream comes quick.

A pristine, stainless-steel kitchen I've never seen before. Everything gleams. It's so quiet I can hear the precise click of plating tweezers between my fingers. The cool steel presses into my skin—steady, familiar. *Click… click… click.*

I'm garnishing. With actual tweezers. It's not a fantasy about sex, fame, or money. It's shaved fennel, microgreens, and truffle curls landing on artful dishes with surgical precision.

I have tweezers in real life. They're in my knife roll, top interior pocket, right-hand zip. I've never used them in a professional kitchen—too much risk of being called a pretentious fuck.

But tonight, in my dream, I belong there. It's quiet and focused. Sacred.

I come to with my hand still curled like I'm holding the damn tweezers. The room's too quiet, and my chest is tight. My dick's hard—I'm not proud of that. But last week, Chef Henri Vallois posted a shot on the Le Début page—a simple dish, elegant as sin, the final curl of truffle placed *just so* by a gloved hand holding tweezers.

That hand might as well have been wrapped around my cock.

Chapter 2

HEARD

Same window, same knives strapped across my back. Same goddamn disappointment filling my chest. But this time, the golden glow is gone. It's morning—bright and unforgiving.

I catch my reflection in the glass. A hoodie, ratty chef pants, beat-up skate shoes. One broken shoelace tied in a desperate double knot. Hair a mess. Face still puffy from sleep and… yeah. Regret.

I don't belong in there.

Down the alley, the delivery truck is unloading for the day. Plastic crates clatter on the cement. I lean against the cool brick and watch—a voyeur, again—into a life that isn't mine.

Chefs are out there laughing, slicing open cartons, smelling produce, tasting for freshness. Leather-strap aprons. *Fuck.* I want leather.

I'm torturing myself.

I drop my skateboard, and just as I start to push off, the reflection catches me. I can't see them clearly inside—but I can see *me.* And I look like someone who should stop chasing things that were never meant for him.

~~~

"Where's Louis?" I look over at the empty raw bar, then back at Vic.

"I don't know, Kyle—something about his car… running late… Who the fuck knows." He shrugs, hoisting plates onto the shelf.
~~~

I hold my hands out. "Who's running the goddamn raw bar tonight then?"

"Looks like you and Ritchie-boy," he calls over his shoulder as he disappears into the back.

I pinch the bridge of my nose. Why don't I tend bar while I'm at it?

Fuck.

The ice dumps from the bucket with an aggressive crash, burying the oysters.

"What are you doing?" Ritchie asks, confused.

"Icing oysters. What does it look like I'm doing?"

"Did Louis not show up again?" He takes the empty bucket from me.

"Yeah, the guy needs to go. This is total bullshit." I spread the crushed ice around the oysters, keeping them organized by variety.

"No call, I take it?" he leans in.

I shoot him a glare before pushing past him into the walk-in to search for… What the fuck was I searching for? Lemons. Of course. Next to the goddamn beef tenderloin—right where they belong.

It's like working in the dementia wing of a nursing home.

Fuck.

The night goes according to plan: fast, furious, and with a menu that underwhelms me as much as spreading margarine on stale wheat toast.

Harsh fluorescent lights beat down while Alice in Chains' "Man in the Box" blasts through the speaker. I scour the flat top with my grill brick like it's going to transport me to another universe if I scrub hard enough. Hopefully, it takes me to a better fucking lifetime.

My phone vibrates in my back pocket and I stop the madness.

It's my roommate, Collin. He's a bartender over at Glass and Brine. As much as he claims to be a sommelier, boasting about his "training," I know better. He's a bartender.

"What's up?" I answer.

"Hey, man. Come out tonight?"

I glance at my watch. Then at my pants. My shoes. The whole outfit screams "line cook on life support," and I know for a fact

Collin's crew will show up looking like they're hosting the goddamn Catalina Wine Mixer.

"Yeah, sorry. Not tonight. It's been a shit day, man. Thanks, though."

"Aww, come on, Kyle. You haven't come out in over a month. One drink. We're just shooting pool at Lizzy's. You don't even have to change." He says it softly, glasses clinking behind him, some moody lounge bass line playing.

I sigh. "Lemme think about it. I'll text you if I change my mind."

"Sweet—that's a yes," he says, and hangs up before I can correct him.

Dim lights. Soft music. *God, I want that.* I stare at the screen for a second, still leaning against the counter, then start scrolling.

I swipe to GigPro. Let's see what's out there.

Prep—no.

Dish—hell no.

Sous—*hello.*

Oh… Vellium.

Collin dragged me there once. No sign, just a black door with a single brass "V." Inside? Silence. Servers in thigh-highs and three-inch heels. I actually thought it was a secret high-society strip joint at first.

The plates looked like museum installations, and one bite of a roasted beet almost had me reevaluating my entire culinary career.

Nope. Not my style. Even if it's definitely tweezer-worthy.

"What are you looking at?" Ritchie hands me a Bud Light.

I take it. It's a far cry from the back-office merlot at Le Début I daydream about, but cold is cold.

I crack the tab and take a sip. "Opportunities… I dunno." I shake my head. "You almost done back there?" I point to his station, or whatever you'd call it. We all do everything here.

"Yeah, almost." He nods toward my phone. "Anything good?"

I hold it up and down half my beer before answering. "Nah. Just that Vellium place. Sous. I guess I'll have to beat the streets. Go hunt for what I want." I shake my head, voice lower. "Maybe I'm fucking

Red Lobster material after all." I laugh. "I mean, I can make scampi in my sleep… and those biscuits? They're the fucking bomb, man."

He claps a hand to my shoulder. "There are hundreds of fine dining gigs in this city. Go get you a piece and stop that shit." He pushes off the counter and walks off. "The French are snobs anyhow."

I stand there, twisting the can in my hand, flipping the tab back and forth until it weakens and snaps off.

What I really want to cook is Asian, but I can't just walk into a dim sum house and apply. Look at me—I have zero Asian training, and the language barrier would wreck me. I need to start in French. It's the base. All culinary training starts there—we know this.

Maybe I need to suck it up, take the fucking money, and go to school.

I grab the grill brick instead and scrub that thought out of my mind. Scrub the thoughts of my father, my inheritance, my inability to make it up the ladder with skill alone.

I'm fucking determined. I don't need his help.

I scrub.

~~~

I walk into the sound of pool balls cracking. Nirvana's playing on the jukebox, and there's no stress, no heat lamps, no expo tickets stabbing me in the gut. No shucking Louis' oysters while tossing shrimp scampi at the same time. No kitchen heat. Just stale beer and the sound of my shoes sticking to old linoleum.

"Holy shit, he lives!" Collin yells across the bar, cue in hand.

I love Collin—I really do—but he's, well… Collin. He's wearing a blazer. A fucking *blazer.* Looks like he just left a finance bro mixer, not in a dive bar with duct tape on the barstools. His cuffs are rolled, his collar's popped, and his whole vibe screams, "I text women 'You up?' at 2 a.m."

The kind of guy who owns six pairs of Armani dress shoes and still can't get laid—probably because he talks about wine like he invented the grape.

I wave, and he meets me at the bar. His cologne drags behind
~~~

him—cedar and sandalwood. Probably eighty bucks an ounce at Saks.

Me? Garlic, fish, and stainless steel cleaner—three bucks at restaurant supply.

"What are you drinking? I've got a tab. Put it on mine." Collin gestures toward the bartender.

I glance at his glass… Stella. In the signature chalice. I'm honestly shocked they have it here.

"Can I get a PBR, please?" I ask, placing a five on the counter.

"Ahh… moving up from that boxed varietal you've been drinking at home, I see," he jokes, taking a sip.

"Actually," I say, taking the can from the bartender, "it's a box of Côtes du Rhône—just a red blend. Bright acid, little thyme on the finish. Went perfect with the sourdough I made last night." I shrug. "But yeah, no cork."

Collin's expression freezes for half a second, like he's buffering.

I nod toward the pool table. "Let's play."

It doesn't take long before I'm leaning over the table, lining up the eight ball, when someone slaps my ass with the cue stick.

"Jesus, Collin." I glare behind me.

"That was an encouragement tap, Berkley. Good luck."

"I'm gonna shove this PBR can up your ass, man." I point at him with my cue. "Don't get shitty 'cause I'm winning."

One of his yacht rock buddies calls from the far end, "Hey, Chef Daddy… tonight's special's coming in hot… one o'clock."

I look down the line of the cue and spot Macy standing at the bar.

Collin leans against the table, his voice low. "Still seeing her?"

"No." I tap the right side of the table with the cue tip. "Right pocket," I say softly, eyes on the ball as I sink the eight.

Laughter erupts, and I slap the twenty clean out of his hand with a shit-eating grin.

"That's right," I say, chalking the cue. "Chef Daddy knows how to finish."

"Bet Macy knows that too," someone mutters.

The laughter turns to oooohs and shoulder slaps. My jaw ticks before I down the rest of my beer and grab a new one off the table.

"I don't shit where I cook, thanks." I lie, scanning the group.

At least I put a stop to it months ago. She fought me on it—*God, did she ever.* The texting, the calling, the seductive eyes in the pass. The sneak-grab bullshit in the walk-in.

All it'll take is a good buzz, those lashes, and my dick's back in her mouth. Then I'm starting from scratch… again. Peeling her off me, out of my bed, out of my kitchen while I'm trying to eat fucking toast.

"Do you want to go to a movie, Kyle?"

No. I don't want a relationship. I don't *need* a relationship. I'm not made for one.

Collin toasts me. "You're tense, Berkley. You need to get laid… or hired. Preferably both."

"You offering?" I smirk, taking a long pull of my beer.

"I'm a generous man," he winks.

I toss a bar napkin at his stupid popped collar and check my phone. One missed call. My world stutters.

Unknown number.

I've said "heard" a thousand times. But staring at that notification, for the first time in my life it feels like it's being said *back.*

Chapter 3
THE PASS

I step into the alley beside Lizzy's, back pressed against the cold brick wall, my breath fogging in the air.

One missed call. *Unknown number.*

I tap the voicemail with a thumb that's suddenly gone sweaty.

"Hi, Kyle Berkley? This is Natalie from Le Début. Chef Vallois has reviewed your résumé and would like to offer you a stage—starting this Wednesday. Please call us back tomorrow to confirm if you are available. Merci."

My stomach drops straight through my shoes. The alley's silent. I swear even the distant hum of traffic cuts out for a second—like the world hit mute just to let me have this moment.

I blink. Rewind it and listen again.

"...would like to offer you a stage..."

I laugh. Just once. One of those stupid, breathless half-laughs that escapes before you can stop it.

I *didn't* fuck this up. They read it and they called.

I stare down at the phone like it's holding the blueprint to my future.

Then I whisper and smile to no one."Holy shit."

~ ~ ~

I burst back through the door like a guy who just got laid, found a hundred bucks, and hit every green light all at once.

Collin's lining up a shot at the pool table, eyebrows furrowed like he's solving global hunger with geometry, when I slap him on the ass.

"Yo," I say, trying not to sound out of breath or manic, or like someone whose entire life just changed.

He glances up, shocked. "What the hell? Did you leave your balls out there or something?" He points to the table with the cue.

"I got the call."

He straightens. "Wait—what call?"

"Le Début. They want me for a stage. Starting Wednesday."

For once, he's speechless. Then, "No. Fucking. Way."

I nod. "Yes. Fucking. Way."

Collin tosses the cue stick onto the felt. "Barkeep!" he shouts into the air. "This man needs a real drink!"

"I'm still drinking PBR," I say, folding down his ridiculous collar, smiling.

"Shut up. You're going to be a fancy French bitch now."

"Well, not yet. And… 'barkeep'? Who are you, Dean Martin? You're a bartender, for fuck's sake. Why did you say that?"

"I'm a *sommelier*, man." He narrows his eyes.

I drape my arm over his shoulder. "Okay, let's grab a beer, Dom Pérignon, and celebrate. Rack the balls again, and let me shake you down for another twenty."

I stand at the bar waiting for our beers and swipe to Ritchie's contact.

Kyle: I got the call. Stage starts Wed.

I slide the phone into my pocket, toss the cash across the bar, and head back to the pool table with our drinks.

"So," Collin says, "when you get it, will you even give that shithole notice?"

I take a long draw from my beer. "I don't burn bridges, even the crappy ones, so yeah." I shrug. "Vic's terrible at running that place, but I'm the one who chose to stay too long. I should've left a year ago."

Collin claps a hand to my shoulder. "You're going to kick ass, man. You're ready for this. You've been training in our kitchen like you're auditioning for *Top Chef* for years."

"Thanks."

The table clears, and he nods toward the sea of green felt. "You ready for me to humble you?" he says, smirking over his fancy-ass Stella glass—now missing half its lettering. Reads more like *Sle la.*

I laugh low and throaty. "Game on." I chalk up the lesser of the warped cues in the joint.

Collin lifts the triangle rack gently off the balls, moving out of my line of sight, and I line up the break. Then my eyes lose focus on the shot, shifting upward... to *her.*

Macy.

Jeans hugging the lines of her legs and ass. Blonde hair waterfalling over her shoulders. I can still feel the way it wrapped around my hand, slipping like silk between my fingers.

Her eyes meet mine. Navy blue.

Fuck.

I drop my gaze back to the table and break. Hard. So hard it redirects the blood flow that's rushing south.

I play like I've got something to prove—precision, silence, full focus. Until I miss it and it's Collin's turn. I step back, and Macy's there. Right beside me, like Velcro.

"Hey. How was work tonight?" she asks, voice light—like she didn't once have her mouth on me in the walk-in. Her perfume hits—tropical and sugary. She smells like the beach, and I want to be the sand stuck to her skin.

I reach past her for my beer. "Sucked. Short staffed like usual." I shrug. "But it's over."

My eyes take a slow tour—head to toe, toe to head. "You were off tonight?"

She seems surprised I even noticed. "Yeah. Helped my mom with some errands." She sips whatever fruity drink she's holding. "Nothing exciting."

That's the thing—she's not exciting. Not really. Just pretty and available and sweet when she wants to be. But there's nothing under the surface. Nothing real. And I've spent too many nights letting *nothing* climb into my bed and pretend to mean something.

The sex? Fire. The connection? Paper-thin.

I want more. I want *substance.* I want someone who looks at me like they want to know everything. I want to sink into someone like smoke—be felt, not just used.

Collin misses. "Damn, I set you up, Chef Daddy." He winces, chalking his cue like he thinks he's getting another turn. He won't.

I wink and run the rest of the table. A light tap with the cue tip. "Right side pocket."

Then I sink the eight… again.

"Damn, he kicks your ass every time, Collin," someone calls from the peanut gallery.

Collin slaps another twenty into my hand.

"Always a pleasure, friend," I smirk.

He glances at Macy, then at me, lowering his voice. "Should I stay out longer?"

I scoff. "Nah. I'm heading home in a minute."

"Alright." He claps my shoulder. "Good game, asshole," he says louder, smirking as he heads toward the bar with the guys to settle his tab.

I turn toward her—her hand wrapped tight around an empty drink, her blue eyes slowly untying my chef pants without touching me.

I reach around her for my beer on the shelf. Her hair sweeps past my chin. Her scent hits me again, and suddenly I'm lying next to her at the damn beach, watching her polished red nail trace over the ink on my arm. Long, slow strokes.

My pulse kicks. My dick follows.

I'm so fucked.

"So… I was thinking." Her voice drops—soft, sweet, already sliding into my mouth. "You want to come back to my place?" She looks up at me with those damn eyes—full of fire and every reason I should walk away.

I'm caught between the red nails, the plump lips, the daring eyes. The trifecta. The Bermuda Triangle of sexual frustration I call *Macy.*

Goddamn it.

This… this is the line. Between being stupid and sinking into something familiar—someone hot and willing. Or actually being smart and going home alone to jerk off in the shower.

"I… I don't know if that's a great idea, Mace," I stammer, borderline daring her to change my mind. "You know what we talked about. I just—"

"I know, Kyle." Her tone shifts—serious, soft, knowing. "I know what you want. I'm not standing here for that."

Her nail drags lazily over my chest, flicking across my nipple like she owns it.

My breath stutters. "Mace…" I shake my head, swallowing hard. "I don't—"

She presses a finger to my mouth. "Shhh… just come home with me. It's been a while. We both want this. It's okay."

I can't stop staring at her lips—the way they part, her tongue slipping out slow enough to ruin me.

And then—they're on mine.

Soft. Warm. Familiar. She tastes like orange, mango, pineapple. Like a goddamn sex on the beach.

While my dick books a flight to Jamaica, my hand's already in her hair, my mouth pressing deeper into hers. Her tongue finds mine—choreographed, practiced—like we've done this a thousand times.

Because we have. But then—

That moment in the walk-in flashes in brutal HD.

"Macy, this just isn't working. Us. I'm sorry." Her face when I said it. The way it carved something sharp down the middle of me.

I tear my mouth away, forehead pressed to hers, hand still gripping her hip like muscle memory won't let go.

"Macy… fuck, baby. I—I just can't."

She studies my face. She's not disappointed. It's something sharper. Hungrier. Challenge.

"I get it. Just not tonight." She kisses me softly—one last brush of lips, then drags her thumb along my jaw, gentle as a sigh, before turning and walking out, leaving me standing there hard as hell and heavy with regret.

"I'm out," I call to Collin, lifting a hand as I head for the door.

He raises his arms. "What happened? That looked like a sure thing."

I shake my head. "Nah. Heading home, man."

I flip my hat backwards and push off into the night. The California air is cool against my face as I carve down the winding streets. Just me, the swoosh of my wheels, my breath, my heartbeat—and Natalie's voicemail looping in my head like a brand-new playlist.

I fly through a quiet intersection and nearly get clipped by a Prius. The horn blares, and I throw up my hands. "Sorry, dude. Chef Daddy's got places to be." I laugh—loud, full, and maybe a little unhinged.

Back home, the dim light on the entryway table greets me. I toss my keys into the ceramic bowl, and they clatter like a bell announcing something sacred.

Shoes off. Backpack on the chair. Knife roll on the counter. I unbuckle the flap and roll it open like a ritual. There they are—my lineup. Each one tucked tight in its slot—six years of hustle, gifts, trade-ups, and late-night obsessions. My two chef's knives. The Japanese blade Ritchie gave me for my birthday. My santoku, which feels like an extension of my hand. Filet. Paring. Bread. Offset spat. My plating tweezers—*fuck yes.*

I grab a beer, crack it open, and put on some music. Low and dirty. Industrial beats and basslines. The perfect soundtrack for sharpening.

I lay out the stones, add water, and get to work. Long, even strokes. A rhythm builds—steady, entrancing—and my mind drifts: Dishes I haven't made yet. Sauces I haven't reduced. Proteins I haven't seared. A life I haven't lived.

But I will.

When the blades are gleaming, I dry them, oil the handles, and wipe down the roll. One by one, I slide them back in—rested and ready. I roll them up and strap the flap tight. No gaps. No fuckups.

I dig into my bag and pull out my clogs. Greasy and grimed.

I scrub them in the sink with dish soap and a utility brush until they look almost respectable.

I check my watch. 1:25.

I strip down and step into the shower. The water hits scalding hot—steam rising, fogging the mirror, fogging everything.

I brace against the tile, one hand flat to the wall, eyes closed. Pressure hits me straight in the chest.

Her hair brushing past my face—I can still smell her.

I tip my head back, shampoo sliding down my spine. God, I can still feel her in here—her mouth on my neck, her hand on my cock.

"You like that, baby?"

Her, on her knees in front of me. Red lips stretched around me, wet and hot. Blue eyes looking up. Water running down my chest.

Again, those damn eyes. Distracting me the next day through the pass as I try not to burn garlic, fish—everything I touch.

You liked that last night?

But then—something shifts. It's not her I'm thinking about. Not anymore.

I'm on the line. *The* line. *Their* line.

Heat. Flash of steel. Flame licking the edges of a sauté pan. The rhythmic whisking of a velvety velouté. The bark of "Yes, Chef." My towel swipe. The perfect wipe of a plate's rim.

The pass.

"Order up."

And then I come hard and fast and silent.

I lean into the tile, my breath shaking out of me.

God, I'm such a fucking nerd. Because yeah, I might be twisted, but I know exactly what turns me on.

Chapter 4

BODY OF DUCK, BLOOD OF CHERRY JUS

"Thanks for the ride. I just didn't want to roll up on my skateboard, ya know?" I shrug.

"You got this," Collin says, fist-bumping me from the driver's seat of his vintage BMW. He's still in his grandpa pajamas—like, *actual* matching pajamas. And, of course, driving shoes. Fucking driving shoes. Who even owns those?

Collin. Obviously.

I glance down at my watch. 8:15. They said 8:30.

Perfect.

I stand at the door—the same pristine glass I've been staring through for weeks. Same reflection. But this time, I see something different.

Hope.

A smile tugs at my lips as I clutch my knife roll a little tighter.

It's dark inside except for a sliver of light bleeding from the back kitchen. The front door's locked—of course.

So, I head down the alley toward the soft thump of music spilling from the propped-open back door, held open by a mop bucket that looks like it's been through some shit.

I knock.

"Hello?" I lean into the opening.

"Yep?" a voice calls. A guy about my age swings the door wider. "Can I help you, man?"

"I'm your stage today?" Not really a question—more like a hopeful confession.

"Oh—right on, man. Come in." He steps aside and gestures at the floor. "Watch it, I just mopped. Spilled a whole-ass Cambro of duck fat. I'm gonna get ripped a new asshole when Chef walks in. Fuck."

I step carefully—the floor's still slick.

"You use degreaser?" I ask.

"Shit. *No.*" He smacks his forehead like he's in a *Looney Tunes* short.

I chuckle and clap a hand to his shoulder. "Here—let me help." I set my knife roll on the stainless and hold out my hand. "I'm Kyle, by the way."

"Joe. I'm dish. And clumsy as fuck." He winces.

"I gotchu, Joe." I grin. "Happens to the best of us."

We're mid-clean when she walks in.

Black chef coat. Dark hair pulled back into a tight braid. A steady, confident presence that hits before she even speaks.

"Ahh, you must be Kyle." She offers her hand.

I shift the mop handle to my left and take it. "I am. Sorry—I got a little sidetracked helping Joe here."

She returns the smile, then glances at the clock. 8:30. "Right on time. I'm Natalie. I'll show you around."

Then, to Joe—"Sorry, I'm stealing your new friend."

"Yes, Chef. I've got it from here." Joe nods at me. "Thanks for your help, Kyle."

"Anytime."

My chest tightens—but in the best way.

I'm *here.* In the kitchen I've watched on YouTube and stalked on Instagram Reels. Post after post. I've mentally photoshopped myself into this place a hundred times. I've whisked roux, seared scallops, pulled a cassoulet from the oven like it was mine. I've already had family meal with Natalie, traded inside jokes—she just doesn't know it yet.

As she walks me through the kitchen, she's all movement and

muscle memory—flicking on hoods, firing up ovens, clipboard in one hand, coffee in the other.

"So, what made you want to stage here?" she asks.

"I want to be proficient in French," I say. Steady voice, steady pulse.

"Good answer. We like proficient here." She raises a brow—sharp, amused. "Follow me… with that." She nods to a dishpan full of tiny mugs and saucers designed for people who drink coffee with their pinky up.

"Sure." I trail behind her as she moves, stopping briefly at the bar to gesture toward the coffee station.

I set the pan down. She waves me onward.

"So—you'll be working with Felix this morning on prep. He should be here any minute to help with the delivery. You can jump in and unload." She stops suddenly, turning to face me.

"You're here for two days?"

"Three."

Her expression shifts—surprised, then pleased. "Sweet. We're short-staffed Friday." A nod. "Cool."

She keeps moving, talking as she goes. "You'll be with Chef Theo tonight and tomorrow. Friday…" she pauses, lips twisting.

I catch it. "Is there something I should know?"

She tilts her head. "Not necessarily. He's just… Vallois. Strict and particular. Just don't fuck up."

She flashes a smile—right as a head pokes into the dining room.

"Chef, the truck's here."

"On the way," she calls back, then looks at me. "Let's get this day started, Kyle."

~~~

"Fine, even chop on that onion, Kyle." Felix doesn't even slow down—barely a glance as he passes behind me.

"Yes, Chef."

I've been chopping for three hours—onions, porcini, more onions. It's beaver bootcamp. And I fucking *love* it.
~~~

I'm not zoning out—I'm tuning in. The soft thud of the walk-in door. The clinking of pans. The rhythm of the line.

Discussions of recipes swirl around me, and I'm mentally filing every detail like I'm running the Dewey Decimal System in my brain. The voices I've only ever heard on podcasts, seen on reels, watched on food TV—they're right behind me.

I'm fucking giddy with electricity and waiting for my next order.

The kitchen hums with a quiet rhythm—knives tapping, fans whirring, music playing softly in the background.

Then Chef Theo walks in.

Like the Messiah, if the Messiah wore tailored chef whites, smelled faintly of smoked paprika and cedarwood, and moved like a man who'd already plated his final dish and set down his knife for the last supper.

He's younger than I expected—maybe late thirties, but he carries a quiet authority that makes time feel slower when he enters.

Someone reaches over and turns the music down. Not off. Just… enough. Not because he asked, but because it feels like the right thing to do.

The chatter trims, and the air sharpens. Not with fear. With *presence.*

Chef Theo doesn't command the room. He invites it to rise to a new level—excellence.

He moves through the kitchen, checking stations, nodding once at Felix, another time at the saucier, before stopping directly in front of me.

I freeze, half a shallot in.

He scans my board, then meets my eyes. "Nice work," he says. "Good knife discipline."

"Thank you, Chef," I reply, heart doing stupid gymnastics in my chest.

He gives the smallest nod—the ghost of a smile, then moves on. No drama. No theatrics. Just… Chef Theo.

~~~

It's 4:30.
~~~

The air shifts again, different from this morning's rhythm and hush. Now it's tension simmering under the skin. The kind that builds before service, before the first ticket drops, when the adrenaline hits, and you're nothing but knowledge, instinct, and the sheer will to make it through the night.

Theo steps into the center of the kitchen, clipboard in hand. Not a yell, not a clap—just a look. And everyone comes.

Line cooks. Prep team. The hostess with the septum ring. What I'm guessing is the pastry chef, already stress-eating a baggie of almonds. Even the dish pit crew dries their hands and drifts in like summoned altar boys.

I find a spot in the back—haven't earned my way up front. Try to look casual while basically vibrating out of my skin.

Chef Theo clears his throat. "Alright. Tonight's specials."

Silence falls like a damn curtain at a kids' dance recital. Even the dishwasher hits pause on the rinse cycle—some kind of collective, involuntary reverence radiating from Theo like steam off a balsamic reduction.

"We're 86'ing the cassoulet—cod came in pristine. We're doing it with a champagne beurre blanc, confit lemon, roasted leeks. Tight sear—don't let it steam. Let the sauce do the talking, chefs."

He flips the page.

"Duck breast. Smoked cherry jus. Don't go heavy on the acid—let the endive do the balance."

Someone in the back murmurs a soft, "Amen."

I want to laugh. I feel like I'm having a religious experience. What's next—holy eucharist?

Theo keeps rolling. "Flat iron's on. Steak frites. We're going traditional—maître d'hôtel butter, shoestrings, bordelaise. Don't overthink it. Just cook it right."

I'm nearly breathless. The sacred service rundown. *The Gospel According to Theo.* Spoken with quiet authority, absorbed like scripture. No flair. No theatrics. Just truth.

He finishes and looks up. "That's it. Clean hands, clean minds. Let's go."

And just like that, the congregation disperses to break bread—a cheap, buttery Italian loaf served with lasagna. Family meal. Something we don't get at High Tide. There, you eat the fuck-ups. And if you have time, you make a fuck-up—just so you can eat.

I'm still buzzing as everyone drifts back to their duties, disposable cutlery and biodegradable plates clattering into the bin.

I stand jobless and without a purpose, still high from Chef Theo's rundown—those dishes etched into my brain like the Ten Commandments. Duck with smoked cherry jus. Steak frites. Bordelaise. I'm ready. I've never felt more ready.

Part of me expects someone to thrust a tray of scallops into my hands and say, *"Show us what you've got, rookie."*

Instead, I get Felix. He slides up beside me, arms crossed, smirk already locked in.

"You look like you're about to be knighted. Or sacrificed."

I blink. "Was just… taking it all in."

He scoffs. "Well, un-take it. You're with me now."

I follow him toward the back, trying not to look too eager. "What station?"

He laughs—actually pauses to laugh at me. "Station? Oh no, no, no. You're floating."

"…Floating?"

He starts counting on his fingers. "Runner. Fetcher. Ice guy. Plastic wrap. Hotel pans? That's you." He taps my shoulder like a coach sending in the second-string.

It hits like a wet rag across the face. All that prep. All that "*good knife discipline.*"

"But I thought—"

Felix cuts me off without even looking back. "You thought you were getting garde? Vallois would sooner hand you his firstborn than a cold plate."

I bite the inside of my cheek and nod. "Got it."

He stops, finally looks at me—like he's scanning for cracks. "You're disappointed."

I shrug. Yeah. I am.

Then he says it. "But you're here." He lets it hang. "You're still fucking here."

And he's gone, calling over his shoulder, "I need lemon wedges, ice, and your dignity—in that order. Let's go, stage boy."

And just like that—I move. Not because it's what I wanted. But because it's exactly what I came for.

~~~

"Thanks for helping me mop, man," Joe says as we roll the bucket toward the back door.

One last swipe of the now deep-gray mop before I dunk it in the filthy water.

I wipe the sweat from my forehead. "Anytime," I say, just before we kill the lights.
~~~

Chapter 5

MISTAKES & MILK CRATES

His voice is right behind me. Low, measured, disappointed.

"Look at me when I'm talking to you."

I don't want to. If I do, I'll flinch. And he hates it when I flinch. But I turn.

We're in the garage. I'm holding a springform pan.

Why the fuck am I holding a pan?

Burnt remnants of cheesecake cling to the sides. I don't remember baking anything.

"Did you think that was good enough?"

He says it calmly. That's the worst part. Calm means it's already over.

I want to explain. Say I didn't mean to burn it. Say that I'm sorry. That I can do better. That I will. But I just stand there, the pan shaking in my hands. Like my bones are weak. Like I'm nine years old again, about to cry over dinner.

He scoffs, voice low and clipped, his jaw locked tight as the words slice out clean, sharp, surgical. "She left to fix your mistake, Kyle. It's your fault. Look what you did."

Then—BEEP BEEP BEEP BEEP.

My eyes snap open.

~~~

I've run so many hotel pans today, I'm starting to think I *am* one—stacked high, slightly warped, emotionally cold to the touch.
~~~

"Kyle, take over these beans," Felix barks.

I spot the massive Cambro. I've seen the episode. I sigh. "Yes, Chef."

I'm pretty sure I left part of my soul somewhere between the foil and the ninth pans. Maybe it's buried in the sliced lemons, peeled garlic, or these green beans.

I'm almost looking forward to going back to the line at High Tide. The line where I actually cook. Where pans matter. Where heat means something.

I round the corner by the line—hands full, head down, and that's when I see it.

A mistake.

Those same dream-words flash through my brain before I can stop them.

Saucepan. Back left burner. Bubbles threatening to boil over. A slick sheen rising. *Shit.* It's emulsified and seconds from breaking. No one's at the station. Saucier's empty.

Before I can think, my body moves—shifting my grip on the hotel pan, sliding the saucepan half off the flame, hitting it with a quick whisk. Just enough to bring it back. Then I walk away.

No theatrics. No ego. Just a half-second save.

I stack the pans, turn—

"Who touched this pan?" Chef Theo.

My stomach drops.

Felix answers before I can. "Your stage. On his fifth hotel pan run."

Theo looks at me. Calm and unreadable. Then, "Nice catch."

Two simple words, but they brand me.

Felix tosses a towel at me. "Careful, Stage. Keep that up, and someone might ask you to cook."

~~~

From the sidewalk, I can see it through the front window—the dim lights, chairs flipped onto tables like tired limbs, a lone shadow pushing a mop in slow, heavy strokes across the dining room. The smear of water reflects the EXIT sign in a way that makes the whole
~~~

place look smaller than I remember. Quieter. Like it's exhaling without me.

I round the corner—the familiar smell of fryer oil and day-old heat sticking to the air like static, and find him right where I expected.

Ritchie.

Perched on a busted milk crate, hoodie half-zipped, smoke curling from his lips. He doesn't flinch when he sees me. He smiles. "Thought you forgot about us little people."

I huff out a laugh. "It's been two days, man." I hold up the six-pack. "Brought peace offerings."

He exhales. Nods. "Holy shit. You remembered my religion."

He drags another milk crate beside him. I pop two beers and hand him one. No cheers. Just the long pull and the foghorn in the distance.

"So?" he asks. "How's the sacred temple?"

I slowly peel the label from my bottle. "Intense. Beautiful. Maybe above my pay grade."

"Bullshit." It's automatic. "You've been ready."

I shake my head. "I'm staging. One more day. Nothing's guaranteed." I gesture to the back door. "I could still end up back here."

He snorts. "You're at the finish line, man. Just finish the race." His hoodie sleeve slides up revealing the faded matching tattoo we got after bourbon and a very bad idea.

He sees me looking. Shrugs. "Still here."

I nod and take a sip, a small smile pulling at the corner of my mouth. "Still fucking here."

For a second, we're quiet. A good quiet. The kind that carries history. The kind where a six-pack means *I love you*.

Ritchie tips his bottle at me, grinning like we're still kids. Like nothing changed. Like we're still two broke-ass dish rats dreaming about getting out.

I grin back, because he's Ritchie-Boy. But underneath it, a whisper: *He's a High Tide chef. He's not Le Début material.*

And I hate myself for thinking it. And I hate that it's probably true. I don't want to leave him behind, but maybe I already have.

He lights another cigarette. I don't stop him.

The foghorn hums again, low and distant—as if it's calling someone home.

Chapter 6

WALK-INS & WEAKNESS

I'm starting to hate the color green.

Haricots verts—another big-ass Cambro full of them, of course. It's actually starting to become meditative now. At least garlic and shallots are next. It'll be a nice change of pace.

I'm standing at the same prep table I was on my first day. Same towel over my shoulder, and same dull ache in my back. And I'm thinking, *Yeah. Back on prep. Good run, Stage Boy.* Was this even worth my time?

The office door cracks open behind me. Low voices—Felix, Natalie, and Vallois. A shift in energy. The kind that makes people stand straighter without realizing.

Felix emerges first, holding the clipboard like it's a weapon. He starts barking stations. "Danny—fire. Zoe—sides. Nate—fish. Weston—garde."

He keeps moving.

Then, he stops and turns to me. A small nod. Almost a smile. "Kyle—Garde with Weston. There's your shot. Don't embarrass me."

I freeze. A glove half-peeled, heart stuttering so hard I nearly drop the bin. I've been snapping beans all morning, but now? I get to plate something cold and clean. Something *mine.*

I finish my prep and wipe down my table just as Chef Vallois enters—yellow legal pad in one hand, espresso in the other, commanding the room without even trying.

Music instantly goes off. Silence doesn't just fall gently; it's sucked out like a vacuum. A spoon falls to the floor somewhere behind me, and nobody even looks. Sara, the pastry chef, swallows too loud next to me, and I think my asshole sealed shut.

Vallois clears his throat and begins like he's delivering a eulogy instead of tonight's menu.

"Cod is in. We're running it with saffron nage, confit fennel, and citrus ash. If it flakes too early, you're off the station.

"The duck is staying. Charred endive, smoked cherry jus. The jus should whisper, not scream—watch the acid."

My mouth is watering.

"Flat iron with pommes anna and sauce foyot. No creative liberties. No flair. For the amuse—compressed melon, pickled shallot, and a basil foam. Foam should hold. If it dies on the spoon, so do you."

He pauses.

"Don't ask me to repeat it. If you didn't listen, you weren't meant to plate it."

Vallois doesn't dismiss us. He just walks away—like the room will either rise to his standard or die trying.

My pulse spikes. Not the inspired holy-shit feeling I got with Theo yesterday. This is sharper. *Hungrier.* A jolt straight to the sternum.

Wake up, Kyle. This is the big time. Don't fuck this up.

Natalie brushes past me on her way to the line, muttering just loud enough, "You heard him. No mistakes." Her voice needles straight into my spine. And suddenly I'm wide awake.

~~~

Weston has the personality of wilted endive in August and refuses to let me touch anything that isn't leafy and cold. He handles every other part of the station like I'm an OSHA violation waiting to happen. Even at that, he watches me plate salads like he's spotting a toddler with a knife.

I watch him assemble the amuse-bouche with so much finesse it feels like a sin to send it out to be eaten. His basil foam holds like a damn miracle.
~~~

Foam didn't die. I guess he lives another day.

I'm doing alright… until I'm not. I overdress the frisée—not once, but twice. The walk-in door hisses shut behind me. Cold air hits the back of my neck, crawling under my apron like shame. I press my spine to the steel shelf and try to breathe. But it's not quiet enough.

His voice slips in—the one from my dream, low and controlled, the look that always came with it. *Did you think that was good enough?*

My chest goes hollow.

Out in the kitchen, I hear it: the scrape of metal on metal as my salad gets dumped. Nobody says a word. I can't see them, but I can picture it—Vallois not blinking, Weston's jaw locking up tighter than the fucking ring mold I mangled plating it.

I stare at the box of limes like it's going to answer for my sins.

This is the part where Tony—this guy I used to work with—would drop his pants and sit bare-assed in here like the walk-in itself could cure humiliation. And for a second, I get it. Like, full-drop get it. Let the cold bite my thighs. Let it punish me for overdressing a frisée like a rookie.

My legs are hot, my pants feel like a vise. For the first time, I understand exactly why he did it.

But I don't. I just stand there. Apron on. Dignity mostly intact.

Greens were overdressed, but I'm not unraveling. Not yet.

I step out of the walk-in with a fresh container of microgreens, the cold still clinging to my skin, and there's Felix—waiting.

"You good?" he asks.

"Yes, Chef."

"Then fix it." He jerks his chin toward the station. "You're still on the fucking line, aren't you?"

I nod, swallowing what's left of my pride.

~~~

The shift ends the way it started—quietly brutal.

No applause. No group high-five. Just the clatter of spent tools hitting metal and the soft hiss of a mop dragging across tile.

I finish wiping down garde, slower than I should—like stalling
~~~

might magically undo the fuckups or convince someone to tell me it didn't count. That I get to come back tomorrow and try again. But then Felix passes behind me—doesn't stop, doesn't look, and drops it like it's nothing.

"You want it? The spot's yours."

That's it. No handshake. No clap on the back. Just six words that gut me harder than any "good job" ever could.

I nod. Just once. Like it's a shift note. Not the thing I've paid for in burns and exhaustion.

It hits differently in the silence.

"Hey, Kyle." Natalie's voice snaps my head up.

"Yes, Chef?"

"This is your locker." She gestures to the far end, to an open metal door like it's a portal or some shit. "Welcome aboard." She smiles and hands me two aprons.

"Thanks." It comes out too soft, but it's all I've got.

She gets a few steps away, then glances back. "Oh—I'll email you your schedule. Have a good night." She waves.

I wave at nobody.

I pull out my phone, thumb buzzing with nerves, and text the only person who will explode with me.

Kyle: Where you at?

~~~

San Francisco has some legendary rooftop bars. Up Top is one of my favorites—locals only, bartenders who actually give a shit, and, on Fridays, a DJ spinning industrial rock or mellow house that somehow fits the skyline.

I spot Collin immediately. He's deep in conversation with the bartender, drinking something fancy in a highball—probably a Manhattan, his go-to whenever he's trying to look like a man of culture.

I weave through the crowd and saddle up next to him. "Hey."

He turns toward me—dark hair artfully disheveled with way too much product, skin glowing like he spent the whole day getting a facial and a massage. Well-rested fuck.
~~~

"An IPA?" I tell the bartender.

Collin blinks at me like I just ordered a trust fund. "Upgrading, are we?"

"I almost took my pants off in the walk-in." I mutter.

He smiles over the rim of his drink. "God, I love when you flirt with me."

I laugh and take my beer. "I was doing great… then I wasn't. Totally fucked up two frisée salads, freaked out, almost dropped trow in the walk-in—then they hired me."

Collin's brows practically fuse together. "So, let me get this straight. You bombed a salad and went full Winnie-the-Pooh? And we're all just pretending frisée is a real thing?"

"It's French lettuce. It's real." I laugh.

The second beer hits different. Not celebration—something closer. Relief. Like maybe I didn't completely fuck it all up.

Collin's halfway through another drink he definitely ordered for the glassware. He waves at the bartender like they have shared custody of a plant, then eyes me. "You're glowing, by the way," he squints. "Did they let you run the whole kitchen?"

~~~

The steam finally fades, leaving my skin smelling like cedarwood and bad decisions. I'm spread out on my bed—towel barely hanging on, brain humming, body loose and slutty from too many IPAs and emotional whiplash.

My phone's in my hand. I'm staring at it like it's supposed to give me permission.

One eye open. One eye already half-asleep. Perfect combination for catastrophic choices.

My thumb moves before my brain does—drunk, horny, and reckless as hell.

Send.

I blink. Wait. No. Did I actually just—? *Sent.*

Suddenly, I'm sober enough to file taxes, and regret floods every pore.

"I might as well have sent her a goddamn dick pic."
~~~

I consider throwing my phone into the ocean, but I don't live anywhere near one. So, I just stare at the screen. Not blinking. Not breathing. Just… dying inside.

"You up?" Total douche move.

Chapter 1

SEX, LIES, & VIDEOTAPE

She's on me before I can say her name.

Her heels click across my floor like a threat. And that dress—*fuck*, that dress—is slit up her thigh, neckline deep enough it makes me dizzy.

I take one step back, and she's there, gripping my bare chest, breathing against my jaw like she owns me.

"Still up?" she whispers.

Her voice is smooth and controlled, but there's a tremble in it, too—something she's trying not to feel.

"You came," I breathe against her ear.

"Well, you texted."

Her mouth finds mine, and it's not sweet, it's not careful. It's want. It's need. All the unfinished shit from the walk-in and that night at Lizzy's—warm, open, and a little wild.

My hands go to her hips automatically, anchoring her. Not guiding, but holding. Because if I let go, I'll lose the thin thread that's barely holding me together. The thread I cut weeks ago and tied back together with one stupid, reckless text.

She pushes me. Back, back, until the backs of my knees hit the bed and I sit with a grunt.

She climbs over me—one foot on the mattress, dress sliding up her thighs, all satin and sin. My hand runs up the back of her leg, her skin so damn smooth it makes my pulse stutter. The fabric shifts, exposing her panties.

It's torture. Beautiful, slow torture.

"Lie down," she says, low and commanding. It's not a request.

My dick hears it before I do. I obey.

She's still dressed. I'm half-naked. We haven't even blinked and I already feel undone.

Her hands move with practiced ease—she palms my jaw, tilts my head just right, and kisses me again like she's memorizing my mouth.

Then she shifts her weight, straddling my thighs. Her hips move—once, twice—slow, deliberate, testing.

"Fuck, Kyle," she breathes, rolling her hips again, slower this time. "You feel so fucking good."

My fingers dig into the back of her dress, searching for the zipper, my breath uneven. I don't say anything. I just grip harder, because she's not mine. She's not staying. This is need—heat—an echo of something familiar, not the start of anything real.

She moves her hips again, drawing it out like she knows I'll break first.

She's not wrong.

My fingers find the zipper, and I drag it down slowly, knuckles brushing the curve of her spine as her breath hitches.

"Don't tease," she says, voice tightening.

"I'm not." Lie. I want her begging. I want her wrecked.

The dress slips down her shoulders, pooling at her waist. Black lace against bare skin. It's the kind of bra designed to be seen, and even though there's something in the back of my mind telling me this isn't a good idea, I ignore it. I inhale like I've been underwater.

She reaches down, palms me through my sweats—*fucking hell*—and my whole body jerks under her touch.

"Still up," she smirks.

Smartass.

I sit up, my hand sliding behind her neck, and kiss her like I need to erase the smirk, and maybe everything else too. She tastes like champagne, celebration, and adrenaline.

"Take it off," I say, low and rougher than I meant.

She stands without breaking eye contact and steps out of the dress like it's nothing. Like this doesn't cost her anything. Like we aren't coming apart at the seams.

I kick off my sweats and boxers, hand fisting around my cock as I take her in like it's the last time. Because this *needs* to be the last time.

But damn, she's beautiful. Perfect curves and porcelain skin. Caramel hair spilling over her shoulders like something I should never touch again but still want to.

I need to quit—she's a drug that keeps calling me back. Crawling under my sheets, breathing across my skin, making me want more than I should. I know she's not what I need, but fuck… I *want.*

She climbs back into my lap, straddling me again—bare now, except for a thin strip of black lace and those sharp black heels.

Her hips move once more and we both groan, because it's not teasing anymore. It's not a game. It's everything snapping loose at once.

My hands grip her ass. Her nails drag down my chest, leaving heat behind in their wake. We're breathing like we've run five miles.

I slide my thumbs under the edge of her panties and pull them aside slow and deliberate—*fuck…* she's right there. Hot and wet and ready for me.

She sinks onto me so slow and I swear I forget my own name.

"Fuck, Kyle," she moans. This time it's not a command. It's the only thing keeping her together.

Her forehead presses to mine, her fingers tangled in my hair, her hips rolling—harder now. Deeper. She takes me all the way, sitting fully, gripping her breasts, head thrown back, mouth open with my name falling out of her.

I hold her tighter, my hips lifting to meet hers, chasing her rhythm, matching it—no words, no thought. Just friction and want, the sharp slap of skin, the heat of her breath on my cheek.

She rides me until I'm right there—chest tight, blood pounding, every nerve wired to her voice.

"Look at me," she whispers.

I do. Unblinking.

She comes with my name on her tongue, falling against me as she shudders apart—and I let go right after, teeth clenched, fingers digging into her ass, the kind of release that feels more like surrender than victory.

~~~

Her fingers run lazy circles over my chest and down my arms—slow, soothing, almost absentminded. It slices right through the reel of questions firing in my skull.

Why did they hire me after that shitshow?

Can I handle Vallois?

What the hell was in that foam?

"So, do all of these mean something?" She giggles, fingertip landing on the flaming chicken leg tattoo on my forearm. "Like that one—does it actually have a story?"

I glance down and laugh. Even packed in with the rest—like a full-body game of Where's Waldo—it's still one of my favorites.

"Actually, it does," I say, settling back on the pillow, one arm behind my head. "Ritchie and I both have it. We went to Nashville for a long weekend. Checked out the food scene, tried to escape for a minute. Thought maybe we'd actually bust out of here for real."

The memory pushes a grin out of me. "We jumped on a discount flight, partied like idiots, and went for the full hot chicken experience before a night out. I knew my spice limit—I played it safe."

She laughs, already knowing. "Oh my god, I *know* where this is going." She props herself up on her elbows, eyes bright, mouth twitching like she's begging me to finish the story.

"Yup. He ordered the extra-fucking-hot, even after the server warned him." I tilt toward her, grinning. "Took it like a champ going down, but let's just say… we didn't make it out of the restaurant. Or to the hotel. It hit fast. The noises—Jesus Christ."

Years later and I'm still laughing hard enough that I can't breathe. Tears sting my eyes and slide back into my hair.

"So, the next day, after a bourbon-soaked lunch, we got matching tattoos. It just… felt right."

She reaches for her phone on the nightstand. "Okay, this is probably stupid," she says, "but I feel like this might be one of those moments. A last."
~~~

She shrugs, something soft flickering there. "I know what you want, Kyle. I've heard you—loud and clear." Her thumb skims my cheek. "But let's commemorate it anyway." She lifts her phone. "Selfie?"

I smirk. "Fine," I say, running a hand through my hair.

"No—sexed up. Just like this." She tugs the sheet up over her chest with a grin. "Well… maybe not with my tits out."

We both laugh. She points, we smile, and there it is—captured. Kyle and Macy. Messy and hot. Not forever, but real right now.

As I zip up her dress, I finally say it. "I got the job. Le Début. They offered it tonight."

She turns. Her expression splits—joy on one side, something heavier on the other. "Kyle, that's amazing. Why didn't you tell me?"

I shake my head. "I don't know."

She kisses me—soft, almost careful. "You're going to be great. You really are."

The belief in her voice wedges itself under my ribs—something I'll end up carrying far longer than I should.

I tuck a strand of hair behind her ear and glance down at us—me, shirtless in gray sweats; her, radiating like a Bond-film dream in silk and heels.

I snort. "Looks like Frank the Tank wandered into a Bond movie. You'd make a hell of a Bond girl."

She swats my arm. "I'll miss you," she whispers.

And I kiss her—hard.

~~~

"Glad you're back," Vic says as I walk through the back door. "How's your aunt?"

My steps don't falter, but Ritchie's snort from the prep sink nearly kills me.

"She's good," I say. "Thanks." I pause. Deep breath. "Hey, Vic… can I talk to you for a sec?"

He nods, and we step into the office. The door closes behind us, and the conversation? It stays there.
~~~

~~~

Same night. Same walls. Same bullshit.

The kitchen's already behind. Louis no-showed—again, and his name is still sitting on the schedule like some ghost of mediocrity we're all pretending will manifest into a human eventually.

Too much pasta. Not enough garlic. Someone left the fryer temp too low, and now the calamari's a soggy, shameful tragedy. The menu still reads like it was phoned in from 2014, and it's obvious that change is prohibited.

I overhear someone say Macy called out sick. I don't react, but I slide my phone from my pocket and text her anyway.

Kyle: You okay?

Nothing.

I tuck the phone back into my coat and keep working. I don't need a reply to know the answer.

The shift drags. The music's too loud, the tickets too long, and the air is too thick with the smell of fryer oil that never really leaves your clothes. Somewhere between peeling eight pounds of shrimp and hearing Vic lose his shit at the new runner, I realize—I'm not coming back tomorrow.

Not because I'm angry. Not because I think I'm better. But because I'm just… done.

When the last plate hits the pass and the kitchen finally dies down, I find Ritchie outside—same milk crate, same cigarette, same hoodie.

He looks up. He knows, and just nods.

I hand him a beer and sit beside him, still in my apron. We don't say anything. We don't need to. Nothing moves out here except the fog. The foghorn moans in the distance like a friendly reminder: *Your time here is up.*

Ritchie takes a drag from his cigarette. "So… aunt's fine, huh?"

I side-eye him. "She pulled through."

He chuckles. "Miraculous recovery. God bless."

We both laugh the kind of quiet and real laugh you feel in your ribs.
~~~

He flicks ash toward the curb. "You're doing it, huh? For real."

"Yeah. I'll probably regret it. That Vallois is a real prick."

He nods slowly. "Le Début." Like he's tasting the words. "You're gonna be fancy as fuck."

"I'm still me."

"You better be." He shifts, pulling up his sleeve. "You forget where this came from?"

I glance down at the ink. That stupid flaming chicken leg.

"Nope."

"We earned that pain," he mutters. "Both ends."

My laugh cracks out of me. "Yeah… yeah we did."

"You just better not change so much you stop calling me."

"I won't."

"Better not forget who taught you how to deglaze a pan and make a proper fucking roux."

"I won't."

He nods again.

The kitchen buzz fades behind us. My hands still smell like fryer oil and lemon peel. But I've never felt cleaner.

The foghorn calls again. I stand. This time, I don't look back.

Chapter 8

FEELINGS & MR. PICKLES

Second week in a row on Garde. Weston's still a grump, but at least he lets me plate alone now. Felix hasn't yelled at me all week. Natalie laughed at one of my jokes—an actual laugh, not just a puff of air and a head shake. The foam holds, and I didn't overdress the fucking frisée.

I've got rhythm in my hands again, and I'm not proving anything today. I'm keeping my pants on, and I'm just working.

The kitchen breathes its own rhythm—oil sizzling, knives tapping, the metallic clatter of pan to rack in a beat that feels like my own damn pulse.

Station by station, we move. Felix calls. Weston plates. And I sweep in with citrus ash and micro tarragon—no hesitation. I know my place now. I know my lane. My heat.

"Garde's smooth today," Natalie murmurs without looking up. "You finally selling your soul or just stopped overthinking?"

"Bit of both," I grin, sliding the next plate forward.

We're cruising—until he walks in. Vallois.

Crisp coat. Eyes scanning like everything personally offends him. He stops at the pass, practically *sniffs* a plate, then turns to Felix.

"Why's the branzino resting so long?" he asks, quiet and condescending.

Felix wipes his hands, but doesn't flinch. "That one's already out. You're looking at the wrong ticket."

Vallois doesn't respond. Just hums like he's disappointed and keeps walking. Someone behind me mutters, "He's unhinged," but no one owns up to it.

And honestly? I believe it. He's got the look of a man watching his own empire develop hairline fractures. He doesn't know where they started, but he sure as hell knows they're spreading.

~~~

Later, during close—when shirts are untucked, shoulders are looser, and the chatter softens into actual human voices—Felix says,"What was that earlier?" low enough that it's almost hidden under the scrape of pans. "My branzino resting too long?"

He scoffs without looking up, scribbling on the back of a prep list while Natalie works beside him. They're relaxed—*too* relaxed for Vallois's kitchen, which makes it feel like a dare.

"I don't know," she says. "Theo slipped in our meeting about a possible new hire."

I arch a brow. "Chef's choice?"

"Yup. Some hotshot from the Bay Area. Right out of CIA, supposedly. She worked in Oakland. Made a grown man cry over risotto, apparently."

"That good?" I ask with a smile.

Felix smirks. "Maybe we'll find out."

~~~

I wake to the sound of whining.

Yeah… *whining.*

I flick on the bedside lamp, groggy and confused.

Silence.

I hold my breath, waiting—there it is again. Soft whimpering. A… puppy?

I drag myself out of bed, following the sound down the hallway. It leads to the living room. In the corner sits a metal crate, half-covered with a blanket. The whining picks up—higher, more hopeful—as I get closer. A tail thumps wildly against the bars, a steady *thwack-thwack-thwack* of desperate joy.

I click on the lamp by the couch and crouch down to find two big, glossy golden eyes staring back at me. A gray face, a twitching nose, and the tiniest, most pitiful howl—a whisper of a plea.

Let me out.

I unlatch the crate.

The second the door opens, he scrambles forward—paws too big for his gangly body, ears floppy, tail a metronome of hope. He stumbles into my lap like it's the only place he's ever belonged and presses his whole weight against me, curling into the crook of my arm.

I sit there, on the floor, his soft body warm against my bare stomach, blinking at the reality of it. Someone left a puppy… with me. And for one ridiculous second, something inside me tightens—like this tiny creature decided I was safe before I ever proved it.

I glance around, half expecting a note. But there's nothing. No food. No leash. Just this tiny, desperate thing who's already licked the underside of my jaw and let out a hiccupped sigh like I'm supposed to fix everything.

"Well," I murmur, scratching gently behind one too-soft ear. "You've got shitty timing, but… same."

He sneezes. Then flops down—just collapses—all trust and bones and warmth.

Guess we're doing this.

~~~

I wake to sunlight cutting through the blinds, and there's warmth pressed against my side.

I pray it's not Collin, but then I remember. It's… a tiny gray monster with floppy ears, curled into the crook of my arm like this is his couch and I'm just lucky to be invited.

I blink blearily at him. He yawns, then licks my chin.

Before I can even untangle his long limbs, the front door clicks open. Footsteps. Keys.

"Dude. Are you spooning my dog?"

I groan. "*Your* dog? Since when do *we* have a dog?"

Collin's leaning in the doorway, holding an iced coffee and looking way too smug for a man wearing vintage tennis whites like it's a personality trait. His blue shorts have an inseam dangerously
~~~

close to a full ball-out situation. His LIVE, LAUGH, LOBOTOMY T-shirt is absolutely stolen from a women's section. And the *iconic blazer* thrown over the whole catastrophe—Papa Runway chic.

When people ask if he's gay, I laugh. He's fashionably confused. Weird, eccentric, shops like he broke into my grandparents' attic… but the man absolutely loves pussy.

"I leave for one tiny sleepover," he says, waggling his brows, "and come home to a full-blown dog-bonding montage. What the hell?"

I sit up. The dog immediately tries to climb inside my hoodie.

"Whose is this—for real?" I ask.

"Oh. That's Bandit." He points at the wriggling lump. "Belongs to that Lotus chick from my work. She's out of town for a few days. Asked me to dog-sit."

I stare at him. "Lotus?"

Collin shrugs. "Yeah."

"Is that her *real* name, Collin?"

"I didn't check her birth certificate, man. She has a septum piercing and makes a margarita taste like salvation. What do you want from me?"

I scratch the puppy's head. "You can't just leave a baby dog alone all night. He was losing his shit."

"Oh damn, I'm sorry. Did he wake you up?"

"No, Collin. I *normally* fall asleep spooning strangers' pets." I cover the puppy's ears. "Yes, he fucking woke me up. How long are you watching him?"

"Like I said—just a few days," he says in a low tone, casually sipping his iced coffee like it's edging him.

I stand and hand him the limp, half-sleeping puppy. "Here. Take Rocco out. I need a shower."

"His name is Bandit," Collin calls after me.

"Yeah, well that's stupid… just like fucking Lotus."

~~~

It's my first day off in weeks, and I have a list. A real, grown-up, get-your-shit-together list. Grocery run. Laundry. Gym. Coffee. Maybe
~~~

sit outside and pretend I wasn't one breath away from losing my entire mind.

Instead, I'm standing on the sidewalk in sweats and flip-flops, holding a chewed-up leash while Rocco drags me toward a dead pigeon.

"Dude," I groan, tugging gently. "Leave it."

He ignores me. Sniffs it. Then sneezes so violently he knocks himself off his own axis.

I sigh from my soul. "You're ruining my life."

Rocco looks up, tongue out, tail wagging in full white-tipped helicopter mode.

Damn, your cute face.

Then it happens. A girl walking past slows, crouches, and buries both hands in Rocco's ears.

"Oh my god, your puppy is so cute."

I don't correct her. I don't even consider it. I stand there grinning like a proud single dad at a school play. Not because *she's* cute—because *he* is.

"Thanks," I say casually. Like it's the most normal thing in the world. Like he's mine.

~~~

It's been seven days—*no* Lotus.

I put it in the universe. I fucking willed this to happen.

Now, I'm that guy at the pet supply store buying more food. I've memorized his brand, the exact bag, the weird toothbrush-shaped dental chews he pretends not to like but always eats first. I even got him a tag—Rocco—with my number. Just in case.

We have a routine now. Walking, feeding, kenneling him before work. Playing and wearing him out so he sleeps hard while I'm gone. I even pay the neighbor to come let him out when Collin and me are both working.

I'm being strategic. I'm being responsible. I'm being *a Dog Dad.*

"I won't be too late, buddy," I say, tossing in his favorite Mr. Pickles and a peanut-butter-stuffed Kong into his kennel before I click the latch.
~~~

I shut the door gently behind me and step out into the sunshine, waiting for the soft whimpers… They don't come.

He's getting more comfortable. With the kennel. With the house. With *me.*

"Good boy," I murmur.

I blink. Weird how fast that flipped the switch. I'm used to hearing that kind of praise in the bedroom.

I strap my knife roll across my chest, drop my board to the sidewalk with a hard thud, and before I push off, I dial Collin.

He answers on the second ring, glassware clinking in the background.

"What's up?"

"Where is she?" I ask, sharp enough to cut myself on.

He sighs. "I don't know, man. All her texts say *read,* so she's not dead." He chuckles at his own rhyme. "She hasn't come back to work." A beat of silence. "There's rumors and shit. People are saying she quit." Another rhyme, another laugh.

I don't feed into it. If I do, he'll go on all night, like a first grader telling bad jokes. And the sad part? He's proud of it.

"No shit she hasn't been back. It's been over a week—that's pretty much the definition of quitting." I clench my jaw, take a long breath, and push my board back and forth with my foot like I'm revving myself up.

"What are we doing with Rocco?" I ask.

He snorts. "Umm… the fact that you have completely changed his identity, his diet, and become his person… Are you really asking?"

I pause.

Am I really going to take on this kind of responsibility? What if I want to travel?

I laugh—at myself, in my own damn head. *Travel*? I barely travel outside my own brain. I work late nights and sleep weird hours. It's not fair to him.

But… I have been making it work. And he seems happy. And I sure as hell can't let Lotus—the incompetent mezcal bar wizard—come marching back and take him now. No way. I would cut her tattooed hands off before I let that happen.

"Are we even allowed to have a dog in our apartment?" One last Hail Mary to change my mind.

"Yeah, I think we could legally raise wild orangutans and nobody would say shit as long as rent's paid. Maybe some pet deposit or something. I'll check."

"Alright," I exhale.

"Congratulations! You're a dad. It's a boy!" He laughs. "Shit, I gotta go. Talk tonight after work—beers over puppy breath." He hangs up.

I push off toward work, my heart doing something stupid and warm, Collin's voice echoing: *You're a dad.*

In just over a month, life's taken on a new shape. Not just a job… A career. I'm learning. Absorbing skill and knowledge like a damn sponge. I'm making friends—real ones—with the same fire and the same drive.

And now… this. It's not just a dog. He's my boy. I gave him a name. That's when it changed. You don't buy a tag for temporary. You don't name his favorite toy Mr. Pickles.

Rocco. My boy.

Chapter 1

WALK-IN REDEMPTION

I'm on Garde… again. The station that just won't quit. But everything's off.

The light's too bright overhead—interrogation bright. The station's too clean—stainless steel mirror-sharp. The cutting board is a blinding white—new.

And my white apron… red-splattered. But I haven't plated a damn thing.

Weston plates beside me in total silence. Natalie's mouthing something I can't hear—like she's underwater. Then suddenly, in my hands: A springform pan.

No.

No, no, no.

It doesn't belong here. Not at this station. Not in my fucking hands. And it's heavy. Cold. Wrong.

"You bring that from home?"

I turn.

Vallois. Towering. Fuming. His coat no longer crisp white but splattered with that same wrong red, matching my apron.

I look down at the pan like it's a bomb I lit myself.

"You think this is a fucking joke?" He steps into my space.

I open my mouth—nothing. My throat is dry. My palms are slick. The pan slips. Clatters to the tile. Spins out, rattling across the floor.

Silence slices like a blade.

"Goddammit, Kyle." But it's not Vallois's voice now.

It's *his.* My father's.

"You always break shit. Always in the way."

I freeze. Don't flinch. He hates when you flinch.

I can't breathe. I bolt upright, drenched in sweat. Moonlight cuts through the blinds in gold bars across my bed, and across Rocco stirring beside me.

I lay a heavy hand on his back and fall into my pillow, staring blankly at the ceiling.

Fuck.

~ ~ ~

Service is in full swing. Short-staffed—tight, hot, but moving smooth, all things considered.

I'm locked in on Garde, fully focused. I've been doing this long enough now, it's become a second skin. I'm working it alone. Weston called out sick—rolled his ankle yesterday playing pickleball. I've come in thinking my leg was broken, but you do you.

Felix is down the line, focused and controlled. Running sauté. Checking down with Natalie like always.

Then it starts.

"Felix." Vallois's voice cuts through, low, sharp, already coiling. "You call this properly reduced?"

Felix stays calm. He doesn't look up. "Yes, Chef."

"You sure?"

I glance just in time to see Vallois lift the saucepan by the handle and tilt it too far—on purpose, like he might throw it. Instead, he sets it down with a clang that slices the room clean in two.

The line goes quiet. Eyes snap up. Hands pause mid-plate.

"This is the third time this week you've pushed a half-finished sauce through expo. You got something going on? You wanna talk about it?"

Felix's jaw tics. "No, Chef."

"Because if you've got problems at home, you can take PTO. Don't fuck up my pass with your personal shit."

The air drops five degrees. Nobody looks at Felix. Nobody breathes too loud.

I just stare at my tickets—my hands moving like muscle memory. Robotic. *Focus, Kyle.* Don't fuck up. Don't swallow wrong. Don't breathe wrong. Just *don't.*

Then Felix responds. His voice is steady. Sure. Unflinching. *"Yes, Chef. Won't happen again."* Like a professional. Like a human punching bag.

Vallois doesn't apologize. Doesn't soften. Doesn't do anything resembling leadership.

He just turns and mutters, "Someone better fix that shit before the next ticket goes out," and disappears down the line like he didn't just detonate the morale of his entire fucking kitchen.

The rush comes and goes. Pristine dishes slide through the pass, but the damage is done.

We all watched Felix crumble like a stale cracker under Vallois' shoe. It was emasculating. This isn't the fucking Army. You don't need to break a man down to build him back up. We're not going to war. We're making goddamn foie gras, escargot, and overpriced one-bite appetizers we serve on spoons and give fancy fucking names.

Why was that called for?

I know what it's like to feel that rage, to stand there cracked open while still trying to keep being you, to slice chives like nothing happened, to wonder day after day if you did good enough. If *he'd* be proud.

The final dishes go out.

Natalie walks past Felix just as he slides the last plate into the pass.

"Behind," she says softly, placing a hand on his shoulder. Just that. One hand.

Felix doesn't speak—but a small smile tugs at his mouth. A crack of light in the wreckage.

A while later, I balance a hotel pan on my hip, stacked with marinating beef tenderloins for tomorrow's service. When I yank open the walk-in door, I'm greeted by… Felix. Mid-bite.

He's hunched on an overturned five-gallon bucket, eating garlic-confit mashed potatoes out of a quart container like it's penance. No spoon. Just a tasting fork. Coat unbuttoned. Steam curling off the potatoes into the cold air like incense. Like it's church, and he's about to eat his sins.

He freezes when he sees me. Fork halfway to his mouth. "What the fuck are you looking at?"

I blink. Shift the pan to my other hip. "I was gonna ask you the same thing." I hoist the pan onto the empty shelf beside him.

He stares. Takes the bite anyway. Chews with quiet, stubborn shame. "They had garlic confit in them," he mutters finally. "Felt emotional."

"I get that." I nod, shrug. "Shit, I almost took my pants off in here after fucking up salad on my second day. Enjoy."

I push the door open and the cold air curls into the hallway behind me.

Just before it clicks shut, I hear him breathe, low and venomous: "Fucking Vallois."

~~~

Rocco's tail pounds a frantic rhythm against the crate as I crack the door—followed by a high, keening whine that hits me like guilt in stereo.

"I got you, buddy." My keys clatter. The knife roll drops. My shoulders finally sag, like they've been fighting to stay square all damn night.

I unlatch the crate, and he launches out—tongue, tail, paws everywhere. A mess of pure, unconditional joy.

"Come on, Rocco… good boy."

After our walk, I open a beer and put on music. Anything to drown out the negativity and the kitchen noise still rattling around in my skull like loose screws.

I lean on the counter and watch Rocco, perfectly content and gnawing his bone as if the world makes perfect sense.

This is what my life started with. Easy. Until it wasn't.

I switch the playlist to *hers*. Crosby, Stills & Nash. Van Morrison. James Taylor. Sunday soundtracks from back when she was still humming and kneading and making magic from scratch.
~~~

She gave life flavor.

My gaze drifts to the shelf—my ever-growing cookbook collection, alphabetized like I'm trying to look more put-together than I am.

And there it sits. Avocado green. The Tupperware from the late seventies. Probably my grandmother's, or bought at a friend's party because she wanted to be supportive. A time capsule I'm scared to open. A reminder I'm not ready to face. A piece of her that still feels too loud, too bright, too gone.

I pop the lid.

Inside are a hundred discolored 3x5 index cards—memories masquerading as recipes. Some with faint grease shadows, others with flour still dusted into the creases like fingerprints frozen in time.

I thumb through them slowly. Meatballs in gravy. Chicken Piccata. Grandma's Spinach. Her warm banana bread—always waiting beside my chocolate milk before school.

Her handwriting is elegant and looping, young and hopeful. Captured and preserved. Just like the version of her that my brain won't let age.

"Okay, Ma... what do we got today?" I murmur.

And then I see it. Like a beacon. Italian cheesecake.

My chest caves. I've never tried it. I can't.

I sit at the table, flipping the card over in my hand as I finish my beer. I can picture the springform pan—buried in the back right corner of the cabinet on purpose. I'm not ready. Not yet.

I slap the card onto the table, too hard. Not today. I need a shower. Heat and steam work like a trance. Soap. Water. Breath. Everything softens.

But the second I step out, I feel it. The air is wrong. Too quiet. Too still.

"Rocco?"

I round the corner and stop breathing. The box is on the floor. Cards everywhere—scattered, chewed, shredded, and spit-slicked. A storm of confetti made from my childhood.

Teeth marks. Drool and paper pulp clinging to his fur. And

there, in the middle of it all: her Italian cheesecake recipe. Torn. Soggy. Ruined.

Of all the recipes—of all the fucking cards, he found *that* one. The one I can't touch. The one I've avoided for years. The one that feels like a wound, and he tore it apart like it meant *nothing*. Like it didn't hold everything I never said. Everything I left because I couldn't stay.

That heat hits my chest—sharp, blind. The kind that lives just under the guilt and waits for a crack.

Rocco lies in the middle of the wreckage… tail wagging, panting, happy. Proud.

I stand over him… and the scream rips out of me. "Goddammit, Rocco!"

He flinches, startled.

"What the fuck did you do?" I grab a fistful of shredded cards. Paper flakes off my fingers, and the sight only pours gasoline on the fire.

"Look at this! Do you know what this is? Do you know what it meant? *Huh*?"

He crawls backward, shaking, wedging himself under the kitchen chair.

"Look at me when I talk to you! This is all your fault!" I shake my fist, and he recoils again, whining.

"Look what you did!"

And then—silence.

Rocco is a trembling gray ball under a chair that doesn't even cover him. No tail wag. No bark. Just fear. And the voice that plays back isn't mine. It's *his.* My father's.

The fear in Rocco's eyes? It's the fear I grew up with.

My stomach drops so hard I swear the floor tilts.

Jesus Christ. What have I done?

I drop to my knees and reach for him—soft, slow—and he hesitates for a heartbeat. Then he melts into me with a wet, frantic lick like forgiveness is the easiest thing in the world.

I'm twenty-four. Forgiving my father has never crossed my

fucking mind. Rocco's known me for two weeks and does it in one second flat.

I cup his face, my fingers buried in the soft folds he's *definitely* going to grow into, tears burning hot tracks down my cheeks.

"Little dude… I will never do that to you again. I'm so fucking sorry." My voice breaks. "I love you."

I pull him into my chest because he's mine. Maybe the closest thing I'll ever have to a kid. And that's enough. Because I'm damaged, and this messy little love sponge stays anyway.

Look at me. On the floor. Screaming like a lunatic over old, torn recipes.

~~~

I'm still on the floor when he walks in. Remnants of cards everywhere. Tape and scissors. A half-drunk beer sweating on the table. Rocco's curled on my foot like I didn't scream him into another lifetime an hour ago.

Collin rounds the corner and stops dead. "Jesus Christ. Did a raccoon break in?"

I don't look up. "Rocco got into the recipe box."

"Yeah, I see that. This looks like a Hallmark movie crime scene—sentimental homicide."

He sets down a six-pack and lowers himself to the floor like we do this every Tuesday. He hands me a fresh beer. "Alright. Let's trauma-jigsaw this shit. You got corners, or am I starting with marinara?"

I hand him a soggy chunk that used to read, *"Grandma's meatballs."*

"That smells like peanut butter—gross," he mutters, smoothing it flat and wiping his hand on his tailored pants. I still don't understand how he's sitting crisscross applesauce in—they're so damn tight.

A beat passes. Then he says, "He's definitely yours now, you know?"

"Yeah… I figured it out somewhere between screaming like my father and getting forgiven with a face lick."
~~~

"Seems like a breakthrough." He taps my beer and gets excited when he finds a match. "How was work?"

I scoff. "Vallois is a real prick. Found Felix emotional eating in the walk-in."

He snorts. "Is the walk-in like a confessional to you guys? Everything always seems to happen in there. Confess your sins. Pants optional. Here's a spoon."

I actually laugh, but just a little. The good kind that lets a little light back in.

"Shut up and find the other half of the cheesecake."

"Yes, Chef. May the peace be with you." He crosses his chest like he's blessing a fallen soufflé.

I whisper, "And also with you."

Chapter 10

FANCY SAUCES & CONSEQUENCES

"We're walking, Rocco, not sniffing. Keep it moving, dude."

The little bugger needs to burn off some energy—and honestly? So do I.

I glance down at my biceps and attempt a weak flex. I used to have guns. Now? Pistols. Reduced to squirt-gun status in just over a month. Turns out, a month of twelve-inch-leg paced strolls and dog-park butt-sniff fiestas will obliterate your gym routine.

Shit.

He's even getting more action than me. Cute little fuck.

I'm over here becoming a walking cliché—early onset dad-bod, dark under-eye circles, and just enough emotional trauma to make me look like a red flag wearing Vans.

I toss the tennis ball again. Rocco barrels after it like it's the last one left on Earth. Tail high, tongue hanging out, and thrilled with his entire existence. I haven't lifted anything heavier than a sauté pan in weeks. But there's something about this dog. About this life. About the way he chooses me—every morning, every walk, every sloppy, unconditional moment.

Yeah. Even squirt-gun-armed, sleep-deprived, semi-feral me loves this.

~~~

The metal door slams shut behind me with a heavy thud.
~~~

"Morning, Kyle," Joe calls, not looking up as he yanks down the dishwasher handle.

The machine roars to life, swallowing the hum of prep like a tidal wave. Steel, steam, motion. My bloodstream finally wakes up.

I head toward the locker room. "Why is everyone here so early?" I ask, dropping my bag and unlatching my knife roll from my chest.

Joe shrugs. "Chef Theo's here. I dunno. I'm just dish, man."

The office door is half-ajar as I pass, and Chef Theo looks up. "Kyle."

I pause, lean my head in. "Yes, Chef?"

He leans back in his chair, totally unbothered, radiating the exact opposite frequency of Vallois's cracked-out storm cloud energy.

"Sauté today." A faint smile. "You good?" A simple question.

And it just… sparks. I grin like an idiot. Like a kid whose mom just handed him birthday cake for breakfast. Except it feels real. Earned.

"Yes, sir. I'm good."

I'm barely done tying my apron before Jules calls out, "Hot damn… It's me and you today. Sweet."

I learned everything I needed to know about Julien Mercado—"Jules"—during a previous day in prep. Twenty-eight. Brooklyn born and raised. The accent is the first thing you taste. Pastry-trained but bailed when he realized he hated measuring anything.

Honestly? He reminds me of Ritchie. Unfiltered. Inappropriate. Low-key brilliant. But also contently lost—floating somewhere between burnout and brilliance like half the people in this industry.

…And that reminds me. I need to call Ritchie. I'm such a dick. He doesn't even know I became a dad. *Damnit.*

Jules moves like he's five steps ahead of time itself. By the time I've reached for a whisk, he's already got two pans down, one fish searing, and half the mise set up like it just teleported there.

"See that shimmer?" he says, tapping the pan. "That's when the oil's hot enough. Throw it in sooner and you're just bathing the bastard." He says it so casually, like we're swapping gossip—while spooning a silky velouté with the kind of grace that makes you wonder if he came out of the womb holding a sauce spoon.

I nod, trying to match his pace, even though I feel like a toddler learning to walk during a goddamn sprint relay.

"How are we doing, guys?" Natalie asks, sliding over as the rush creeps closer.

"Kickin' ass, sea bass," Jules fires back without missing a beat.

I freeze. *Jesus.*

No "We're good, Chef." No "Ready to go, Chef." Just pure chaos in poetry, served medium rare. If he ever said that to Vallois, we'd all be vaporized on the spot.

Natalie blinks once, almost smiles, and walks off without a word.

"What?" Jules says, glancing at me, hands up. "You want me to curtsy next time?"

I shake my head, swallowing the laugh that wants to escape.

And the thing is? He's really teaching me. He corrects my heat, calls out timing cues, makes me redo a vin blanc mid-pan, but never like he's trying to break me. He just… gives a shit. *Loudly.*

For all his noise, Jules runs like a metronome. And I'm starting to find the rhythm.

The tickets start slamming in, the rush hits, and suddenly I'm locked in.

Fish down. Sauce reduced. I'm plating tight.

Not perfect—yet—but something's clicking. The rhythm's in my wrists. The timing's in my gut. And I catch Jules watching me finish the sauce with a smooth little drizzle, like I actually meant that shit.

"Look at that sexy beast. You did that shit. See? Nothing to it." He points like a proud dad—like I just colored inside the lines for the first time—and slides the plate into the pass with a smirk.

I grin. Big. And this time, it's earned.

Across the line, one of the sous walks by wearing *the* apron. The thick blue one with the brown leather straps. The weight of it—literal and earned.

I want that. Not like I used to. Not for ego. I want it because I can now.

Because today? I'm not just keeping up. I'm cooking. I'm doing the work. And for the first time, it feels within reach.

"Here, man." I place the stack of sauté pans onto Joe's ever-growing pit.

He just bobs his head and smiles lightly, oblivious to our world out in the kitchen.

Whatever he's listening to—Metallica, Jane's Addiction, or hell… Beyonce—it keeps his rhythm steady among the steam and the soggy shoes.

His job sucks balls. I've been there. Hell, they can always throw me back here if they see fit.

I pass Felix on my way back into the kitchen.

"Good job tonight," he says flatly.

"Thanks, Chef."

And that's it. No fanfare. No slap on my back, but it was perfect praise from someone wearing the coveted blue and leather.

I'm at my locker gathering my things when the dishwasher finally stops whirling, the last of the trash rustling out the back door, and the swish of a mop tracing arcs across the tile. Finally… quiet.

Then I hear voices behind the office wall—Theo and Felix.

"I don't know what to do." Theo's voice is low, tight.

"Theo, how do we put this genie back in the bottle? He really fucked up."

"Goddamn it. It's going to be all over the local news. Social media. We're gonna be fucking toast. He's out of control."

My pulse kicks up and I don't move. *Who are they talking about?*

Felix scoffs. "Well, the group doesn't have to figure out how to fire him. Vallois has done it all on his own. I can't believe he fucking gets a DUI with a prostitute in his car. What an idiot."

A chair scrapes across the floor with a screech, pulling me back to now.

"I'll wait to see what the group wants to do tomorrow. Maybe we can still get that Bay Chef in to stage." He sighs. "Fuck, what a mess. Let's get out of here. Talk about this tomorrow. Thanks, Felix."

"Okay."

I shut my locker softly and slip out the back door.

Vallois gone? Holy shit.

The night air hits like a reset button—cool, quiet, the weight of the kitchen still clinging to my clothes. I tell myself I should feel bad for him, feel something… but it slips away with a laugh I can't swallow. The ground shifts, and what rises in its place is terrifyingly simple—freedom, hope, and the thrill of wanting more.

~~~

Rocco's curled up in his crate when I walk in. Ears perk. Tail thumping. Like he heard me coming from a mile away. I let him out, give him a lazy ear scratch, and collapse onto the couch with my phone.

I scroll through my camera roll. Good lord, I take a lot of pictures of him. Like some proud parent who can't believe their newborn exists. Measuring his tiny life through snapshots and videos. I stop on one of him curled in my hoodie against my chest. A selfie of us. His tongue out. Proud and ridiculous.

I open the thread with Ritchie first. Haven't touched it in… too long. Something I swore I wouldn't let happen again.

> Kyle: Look who I adopted. His name's Rocco. Total menace, but he likes me. So that's new.

Send.

It feels good. Easy.

Then I scroll.

Macy. My goddamn drug. The second her name hits my screen, something in my chest tilts toward her. I know I shouldn't text. I should let her go. But the pull is strong. Just one last hit. One more time.

My last text is still there.

"You okay?"

Read. Never answered.

I sit with it. Thumb hovering. Heart doing that stupid tilt it always does when her name comes up. And then… I choose a different photo. Rocco at the dog park, looking up at me like he's laughing.
~~~

Kyle: Look. I'm a dad. Thought you should know. I think he has my eyes. I hope you're doing okay.

Send.

No question. No hook. Just that.

I set the phone down. Rocco shifts beside me, sighs, presses his warm little body closer.

It's not that she's ignoring me. She's just matching what I've always given her—half-interest, half-availability, half a heart. Turns out I don't love the view from this side.

Maybe this time… I finally let her go.

Chapter 11

BONE BROTH & BRUISES

The sun cuts through the slats in the blinds. A blade of light runs straight across my face. Sharp. Warm. Unforgiving.

I blink against the light, groaning as I roll onto my back. For the first time in weeks, I don't have to rush into the scent of bleach and fryer oil. No prep list running laps through my head. No imaginary timer ticking down.

Just stillness.

I tug on sneakers, throw on a hoodie, and whistle for Rocco. He barrels toward me, all legs and ears—still growing into himself, his skin loose in places like a suit he hasn't tailored yet. But he's filling in fast. Thick and muscular.

He's going to be a monster. *Jesus hell.*

Outside, the air has that clean-crisp bite. It smells like wet pavement and something green waking up. Morning birdsong hums around me, layered with the distant thrum of the city coming alive.

When was the last time I noticed birds?

I clip on his leash and we start walking.

We don't go far—just a loop around the neighborhood. A stretch. A breath. I let Rocco lead. The tension in my shoulders unspools a little, muscle by muscle, minute by minute.

My phone buzzes in my pocket, and I almost don't answer.

Then I see the name: Wallace. "Uncle Wally." My father's brother. The only sliver of family I still have on that side. The only one I still talk to, anyway.

I hesitate for a second. Then I press Accept.

"Hey, Wally."

"Kyle. How are you?" His voice is warm and friendly. *Not* my father's.

"I'm doing great. You?"

"Oh, you know. Retirement life. Your Aunt Becky's got me booked solid with trips. We're doing well." He pauses. "Kyle..."

I stop mid-step. There's more coming—I feel it.

"Wally, is everything okay?"

He lets out a laugh that doesn't quite land. "Oh, yeah, yeah... Everything's fine, Kyle. It's... your dad."

My heart drops straight to my feet. I look down, half-expecting to see it sitting on the sidewalk.

"What about him? Did something happen?" My voice comes out shaky, low.

"Yeah, Kyle. He's fine."

Somehow, that doesn't sound like good news.

"Okay. Spit it out, old man. What?"

He chuckles. "Him and Caroline are coming into town next week. He wants to see you, son."

"No." It comes out sharp, reflexive.

"Kyle, come on. It's been—what? Five years since you've seen him?"

"Yeah. And it can be another."

I lean against a brick building. Rocco plops down beside me with a huff, giving up on the walk entirely.

"Why don't you just think about it?" Wally asks.

I pinch the bridge of my nose. My head's buzzing.

"Wally... How long are they staying?"

"A week. They're booked at the St. Regis. We can work around your schedule. You still over at that seafood place?"

Of course he's at the St. Regis. Caroline needs her butler service. Father needs floor-to-ceiling windows, so he can look down on the little people. *Good god.*

I scoff. "No. I'm at Le Début now."

"Oh! Nice, Kyle. That's really nice."

Not that I needed his approval. Or his praise. But… It felt good. And I know it'll make its way back to Father Dearest. Maybe he'll be proud of me. Maybe he'll think I'm worth a table reservation now.

Anger rises—burning low in my gut, climbing up to my ears. His voice is already churning in my head.

"Becky and I will have to come check it out. I'm proud of you, son."

Wally's voice steadies me. Calms the boil. Pulls me back from the edge.

"Anyway… think about it, okay? Just dinner. That's all."

I swallow the chunk of cement lodged in my throat. "Yeah. I'll give it a thought. I'll have to check my schedule. I'm really busy."

"Okay." A long beat of silence. "We miss you, Kyle. You know we're always your family. Always here… right here, son."

I take a shaky breath. "Thanks, Wally. I know." I pause. "Give Becky my best, will you?"

I hang up and then tug lightly on the leash. "Come on, buddy."

Rocco looks up at me like I've just interrupted the greatest nap of his life.

I don't hear the birds anymore. Don't feel the sun. Don't see the trees or the people passing by. Instead, I'm back at their goddamn wedding. Eighteen years old, sitting at a table weighed down by flower arrangements that needed their own security detail because they were so fucking expensive.

And the anger rushes in—flooding my body like it never left.

I wasn't seated with my family. Not up front, but not in the back with the chick who did Caroline's hair. Somewhere in the middle. Lost in a sea of names I barely knew. Strategic placement.

I could practically hear the conversation.

"Oh, Whit… where should we put Kyle so he blends in?"

His deep laugh echoing off the marble walls, casual as a discarded paper napkin.

"Toss him in with those cousins… Ricky, Joseph… I don't know who they are. Somewhere in the middle. I don't care."

The story of my life. "I don't care."

Ever since my mom died, he stopped caring. I turned eighteen, and he got married. He moved on—with *her*. Left me drifting, surrounded by beautiful things I didn't ask for. Expensive things I'll never touch.

I stop walking. Somewhere in the fog of memory and rage, I've managed to go blocks. Maybe miles. Rocco's tongue hangs out, tail wagging, happily oblivious to my emotional collapse.

At least one of us is thriving.

My phone buzzes again. A text.

Ritchie: You're a dog dad? I see the resemblance.

I huff a laugh. Barely. But it's there.

I look up and realize I'm at the waterfront. Close to High Tide.

Kyle: You at work yet?

His reply comes fast.

Ritchie: Yep. Here early. Grease trap day. Another day in fucking paradise.

I pick up the pace.

Kyle: We're in the hood. My boy needs water.

Ritchie: I gotchu.

We walk up just as Ritchie pushes open the back door with his foot, a quart container in hand. The heavy door thuds against the mop bucket propping it open.

Rocco's tail starts beating double-time when he sees Ritchie crouch with his arms open. He just knows—this guy's my friend.

"Oh my god. He's fucking awesome, man," Ritchie says as Rocco launches a full tongue assault on his face, butt wiggling so hard he almost knocks himself over.

"Yeah," I say, smiling despite myself. "He's pretty cool."

Ritchie stands and points to the container. "Here, buddy."

Rocco goes face-first, water flying. He pauses mid-slosh to look up at me like, *Am I doing it right?*

"Go on," I nod, and he dives back in.

"So?" Ritchie lights a cigarette. "How's the new gig? You speaking French yet?"

"Not yet." I look down, kick a rock with the toe of my shoe, then glance up at him, squinting against the glare. "It's hard. But I'm learning a lot. How are things here?"

He exhales a laugh, smoke curling into the sunlight. "Same shit." He points at me with his cigarette. "Vic finally fired Louis. Hired a couple new guys. It's not the same." His voice drops. He's tired. "It's not fun." He gives me a half smile and taps my arm.

"I'm sorry, Ritchie."

"Fuck… don't be. I'm happy for you." He smiles again, takes a drag, and nods toward Rocco—now sprawled belly-down in a puddle of spilled water, panting with a goofy grin. "You're doing good shit."

I smile at Rocco's ridiculously cute face.

"Hey… how's Macy?" I ask. The second the words leave my mouth, I want to cram them back in.

Ritchie stubs his cigarette out with his shoe, shaking his head. "I don't know. She quit like… maybe two weeks after you. Better job, something with her mom. I don't know. Front-of-house drama. I had my own crap to deal with—working your job and mine."

"Oh. Damn."

He nods. "Why? Thought you stopped seeing her anyway."

I sigh. "Yeah. I did. I just texted her a few times. She didn't answer. Just checking on her."

He laughs—throaty and obnoxious. "Ahh… two a.m. booty call? She ghost your ass?"

"Fuck off," I say, smirking.

"Anything else going on?" he asks.

I chew my inner cheek. Ritchie's known me since high school. The only one who knows the whole story.

It blurts out before I can stop it. Like a spark catching air.

"Whitmore and Caroline are coming to town. They want to… do dinner."

I exhale like I've been holding those words underwater.

"Ho—ly shit. What the fuck? He actually called you? What'd you say?" Ritchie fires the questions off rapidly, like rounds from a gun.

I shake my head. "Nah. Wally called. Whit's too much of a pussy to actually do that himself."

"What are you gonna do, Kyle? Are you going?" He snorts. "Low-key, I want you to go just so you can take pictures. Show me how much plastic surgery they've had. Like—text me mid-salad."

I huff out a laugh. Ritchie has a way of making it funny. He always has.

"I haven't said yes." I shake my head. "I don't know." I bend and pet Rocco—my new support animal.

"What do you think he wants?" Ritchie asks, voice quieter now.

I don't look up. I keep my eyes on Rocco, fingers ruffling the fur between his ears. "I don't know, man," I mutter. "I don't know."

~~~

I stare blankly at the text.

Uncle Wally: Just dinner. Come on, Kyle.

If he only knew—it's more than just dinner. It's selling my soul to the devil. I don't respond.

Instead, I get back to work. Busy hands. Quiet head. Sink into the list, one task at a time.

I've got a stockpot the size of a toddler warming low and slow on the back burner. Bones, mirepoix, peppercorns, and bay leaf. Everything is submerged and still.

I lift the lid and stir gently, the scent rising like a memory. Earthy, rooted, and honest.

I don't know why I picked broth. Maybe because it takes hours. Maybe because it's ugly at first—bloody bones, scraps, fat, heat—and then it transforms into a beautiful base, a foundation to build on. Something that holds.

Maybe because I want to believe I can do the same.

There's a shuffle of feet from the other side of the kitchen. Voices. Theo's.
~~~

"…she's staging with us this week. Possible replacement for my position, if she doesn't burn the place down."

I don't even look up at first. I just keep stirring.

And then: "Cassie Patterson."

Everything inside me stills. Just for a second.

I look up and there she is.

Hair pulled back. All in chef blacks. Eyes sweeping the room like she already knows where everything belongs.

I don't know why that thought even crossed my mind, my chest tightening like I've missed a step in a recipe I've never made before.

Later, when I tell this story to myself, I'll pretend I didn't feel it. That it didn't hit me out of nowhere. That I didn't feel the world narrow to the shape of her shoulders and the certainty in her stride.

But this is the moment. Right here. The exact second everything in my life branches off in two directions: Before Cassie Patterson walked into my life. And after.

Chapter 12

STIRRED, NOT STRAINED

She floats.

That's the only word for it. Not glides, not walks—floats from one station to the next, like she's already worked every corner of this French kitchen in another life. Like the knives and pans remember her.

It's her third day staging, and I haven't stopped watching her since she walked through the door.

Cassie Patterson is the kind of chef who makes the kitchen quieter. Not because people are scared—because they're listening. She doesn't raise her voice. Doesn't throw pans. Doesn't carry the weight of her authority like a threat. She just moves like she belongs. Like this line was always waiting for her.

And when she messes up—and she does, once in a while—it doesn't rattle her. She laughs. Shakes her head. Keeps going.

She just smiles.

Jesus Christ, that smile.

It's not flirty. Not even aimed at anyone. It's the kind of smile that says, *I'm going to get this. Just give me a second.* It's grace. The real kind. Not polished. Not performative. Simply earned.

And my heart? Yeah. It fucking melts. Every single time.

"So, do you think they'll offer her the job?" I ask Natalie during closing, balancing a stacked hotel pan.

She shrugs. "I think it's more—will she take it? Rumor has it this isn't her only option." She heads into the office.

That tracks. Who wouldn't want her?

I glance down the hall as the doors swing open. She's breaking down sauté with Felix. Wiping down the station. Talking. Laughing.

Felix is laughing. Like… full-body, throaty laughing.

She's been here three damn days and has already managed to change the entire atmosphere—from Vallois' suffocating foot-on-your-chest pressure to… this. Everything feels lighter.

"Hey! Berkley," Jules calls from the pass. "We're heading to Lowball for drinks. Ramen pop-up tonight. You in?"

"Yeah…" I check my watch. *Shit. Rocco.*

"Yeah, let me see if my roommate's going home to take my dog out. If not, I might meet you there." I smile, a thing I'm somehow doing more lately.

"Cool. I think we talked Chef Cassie into going," he adds before disappearing.

My hand's already in my back pocket, fumbling for Collin's contact.

Kyle: Hey. You going home after work?

I stare at the screen, willing him to answer faster.

When the reply buzzes in, it hits like a jolt.

Collin: Just walked in. Sup?

Relief washes over me.

Kyle: Sweet. Can you take Rocco out for me?

Collin: Already did.

Kyle: Thanks, man. I'm going out for a bit with the guys. I won't be late. Just put him back in the crate if you go out or to bed.

Collin: Oh, we're gonna party. I got some bitches on da way. By the way, he's panting and staring at me. I think he's down.

I shake my head and laugh. Between me and Collin, this dog

has become our entertainment and replaced any resemblance of a dating life.

I tug off my apron, fold it once, and slide it into my bag. My hands are still warm from helping Joe in the dish pit so we could get out faster, wrists sore from breaking down boxes, but I don't feel tired. Not really.

More like… wired.

I shove through the back door into the cool night air. The walk to Lowball is short, maybe ten minutes, but long enough for my brain to start up again. Thinking too much. Thinking about… *her.*

By the time I round the corner and see the flicker of the red light above the door, I've already imagined what it'll feel like to sit near her. Not *with* her. Just close enough to watch the way she tucks her hair behind her ear or laughs at something no one else noticed.

Lowball is already humming—music low, lights warm, that trendy vintage vibe everyone pretends not to love. A few bodies are tucked into booths, voices climbing over each other in that way service industry people talk after closing: fast, loud, and uncorked.

Jules waves from the bar, already holding a drink.

"Berkley!" he yells. "You're late. The broth's hot, but the bartender's hotter." He winks at the bartender, who just shakes her head with a forced smile.

I smirk, weaving toward the group. And then, I see her. She's here. Cassie fucking Patterson is here.

Sitting in a booth near the back, laughing. Same laugh. Same ease. Her chef coat's off, a cold cocktail in one hand and a bowl of ramen steaming in front of her like she's getting a sexy little soup facial.

My chest tightens.

Deep breath, Kyle. Why the hell is she having this effect on me?

I've worked with plenty of talented chefs. I've laughed with plenty of beautiful women. This is different. This feels like a damn wire wrapped around my ribs and someone just tugged.

I force my feet toward the bar. I need a drink.

I slide onto a barstool, still watching her from the corner of my eye. She doesn't see me. And maybe that's for the best.

Jules slaps my shoulder. "Sorry we left you behind with Joe."

I smirk. "I get it… I'm the new guy." I shrug. "We got it done. All good."

"What can I get you?" the bartender asks.

"Just an IPA… whatever's on tap. Thanks."

Then she appears at my side. Her voice slices through the noise—low and easy. "So… you just started?"

I turn, and she's right there, propped against the bar like she's been doing this for years. Vintage tee, chef pants cuffed, hair loose and a little wild from the walk. The lowball glass in her hand is nearly empty. She was drinking something dark.

For a second, I don't even know if she's talking to me.

"Yeah," Jules says beside me. "This is Berkley… Kyle. He's been with us a little while now. Likes to keep a low profile."

She arches a brow. "Low profile, huh?"

I shrug. "Mostly just tired."

She smirks, lifting her glass. "Well, I'm glad you came out. Sorry I didn't get a chance to work with you."

"Yeah, maybe next time." I smile—too small, too awkward. "What are you drinking?"

She chuckles, glancing at the nearly empty glass. "Their signature cocktail. The Line Cook. Mezcal, cold brew, Fernet, smoked salt rim… something like that. It's really good. Dirty and funky."

"That sounds like us." I laugh. "Also sounds like you could climb back there and make it yourself."

She tilts her head like she might. "Maybe. If they let me." Then she sips.

And Jesus—when her head tips back, ice clinking against the now empty glass, my eyes fall down her neck to her chest. A faded black T-shirt with the picture of a little toaster with oversized hands. And in white block letters: *Emotionally Overcooked.*

Of course she's wearing that. Of course she's the kind of person who can command a kitchen all day, then walk into a dive bar in a thrifted tee that sums up the entire service industry's mental state, and somehow make it look cool.

She sets her glass down just as my beer hits the bar.

I nod to the bartender. "Can she get another one of those, please? Put it on my tab."

She blinks. "Oh… thanks, Kyle."

That smile.

We end up taking over half the place—multiple booths and tables shoved together in a way that would make any server roll their eyes, even if they know our tip will make up for it. Drinks flow freely. Funky food hits the table in waves: dirty fries, béarnaise with pickled onion, duck-fat grilled cheese with bacon jam—everything torn apart like it's the back prep table at the restaurant.

It feels like family meal.

This is family.

This is easy.

This is fun.

I can't stop glancing over at her. I can't stop watching her.

Her hair's loose now, curled at the ends from the humidity. She tucks it behind her ear and slurps a noodle without shame, laughing at something Jules just said. Felix and a few front-of-house staff tell nightmare stories from past services. She's not appalled. She's lived these same stories.

I swear to God, she glows. Not in a glittery, manic-pixie way. Not in the filtered kind of glow you see on social media. No—this is a slow burn. Stove-light glow. The kind that makes you lean closer without realizing it.

By the look on her face, I think she's in. I think we sold her on… *us.*

~~~

The overheads are off. It's dim, and everything glows like melted honey. The air's thick with garlic and something sweeter—herbs and tomato. Warmth wraps around my body, slow and indulgent.

Something sizzles low in a pan. The rhythmic sound of a knife on a board beside me—basil chiffonade, the green ribbons scattering like confetti under her delicate fingers.

A pot rolls at a low boil. Pasta, handmade, slips through my
~~~

fingers and sinks like wishes to the bottom of a well. Flour coats my hands. A dusting clings to my apron, blue and broken in, the leather soft from use and the ties hanging low on my hips.

She's behind me. I don't see her. But fuck if I don't feel her.

Her arms slide around my waist, under my shirt, palms splaying across my stomach like she owns it. Her body molds to mine, hips pressing into the backs of my thighs. Her chin rests on my shoulder. Her breath—hot and humid—tickles my jaw.

"I've been thinking about this all day." Her voice is low. Not a whisper. Not a tease.

Just the truth.

My grip on the wooden spoon falters when she turns me, and I let her. Like gravity. Like we've done this before—over and over. Like my body remembers even if my mind's still catching up.

She slides my apron off slowly, looping the ties around her hand like a dare. Flour streaks across my forearms, my black T-shirt, and the sides of my jeans. Her eyes lock with mine. Her mouth parts.

She leans in. Her kiss lands beneath my jaw, teeth dragging across the column of my neck like a brand. My breath catches.

"You gonna get that pasta?" she murmurs.

"Nope." My voice sounds foreign. Rough and starved.

We crash together like a slow-motion wreck—hands greedy, bodies sliding into each other, backs hitting the counter. I lift her onto it without breaking the kiss. Her thighs part and pull me in, gravity snapping us into place. Like I was always meant to be here.

Flour. Heat. Basil. Her.

I bury my hands in her hair and tug—just enough to make her gasp. That sound. *God.* That sound practically brings me to my knees. She lightly bites my lower lip, and I nearly lose it.

Her fingers ghost the waistband of my jeans, then down over my cock—so hard it's almost painful against the zipper.

"Fuck, baby. We need to do something about that." She whispers against my chin. Teeth grazing my jaw. Her smile tugs at something deep inside me.

The button, the zipper, then her warm hand wraps around me. I kiss her hard, her hand working me in long, slow strokes.

My hands slide under her shirt. Her skin is so damn warm. My thumbs find her nipples already hard.

Behind us, a sharp hiss cuts through the room—the pot boiling over, water hitting flame. A sizzle like the heat rolling off our skin.

"The pasta," she whimpers in my ear.

She's everywhere—her scent, her breath, her hands ghosting fire across my skin.

"Fuck the pasta. God, I want you, Cassie."

BEEP… BEEP… BEEP.

No no no. *Don't stop.*

I jolt awake in my room—hard, panting. Sheets kicked halfway off, pillow damp behind my neck.

Jesus.

I rake a hand through my hair, trying to shake the static. My heart's still racing. My skin feels tight. At least it's not the usual nightmare.

No screams. No fists. No Dad.

But still… cold shower. Now.

I glance down.

Maybe if I'm lucky, my brain'll cue the sequel.

Chapter 13

BURNED IN SPRINGFORM

"Go, Rocco," I hiss, glancing at my watch.

I can't believe my life is now at the mercy of my dog's bowel movement schedule.

"Dude, I'm gonna be late for work. Stop with the circles and poop already."

My phone dings in my pocket. I pull it out.

Uncle Wally: Are you going to make it to dinner Friday?

I groan and shove it back into my pocket. I'm not answering. I still haven't made up my mind if I'm going, even though I already requested the day off. I can't believe I'm even contemplating it.

I swore the bastard off years ago. Never letting him in. Never letting him under my skin again.

I glance down just in time to see Rocco straining in his awkward poop stance. I stand there, ready with my bag-covered hand like a proud dad watching his kid use the potty for the first time.

God, my life has taken a weird turn.

Between this and the hopeful sex dreams of Chef Cassie, my existence has become… pitiful.

~~~

"Three fish all day, and eighty-six the rabbit confit," Natalie calls.

"Heard," I say, sliding a pan onto the flame. Butter, a swirl of
~~~

oil, one plume of smoke—perfect. I lay in the branzino, the sizzle rising like an orchestra in my ears.

"Sharp behind," Jules says, passing with his knives on the way to the dish pit. He glances at my pan. "Nice sear, friend… nice." His northern accent paws at my ears before he disappears again.

I'm on my own at sauté these days—comfortable and at home. Earning nods from everyone on the line.

The rhythm hits.

Sauce down.

Flip.

Plate.

Garnish.

"Runner to expo," I call, placing a plate in the pass.

"Three fish walking!" I call out, sharp and clear.

Poor bastards. Like they're on death row, and someone just handed them their last cigarette.

Calls come fast, but I'm faster.

There's this stretch in the middle of service where everything just clicks—like a song you didn't know you knew. Muscle memory and instinct. Fire and steel.

I'm mid-scrub on my station during breakdown when Natalie passes behind me, balancing a stack of dirty pans.

"Oh—hey. Guess what?"

I smirk, not looking up. "If you say I'm back on Garde tomorrow, I'm walking out."

She grins. "Chef Cassie said yes."

I pause. Just enough for the silence to say too much. "She took the job?" I ask, trying to keep my voice neutral.

"Theo's position. Yeah. Theo's officially head chef."

I nod once. "Cool."

Just cool. Just information. Inside? I'm a goddamn firework show. I'm twelve espresso shots deep on an empty stomach. I'm trying not to smile.

~~~

I ride my board home through the hum of the city, wheels buzzing
~~~

underfoot. The air's soft and cool as it brushes my skin. Streetlights blink overhead like someone breathing slowly.

And all I can think about is her.

Cassie, slurping ramen like it was a Michelin dish. Laughing like she's got a secret. That thrifted tee with the toaster and the words *Emotionally Overcooked.*

I don't want to be obsessed. But fuck… I think I might be.

I hit the intersection too fast, nearly eat it on a crack in the pavement, and just laugh—alone, breathless, a little unhinged. I don't even care.

She's coming. Cassie's coming.

When I walk in, Rocco's waiting at the door with a full-body wiggle like I've been gone a week. I leash him up, and we walk.

The streets are quiet. The sky is heavy with stars. Something's blooming—jasmine, maybe. He sniffs everything like it's sacred, and I let him. My hand stays in my pocket. My mind doesn't stay anywhere. It drifts straight to her.

Back inside, I crack a beer and drop onto the couch. Rocco circles once and flops against my shin with a long dog sigh.

And then I see it. The box.

Still on the top shelf, a little landmine I keep pretending isn't there. Still untouched since Rocco's shredding frenzy exposed it.

I take a long pull from the bottle, eyes glued to it. I don't want to go there tonight. But I know I will.

~~~

The steam climbs over my shoulders, steady as breath, trying to soothe a mind that won't shut up.

I drag my fingers through my hair, trying to untangle the mess in my head—her, my mom… and then, like always, him. My father. The dinner invite I haven't answered. The weight I haven't lifted.

Fuck.

Wally.

I shut off the water and step out, feet hitting the cool tile. The mirror fogs, and I wipe it clean, revealing the version of me I've been avoiding—hair longer than I ever keep it, stubble creeping down my
~~~

jaw. Unkempt. Not the guy Cassie Patterson's gonna notice when she's back on the line.

And definitely not the kind of son my dad wants to see sitting across the table Friday night—*if* I even go.

I throw on sweatpants and walk into the kitchen. It's late—but in this world, late doesn't mean tired. It's *after-shift* late. That strange, wired stretch where your body's still buzzing from service—heart pounding, hands tingling—and the rest of the world's already asleep. This is when most food and bev people head out drinking, blow off steam, and make bad decisions.

This is when a lot of people get in trouble.

I'm the guy who goes home and cooks like a lunatic. Nerds out on vintage recipes that say things like *scant* and *smidgen*, tests sauces at midnight, blasts jazz or Led Zeppelin while I make three kinds of gnocchi just because I can. Same energy—just aimed somewhere that won't wreck me.

Collin loves this shit when he comes home buzzed at two a.m. with an appetite built like a death wish.

So, here I am, barefoot, bone-tired, still twitching from service… and staring at that damn recipe box like it might break my soul in half.

"Fuck it," I say to my four-legged support system, pulling it from the shelf.

"Don't even think about it," I add, glancing down at Rocco, already sitting like I'm about to whip up something life-changing.

"I'm surprised this thing doesn't give you PTSD, dude." I wave the avocado-green box in the air.

He just smiles and wags his tail—his forgiving heart thumping like none of that ever happened.

I wish mine had the same capacity.

I open the lid and smirk down at him before going back to the search.

One by one, I flip through them—sauces and Italian sides that deserve to be kept in a museum, not jammed into this old plastic box. All handwritten cards, flour-smudged edges, ink fading with time. All patched together with too much tape from the Rocco incident.

My mom's handwriting curls across every one—strong, confident strokes, like she never doubted a single outcome. Each card is a gateway. A ghost. A pulse of memory: her at the stove, stirring something deep and slow; pasta rolled thin across the counter; the whole kitchen warm with the scent of vanilla and hope.

I run my thumb along the edge of the card, patched like a wounded soldier. My breath tightens.

I remember her humming that day. She always hummed. Still in her apron, barefoot, swiping flour off the counter with the side of her hand. Measuring cream cheese. Scraping vanilla beans with the back of a paring knife. Calm and methodical. Magic.

"We just burned the first one, kiddo. It's not the end of the world."

Except it was. I just didn't know it yet.

My finger drags down the ingredients, and suddenly I'm not twenty-four in my kitchen—I'm a kid again, my hand half this size, tracing these same words while she hummed beside me.

The card is soft around the edges—worn down by time, dog teeth, and tape. Her handwriting still curves across the top like a whisper: *Mom's Italian Cheesecake.*

I exhale slowly and carefully. Because if I breathe too hard, I might fall apart right here on the counter.

It's not New York style. It never was. This was her version. Lighter. Tangier. Sweet in the way memories are sweet. Always made in my grandmother's old springform pan, the janky latch you had to finesse open like it was part of the recipe.

I trace the list with one finger:

- cream cheese
- sugar
- eggs
- lemon zest
- vanilla
- ricotta

I stop.

Tears well in my eyes, hot and sudden. I blink hard, but they come anyway. My throat pulls tight.

Ricotta.

I told her I'd set the timer. But I didn't.

The word hits like a gut punch. The missing ingredient. The reason she went out. The reason she never came back.

Fuck.

My vision blurs and the card trembles in my hand. I set it down too fast, like it burns.

Because it does.

I know her springform pan is in that cabinet—back right corner—exactly where I've avoided it for years. I press my palms to the counter, anchoring myself. The card sits beneath my fingers, fragile and crooked and still here. Still waiting.

I whisper it, more breath than sound: "I want to make this fucking cheesecake."

Chapter 14

NO REGERTS

Rocco skitters across the kitchen, nails tapping against the tile as he beelines for the door. I don't even look up.

The lock clicks. The door swings open.

Collin breezes in with a six-pack swinging from one hand and what is absolutely someone else's flannel draped over the other. His boots are half-unlaced, jeans cuffed like he didn't quite finish getting dressed. And he's sporting a long silk scarf in a pattern so chaotic it might trigger a seizure. It's somewhere between vintage paisley and acid trip. And he's humming… yep. ABBA. "Mamma Mia," clear as day.

Then he freezes. Mid-step. The hum dies.

"Oh fuck," he says, tone flat. "Not that box."

My head lifts, barely.

He sets the six-pack down like it might detonate. His eyes lock onto the green plastic container like it's a live explosive.

"Please tell me you were looking for a meatball recipe?" he asks carefully, already knowing he's wrong.

I don't say anything.

He exhales hard through his nose, the smirk he usually wears like armor softening at the edges. "Shit, Kyle." He steps closer, ruffling Rocco's ears automatically, grounding both of us.

"Okay," he says, dropping his voice like he's afraid to spook me. "Are we about to make something? Or are we just… standing in the wreckage right now?"

I shrug. That's all I've got.

Collin loops around the island, pops the caps off two beers, and sets one in front of me without asking.

"I figured," he says. "You've got that 'I just emotionally relived my childhood over a recipe' look."

A breath slips out of me—something almost like a laugh, but not quite.

He leans on the counter, eyes soft, voice low. "We making some shit?" he asks, shrugging off the scarf and taking a pull from his beer.

I look down at the recipe card. "Not this." I slide it back into the front of the box like it's too fragile to press on. My fingers shuffle deeper until I find *Aunt Rosie's Crostini with Ricotta, Lemon Zest, and Olive Oil.* I hold it up.

"Here. I'll make this." I wave the card like a winning lottery ticket.

"Sweet. I'm starving." Collin turns toward the entryway to kick off his boots—completely unaware he just dodged the emotional equivalent of a commercial-grade grease fire.

"How was work tonight?" Collin calls, walking back in with a stack of mail—completely oblivious.

"Good," I say, pulling ingredients from the fridge. "You?" I flick on the music, grateful he's home, grateful for the shift in energy. The air lightens. The kitchen exhales.

"Busy. It was good." He discards half the mail straight into the trash. "Oh shit. Lotus came in."

My head snaps up so fast I nearly slice my finger off along with the lemon. "Jesus Christ, Collin. This should've been the first thing you said to me." My pulse spikes. "Did she ask about Rocco?"

He snorts. "Yeah, she did."

I raise both hands. "And?"

"She just asked how he was."

I let out a long breath. "Jesus. Does she even care? She just abandoned her goddamn dog."

He takes a sip of beer. "Well, I didn't want to say too much. I was worried she'd say she wanted to come get him. And you're not… you know… prepared for that now, right?"

I glance down. Rocco is sprawled in the middle of the kitchen like a failed cinnamon roll—bigger now, belly up, snoring softly. Completely at peace.

He knows where he belongs.

"Yeah," I say, laughing under my breath. "I'd have to take her out if she tried to take him now." Not entirely a joke.

"So, yeah. I didn't ask too many questions." Collin's voice is casual, but the protectiveness underneath it is loud.

"I need to take him to the vet," I mutter, slicing a baguette and laying the rounds on a sheet tray. "I have no idea what shots he's had. That would be nice to know."

Collin flops onto a barstool, still nursing his beer like it's a prop in a one-man show.

"Well, since we're playing show and tell," he says, gesturing dramatically at the ricotta, the lemons, the emotional crime scene still hovering in the air, "how was *your* day at work, honey?"

I roll my eyes. "I made a sexy-ass branzino special, and they're still letting me roam free in sauté."

He smirks. "God, I love when you talk dirty."

I finish brushing oil over the bread and slide the tray into the oven. "Cassie's coming back," I say—like it's nothing. Like it doesn't make my chest tighten every time I say her name.

Collin's head tilts. "That chef who was staging?"

I nod. "Yeah. She's taking Theo's position. He's head now."

There's a silent beat.

"And how do *we* feel about that?" he asks gently, in a voice that tells me he knows I brought it up for a reason.

I grab a bowl and start whipping the ricotta with lemon zest like it's suddenly a matter of national security.

"I don't know," I say. "She's… good."

"Mm-hmm," he says, watching me too closely. "Good at cooking? Or good at making you look like a teenager with a boner in sweatpants?"

I snort. "Jesus, Collin."

He raises his beer in salute. "I'm just saying. I know that look.

You get all weird and serious. Like you're trying to decide whether to make her dinner or tell her your trauma."

I spread the ricotta onto the toasted bread. "Nah. No trauma here."

I line up the baguette slices, garnish each one with a dusting of lemon zest from the microplane, then finish with a clean drizzle of olive oil. Simple. Classic. Emotional support crostini.

I slide the plate between us.

"Dig in, bitch." I smile.

He takes a bite like it's communion. His eyes roll back. "Fuck. If I were gay, I'd bend you over nightly, I swear."

I laugh and grab one for myself.

"How does something this simple taste this good?" he asks.

I lean on my elbows, the tension finally easing from my shoulders. "Love, fucker." I say softly. "It's love."

And just like that, the avocado-green box stops staring. Just for a little while.

~~~

I stare at the text.

My thumb hovers. And before I can talk myself out of it, I hit send.

The phone buzzes back almost instantly—like he's been waiting all week, phone in hand, breath held.

Uncle Wally: It's going to be okay, Kyle. I promise.

My throat tightens. I blink at the screen.

Can he *really* promise that?

~~~

I stand with one foot on my skateboard, rocking it back and forth. Leash in one hand, phone in the other.

Kyle: Gym today? You still off?

I chuckle at the thought of *Ritchie* at a gym, but I need to catch up. I seriously need to move—bleed off some of this stress before dinner tonight.

The dots appear. Dance a little.

Ritchie: Fuck. Why did I tell you? Can I smoke while I lift?

...and there it is. Right on cue.

Kyle: Come on. I said yes to dinner with the King and Queen. I need emotional support and to throw around some weights. It's this or I jump off the Golden Gate.

Ritchie: You know you can't jump off that thing anymore with all those fences, nets, and shit. Fine.

Kyle: I go to The Yard now. See you at 10.

Ritchie: Oh Christ. The place with the truck tires and crap?

Kyle: Be a man and sweat.

I can practically hear him groaning from here.

"You too, asshole," I say to Rocco's smiling face. "You're learning to run today."

I push off gently, skateboard rolling beneath me, leash pulling lightly. Rocco trots beside me, catching on fast—tongue hanging out, tail high, happy.

We reach the waterfront. Running paths curve along the wharf, water lapping against the sea wall. Sea lions roar, tourists gawk, and we weave through the chaos until the path opens into a long stretch of green—runners, bikers, strollers.

I stop and check my watch. 8:05.

"We need to get back, buddy."

I glance down just as Rocco sets a paw on the skateboard. Just a tap. A... *try me.*

I scan the path. Clear enough.

"Here. Get on, buddy," I say, crouching to help him up.

He settles on the board without a flinch. Gangly, awkward, all legs—but calm. Trusting. I steady him with both hands and start to push. And then... we're moving.

I'm laughing. He's locked in. Tail wagging. Tongue lolling. Not a tremor in his body. Just pure trust. In me. I let him go, guiding him only with the leash.

He's *skateboarding.*

"Rocco, look at you!" I shout, grinning like an idiot—like he's my kid riding a bike for the first time.

I fumble for my phone, hands shaking as I dig it out of my pocket. He keeps rolling down the path—ears flapping in the wind, totally locked in.

My heart pounds against my ribs. My smile stretches all the way to my ears for the first time in… God, I don't even know how long.

I reach down and unlatch his leash.

"Alright, buddy," I whisper, giving him a gentle push.

He glides forward, steady and sure.

I take off ahead—sneakers slapping pavement—fumbling to hit record on my phone.

I catch it all: his tongue out, ears bouncing, tail wagging like it's keeping time. Rocco, rolling like he was made for this. Pure joy—mine, his, ours. *Free.*

~~~

I'm finishing up my twenty-minute run on the treadmill when my phone buzzes with a text.

Ritchie: I'm here and I hate this already.

The double doors swing open and there he is.

Chuck Taylors, unlaced. A faded AC/DC shirt with the sleeves cut off and the collar stretched to hell. Jeans turned into cutoff shorts so freshly hacked they're still fraying—like he destroyed them in the parking lot just to prove a point.

And on his head? A beat-up white trucker hat that reads: NO REGERTS. Possibly permanent marker. Totally crooked.

He walks in like the concept of personal hygiene is optional.

"Let's get this over with," he mutters, stopping in front of my machine. "This place smells like if a gym sock and a tire store had a baby."
~~~

My mouth twitches, fighting a full grin. "Nice shorts."

He looks down. "I cut them five minutes ago with kitchen shears."

I snort, grab my towel, and wipe my face.

"Wanna stretch?" I nod toward the mats.

He shrugs. "I'll follow your lead."

I drop into a hamstring stretch while he literally just reaches for the air. That's it.

"So," he says, like he's mid–Olympic warmup, "where are you going for dinner?"

"The Ledger." I exhale, letting my leg fall to the floor.

His eyes widen. "Oh hell. Do you even have anything to wear?"

"Yes." I rake a hand through my hair. "I need to cut this shit, though. Seriously, the world stops for that man. God forbid anyone be themselves when Whit and Caroline come to town."

"Hear thee, hear thee," he intones, dropping his arms from some half-assed non-stretch. "Roll out thy red carpet for the plastic King and Queen."

He smirks. "You *have* to send pictures, dude. She's gotta be full-on silicon by now." He bends over, maybe ten degrees, then gives up entirely.

"Come on," I say, standing up. "Let's go out there and push some sleds. Flip some tires around."

He snorts. "Why don't you just go work out at the landfill? Same vibe, less pretension."

I shake my head and sigh. This is exactly what I signed up for. And honestly? I need it.

Comic relief served hot before the entrée of hell my father's got planned for tonight—some legacy-laced lecture, a guilt glaze, judgment slow-roasted until it falls off the bone.

I'll take Ritchie in cutoffs and a hat that says *No Regerts* over Caroline in an overly expensive couture gown and quiet disappointment any day.

Every time he grunts, I laugh.

He barely moves his awkward body, and somehow it makes my abs hurt more than anything I've done all month in this damn gym.

This. This is why he's my best friend.

"So," he says, placing an exhausted hand on my shoulder like he actually worked out. His hat is now backwards, sweat soaks his AC/DC shirt, and I'm pretty sure his thighs are chafed from those damp denim nightmares.

"If you need me tonight," he adds, tone shifting just a little, "I got you." Then he smirks. "But seriously—pics."

I shake my head, smiling.

I leave the gym sore, loose, and slightly more prepared to face the firing squad. Then I walk into the apartment, and Collin takes one look at me, fresh haircut and all, and just says, "What are you wearing tonight?"

The mirror doesn't lie.

Tailored black pants, pressed so sharp they could cut glass. A crisp white shirt, collar open, sleeves cuffed with surgical precision. A dark blazer. And that subtle, vaguely illegal cologne from the underground dealer Collin swore me to secrecy over.

My hair is shorter now. Clean lines. Styled like I invest heavily in emotional detachment.

I barely recognize myself.

"Perfect. You look like someone with a complicated relationship with their father," Collin says, circling me like a backstage stylist at Fashion Week. "And also… like a thirst trap on Instagram."

I glance down and adjust the cuffs.

Everything fits. None of it feels like armor. Just a costume.

The jacket slides over my arms, smooth and quiet. I tug the sleeves down just enough to hide the ink winding along my forearms. Whit doesn't need to see that part of me—the part I chose, the part that doesn't belong at a table with his name on the reservation.

"Thanks," I murmur.

Collin hands me his keys and straightens my collar.

"Go make peace with the devil, man." He grins. "And if you don't, go out and get fucking laid."

~~~

Inside, it's all glass, dark wood, and warm lighting. Muted
~~~

conversations were underscored by the soft clink of silverware and crystal. Everyone is power dressed in pressed linen and pretentious low laughter.

I'm early. On purpose.

I take a seat at the bar. The stool is leather—the kind that squeaks like it's been expensive longer than I've been alive. The bartender nods once. "What can I get you?"

"Manhattan. Rittenhouse, if you've got it."

He doesn't blink, just slides it over in a heavy crystal glass.

I swirl the drink once, take a sip, and let the burn settle. Then I see her. Far end of the bar. Red lips. Black dress wrapped across her chest like a curse. She's watching me.

I look away and breathe. Before I can even check my watch again, she's standing beside me.

Her voice is velvet and casual. "Is that a Manhattan?"

I glance over. She wears confidence like a second skin. "Yeah," I say. "Rittenhouse. Want one?"

She smiles. "Only if I can sit."

I gesture toward the empty stool and the bartender's already moving. We talk. Light stuff. Names unspoken. Just a slow, steady flirt—the kind that smolders before it sparks.

And then the air shifts.

I feel it before I hear it. The tone of the hostess—polite, polished, reverent—the way people get when they greet names with weight.

I turn.

Whit and Caroline.

His eyes lock on mine immediately.

"Well," he says, voice edged with amusement, "you didn't tell us you were bringing a date?"

She stiffens beside me. Caroline's brow arches, a smile tugging at her mouth like she's auditioning for a soap opera.

"She's not…" I start, but Whit's already waving it off.

He turns to the hostess. "Can you add one more to our table, please? My son didn't tell me he was bringing a guest."

"Yes, of course, Mr. Berkley." She practically bows before gliding away.

I stand. "Dad. No—"

"No worries, son. You clean up well." He claps my shoulders, giving me a once-over. "Didn't think you had it in you."

And just like that, the floor cracks beneath my polished shoes.

I turn. She's already walking off. Black-draped sin with her Manhattan in hand. Gone.

I sit. Fake smile stretching thin. And I pray I don't throw the first fucking fork.

Chapter 15

THE SMOKE SHOW

I'm looking at the menu, but I'm not reading it. It's just rows of letters printed on paper, wrapped in leather binding. A stage prop. Background noise dressed up as conversation. Strangers with familiar voices tossing words across the table like napkins—polished, useless, easy to discard.

"Kyle, I was telling your dad that you just started a new job," Uncle Wally says casually.

I lower my menu just enough to see my father looking back at me. The face I haven't seen in five years. The face that looks disturbingly like an older version of me. And I want to punch it. Over and over.

"So," he says, smug, before sipping his scotch. "Tell me about it, son."

"I'm on the line at Le Début now. One of the top French restaurants in the Bay Area."

He tilts his head. "Is it Michelin?"

I scoff. "Is that all that matters? Stars?"

"Okaaay," Wally cuts in quickly. "So… what are we ordering?"

"This menu looks fantastic," Aunt Becky says, eyes dropping to the page. "What are you getting, Caroline?"

"Oh, probably just a soup and salad," Caroline says breathily, sipping her prosecco.

She crosses her legs, unfolding her napkin like she's at a Vogue luncheon.

Becky tries again. "So, how long have you been at Le Début, Kyle?"

"A couple of months," I say, eyes on the empty glass, turning it slowly in my hand like it's the only thing keeping me tethered. "Sauté now. Worked Garde for a bit at first."

Whit gestures with his glass. "So, why not just go to culinary school? You've got the means. The time. You'd move up faster. Stop playing around, son."

And there it is.

That word. *Playing.* Like this is a hobby I picked up between poker tournaments.

I meet his gaze. "Because this is how I want to do it. I like learning every station. I like learning on the job—from chefs who've been doing this their whole lives. Not in a classroom."

What I want to say is *I don't want your goddamn money.* I don't need your handouts to build a life. I can do this on my own. My way.

Caroline chuckles softly. "That's noble. Though not exactly efficient."

"There's something to be said for working your way up," Becky murmurs, fidgeting with her silverware.

Wally opens his mouth—probably to agree, but Whit steamrolls right over him.

"You're not getting younger," my father says, pointing his glass at me. "You could've owned a place by now if you'd enrolled years ago instead of screwing around at that low-grade fish house."

"I don't want to own the place," I say quietly. "I want to be a chef. I want to cook. I want to be good at *that.*"

"Well, Frank said you haven't touched your account. Not one cent in all these years." He shakes his head. "How are you even surviving on that measly pay—here, in San Francisco?" He gestures around us, like I should be dining in places like this on the regular.

Like I'm an embarrassment. Berkleys live better than this. Always have.

A beat passes.

"At least pay your bills with it, son."

Stop calling me that. The word catches in my throat like a fishbone. I glance at Wally, who looks like he might jump in, but even he knows better.

Caroline smooths her napkin like she's prepping for surgery. "I suppose pride tastes better than rent."

Fire climbs my throat, hot and fast. This—from the woman who thinks she replaced my mother. Who's never worked a day in her life. Who's only eight fucking years older than me.

"Hey—Whit… Kyle." Wally lifts his hands. "This was not supposed to be about this. You two haven't seen each other in years. Come on. Please."

Our server appears at the table like an answered prayer, oblivious.

"Is everyone ready to order?"

Caroline doesn't even glance at the menu. "Could we start with a wine recommendation?"

"Of course," the server says.

Caroline smiles, folding her hands in her lap. "Something… *special.* To celebrate."

My head snaps up. Celebrate? My job? The fact that I showed up? The fact that I'm still sitting here?

The server nods, already smiling. "If you're celebrating, I'd recommend the *Château Margaux.* We have a beautiful two-thousand-three."

My fingers tighten around my empty glass. That bottle costs more than my rent—and I should know.

Caroline doesn't blink. "Perfect," she says. "We'll take that."

Whit nods once, satisfied. Of course she wouldn't flinch. Why would she? This is just another Tuesday night to them.

The server glides away, already uncorking my humiliation.

~~~

I sit in the parking lot of the restaurant in Collin's BMW, headlights reflecting off the rows of expensive cars like some dignitary's funeral procession. I don't want to go home. Not yet. I'm too full of rage. Regret. Words I should've said but swallowed instead.

I can still hear Whit's voice—sharp as the steak knife I imagined
~~~

sinking into the table just to feel something solid. I can still see Caroline's tight-lipped fake smile like she'd just won a fucking pageant.

Wally and Becky tried. They always try. But trying doesn't change the fact that everything about that dinner felt like a goddamn performance. And I was the opening act and the punchline.

I stare out the windshield, the city lights smeared through the vintage glass. I exhale, slow. Then I reach for my phone on the cracked leather seat.

I type:

Kyle: Where ya at?

Ritchie: Is this a booty-call or an SOS?

Kyle: Funny. Those shorts didn't do it for me today. So, I guess an SOS.

Kyle: BTW, tons of plastic surgery.

Ritchie: Pics or it didn't happen.

Kyle: I was too busy not throwing a fork into their skulls.

Ritchie: Proud of you for not doing that. Also, disappointed. Those would have been cooler pictures.

Kyle: You still got that weird whiskey in the freezer?

Ritchie: Always.

Kyle: On my way.

Ritchie: Door is open. I'm so sore from today I can barely stand.

He seriously broke a sweat just standing in the sun, talking shit. The man worked harder avoiding exercise than actually doing it. I toss the phone onto the seat and laugh.

~~~
~~~

Ritchie lives in a converted Victorian with bad plumbing, thrift-store furniture, and a record collection so large and eclectic it feels like a personality disorder.

I let myself in. The lights are so low I almost think he's setting the mood for me.

"Hey," I call out. "Where you at?"

"In here," he says from the kitchen. Then he appears with two rocks glasses and a look of shock. "You look too good to be wasting that… *here.*" He gestures towards me with his head before handing me my drink.

"Yeah, I totally got hit on in the bar before dinner. Total smoke show, too." I blow out a breath, trying to extinguish the memory of tonight's never-ending dumpster fire.

He splays his hands out in question.

"Don't even. Fucking Whit." I take a sip, letting the whiskey burn, holding a hand up in protest.

He pats the couch. I sit. We drink. We talk about everything *but* dinner. That's the rule.

But later—when I'm in his guest bed, staring at the ceiling, too buzzed, too wired to sleep—I eventually doze off. And it's not my dad I dream about.

The cold hits first. It always does. Like grief.

The hum of the walk-in pulses around me, steady as a heartbeat. And she's there. Her bare arms in her chef coat, sleeves rolled high. Hair twisted back. A faint sheen of sweat clings to her collarbone.

She doesn't speak. She doesn't need to. She walks toward me like she owns every square inch of this space… of me.

Her fingers trail up my chest, brushing the front of a chef coat I'm not even sure I was wearing a second ago. Then it's gone. No coat. No space between us.

She presses me against the shelves—lips at my throat, fingertips skimming my jaw. My back hits the cold metal. I don't care. Her mouth is fire against my skin, and she smells like citrus and recklessness.

She slowly sinks to her knees, tongue blazing a path down my chest.

"Cassie," I breathe. Not a command. A wish. A prayer.

She looks up at me, eyes dark—hungry, knowing.

"You need to let go, Kyle," she whispers.

Hearing my name from *her* lips melts me.

Then, her mouth closes around me, slow and deliberate, and I grip the shelf behind me just to stay standing.

Breath fogs the air. My jaw goes slack. My knees threaten to give.

She hums—*hums*—and the sound ricochets through my cock—through my entire body.

I'm unraveling.

She looks up again, lips slick, breath visible.

"When you're ready," she says, voice low, "come for me, baby."

My hand slides into her hair, guiding her. "Don't stop. Keep going, baby." My head falls back.

Her mouth, wet and warm around my dick.

"Fuck yes… just like that. What a good girl." I groan. Her rhythm quickens and her hand strokes up and down my shaft along with the coolness of the air, the warmth of her lips. I'm losing it. "Goddamn, Cassie. I'm going to come."

She slides me from her mouth, "Yes, Kyle, come for me. Then make me that fucking cheesecake."

I wake gasping—ripped straight out of heaven.

Sweat-slicked. Sheets twisted. Hard and shaking.

I stare up at the ceiling, breath ragged, throat dry.

"Cassie…" I whisper.

My heart won't slow down. And then it hits me—

Today's her first day back. On the line.

With *me*.

Chapter 16

HEART IN THE PASS

I'm already in the walk-in when the door creaks open.

She steps in like it's just another shift. Like she hasn't been living rent-free in my head for the past three weeks.

Her sleeves are rolled up. Hair back. Cool as ever.

She barely looks at me. Just casually grabs a quart of cream and the mascarpone like she doesn't have a starring role in my most X-rated REM cycle.

"Morning," she says, like her mouth wasn't just around my cock in my subconscious a few hours ago.

"Morning," I croak.

She turns and walks out, the door swinging shut behind her.

And I'm left in the cold, surrounded by fresh produce and imported dairy, trying not to implode on the spot.

Breathe in. Breathe out.

What was I getting in here? *Frisée. Back on fucking Garde.*

I push the walk-in door open to the clatter of kitchen noise, and it clears my head. Puts me back in my place. Salads and cold plates.

Focus, Kyle.

Go anywhere but sauté. Look anywhere she isn't.

It's no good because she's only ten feet away.

The flame lights her face like it's seducing me on purpose. She moves with this quiet precision—confident, clean, fucking effortless. She calls tickets like she's conducting a symphony, and I'm just a guy holding a goddamn triangle.

And then there's her tongue—caught in the corner of her mouth while she plates—focused, deadly serious. I get wood watching her garnish. *Garnish.*

I should volunteer for dish. Demote myself. Fuck it—maybe quit altogether.

Felix passes me, head down in deep focus with his clipboard.

"Hey, Felix. Why is Cassie on the line if she's taking Theo's job?" I ask.

He glances up. "She wants to work every station… get to know every part of this kitchen before she goes into the management role." He shrugs. "Her call."

"Oh, cool." I say it like it doesn't bother me. Like it's totally fine she's going to be shoulder-to-shoulder with me every damn day.

But also… when she starts barking orders? That'll probably do it for me too. Yeah. I should just quit. I turn.

I'm so fucked, I think, and this time it's not even funny.

Later that night, when it's time to close it all down, a pause settles over the kitchen. A hush.

"Hey. Everyone." Her voice cuts through the chatter like an archangel delivering a speech from the pearly gates. "I just wanted to say thank you for a great first night as an official member of the staff here. I hope to learn every position and work together as a real team." She places a hand on her chest. "Thank you for making me feel so welcomed. Now… closing beers for everyone and turn up the music!" she cheers, clapping along with everyone and smiling that gorgeous smile.

That.

That's when I went from infatuated to something way worse.

~~~

It's a Pink Floyd and Bolognese kind of night. I either cook or I'm going to jerk off so much I rub the skin clear off my dick.

They invited me out after work.

I can't. For one, I can't afford to go out all the time now that I have taken on another mouth to feed. For two, she went. I'll just stare and dream, and I've done enough of that all night.

So, here I am, stirring my Nonna's Bolognese, drinking the best
~~~

seventeen-dollar bottle of Chianti the corner store had, and chilling to *The Dark Side of The Moon* with my best boy sprawled out on the kitchen floor.

Just a guy in a borrowed apartment, stirring sauce to an album older than me, pretending it fills the space everyone left behind.

My dog snores. My dick aches. And I'm trying to make peace with the fact that I'm in love with my boss.

I hold my hand under the spoon and cradle the old-world goodness to my mouth.

"Damn. That slaps."

Just then, the door bangs open with a clatter of keys and the crash of stumbling limbs bouncing off the walls.

"BROOOO. You cookin'?" Collin's voice crashes through the calm like a cymbal dropped down a stairwell.

I look up just in time to see him stumble in, with nothing short of glitter and giggles attached to his side.

"This is Shandy," he manages, like he didn't just make that up on the stairs.

I give him a knowing look. "Shandy?"

She laughs and slaps at his arm. "Collin, you know that's not my name, silly." She glances back at me. "I'm Dalia."

Collin twists up his face and shrugs from behind her.

"I'm Kyle."

"Wait, is that, like, soup?" she asks excitedly.

I blink. Rocco lifts his head, then wisely puts it back down. Completely unfazed.

She walks around the island and goes for the spoon, about to dip it in my pot.

"Please don't touch anything, Rhonda."

"Dalia." She pauses mid-dip. "Oh." She giggles. "Is it like… sacred?"

I shake my head, "No. I just don't want you to contaminate an hour and a half of my life, that's all." I hold up my finger and open a drawer. "Here." I grab a clean spoon, heap it full, and hold it out to her.

She blows, and the second it hits her mouth, her eyes go wide. "Oh my god." She covers her lips. "That's so good!"

"Thanks." I take her used spoon from her and toss it into the sink.

"Yeah, I'm amazed I'm not on *My 600-lb Life* living with him," Collin says, reaching for her hand. "Let's go to my room, Shannon."

"Dalia!" She giggles… again. "You guys are so funny."

Collin winks at me over his shoulder as he leads her down the hall.

I turn the music up a little louder, knowing Collin moans like a little bitch.

~~~

I haven't even made it to my locker when I see it. The whiteboard. Freshly updated with today's schedule. Our names lit up like a lighthouse beacon.

Grill: Kyle — Cassie

I stop walking and just stare blankly at the line-up.

Fuck. I stop breathing.

There it is. My name. Right next to hers.

Like a dinner invite or a wedding invitation: *We cordially invite you to the marriage of Kyle and Cassie.*

Oh my God. *What is wrong with me?*

I squeeze my eyes shut for half a second, willing the intrusive thoughts to die in a grease fire. But they don't. They multiply.

She's going to be next to me all night. Calling temps. Slinging steaks and lamb chops, handing off plates, dodging flare-ups like it's foreplay.

I'm so fucked.

I stare at the board long enough that Natalie almost crashes into me from behind.

"Whoa. You good?" she asks, following my line of sight. "Are you okay with that?" She looks confused. "You can't stay on the same two stations your whole career." She smirks, clapping me on the shoulder.

I don't respond. I'm still trying to remember how legs work.
~~~

"Don't forget to hydrate," she adds, patting my shoulder before walking away, "That station gets hot."

~~~

We're ten minutes from the pre-service meeting, and everyone's gathered around prep and sipping shitty gas station coffee.

Cassie steps forward, wiping her hands on a towel like it's a damn security blanket.

Theo nods toward her. "Hey, listen up. Cassie's got the specials tonight."

She freezes for half a second. Just long enough for me to notice the subtle inhale. The way her fingers tighten around the edge of the towel. The way she looks down, then up again, shoulders set.

"Okay. So… tonight we're running the grilled lamb chops. Medium rare unless requested. Served with charred leek puree, rosemary jus, and crispy sunchoke chips." She clears her throat and keeps going.

"For fish, we have a grilled swordfish marinated in garlic and thyme. Served with fennel two ways, preserved lemon, and a warm olive oil sauce."

Someone whistles low.

"Right?" she says with a smile without even looking up. "And Pastry's got a cornmeal polenta cake with a blackberry compote and lemon verbena cream." She looks up, searching the room, "Is that right, Reese?"

"Yes, Chef." Reese calls from the back.

"Sorry. Pastry is not in my wheelhouse, girl."

She folds the towel once on the prep table. Perfectly squared. Nerves still humming beneath the surface. "That's it. Thank you."

Just silence and a few nods. Then the usual shuffling and chatter. But I'm still stuck there. Watching her. Watching how hard she tries to play it cool.

She nailed it. But I saw it—that little flicker of nerves beneath the surface. And God help me, I want to kiss the confidence right back into her.

Wait, where's the amuse?
~~~

The room's already shifting back into motion with aprons being tied and everyone starting to shift into family meal.

I raise my hand. "Chef?"

Cassie turns and blinks. "Yes?" She's trying for serious, but there's a flicker of a smile at the corners of her mouth.

I try to keep a straight face. "What's our amuse, Chef?"

A few heads turn.

She doesn't miss a beat. "Oops, sorry about that." She looks down at her notepad, scanning, then looks up. Looks right at me.

"Compressed melon with a balsamic reduction and mint foam. One bite. Refreshing and bright. Just like your attitude, Berkley."

Laughter ripples through the room. Theo smirks. Natalie full-on giggles. But I can't move.

Because for half a second, she was looking right at me. Not across the line. Not as my boss. Just… *at me.*

And like an idiot, I let myself think it meant something.

God help me.

~~~

Cassie hands off a plate, spins, and wipes down the board.

I'm still recovering from nearly overcooking a swordfish and watching her casually save my ass with a single, silent head shake.

She sets down her tongs and leans against the prep table beside me. "You okay?" she asks.

I glance sideways. "Define okay."

She huffs out a laugh, then picks up a ramekin of herbs and starts sorting them. "You're doing fine. Grill's just… different. More aggressive and fast-paced."

"Yeah," I say, wiping my hands on my towel. "It's like juggling chainsaws. On fire. While someone yells at you about meat temps."

"That someone is me," she says, deadpan.

Yeah. And I'm loving every minute of it.

"Look, I know it's a shift," she says, softer now. "Going from Garde to Grill. And having me… " she trails off, gestures to herself. "I get it."

I cock my head. "What, being trained by someone terrifyingly competent and… well, you… "
~~~

Her mouth twitches. "I meant… being your boss."

"Right." I nod. "That too."

She looks at me then—really looks. Not the chef-eyes-scan-the-line look. But *woman registering man*, and for a split second, we're just two people standing way too close over a tray of raw lamb chops. At least… that's what I think we're doing.

"I'm not here to make anyone feel small, Kyle," she says. "I just… want to earn it. Every station. Every shift. And I want *you* to feel confident in working your job, too. I want you to be the best."

I swallow. "You already have."

Her eyes flick away. She reaches for her tongs. "Call it," she orders, eyes staring directly into mine. My dick jumps at her command, and I almost forgot what we were doing here.

Oh, cooking. We're cooking. "Order up." I call.

And just like that, we're back in motion. And something cracks open between us—and I have no idea how I'm supposed to survive the rest of this night.

Grill station is hell.

It's all open flame and flying fat, the air is thick with meat smoke and barely contained panic. But tonight, I'm on the line with someone who moves like she owns the damn line. Controlled. Efficient. Not a single wasted motion.

Me? I'm sweating through my apron trying to keep up, but learning fast and furiously.

We're shoulder to shoulder, elbows brushing every few minutes. She smells like heat and rosemary and the faintest whisper of citrus—probably that lemon verbena cream I'd like to eat off her collarbone.

Jesus.

She calls out, "Two lamb, one sword, fire now."

"Yes, Chef."

Don't fuck this up. Don't burn the chops. Don't let your dick call the temps.

She plates one, leans past me, and brushes the jus over the lamb with this slow, deliberate stroke. Her tongue catches in the corner of her mouth again. Same way it did when she was garnishing. I swear to God, I could die happy under this broiler.

"Lamb, medium-rare, behind." Her voice is clean. Commanding. Almost cocky.

I pass her a plate. She doesn't look at me, but her fingers graze mine. Barely. A whisper of touch. Like she's testing the current.

I flinch. Not visibly. But inside? Full internal explosion.

"More radicchio, Kyle," she says, stepping around me.

I nod, wordless, because speech is too dangerous. One wrong syllable and I'll confess to everything—how I dream about her, how I count her smiles like inventory, how I'd happily be a fork if it meant getting that close to her mouth.

Theo passes behind, checking plates, nodding once.

Cassie stays cool, even under his watchful eye. I feel like my apron's about to catch fire.

We finish a rush and fall back for a beat. Cassie grabs her towel, wipes her hands, then leans back just enough to mutter without anyone hearing. "You good?"

I nod, too fast. "Yeah. Just… hot," I say, chugging water from a quart container.

She smirks and fans herself. "I love it. I love the rush. I love to sweat."

And then she turns away, already firing the next round of orders like she didn't just turn my ribcage into a fucking percussion section.

We push through the last rush of the evening. My shirt is soaked. My forearms are scorched. I've got lamb fat in places that will never be the same again.

Cassie calls the final ticket. Her voice doesn't waver, not once.

I plate, wipe, and send it out. And then… the stillness.

The low hum of clean-up chatter starts as knives hit boards and towels hit shoulders. Cassie's already moving, breaking down the station with practiced efficiency.

I start stacking pans when I feel someone step behind me.

Theo. He nods once, sharp and brief. "Good work tonight, Kyle."

That's it. No smile. No pat on the back. Just a two-second miracle of praise.

"Thanks, Chef," I manage, trying not to visibly swell with pride.

Cassie glances over and we lock eyes.

She doesn't say anything—just lifts one brow, nods once, then turns back to our station. And somehow, that single nod lands harder than anything she could've said.

I wipe my hands on my towel. My body's wrecked. My heart's a disaster. But tonight?

Tonight, I made it.

Chapter 17

CUTTING STRINGS & BUILDING DREAMS

Rocco is absolutely shredding.

Well—wobbling, confidently, at a whopping seventy-five pounds now. But in his mind? He's Tony Hawk.

He cruises the sidewalk beside me, tail flapping on the beat-up board I found secondhand, his tongue flopping out like a kid who just discovered what happiness is.

I snap another ridiculous picture.

We stop on the side of the asphalt path. The sun breaks beneath the clouds, warming the day as the city stirs awake. Runners and cyclists begin their early morning rituals, breath pluming in the cool air.

I pull up my Instagram and post.

@ChefKyleBerkley: My sous chef, Rocco. Great with mise, terrible with wheels. #SkateDogsofSF #FloppyButFocused

Social media wasn't my thing before. But lately, it's something to build. A place to pour my time into. Food porn and Rocco. Maybe the occasional shameless selfie. It helps.

I check the time, tucking my phone back into my pocket.

"Come on, buddy."

I've got just enough time to swing by the Asian market for a jar of that chili crisp Cassie likes. She didn't ask for it. But I know she's running low—from that conversation the other night, when we were geeking out about dumplings.

I always notice.

~~~

After dropping everything off in my locker, I lightly knock on the cracked office door.

"Yes?" her voice calls out.

I push it open, the jar knocking lightly against my palm, a small smile on my face.

"Good morning, Kyle," she says, looking up from the laptop.

"Morning. I grabbed you some more since I was already there." Lie. I needed nothing.

She reaches out and takes the jar. "Oh hell. You are the best. This is my crack."

And I am your new dealer.

"Yeah, all that dumpling talk, I figured."

Her eyes roll back as she clutches the jar to her chest.

Where I want to be.

"I've been dreaming of dumplings ever since that conversation. Ugh." She slaps her hand on the large stack of paperwork in front of her. "I'm so swamped with mine and Theo's work since he's out on vacation." She blows out a breath. "I've had no life outside of here to even think about eating out."

"Do you need help?" I offer.

She glances around at the mess, clearly weighing it.

"Well… can you help Felix with the delivery trucks this morning? That'll free me up here to finish this order." She gestures to the computer. "And can you send Natalie in when you see her? I need to lock in next week's schedule."

"Sure."

She hands me the delivery clipboard and lifts the jar again.

"Kyle, thank you for thinking of me," she says with a smile. "That's really thoughtful."
~~~

~~~

Back in the kitchen, the scent of roasting chiles hits me first.

Tonight, Mateo Rivas, our newest member of the Le Début family who started a month after me, volunteered to make family meal. He recently moved from prep to the line and is probably the most chill guy in this place. I've never seen him rattled—especially for someone so professionally green.

When I asked him how he stays so calm, he says, "I learned how to cook from my mom. She used to swat me with a wooden spoon if I didn't move fast enough, amigo."

Mateo's plating family meal—enchiladas, bubbling and golden, with sides of rice and what looks like a lime-heavy slaw.

"Hot behind," he calls, setting the pan on the prep table.

I raise my eyebrows. "You do all this?"

He shrugs, wiping his hands on his apron. "My tía's recipe. Don't tell her I added some mozzarella. She'd murder me."

Cassie walks by, grabs a paper plate, and takes a small serving of everything. She leans against the stainless-steel table, takes a bite, and lets out a low groan.

"Mateo, these enchiladas are insane," she says, pointing her fork at her plate.

He just smiles, eyes crinkling at the corners. "Glad you approve, Chef."

Everyone joins in. This is what it's about—sharing family recipes. Growing our family.

"Let's have a great service, everyone," Cassie calls down the line.

I slip my apron over my head—fresh white. Always clean to start. It's stupid, but I like the ritual. Like I still believe I can stay untouched in the kitchen chaos.

I glance down the line and there she is.

Cassie. Already in her dark blue apron, leather straps tied snug. Her hair's tied up in a bun on her head. A few pieces falling freely around her face. Her gaze is sharp. She runs the line now. It's all hers.

She doesn't need to say anything. Her presence sets the tempo. You feel it in the way the kitchen leans forward when she speaks.

She scans the room, doing her own silent inventory. Her gaze
~~~

catches mine for a half-second. Just long enough for my throat to tighten and my grip to loosen on the towel. Then she looks away.

The sound of the first ticket hits. Service starts.

~~~

I didn't know it then. Didn't know that night was the end of something.

The end of us as we were—Cassie running the line, me one station over, learning her rhythm. Hearts steady, future unknown.

It felt like just another night of service. Mateo's enchiladas. Store-bought chili crisp. Her smile when she tasted a sauce I made. But things were already shifting.

Theo had put in his notice that week. No big announcement. Just a quiet "I'm taking something new," followed by the usual handshakes and a final closing beers.

Cassie didn't even blink. She stepped in and filled the space like she'd always belonged in it. And she had. A few weeks later, Felix told us he was leaving for Seattle. A new job. A new partner. A new chapter. He was next in line. Should've been, anyway.

But Cassie pulled me aside, handed me the clipboard and apron, and said, "You're up."

"What?" I asked, confused.

There it was. Pristinely rolled. The coveted blue apron, leather straps binding it tight.

Suddenly, I wasn't just a line cook. I became her sous… then, shortly after, her Chef de Cuisine. I *earned* my place. Standing where she used to stand. Watching her run the whole damn kitchen with that steady hand and wild brain I was still trying not to love every damn day.

During closing, we talked late into the nights while she did paperwork, and I ran the kitchen. Joked about cassoulets and butter-soaked sauces. Whispered about the restaurant we'd open someday over closing beers. We talked about her travels to places I'd only dreamed of, and the food we *really* wanted to cook.

We talked about new dreams.

We joked about a crazy idea.
~~~

We started sketching out a new concept. A name that rolled perfectly off her tongue, then stayed between us—folded into notebooks and late-night conversations—waiting to be born.

Chapter 18

ONE HEART WALKING

The light is low. The music moves slow and deliberate—glass tinkling, silverware clicking through quiet conversation. The air is heavy with leather and expensive whiskey.

"This is what you want, Kyle." His voice slices through the room like a blade.

I turn. He's standing behind me—my father. Pristine suit. Cuffs gleaming like diamonds. Eyes full of pretension and accusation.

"Not if it comes at the cost of being like you," I say.

Jesus. I can't believe I just said that. The one thing I've bitten back my whole damn life.

"You're just like her," he spits. "Always dreaming. That's not what life's about, son."

Stop calling me that.

"Look what you did, *son*." He gestures toward my hands—they're covered in blood.

Jesus. What the hell?

I shake my head, stumbling back a step.

"I… I don't know where this came from." I wipe them on my immaculate blue apron, but it only smears the red deeper into the fabric, thick and unforgiving.

I glance down. My chef whites are splattered in blood.

Jesus.

"I've had enough, Kyle. I can't keep doing this with you." His hand lifts. The impact knocks me back. The sting—sharp, hot, familiar.

"Take it like a man, *son,*" he growls.

I cower.

Don't flinch. He always hits harder when you flinch.

I slowly rise. Shoulders square. Breath steadying.

"I'm not taking this anymore. I'm not twelve. I'm not fucking scared of you." My voice is ice. "Go to hell."

"Kyle…" But now it's *her* voice. "Kyle, wake up."

Her hand is on my chest, shaking me gently.

"Kyle, you're dreaming."

"Shit. I'm sorry." I rake a hand through my sweat-soaked hair. "Was I talking? Sorry if I woke you."

I roll to face her in the dark. Her thumb brushes my brow, and I flinch. The shadow still lingering there, just behind my eyes.

"Damn," she says, voice uneasy. "Are you sure you're okay?"

"Yeah. Just a fucked-up dream… that's all."

"Maybe I should go."

She starts to climb out of bed.

"No—Arden, wait. Don't."

She hesitates. Sinks back into the sheets.

"Kyle, you've been so distracted lately. I… I just don't know."

I reach over and flick on the bedside lamp. A warm, golden glow spills across the room.

There she is. Arden Hendricks. Beautiful. Blonde. My girlfriend of six months.

At least, I think that's what she is. We never really talked about it. It just… happened. More time together. Less with anyone else. We started having sex. I haven't slept with anyone else—and I'm hoping to hell she hasn't either.

Between my insane hours at Le Début and her long hours at the law firm, neither of us have much time for anything else.

"What do you mean?" I ask. "Babe…?"

She gives me a look. *That* look. The one that tells me she's already halfway out the door.

"You're always thinking about work. Menu stuff. Ordering. Staffing. Anything but *us.*"

She gestures between us.

I close my eyes, hard and exhale. "I'm sorry. It's my job. Cassie's got me on edge, and I'm just… trying to prove myself."

Her expression softens. She traces my jaw with her thumb. Kisses me, slow and sweet.

"Cassie," she whispers. "I can't compete, Kyle."

I laugh, but there's no humor in it. "What does that mean?"

"It means," she says quietly, "since this started—*us*—I've had to listen to you talk about her like she's your girlfriend. Like she's *everything*. Every conversation. Every day." She lets out a dry laugh, tossing her head back on the pillow. "I'm surprised you haven't accidentally called me by her name in bed."

"Come on. That's ridiculous."

She turns to look at me. Blue eyes. Devastatingly serious.

"Am I? *Am I*, Kyle?"

I want to say yes. I want to tell her she's wrong.

But she's not.

Every relationship, every hook-up—it's just a Band-Aid. A placeholder. Someone to keep my bed warm while I wait.

Wait for *her*. For the one I've never truly let go of.

"Arden… don't."

She scoffs and climbs out of bed. Golden hair down her back. Legs that don't quit. And she's already walking away.

"It was great, Kyle, but I need more." She pulls on her sundress. "I'm twenty-eight. I want something real. Commitment. You said you did too."

She pauses beside the bed, runs her hand through my hair, and kisses my forehead.

"I hope she realizes what she has. You are really special."

And then she's gone.

The door didn't slam, but it might as well have.

I wish I could be the guy she wants me to be. The one who chooses the woman in his bed instead of the one in his head.

Fuck.

~~~
~~~

I yank open the back door of Le Début and step into the alley just as the delivery truck hisses to a halt.

Franko's already sliding boxes onto the loading dock.

"Morning, Kyle," he says, like he didn't bring me swamp mushrooms seven days ago.

I crouch, flip open a box, and gag.

"Franko," I mutter, lifting a slimy pack of creminis with two fingers like it's radioactive, "this is trash, dude. You see this?" I toss the whole pack back into the crate and stand up. "Second time. Don't make me switch vendors over this crap."

Franko's smile wavers, but he's still looking smug like we didn't just have this conversation *last* week. "I'll make it right. I'll swing by this afternoon."

"You said that last week and never showed."

He nods, scribbles something on the clipboard. I keep going—checking spinach, fennel, and herbs. I'm fast but thorough. I don't miss much anymore. I slap the lid closed on the last box harder than I need to.

This is my kitchen now. I run it like a goddamn tightrope act. No wobble. No slack.

The back door creaks again and I know it's her before I even look.

"Problem?" Cassie asks, stepping out into the alley in her navy chef's coat, sleeves rolled to her elbows. Clipboard in hand, brow raised.

"Swamp shrooms again," I say. "Franko's trying to sabotage me."

She grins and takes the clipboard from my hand, glancing over it. "You want me to call?"

"Whoa, don't shoot the delivery guy. I didn't grow and load this order," Franko protests, hands up like I pulled a knife instead of creminis. "I said I'll make it right, and I'll make it right."

I shoot him a side eye, then a smirk at her. "Nah. I've got it. Just needed to vent."

She nods. "Good. Because we're down two today—Jules called out, and Mateo's going to be late. Again."

I blow out a breath and run a hand through my hair. "Roger that."

Cassie lingers for a second, watching me. "You good?"

"Golden," I say, already turning back to the crates.

What she doesn't know is that I'm feeling everything but golden. I was slapped across the face in my dreams and had my heart slung against the wall—all before sunrise. Definitely not golden.

But here I am, taking my frustrations out on Franko and mushy fungi.

She doesn't say anything else, just taps the clipboard against her thigh once before heading back inside.

Her trust means everything. And the fact that I've earned it? Even more.

~~~

Since Jules called out, I'm on sauté tonight—sweating through the fire while trying to hold it all together. Mateo showed up an hour late, breathless and still buttoning his coat.

"Sorry, amigos! I'm here, I'm here!"

Typical.

I keep my head down, focused, but I catch movement from the corner of my eye.

Cassie. She's in the office, door cracked, checking herself in the mirror. Clean chef's coat. Lip balm. She smooths her hair, tilts her head, checks her teeth.

She hates this part—going out into the dining room to schmooze and play the part of front-facing executive chef. She's an introvert. I know this. Hell, I know too much.

I'm working a pan of veal medallions with sauce chasseur, steam curling around my arms while I try to keep my heart out of the fucking mirepoix.

Fuck, I have a problem. Watching her every move like a voyeur. I should be arrested.

I turn—and she's gone. Out to do the part of the job she hates, while I pretend it doesn't gut me when she walks away.

She returns thirty minutes later, cheeks a little flushed, paperwork in hand, saying something about the duck confit needing to come off the menu.
~~~

"It's tired," she mutters.

We go over closing together. She smiles at something I say.

God help me.

I smile back, like nothing's wrong. Then Stacy bursts into the kitchen waving a napkin like it's on fire.

"Hey, Chef. Here."

Cassie blinks and takes it. "What is this?" Cassie reads the note, and something shifts behind her eyes—subtle, like a shutter clicking closed.

Stacy just grins and tosses her ponytail over her shoulder.

"Which one was it?" Cassie asks.

She points with her chin, "The brunette with the dark eyes. You got it, Chef, and you don't even know it."

She slides the napkin into her pocket without a word.

And that's when I know. She's not mine. Not really.

Never really was.

~~~

The office door is closed.

Closed.

It's never closed unless Cassie and I are talking shit about staff or roasting the owners.

I knock.

"One second," her voice calls out.

I lean in, ear to the door like an idiot. There's movement inside—shuffling, maybe the sound of fabric.

What is she doing in there?

Then the door swings open, and there she is.

Dark jeans—jeans that, *holy hell,* had to be stitched directly onto her body. A white shirt that clings in all the right places, just sheer enough to flash the outline of a black bra. Her hair's down—chestnut waves falling around her shoulders like it's on purpose.

And black heels.

My mind stutters.

Jesus.

"Oh, hey," she says, practically stumbling into me.
~~~

"Hey." I blink. "You... look... good."

She glances down at herself. "Oh. Thanks." Then she spots the clipboard in my hand. "Do I need to sign off on something?"

"Oh—yeah. For tomorrow." I hold it out.

She takes it, along with the pen. Her tongue flicks out, just barely, as she traces the list with one finger, scanning before signing. I look away, trying to keep my dick from launching a rebellion.

"Anything else?" she asks, handing it back with a smile.

I shake my head, swallowing the hunk of concrete lodged in my throat. "No. All good." Then I gesture vaguely with the clipboard. "Hot date?"

Instant regret.

"Sorry, that's—"

She laughs. "It's okay." She looks down again, smoothing imaginary wrinkles from her jeans. "I'm... trying something new. Breaking out of the box, for once." She winces. "Am I trying too hard?"

Fuck. Am *I* too hard?

I shake my head fast. "No. No—you look... great. Lucky guy." And god, I meant it.

"Thanks, Kyle." She smiles, claps me on the shoulder. "You need to get out there too, you know. This doesn't have to be our whole life."

And then she's gone. Swinging her purse over her shoulder. One flip of her hair.

"Have a good night," she calls back with a casual wave.

The heavy metal door slams behind her. So does my heart.

Ritchie shows up just as I'm finishing the week's inventory reports, knocking once before pushing through the back door like it's High Tide.

"So... this is where the fancy people work, huh?" he says, stepping into the kitchen with a low whistle.

I chuckle. "Don't touch anything. You'll lower the average IQ of the whole place."

He follows me out to the front, past Mateo coming out of the walk-in and Natalie writing up tomorrow's line-up on the dry-erase board.

"Damn. This place is efficient as fuck," he says, shocked.

We walk out front where Matt, the bar manager, is printing his credit card report.

"Hey Matt," I say, pulling out two barstools, "You out?"

"Yeah."

Matt nods, pours us each whiskey on the rocks without needing to be asked, and heads out with a wave. "That's our bottle. Lock up behind you."

Stacy swings through, purse over one arm. "Night, Chef."

"'Night, Stacy."

And then it's just us—me and Ritchie—sitting at the dim, silent bar with nothing but the hum of the fridge and the sound of people passing by on the sidewalk.

He doesn't say anything at first. Just lets the silence stretch.

I twist my glass. Watch the ice spin and swallow hard.

"Arden left me this morning," I mumble.

Ritchie leans back on his stool. "Shit."

I nod. Take a sip, and feel it burn all the way down.

"You okay?" he finally asks.

"Nope."

He watches me for a long beat. Then shrugs. "Maybe you need therapy."

I snort, nearly choking on my drink. "You? You're telling me *I* need therapy?"

"I don't know," he says, grinning. "All the SoCal people seem to go. I think I'm supposed to tell you that as your best friend. Plus… your fucked-up childhood alone warrants it."

I laugh, despite myself. "Touché."

I stare blankly into my glass, my voice low. "I also think I'm in love with my boss."

Ritchie's head snaps up like I just punched him.

"What?"

"Yeah." I knock back the rest of my drink, then slide off the stool, round the bar, and pour myself another—just a finger this time. I hold up the bottle toward him.

He nods, eyes wide with my new revelation. "Cassie?"

"Yep."

He lets out a low whistle. "Since when? I mean… I know you're infatuated. It's always 'Cassie this, Cassie that.' She's the best at plating, poaching, deglazing, reorganizing the goddamn walk-in—but I figured that was just chef worship. You never said it was because you wanted to bone her."

I tilt my head at him. "*Bone her*? What are you, fifteen?"

He grins, unbothered. "I'm trying to keep it light. You're spiraling."

I scrub my face and laugh, because yeah—I am spiraling. Hard.

"You ever tell her?" he asks after a beat.

I shake my head. "Nope. Just been… watching. Cooking. Smiling when she smiles. And dying a little every time she leaves to go on some mystery date with a guy who isn't me."

Ritchie raises his glass. "Jesus. You're in it."

"Yeah," I whisper. "I really fucking am."

Chapter 19

SAUSALITO WET DREAMS

Rocco's already at the door, his tail thumping in rhythmic anticipation.

He knows. It's Sunday. Which means iced lattes. Which means Collin.

He lets out a low whine, then trots in a tight circle, nails tapping across the hardwood like a percussion line warming up. His eyes flick to me, then back to the door, like he's trying to summon Collin with pure big-dog willpower.

I take my time. No rush today. No prep lists, no purveyors to threaten, no mushroom autopsies in the alley. Just me and this stupidly silent apartment that still smells like fresh paint and ambition.

I open the door. And there's Collin, all sunshine and sparkles, wearing a worn-out tee that says *Kale Is a Scam*, mirrored aviators on his face, holding two sweating plastic cups like some kind of caffeinated savior.

"Praise be," I mutter, taking one from him.

Rocco practically explodes.

"Oh goodness." Collin ruffles his head aggressively, somehow making him even more excited. "My big boy missed me. Yes, he did."

"Stop, you're getting him all riled up. He needs a serious run," I groan.

Collin walks into the kitchen and leans against the counter, Rocco now bouncing like a pogo stick.

"Oh shit. You better stop. Your daddy's gonna get pissed." He laughs, the instigating uncle to his core. "What the hell are you feeding him? He looks bigger."

"He's managed this weight for over a year. One-ten, swear. Why couldn't Lotus leave me a thirty-five-pound Frenchie? Instead, I get… *this.*" I nudge him with my bare foot. Drool stretches from his mouth to my kitchen floor in one continuous string. "He's so nasty."

Collin drops to his knees and scratches his chest. "He is not. He's the bestest. Look at you."

As if on cue, Rocco lets one rip. Audible. Unapologetic. Lethal.

Collin recoils, gagging. "Oh my god. You are disgusting."

"Told you," I say, nudging him again with my foot like I'm punting a sandbag.

I fold my arms across my chest. "So, how was your first week at your big-boy job?"

Collin sighs. "It was alright. I only have to go in two days a week once I get the hang of it. Remote the rest."

"Grava?"

He chuckles. "Trava."

"Look at you." I tap his shin with my foot. "Big logistics guy in the IT world. I have no fucking clue what you do, but I'm happy you got out of bartending."

Collin smirks. "Same. My liver sent a thank-you card."

I take a long sip of my latte. "Yeah. Our schedules in this industry. The constant temptation." I shake my head.

He shrugs. "It worked. Until it didn't."

Rocco groans and flops dramatically onto the floor between us, tail thudding like a dying metronome.

"Speaking of things that don't work," Collin says, side-eyeing the dog. "You gonna tell me what's going on with Arden, or do I have to drag it out of you like a therapist with a sock puppet?"

"Wait… how do you know?" I hold up a hand. "It's been like… twenty-four hours."

"Ritchie." He jerks his chin upward. "He was at Lizzy's last night, shooting pool. I thought it was going good between you two?"

I scoff. "Yeah. Me too." I turn to the fridge, searching for nothing. Deflecting. I don't want to talk about it.

"Anything else you want to tell me?" he asks from behind me.

Fucking Ritchie.

I shut the fridge and turn back. Collin's leaning against the counter, arms wrapped around himself, ankles crossed. He looks like he ate the canary.

I shrug. "What?"

"Are you going to tell her?"

I play dumb. "Tell who… what?"

He chuckles into his drink. "Pussy."

"What did you just call me?" I ask, brow lifting.

"You heard me. This is ridiculous. Just tell her." He tilts his head. "What do you have to lose? I mean, not Arden."

"Um… my job." I pinch the bridge of my nose and close my eyes. "I can't fuck it up. We're making big plans, man. Some cool shit for the future."

"What, this new restaurant?" he asks.

"Yeah. I don't want to fuck it all up with… *feelings.* This is my career we're talking about."

Collin checks the time and grabs his empty cup. "Alright. I gotta go."

I lift a brow. "Where to?"

He grins like a kid with a secret. "Succulent scavenger hunt."

I blink. "What?"

"Yeah, it's a thing. Archie's in the Mission. This guy Carl hosts them. He hides rare succulents around his building. You bring a trowel, a reusable bag, and a good attitude."

"You need a support group," I laugh.

"You say that like it's an insult."

He tosses his empty cup into the recycling and salutes me. "You should come with me. It'll be fun. You might even touch grass. Chicks dig this shit. Oh. They also like anything with books. I joined a book club on Thursday nights."

"I can't. Grown-up shit." I tick them off on my fingers. "Gym. Laundry. Run the dog. Maybe clean out my spice cabinet if things get real wild."

He shudders. "You're like twenty-six going on seventy-four."

"And you're a succulent-hunting toddler."

He winks. "And yet, here we are. Later, Chef."

He leaves in a swirl of linen joggers and questionable choices. Rocco sighs, like he's disappointed I didn't go.

~~~

I leash Rocco and head toward the marina on my board, letting him drag me past tourists lining up for steaming sourdough bowls of clam chowder. He's living his best bulldog life, tongue flopping, tail wagging like a flag in a storm.

Me? I'm dragging a dog with IBS and trying not to think about Cassie. I'm failing. Miserably.

What if I told her? It's not like I haven't imagined it. Hell, I've written entire fantasy scripts in my head.

We open a restaurant together. Asian, chic, but not pretentious. It becomes the hottest reservation in the city. We get matching tattoos, a chef's knife and a whisk crossed like swords on our wrists. I even have the space left. I glance down at my right pulse point.

Then we fall in love. Well, she does. I'm obviously already chest-deep, like it's quicksand.

Then comes the wedding. Simple. Sweet. A vineyard. Something like my grandparents' place in Napa, rows of vines and folding chairs under the trees.

Two kids, Olive and Basil, because apparently I hate myself and I'm naming children after antipasti.

I laugh out loud, startling a woman in Lululemon. She clutches her green juice like it's a shield.

"Sorry," I say, lifting a hand.

But my mind keeps going.

A house in Sausalito. White with black trim, overlooking the bay, an exceptional deck. We drink good wine and watch the fog roll in. She wears cozy sweaters, and I make mushroom risotto barefoot. Rocco gets fat and lives to be twenty because she feeds him scraps under the table, and I refuse to let him die.

I shake my head. None of it's real. Because in reality, she's probably with a guy who wears loafers without socks and says "return on investment" when talking about opening a restaurant.
~~~

He probably hasn't even used the expensive six-burner stove in his brownstone. He drives a Porsche. His name's probably Blaine.

God, I hate him and his popped collar already, and I haven't even met him.

And I'm here, with a farting dog, worn jeans, scuffed Chucks, and a very real fear that if I tell her, if I really tell her, I'll lose everything.

So, I skate. And I wonder what it would be like if I could stop pretending I didn't love her.

~~~

I'm staring at what's left in the walk-in, cross-checking it against our incoming order for tomorrow.

Mussels. Clams.

Shit. I forgot.

The door hisses open as I push back into the kitchen. Jules is at prep, wrapping up tonight's mise.

"Jules, eighty-six the bouillabaisse for tomorrow."

"No problemo."

I never expected him to call me Chef. Hell, Julia Child herself could be on our line and Jules still wouldn't bother. It's just not his style. But the guy shows up every shift, nails his prep, and makes me laugh harder than anyone else here. I'll take that over formality any day.

I drop into the office's cracked leather chair and pull up the order screen, scanning line after line, trying to figure out where I blew it.

And then—she walks in.

"So… I was thinking," she says, voice low, eyes darting around like we're being watched.

God, I love when she does this. It's like we're in our own secret society. Just me and Cassie. Cassie and me.

"What is it?" I lean forward, instantly hooked.

She hops onto the corner of the desk, legs crossed, lip caught between her teeth.

Jesus. That lip.
~~~

My eyes drop. My dick mutters mercy.

"I think I came up with the perfect name for our restaurant."

Our. She said our.

"Okay…" I say, sinking back into the chair. Her excitement is magnetic. I'd follow her into a burning walk-in if she smiled like that at me.

"So, since we're not Asian, and we're doing this whole fusion thing—we've always joked we're imposters, right?"

I nod, grinning. "Yeah. I'm with you."

She leans in, eyes sparkling. "Sagi-Shi."

She waits.

I blink.

"It means 'imposture.'"

I blink. Then blink again. And smile like a fool. Because of course it's perfect.

Because she's perfect.

"I love it," I say.

Of course I love it. She could call it whatever Japanese is for *The Shithouse* and I'd smile and agree.

"I knew you would," she says, hopping down from the desk, already halfway out the door.

And in a desperate attempt to stop her from leaving, Collin's words crash through my head.

What do you have to lose?

"Wanna go celebrate?" I blurt.

She turns, holding the doorframe. Her eyes practically smiling on their own.

"Oh damn. I wish I could, but I'm going out with Jack. Raincheck?"

Something caves in behind my ribs. "Oh… yeah. Of course." I smile. Or wince. I'm not sure. "Have a good time."

"I'm so excited, Kyle. Sagi-Shi. I love the way it rolls off my tongue."

And she's gone again.

His name isn't Blaine after all. *Jack.*

I stare at the empty doorway for a full ten seconds after she leaves, waiting for some kind of rewind button to appear. Nothing. Just the low hum of the dishwasher outside the office and my own idiocy buzzing in my ears.

Of course she's going out with Jack. Of course I waited too long. Of course I said *celebrate* like we'd just gotten engaged.

I lean back in the chair and exhale through my nose, long and slow.

What did I think was going to happen? That she'd fall into my arms and feed me dumplings in the walk-in? That we'd christen dry storage and spend our days naming appetizers and our unborn children?

Jesus. I'm a wreck.

I glance at the computer screen, still glowing with my half-finished order, and mutter, "Eighty-six my dignity too, while we're at it."

Right on cue, Jules sticks his head into the office.

"Dude, do we still have microgreens coming tomorrow, or should I just go forage in the alley?"

I blink at him. "Why are you the way you are?"

He grins, brows furrowing just a touch. "Born this way. You good?"

I nod. "Totally. Just sitting in here… celebrating."

He squints. "Alone?"

"Yep. It's a solo party now. Bring your own shame."

He backs away slowly, thumbing behind him. "Cool, cool, cool. I'm gonna go finish not crying in the walk-in."

I chuckle, but it's brittle. Because I should've told her. And I didn't.

But dammit, tomorrow's a new day. And Sagi-Shi is still ours.

Sort of.

~~~

She's humming. Always humming.

We're back in my childhood kitchen. Me at the stove, her behind me, like this is how it's always been. Smoke curls through the air like a warning, but I don't see it. Don't smell it.
~~~

I turn.

"Mom," I say, my voice too small for the room. "It's burning."

She smiles over her shoulder as she opens the front door, car keys jingling in her hand.

"We just burned the first one, kiddo. It's not the end of the world."

"Don't go, Mom." My voice cracks. "Don't go. I didn't burn it. See?"

I look down. My hands are covered in blood.

I glance up. I'm standing on the porch. She's at the open car door, exhaust pouring from the tailpipe into the dark.

I squint.

"Cassie?" I call, confused.

She doesn't turn back. Just slips into the passenger seat next to *him*. The engine roars to life. The only answer is the taillights disappearing into the dark, red flickering against the trees.

I wake up tangled in sweat-soaked sheets and regret.

Rocco's snoring at the foot of the bed like nothing happened. Like my heart didn't just get steamrolled in technicolor while I slept.

I drag a hand over my face.

Maybe Ritchie's right. Maybe I do need therapy.

Chapter 20

THE GOSPEL OF FARCE

The kitchen is still. It's that early-morning hush where everything breathes a little slower—ovens ticking as they warm, the hum of the walk-in, the rhythmic clinking of glassware being carried to the front in a dish pan. *Clink… clink… clink.*

I stand in front of the prep table, hands idle.

I should be slicing or organizing my mise. Or doing literally anything to stop replaying the moment from last night—the soft lift in Cassie's voice when she said *Jack*, like it was a name she liked the taste of.

I grit my teeth and turn toward the walk-in. No use thinking about it. No use thinking about her. Or the way she'd said *our restaurant.* Like we were building something. Like I wasn't just a fucking employee in this made-up fantasy called my career.

I pull the door open, letting the cold slap me in the face. I welcome it. Better that than the heat burning behind my eyes.

I stand in the walk-in too long, pretending to check inventory. Pretending to reorganize the duck. Pretending I wasn't just cooling off the part of me that wanted to punch something soft and stupid.

She left me.

Not last night. Not technically.

But in my dream—*our* dream.

The one with the house and the deck and the fat dog and the sweaters and the goddamn risotto. The one I'd built quietly in my chest without permission, without insurance, without an escape hatch.

And just like that, she was out the door. Talking about Jack. Saying his name like it meant something. Like he was already meant to be there.

I stare at the stack of freshly stocked produce in front of me. I don't know what to do next.

I don't know how long I've been in here—long enough to start thinking unhinged thoughts, like maybe if I just dropped my pants in the walk-in, felt the cold, I could reset the spiral.

Not in a sexy way, but in a make-it-weirder-than-the-pain kind of way. The *my life's a mess, but at least my thighs are cold* kind of way.

I mean, it worked for that one chef. I swear, I'm going to do it someday.

I laugh to myself. "Now I'm really losing it."

Just then, the walk-in door creaks open behind me.

"Jesus, Kyle. Did you fall asleep in here?"

Jules. Of course.

He's already in an apron, already too loud, holding two coffees like he came prepared for my bullshit.

"I brought you caffeine and judgment," he says. "In that order."

I grunt and take the coffee. Sip it like it might remind me how to be an actual person.

Jules leans against the shelf, unbothered. "You look like a man who saw his ex on a yacht with Jeff Bezos."

"Worse," I mutter.

His brow lifts. "Man, if someone died and I'm making jokes…"

I let out a laugh. "No. Nobody died, Jules." I shake my head. "I'm just being dumb, that's all."

"Oh, thank god." He sighs. "I thought I fucked up making jokes again when someone died."

I raise a brow. "Again?"

"Yeah." He lifts his coffee toward me and shrugs. "Why are we still in here?"

I step out of the walk-in, blinking like I've emerged from a sensory deprivation tank and straight into judgment day.

The kitchen lights are too bright. The clang of pans, too sharp. The prep table feels like an altar now, somewhere to confess all the shit I'm not proud of. Desire. Bitterness. That dream I built in silence and watched her walk out of.

I move past it, shaking off the chill. And then I see her through the half-open office door, sitting on the edge of the desk like nothing happened.

An angel, backlit by the hum of bad fluorescent lighting and my misplaced hope. Fingers innocently twisting pieces of her hair. One ankle crossed over the other, swaying to some imaginary beat. Head tilted, eyes on something she's reading. Calm, in deep thought, like she didn't just detonate my chest twenty-four hours ago.

And for a second, I almost forget. Forget Jack. Forget my pride. Forget that I was two seconds away from dropping my pants in front of the fennel.

But then she looks up. And I remember everything.

I push the door open wider. "Good morning," I say, shifting into the leather chair, pretending to need pertinent information from the computer. "What's going on?"

"I was just looking over the specials for tonight." She places the menu on the desk. "Looks great. Good job, Kyle."

I don't look up. Tap away at nothing. "Thanks."

"Is something wrong?"

I glance up. She's watching me too closely. Like she can tell something's cracked, but she's not sure where the fault line is yet.

I shrug. "Nah. Just tired."

She nods, but doesn't move. Doesn't look away.

"Can I talk to you about something?"

I pause. That edge in her voice, the one she gets when she's about to pitch something big. Bigger than specials. Bigger than service.

"Sure," I say. Still pretending to scroll. Still pretending I'm not half made of bruises.

She folds her hands in her lap. Takes a breath. "I want you to cook with me. For the investor dinner." She smiles wide.

"Investor dinner?" I ask, my brow lifting.

"I think I have ten people interested in looking at this idea, Kyle." She looks at me with those big doe eyes. "Please help me pitch our idea," she pleads.

My god. Not the pleading.

She hops from the desk, shuts the door, then leans down, eyes searching mine.

"I think I found the perfect location. Come look at it with me." Her shoulders drop—and so does my heart.

I sigh. "Of course I will, Cass." I say it. Cass. Not Chef. Not Cassie. But… Cass.

She doesn't move. Not right away. She just stays there, crouched in front of me like we're kids. Like we're simply in this borrowed kitchen, feeding each other ideas and stealing bites of things we hadn't named yet.

She's so close I can smell her shampoo. Vanilla, heat, and everything I've been trying not to forget.

I could tell her right now that I have the money. I could invest in this dream… *our* dream. That I'm ready to break every rule I made about that trust fund and put it all on the line for us. For this.

But before I can speak, she touches my arm. "I asked Jack to help with some of the logistics," she says, like it's nothing. "You know, spreadsheets and proposals. He's been amazing. He can look over any legal stuff that my dad can't get to fast enough. Did I tell you my dad is a contract attorney?" She rambles.

My heart drops so hard I feel it in my knees.

Of course she did.

Of course Jack is also a lawyer. And of course her dad will approve.

I lean back in the chair and clear my throat. "Yeah. Sure. Great."

She doesn't notice. Or pretends not to.

But in that moment, I make a decision. I won't offer the money. Not yet. Not while *he's* still in the picture. Not while I'm just a broke chef she wants to help pitch the dream.

~~~

The apartment smells like sesame oil and garlic and the sharp sweetness of ginger blooming in a hot pan. Steam curls from the pot on the stove. There's flour dusting my forearms, clinging to my skin.
~~~

Music plays low from the speaker on the windowsill—something instrumental and funky, Japanese electronica.

It's late. But I'm so wired from work, I can't stop thinking.

She asked me to cook. For them. But I'm doing it for me.

Ten investors. Ten plates. Ten perfect bites. And I want every single one to taste like I bled into it.

I fold the mixture by hand—pork, ginger, scallion, soy, a whisper of fish sauce. The farce I always come back to. I've made this one so many times I could do it in my sleep, but tonight I'm tasting every element. Adjusting. Honing it to perfection.

Because if I'm not giving everything, what the fuck am I doing?

I turn toward the shelf to grab more parchment and freeze.

The box. That avocado-green plastic, like a prized trophy in its new place high on the shelf with my favorite cookbooks. Like it's been there for years.

I wash my hands, dry them on a towel, and pull it down.

The cards, still the same, their tattered, floured edges taped in all their glory from Rocco's escapade.

Anise biscotti. My Nonna's chicken cacciatore, written in her slanted Italian, and grease marks like battle scars.

There, still in the very front where I left it—Mom's Italian cheesecake. I pull it out and stare, as if it might offer some divine intervention. Some answers. Some healing. Instead, the pain bubbles back up, and I push it down into the box, just like I do with my feelings.

My throat tightens. I look over at the steaming pot, to the ingredients that would be so foreign to them, and my handwritten notes on notebook paper.

Would they be proud of this? Of me?

Would they understand this grind? This hustle? This quiet obsession to make food that speaks even when I can't?

I stare at the box for a long moment. Then I reach for a fresh stack of 3x5s from the drawer and a ballpoint pen.

I write: *Pork Dumpling Farce.*

Chapter 21

THE SILENT PARTNER

The prep sessions start to blur together.

Late nights at Le Début, long·after the staff has gone home.

It's wrong—we know it.

This place isn't ours anymore. Not really. Not since we decided to leave it behind. But it's the only space that still feels like us. The only one we know how to move in.

So, we stay. Quietly. Cooking like thieves in the night.

Sometimes I catch her leaning against the prep table, hair tied back, eyes lit with a kind of fire I haven't seen since she first came to Le Début.

And for a second, it feels like we're still building something. Like it's still just ours.

But then she talks about him. Jack this. Jack that. Like the man is personally seasoning her every thought.

They're full-on dating now. So wrapped up in each other it's like they're stitched at the seams.

"He's so helpful. So supportive," she says.

She's crashing at his place more and more.

Then one day she says it like it's nothing: "We should practice the dishes at his house."

So, I do what I always do—I show up, I shut up, and I kill it in the kitchen like my heart isn't peeling away with every swipe of the peeler across a scallion.

We stand at the massive granite island, our makeshift altar of intention and chaos. Spread out in front of us is a labyrinth of 3x5 cards—tonight's playlist, tonight's plan.

Flour-dusted. Smudged with soy sauce. A mess of my chicken scratch and her elegant script. Farce notes and flavor pairings. The blood and breath of every late-night prep session leading to this. An Asian-inspired menu meant to seduce ten wealthy investors into seeing what we see—our dream, plated.

We hover over the granite like it's a war table. Flour streaked across the stone. Sesame oil haloing one corner. Steam still curling off a test batch of duck.

Cassie taps at the cards with the top of her pen, biting her lip like the menu sequence holds the fate of the whole damn thing.

"I still think we open with the daikon and shiso. It's bright, clean. Starts on a punch with just a touch of bird's-eye."

"No." I shake my head. "We save that acidity to cut the duck. Start softer. Sichuan baby corn. Chili crisp. Toasted coriander oil. Something unexpected."

"Numb their mouths right off the rip, Kyle?" she says, grinning as she bumps me with her hip.

She shifts the cards, reshuffling combinations. My scribbled margins bleeding into hers.

Duck with yuzu glaze. Black sesame crunch. Umeboshi foam.

Pork dumpling with XO butter. Tempura shiso leaf.

Green tea soba with wild mushrooms and sake broth.

Matcha financier with burnt miso caramel.

"What if we slide the soba up?" she murmurs. "Fourth, maybe? Right before the duck?"

She shifts the card.

I move it back. "No. That broth is too subtle after the tartare. It'll disappear."

I tap my lip, studying the lineup. Mouth watering, already tasting the explosion across ten perfectly choreographed bites.

We go quiet. Both staring at the layout like it's a confession neither of us wants to read aloud.

"I think," she says, "this could actually work. All of it. The space. The menu. The name."

I'm about to answer when the flow shatters.

Jack enters. Barefoot. Smug. Ridiculous.

Dark designer jeans. A starched white button-down with the cuffs rolled like it's a goddamn cologne ad. Hair perfect. Smile rehearsed. A wine bottle in his hand, pulled from some imaginary private cellar.

"Hope I'm not interrupting."

You are. You always are.

He heads to the bar, pops the cork with practiced flair, pours two glasses like he owns the place. Well. I guess he does.

Like this is a dinner party. Like I'm the fucking caterer.

He swirls. Sniffs. Sips.

"Cabernet Franc. From Walla Walla. Subtle cherry notes with a little tobacco on the finish."

Congrats, man. You can read a fucking label.

He hands one to Cassie, eyes never leaving hers. Their fingers brush.

"Babe, get Kyle a glass." Cassie lets out a small, nervous laugh.

"Oh—sorry, man," he adds, like it's an afterthought, already turning back toward the bar.

I step back. "I'm gonna hit the bathroom."

Because if I don't get out of here, I'm going to jam that bottle down his designer throat.

As soon as the door closes, I hear their laughter echo down the hallway. Echo through my hollowed-out chest.

Breathe, Kyle. Just breathe.

I finish up. Wash my hands and try to steady myself. But I'm barely out the door when I hear it.

"I mean, he's talented, sure," Jack says, voice low but clear. "But let's be honest—he's not bringing money to the table. You need someone who can build the foundation, Cass. Not just plate it."

And then her voice. Softer. Hesitant. "I know. But… all this feels like his too, you know?"

Jack laughs. "Then let him run your kitchen. That's what guys like him do."

I freeze. Just behind the corner. Heart pounding. The only thing worse than being underestimated is being reduced.

I walk back into the kitchen. No one notices the shift. But my hands are shaking as I plate her future plans.

~~~

Later that week, we're not at Le Début. We're not even in a space that feels like ours. We're in a borrowed restaurant. A borrowed kitchen. Gleaming stainless steel—too sterile, too staged. Jack pulled some strings with a buddy who owns the place, a favor wrapped in charm and real estate law.

And somehow, it worked.

The food was ours.

But the stage? It was his.

Jack pops the champagne like he's proposing to himself.

Veuve Clicquot, of course. Can't offend anyone with the yellow label. Safe. Predictable. Like Jack.

Everyone applauds. Cassie laughs, and I just… step back.

Six. Six brilliant, ambitious, money-drenched people said yes tonight. They believed in us.

And now they're toasting the dream like I'm just the guy who handled the plating.

Then Sam Patterson, Cassie's dad, enters. All Southern charm and quiet power. This man could be Ted Danson's stand-in—tall, white hair, calm as a still lake. Less pretentious than his counterparts. This is the guy who gave Cassie her ease, her warmth. You can see it in how he smiles.

And he's so proud.

"Well I'll be," he says, shaking Jack's hand with genuine warmth. "You're just as polished as she said. Damn fine presentation, son."

Jack beams. Cassie glows.

And me? I'm over by the counter, wondering if I could chew through the stem of this champagne flute without cracking a molar.

That's when Ritchie slides in. No warning. No filter. Just… full Ritchie.

"Damn, man. They really like him, huh?"
~~~

"Who?" I mutter.

"Captain Cuffs & Champagne," Ritchie says, sipping from my untouched glass. "Guy looks like he's never sweat in his life."

I snort. It slips out too fast.

"No, seriously. He's got that *I do yacht law in Monaco and CrossFit on the roof* energy. I bet his sheets are wrinkle-resistant—and so is his heart."

"You're on fire tonight. You done?" I mutter with a quiet laugh, wrapping up our extra ingredients.

"Nope," he grins. "But I'm pacing myself. You want me to push him down the stairs or something subtle? Like a minor email scandal?"

I shoot him a glare. "Stop. She's happy." Then I laugh. "Do you even own a computer?"

"Yes, I do, smartass." He throws back the rest of my champagne, grinning. "And she just doesn't know she *could* be happier." He raises a brow. "I can make him… less attractive."

"Come on. Help me clean up this kitchen. We promised we'd be out by eleven."

"Fine." He groans, but he moves.

"Dad, I want you to meet Kyle." Cassie's voice cuts in again, pulling Sam gently by the arm. "He's the real talent and brains behind all this."

"Yeah, I just sampled and made spreadsheets, Mr. Patterson," Jack says, smiling like it's charming.

And finally, I'm pulled from the shadows.

Sam steps forward, extending a hand with that Southern charm that makes you feel like you've just been invited to stay a while.

"Kyle, I've heard a lot about you. Cassie says none of this would've happened without your incredible talent. I sure believe her after what I ate tonight, that's for damn sure."

I nod, gripping his hand. It's firm, warm, and just… good. Like everything I've been reaching for and never quite got to hold on to. The kind of dad warmth I wish I'd had.

"It's been an honor working with her," I say, and for once I'm not lying. Even if it guts me.

Cassie glances over, her smile soft. Something unreadable flashes in her eyes—a quiet pause in the noise.

"How much longer before we get out of here, guys?" she asks me and Ritchie.

"About thirty or forty minutes?" I say, looking back for confirmation from Ritchie, who's humming and loading the dishwasher like he works here.

"Yeah, sounds about right," he calls over his shoulder.

"How about I give you a ride to your hotel, Sam?" Jack asks.

"Actully, I was going to meet the rest of the new partners out for a drink."

Sam claps Jack on the shoulder. "Can you drop me off there?"

"You got it." Jack juggles his keys, then leans in and presses a kiss to Cassie's cheek. "I'll be right back to pick you up, babe."

Bile threatens to rise in my throat. What's next? Picking out china patterns?

"Okay. I'll see you tomorrow, Dad."

"Great job, Bug. I'm so proud of you." He hugs her, kisses the top of her head, and then he's gone.

The door shuts. Ritchie's earbuds go in, and the kitchen shifts. And for just a second—it's only us.

The tension of the night—champagne, clinking glasses, and Jack's polished perfection—blurs as we pack and clean side by side.

Her hand brushes mine as she passes the last plate. A look. A heartbeat.

Maybe… But then she turns, and the spell breaks. She hops up onto the stainless-steel prep table. Her legs swing like a kid's—free, careless. A mischievous smile tugs at her lips.

"What?" I ask, catching myself smiling.

She shakes her head and stares at her feet.

"I couldn't have done any of this without you, Kyle. I want you running the line. Chef de Cuisine."

My chest tightens.

"Please tell me you won't ever leave me," she adds quietly. "Be my partner in crime forever?"

I'd walk through fire for you, Cass.

I swallow it down. Say something safer. "Well, that all depends on how much you're willing to pay me," I say, smirking.

She pulls an envelope from her chef coat like it's nothing. But to me, it might as well be a marriage proposal.

"Let me know if this isn't fair. It's a whole package we put together. You're worth it, Kyle."

I take the envelope. Start to open it.

"Not with me here." She puts a hand up, stops me cold. "Just let me know later if it's not enough."

Then she hops down, patting my shoulder like I'm the family dog who just did a really good trick.

"You're not going anywhere, my friend."

My friend.

The words echo in the kitchen long after she's gone. Louder than the clatter of dishes. Sharper than the edge of a chef's knife.

~~~

The hot water pours over my back, stinging where the tension clings to my muscles. My palms press into the cool tile like I'm trying to hold myself together.

Her words echo, sticky and soft in the steam: *my friend.*

I lower my head, let the water pound against the back of my neck.

My friend.

Not my partner. Not my dream. Not *stay, and make my legs quiver.*

Just… friend.

I squeeze my eyes shut. Try to shake the image of her legs swinging from the prep table. The way she looked at me like I was solid ground. And then—*you're not going anywhere.*

Like she owns me. Like I'm some rare, discontinued KitchenAid mixer in the exact shade of her dream. The one she'll never use, but can't bear to let anyone else have.

My jaw tightens.

"I'm not going anywhere."

No. Not tonight. Not unless I want to drown.
~~~

I kill the water, step out into the cool air, and grab a towel with more aggression than necessary. Rocco lifts his head from the bedroom floor, ears perking up like he knows something's cracked open in me.

"I know, bud. I've been gone all day," I mutter, rubbing at his ears. "I'll make it up to you tomorrow."

I pull on jeans, a black tee, and a leather cuff from the back of the drawer. No apron. No chef coat. Just simplicity and impulse.

"But tonight…" I exhale. "I gotta get the hell out of here."

Rocco whines softly as I grab my keys.

"Guard the place," I say, pointing at him. "And no counter surfing. I mean it." I eye the fresh sourdough on the counter.

I don't wait for him to respond. I shut the door behind me and step out into the cool California night air.

~~~

This bar isn't my usual scene.

It's too loud, too weird, too unpolished. No curated playlists. No twenty-dollar smoked cocktails. No conversations about food trucks and Michelin dreams. Just funky beats bleeding out of warped speakers, sticky floors, and a bartender who doesn't give a shit if your ice is cloudy or the perfect shape.

Which is exactly why I'm here.

I don't want to run into anyone I know. Don't want to talk about Sagi-Shi, Le Début, or what it means to be part of something. I want to be invisible tonight.

I post up against the wall near the back. Sip whatever whiskey they handed me and let the bass hit my ribs like a defibrillator.

The place pulses with people—laughing, swaying, grinding against each other in dim light. Bodies everywhere, but none of them looking at me.

Until she does.

Across the floor, backlit by red and violet strobe lights, she moves like the beat is hers. Like she came here to feel something and doesn't care who's watching.

Except she's watching… me. Eyes locked. No smile. Just intention.
~~~

She's not subtle. And I'm too wrecked to care.

She leaves the dance floor slowly, scooping up her drink from a side table before heading my way. Her long blonde hair trails down bare arms as lights flash across her skin, catching the sheen of sweat on her chest.

I already know this is the kind of woman who disappears before sunrise but still leaves the scent of sandalwood and sweat on my sheets.

She closes in, taking up every inch of personal space I didn't invite her to fill.

Yeah. Sandalwood—and something floral.

She takes a sip of her drink. She's so close I can hear the ice clink against her glass over the bass of the music. I catch the shimmer of her tongue as she licks her lips.

"I'm Mira." Her voice is low. Sultry.

"Does it matter?" I say, eyes still on her mouth.

She smiles like she's in on a secret I haven't earned yet.

"Fair enough."

She doesn't move back. The silence stretches between us, thick and pulsing. The kind that makes it hard to think. Harder not to.

Her fingertips skim the edge of her glass. Mine flex around mine.

"Rough night?" she asks, voice like a match strike.

"Something like that."

Even as the thought hits me—I should be celebrating what was in that envelope—I know the truth. It came at a cost. Trading one dream for another.

"You look like a man who needs a reason to forget."

She tips her head, one brow lifting. She's not offering small talk. She's offering oxygen. An escape hatch. Fire.

I down the rest of my drink in one swallow.

"Can you help me do that, Mira?"

She throws back the rest of hers and sets the glass on the table.

"I sure can try."

"Let's go," I say, taking her by the hand.

We don't talk on the way out. No names. No questions. Just the heavy silence of two people who know exactly what this is.

My place is close. Small. Dimly lit. It still smells like incense and faint dog as I pull the door open.

The door barely clicks shut before I press her against it.

She doesn't gasp. She grabs—fist in my shirt, lips crashing into mine like we're already halfway gone.

"Fuck," I breathe against her mouth.

Clothes come off in pieces. Buttons from her top skitter across the floor. She pulls my shirt over my head in one hard, impatient motion. I spin her, drag her into the kitchen. She hits the cabinet with a thud that startles Rocco curled up nearby in his bed.

"Sorry, Rocco," I mutter, breathless, as she pulls me back in.

She tastes like tequila and trouble. Her mouth moves like she's trying to erase someone else's name from her mind. Like she had a rough night too.

My hands slide down the smooth line of her thighs—lift, spread, claim. She wraps around me like she's been waiting all night. Maybe longer.

"Wait…" she gasps.

"What?" I murmur, still moving.

"I'm doing this, but I want to know your name." Her eyes lock on mine. "I want to know what name to call out when you make me come."

Fuck. That's hot.

I lean in, bite her shoulder just enough to mark, and breathe hot against her skin.

"Kyle."

And then it's all motion.

It's not gentle. It's feral. There's sweat. Cabinetry abuse. And not a single moment where either of us pretends this is love.

This is survival. This is forgetting. This is losing Cassie one gasp, one thrust at a time.

She balances on the counter, my hand cradling one thigh, and I watch as my cock slides in and out of her. Then I close my eyes, pretending I'm somewhere else. Inside someone else.

"Damn, you feel so good."

Her fingers thread through my hair while her other hand fists at my shoulder, then slides to clutch the bottom of the upper cabinet like it's holding her to the earth.

"Yes," she moans, breath sharp and shaking. "Fuck me like you want to fuck her, Kyle."

Frustration spikes. Lust surges. And for the next hour, I stop pretending.

Chapter 22

CHILI JAM & WHO I AM

The dining room is empty. Morning light filters through the bamboo blinds, soft and golden. I'm pulling chairs down one by one, adrenaline buzzing with caffeine and a hundred ideas swirling in my head, my mind already racing toward tomorrow.

"Hear me out. We build the specials menu like a journey, right?" I say, dropping a chair with a soft *thunk.* "Then for each table, a little write-up. Just a card. Something personal. Something that tells them why that one broth matters."

Cassie follows, doing the same. *Chair. Chair. Chair.* She's smiling—head tilted, eyes lit.

Like it's still just us. Like we never cracked down the middle.

"For example," I say, "tonight's soba—Kawachi style. It's specific to a region in Osaka. Earthier flavor. Different grind on the buckwheat. We give them the story, they taste the depth. It matters."

"You and your soba," she laughs, shaking her head. *Chair. Chair.*

My hands move faster. I can't stop. The idea's got me.

"Same for the black garlic—fermented over ninety days. It's transformation. It's loss. It's—"

"I'm pregnant."

She says it just like that. Like she's telling me we're low on daikon.

I freeze. My fingers wrap around the legs of the next chair, but don't lift. The silence stretches longer than it should. Too long.

She keeps going like she didn't just gut me like a fish in the middle of the dining room floor.

"Just found out. We haven't told many people yet, so keep it quiet." She grins—and her hand drifts to her stomach, like she's already imagining it. Like there's already a round belly for me to see.

I nod. Say nothing. Because I can't remember how.

I just got used to her being married. Jesus. Has the ink even dried on their marriage license?

One year. One year in this space.

Two awards. One for her. Rising Star Chef. One for the restaurant—Top Interior Design or some shit.

Guess who's still in the goddamn shadows? Still the loyal friend. Her Chef de Cuisine. The background noise to her bright, shining story.

But hey… maybe there's an upside. Maybe I get to be Uncle Kyle. Carve duck bao into animal shapes. Make the ears perfectly round. Steam them just right. Smile for the photos. Pretend I'm not dying inside.

God, what the hell am I even thinking?

"Come on… are you not excited?" Her voice is soft, but the look on her face says it all—hope crumbling under the weight of my silence.

"Oh god. I'm sorry." I place a hand on her shoulder, anchoring myself to the moment. "Cass, this is… great news," I lie. "You just caught me off guard, that's all."

She lets me pull her in. Her hair brushes my jaw. That scent—green tea and something warm, vanilla—snuffs out the flames rising in my blood. Not gently. Her embrace turns them to ash.

"I'm glad." She pulls back in my arms, eyes shimmering. "We're so excited," she says.

Then, quieter, like it's sacred: "You're the first person I've told here."

"Oh—wow," I say, stunned.

"Okay." She wiggles free and brushes invisible lint from her chef coat. "We have a ton of work to do today." She flashes a bright smile. "And by the way—I love your idea."

I blink. Still trying to summon words. Still hoping she'll crawl back into my arms.

"What idea?"

She laughs, shaking her head. "The cards on the table… soba noodles… black garlic?" She waves a hand in front of my face. "Hellooo. Earth to Kyle."

"Oh—yeah. Sorry…" I glance toward her stomach, gesturing vaguely. "You kinda distracted me with… that."

She pulls the last chair from a table. "What else do we have on the agenda?"

"Uh-uh." I step in front of her, hand on the chair leg. "I got that."

"Lord, Kyle." She rolls her eyes. "I'm pregnant, not broken."

I grab the chair anyway. "We've got someone coming from The Redemption Kitchen at ten."

"That's the group that rehabs non-violent offenders and trains them as line cooks, right?" she asks.

"Yeah." I nod. "They reached out after they saw our article. Figured I'd hear 'em out."

Cassie shoots me a look—familiar, knowing. "Umm… yeah… Jack was a little worried about safety when I mentioned that."

I shake my head. "They wouldn't be sending anyone dangerous. And you seriously think I'd let someone into our kitchen who wasn't ready?"

A beat. "Tell Jack to chill."

~~~

It's been over four months. Almost five.

Cassie's stride has taken on the cutest waddle as she moves through the kitchen—and somehow she still manages to look more polished than anyone else here, despite the belly, the bun, and the compression socks she refuses to admit she needs.

Our new line cook, Diego, moves around her like he's been here for years. Technically, he's still a Redemption Kitchen trainee, but nobody's questioning it. The guy's sharp, fast, and respectful as hell. He doesn't just want to be here. He knows what it means to be here.
~~~

"You're cutting the shiitakes too thick," I say, sliding past him.

"Yes, Chef," Diego answers without flinching, already adjusting.

Cassie leans against the counter, one hand on her back. "We need more Diegos," she mutters.

I glance at her. "No," I say, flipping a pan onto the burner. "We need to clone you."

She smirks, then groans, shifting her weight. I don't say it out loud, but I notice. She's slower today. Tired. And still impossibly beautiful.

"I'll be in the office," she says, already turning like her body isn't protesting every step.

She shouldn't be on the line—not this pregnant, not as the executive chef. But she can't help herself. This is where she feels most alive. Not behind a desk. Not balancing invoices or talking to vendors. Here. With the fire. The noise. The knives. The chaos. This is home for her.

And even now, swollen with someone else's future, she moves like this kitchen still belongs to us both.

I watch her walk away. The way her hand supports the small of her back. The way her shoulders are still square, proud.

The door swings shut behind her.

I exhale slowly, barely noticing Diego setting down a fresh tray beside me.

"You good, Chef?" he asks.

I nod once. "Yeah. Just thinking about something."

"Anything I can do for you?"

"Just make sure the mise is tight for this station tonight." I clap him on the shoulder. "I'm perfectly good, thanks."

He smiles, but I'm only telling half the truth.

~~~

Some people journal. Some people go to therapy. Since I found Mira, I decided to fuck the ache out of my system.

One text. One knock. No questions asked.

She's not love. She's not comfort. She's friction and relief—the exhale I probably don't deserve.
~~~

Tonight, it's the shower again. Multitasking.

"God, I needed this," I whisper, voice low and cracked, fingers pressing into the tile.

I lean my head against the shower wall, hot water running down my chest. Her mouth wraps around me—wet, demanding—like she's trying to pull the pain straight from my bones.

"Dammit," I groan, threading my fingers through her soaked hair, pressing her deeper.

Her hands grip my thighs to steady herself, one sliding up to wrap around the base.

She pulls back, lips swollen, eyes glassy and wild.

"You like that, huh?" she asks, voice thick and teasing.

"Fuck yes," I hiss, brushing hair from her cheek. "Don't stop."

Her hand finds my chest. Her mouth twists around me like she's missed it. Like it's hers. And maybe—for the next twenty minutes—it is.

"Goddamn, that's too good." I pull her up, crash my mouth to hers, kissing hard and hungry.

Then I spin her, press her body against the cool tile. She whimpers low and aching, a wicked smile curling at her lips.

I lean in, my breath hot at her ear. "You first," I whisper, sliding two fingers between her thighs. Slow and intentional.

"Oh god, Kyle," she moans, reaching back, threading her fingers through my hair, hips arching into me. She's soaked—warm and greedy—wrapping around my fingers like she's been waiting all damn day.

"Give me more," she begs. "I need more."

I stroke myself, dragging along the curve of her ass.

"Where do you want it?" I ask, teasing, letting her feel just how ready I am.

Her eyes glance back, sharp and shining. "Not my ass," she says, firm. "Not tonight."

I grin. "What a shame."

She spreads her legs wider. "Kyle..."

That's all I need.

I sink into her—slow and hard. One palm flat on the tile, the other locked around her hip as I fill her inch by inch.

She lets out a sound stitched from want and relief.

And I don't rush. I let her feel every second.

~~~

"So, why the text tonight?"

Her fingernail traces slow, lazy circles across my chest, like she's not really looking for answers, but she is.

I stare at the ceiling for a beat, still catching my breath. "Stressed, I guess. I needed a win," I say. "Knew you'd deliver."

She hums, not buying it. "That all?"

My fingers skim the curve of her hip, thumb brushing just beneath her ribs. I shrug. "Stop. This is what we do. Don't complicate it."

That earns a small smile. The kind that says *danger, danger,* but her body doesn't move away.

She's quiet for a beat, then says it like she's just thinking out loud. "You know… at some point, you're gonna have to stop building your whole life around someone who already picked a different future."

My fingers still. My breath catches. It's just a hitch, but she feels it.

"I'm not judging," she adds quickly. "I just… hate watching someone like you shrink."

She lifts my hand and kisses my knuckles.

"I'm not shrinking," I snap.

"Easy." Her voice softens. "We've been doing this dance a long time, Kyle. Someday I might just stop answering your cries for help." She shrugs.

I glance over. "And yet, you keep showing up at my door."

Her fingers rest against my chest. The air between us shifts—something quiet settling there, like steam on glass.

"I should go," she says, soft but steady.

"Yeah." I don't move. Neither does she.

When she finally sits up, I reach out and catch her hand. Just for a second. My thumb brushes over her knuckles.
~~~

"I wish I could be different for you, Mira." I swallow. "You really should quit me."

She sighs, leans down, and kisses my forehead. "Nah," she says. "I'd rather be alone and fuck your fine ass on occasion. Saves me a shit ton of grief with other men." She shoots me a wink, already pulling her shirt over her head—still inside out.

At the door, she glances back once. "No feelings, remember?"

I nod. "No feelings."

The front door clicks shut. I go back to staring at the ceiling, wondering why it still hurts.

I throw off the covers, and Rocco groans like he already knows what's coming.

I grab my phone off the nightstand before I can talk myself out of it.

Kyle: Hey... you hungry? If so, come back.

No overthinking. No meaning layered under meaning. Just hunger. Mine. Hers. Maybe something in between.

By the time I've pulled the ba mee from the pantry and whispered, "Hello, friend. Haven't used you in a while," there's a knock at the door.

She steps back inside, kicking off her sneakers. Hair still damp. Her inside-out T-shirt hanging off one shoulder. Freshly fucked, and she couldn't look sexier.

"You good?" she asks, voice low. That smirk—because she knows exactly why I texted.

I nod. "Getting there."

Mira leans against the counter, watching me move.

I don't explain. I don't fill the silence. She just watches—eyes tracking my hands as I crush garlic, swirl oil, lift the noodles from the water and let them fall like silk.

I let her watch the broth build, slow and low. I roll the lime across the counter to wake the juice before I char it. I swirl the chili jam like it's sacred. It coats the back of the spoon—thick, red, glistening. I drag my finger through it. Taste. Adjust.

Her eyes flick to mine.

"You're really cooking," she says, voice low and breathy. Not teasing. Not playful. Just honest. The same look she gave me in the shower—like I'm the thing she can't swallow down.

"Figured I'd try doing something that doesn't end in self-destruction."

She laughs, soft and surprised. "Growth looks hot on you, Chef." Her bare feet swing from the stool, childlike.

I smirk, but keep moving.

I slide the noodles into the bowl. Ba mee—springy, golden, tangled like my head was just minutes ago.

Now? Clear as glass. Precision. My space. My element.

I ladle the broth. Let it spill slowly. It's deep, dark, and umami-rich. One perfect spoonful of chili jam melts into the center. Not stirred. Not hidden. Just there. Present and bold.

Crispy shallots. Translucent daikon matchsticks. Bright Thai basil wilting on contact.

Half of a farm-fresh egg, nestled gently on top. Yolk glossy, sun-orange.

I set the bowl in front of her.

She looks down. Then up. "Is this for me?"

"For you," I say. "But not about you."

That catches in her throat. She doesn't answer. She lifts her chopsticks. Takes a bite. Chews slowly.

"Holy shit," she whispers.

I smile.

Not because she's impressed. Because I finally am.

Chapter 23

WHEN THE LEVEE BREAKS

Prep is done, and we're wrapping up family meal. The kitchen's clean and organized. Everything's tight. Knives honed. Mise en place, locked.

I step into the center of the room and give the pass a single tap with my knuckle.

"Alright. Let's go over these specials again. Listen close."

Everyone stops and turns. Nate dumps his plate into the trash and leans on a prep table. Diego tosses a towel over his shoulder. Front of house trickles in—hostesses, servers, that new guy who still thinks truffle oil belongs in Asian cuisine. They all stop. They all listen.

I feel like… *Theo.*

"Tonight's a tribute to balance, with some bold Indian flavors." I flip the page on my legal pad. "We're starting with carrot-ginger soup. Roasted, then blended with ghee and garam masala. Finished with coconut milk and chili oil. It's silk. It's heat. It's comfort."

I point to Garde. "Garnish this right. That perfect barista swirl. Otherwise, it just looks like a bowl of baby poop."

The room murmurs. Noah nods.

"Next—grilled halibut. Brushed with mustard seed oil and turmeric. Plated over green mango chutney. Micro cilantro. Clean plates every time."

I catch Diego smirking.

"Yes, it's spicy. No, you don't need to ask for sriracha."

Scattered chuckles echo through the kitchen.

"Our veg is charred eggplant with cumin yogurt and pomegranate—bright, earthy, and sweet. Dessert's the wildcard—rose cardamom panna cotta with pistachio crumble. If it makes them cry, that's normal."

"Hey—that's my line," Reva calls from pastry.

I smile. "And it's a good one."

Noah mutters, "You're such a showoff."

"Our Fishbowl Table tonight is Cameron Vale, —Creative Director for…" I read from my pad, "Vera Luxe Hotels."

A few murmurs ripple down the line.

"Relax." I lift a hand. "He's not a critic. Just money."

That earns a couple of smirks. Diego mouths *just money?* Nate grins.

"Yeah. We like people to spend it here." I nod. "So keep your lines tight. Keep it clean. And remember—" I thumb toward the glass wall. "We're on display. Clean hands. Quiet confidence. Smile when you need to curse."

Silence.

"Any questions?"

No one moves. They're locked in.

"Alright then." I nod once. "Slay it tonight."

Front of house peels off. The line breaks into motion.

"Let's cook."

The back door slams open—hard enough to echo.

"Nope. Go home, Cass." My hand shoots up before I even turn.

She marches past me, already tying her apron over a very-obviously-about-to-pop belly. Her hair is shoved into a messy half-bun. Her chef coat is unbuttoned, with her stretched-out vintage tee underneath. Determined as hell.

"Kyle, I can't," she says. "I'm losing my mind at home. I've cleaned everything twice and Jack won't stop coddling me like I'm a Fabergé egg."

I face her, arms crossed. Inked and unmoving.

"That's because you're the size of a beach ball and could go into labor any second. Does he even know you're here?"

She walks right past me. "I'll just hang at expo," she says. "I promise."

"Stay off the line."

That stops her. She tries to pivot sharply, but it turns into a clumsy, slow-motion wobble between prep tables.

I reach for her instinctively.

"I'm not fragile," she says, steadying herself.

"I didn't say you were. I said you're done working the line. Tonight's heavy. Let the team run it."

She narrows her eyes. "You're being a pain in the ass."

"And you're being reckless and stubborn," I snap back.

A beat. "This kitchen is the only place that still feels like mine," she whispers, teeth clenched. Her eyes gloss. "It could be…" Her lip trembles. "The last time I'm here for a while."

Oh no. Not the tears.

I really look at her. The early days flicker back—her laugh in the walk-in, the late nights, the 3x5 cards at Le Début. The way we built this place out of nothing.

"Fine," I mutter. "Expo only. No running dishes. No cooking. Understood?" I point at her like I'm laying down the law. "And for the love of god—stand still."

She looks like she might actually pop. Glowing. Radiant. Impossible.

She grins.

And I know I'm screwed.

Service runs smoothly. Kitchen chatter, pans clattering, a team firing on all cylinders.

Cassie's at expo, arms folded beneath that belly, calling pickups like nothing's changed—like she's not about to bring a human into the world in less than two weeks.

I'm floating—CDC and Exec, managing the pass, watching plating, clocking front of house flow. Everything tight. Smooth as silk.

At the ticket rail, Cassie barks over her shoulder, "Fire fourteen. Hold panna cotta on fifteen—grandma's still working on her entrée."

I glance up. She's glowing. That Cassie glow. The kind that comes from kindness, adrenaline, and a dangerous level of control.

She's still got it. I don't know how, but she does.

I check a final plate in the pass, wipe the edge, and lean toward her. "Hey—I'm going to swing out, say hi to the Fishbowl table. Can you just… stay here? Be eyes. That's it, Cass."

She waves me off. "Yes. Go."

I step into the dining room, cool air and ambient noise swallowing me whole. Cameron Vale sits with three guests—black suit, cufflinks, polite smile—watching the kitchen like it's performance art—chefs behind glass, the whole line on display.

"Mr. Vale," I say, offering my hand. "Hope everything's meeting expectations."

He nods. "You run a tight ship, Chef Berkley. Your team's got a kind of… choreography going on back there. It's nice to watch."

I open my mouth to respond—

"Oh my god."

One of the women at the table is pointing past me, eyes wide.

I turn.

"I think her water just broke!" she yells.

Cassie stands dead center in the kitchen. Completely still. Wide-eyed. Hands hovering like she doesn't know where to put them. Her chef pants are soaked through, a massive puddle spreading beneath her feet.

She's staring straight at me through the glass.

The kitchen freezes. Then it stirs again, jerky and soundless, like a silent film.

Diego's got a spoon suspended mid-air. Reva comes barreling out of pastry, mouthing, *Oh shit.* Diego backs away like Cassie's radioactive.

Cassie mouths something I can't hear, but her face says it all: *Don't freak out. But also—freak out.*

The dining room dissolves. Cameron Vale says something, but I don't hear it.

I'm already moving—through the service door, back into the heat and noise and the suddenly silent kitchen. Every head turns to me like I've done this before. Like this is somehow on the goddamn menu.

"Nate, Reva, Diego—keep going," I bark. My voice is calm. Too calm. My brain is on fire.

Cassie stands there, breathing shallow. One hand on her lower back and the other clamped over her mouth.

"Holy fuck," she says, letting out a shaky laugh. "I'm so embarrassed. That just happened in front of everyone."

"Danny!" I call toward dish. "I need a mop."

I guide her gently by the elbow, steering her toward the office. "It's okay, Cass. We're good. You're okay. It's not like you shit yourself in front of the President."

She snorts, then winces. "Oh my god, Kyle—don't make me laugh. It's still running down my leg."

She stops short and doubles over.

"What is it?" I ask, already leaning down.

"Ooooh fuck," she moans.

"Somebody call Jack," I shout over my shoulder.

"No! Don't call Jack," she gasps.

"Cass—"

She looks up at me, pain and panic colliding. "He's working late on a case. He doesn't even know I came in."

Another contraction hits. She bends, bracing herself against the wall, breath hitching.

"Dammit, Cassie."

We hit the office. I get her into the little leather chair—older than both of us, and she grips the armrests like she's anchoring herself to the earth.

She winces and lets out a long, low groan. Then she looks at her watch.

Oh fuck.

"Are you already timing contractions?"

Her brows knit. She nods quickly, already breathing in through her nose and out through her mouth, steady and practiced.

"Deep breath," I say, kneeling in front of her. "You're safe. You're okay. Just… let it happen." I shake my head. "But—don't."

She locks eyes with me. "I don't want to do this here."

"How about I call 911?"

"No." She shakes her head. "It's my first. I'm not going to have her that fast. Just… take me to the hospital."

Her.

She was keeping that a surprise.

It's a girl.

"Damn, you're stubborn." I grab my phone and keys off the desk. "Jack's going to kill me. Come on."

Diego pops his head in. Eyes wide.

"Chef? What are we doing?"

"You're running the line," I say, calmly. "You can do it." I nod once. "I'll be back as soon as Jack gets there."

He nods from the doorway like he's watching a damn soap opera.

"This is happening," Cassie says smiling, breath hitching.

"Yeah," I say. "But not in my kitchen."

~~~

Cassie's lying in the hospital bed, breathing through another contraction. The monitors beep softly. The lights are dim. It's the first calm moment we've had in almost an hour.

I glance at my watch before handing her a cup of ice chips. She takes it without looking at me.

"Thanks," she mumbles.

I sit beside the bed, elbows on my knees. Watching her, not the machines. And before I can stop myself, the words slip out. Low. Sharp. Quieter than they feel.

"Where is he? And why is he working late when you're this close to delivering?"

She flinches. Just a flicker.

Her lips press together as she stares at the wall. "Don't do that."

"It's a valid question."

"Kyle—"

"You were soaked, shaking, terrified—and he didn't even know where you were." I keep my voice even. "That's not judgment, Cass. That's fact."

She closes her eyes. "He's trying. He just… he didn't know I left. I didn't tell him."
~~~

"Why not?"

"Because he was working late on a big case. I just… left."

A beat.

"He shouldn't be working late," I say. "You're—forget it." I shut up. Because if she were mine—if this were my baby—this wouldn't look like this.

She shifts again, one hand on her belly, breathing through another contraction. I gently take the cup from her hand and set it aside. The monitor beeps steadily beside her.

I squeeze her hand. "Just breathe. You've got this. You're a rock star."

The words barely leave my mouth when the door bursts open.

Jack rushes in—suit rumpled, tie crooked, voice too loud for this dim labor room.

"Baby, baby, I'm here. I came as fast as I could," he pants, like he ran a half-marathon.

He crosses the room in two strides, and kisses her temple like he's trying to erase time with affection.

"How are you feeling? Are you okay? Did they check you yet? Where are we in this?"

She nods, breathless. "They admitted me. We're still early."

Jack scans the room like it's a crime scene. Then he sees me.

His mouth tightens. "Thanks for getting her here, man."

"Mmhm."

I don't stand. I don't move. I let the silence stretch until it stings.

He turns back to her. "You should've called me, babe."

"I told Kyle not to." She shrugs. "Didn't want you to worry. It was fine."

"You didn't want me to worry? Jesus, Cass."

"She didn't want to interrupt your busy work schedule," I add, casually.

Jack turns to me, jaw tight. "Appreciate the concern. But this is *my* wife."

"Yeah," I say, standing now. "That's what I've been trying to wrap my head around."

His eyebrows lift. "Excuse me?"

"Nothing." I wave it off. "You're here now."

Another contraction hits. Cassie groans, gripping the rail of the bed.

We both freeze, watching her.

She breathes through it like a pro, then lets out a shaky sigh.

"Can you two just… *not?*"

Jack steps back. I step forward, lifting another cup of ice chips. Cassie takes them without looking at either of us.

"I'm not doing this while in labor. Not with both of you posturing like a couple of chefs in a chili cook-off."

That earns a laugh from me. Quiet and bitter.

"Pretty sure I'd win that."

"You're not even in the damn competition," Jack mutters.

"You can't even boil water," I say under my breath.

Cassie groans again—this time, not from a contraction.

"Oh my god. If either of you says one more word, I will rip out this fucking IV and strangle one of you with the tubing."

The nurse breezes in, clipboard in hand. Bright smile. Zero awareness she's about to light a match and walk away.

"Alright, Daddy, we're going to check dilation and get things rolling—"

She looks straight at me. *Me.*

Jack's head snaps so fast I swear I hear cartilage protest.

"Oh." The nurse blinks. "I'm sorry—are you not the…?"

Cassie closes her eyes, like maybe if she doesn't look at either of us, the room will dissolve.

"He's not," Jack grits out. Tight. Cold.

"Right," I mutter, still gripping the bed rail like a total dumbass. "Just the driver."

The nurse lets out a nervous chuckle and scurries toward the monitor.

Cassie mutters, "God, just kill me."

Jack paces. The silence is loud—his Armani dress shoes scuffing across the floor.

"You want me to leave?" I lean down and ask quietly.

She doesn't answer right away. Then, "No. But maybe just… say less."

The nurse touches Cassie's arm. "We're going to check your cervix now." She glances in my direction.

Cassie's eyes lift to mine, wide. Jack stops pacing.

"I think it's time to go, Kyle. I've got it from here," Jack says, smug.

I nod. Step back. And swallow the thousand things I'll never say.

~~~

The restaurant is quiet now. Just the hum of the refrigeration units.

I walk the line one last time—checking every station, giving the pass a final wipe-down. The tile gleams. The steel shines. The space feels too clean and quiet after the chaos that tore through it earlier.

At the front, I flick off the lights.

Click. Darkness.

I head to the back and grab my things from the office.

My phone buzzes in my hand. I look down. A photo fills the screen—plump newborn cheeks, a tiny pink hat, a blanket pulled snug.

Cora Anne Buckley

8 lbs, 2 oz

19 inches

She's perfect, Kyle.

"You all good?" Danny asks, backing down the hallway, finishing the last slow swooshes of the mop.

I look up. "Yeah… yeah, Dan. I'm great." I hold up the phone. "It's a girl. Chef had a girl."

I smile and scrub a hand down my face, staring back at the picture until the screen blurs.

"Oh, right on. Right on." He says, then he keeps mopping.

I push through the back door. It slams shut behind me with a finality that makes my chest ache.

I lean against the brick wall and exhale hard. The parking lot glows beneath a single buzzing overhead light. Bugs swarm it like static.
~~~

My thumb hovers over the screen, already knowing what I'm looking for.

Then I type: Are you up?

Chapter 24

DIAPERS & DUMPLINGS

I keep staring at my phone, waiting. The silence cuts deeper than it should.

I'm always here for you, Kyle. Anytime.

The words loop in my head, like maybe I imagined them. Like maybe I believed a lie. My phone buzzes, and I hate how fast my pulse spikes.

Uncle Wally: I'm here. Are you okay?

I exhale. The message I actually needed.

Kyle: Yeah. I just have questions.

Uncle Wally: Okay. Like what? Do you want to talk?

I look at the empty parking lot. The buzzing light. The bugs. The restaurant behind me. Then I head to my car.

I slide in and shut the door. The only sound is my breathing. I press call.

He answers on the second ring. "Hey. What's going on, Kyle?" His voice is gravelly. Familiar.

I toss my hat onto the passenger seat and drag a hand through my hair.

"I don't know. Today was a weird one. Got me thinking."

"Okay… about what?"

A beat. "My father."

"Alright." Another pause. "What about him?"

I shake my head, scrub my hand down my face. "What happened? Why does he hate me so much, Wally? I'm his kid."

"Oh, Kyle. He doesn't hate you. He—"

"Wally," I cut in. "You see the way he talks to me. The way he belittles me. He can't stand me."

Silence.

"I don't know," he finally says. "When your mom died…" He pauses, like the words sting. "Your dad didn't know how to raise you. He didn't know how to… love. That was her gift. God, she loved you, Kyle. With everything she had."

I swallow hard.

"Then why did he make me feel like I ruined her?" My voice cracks. "Like it was all my fault?"

Wally goes quiet. Too quiet. I hear the shift of fabric—he's sitting up now. Bracing.

"He never said that, Kyle."

"Yes, he did," I snap. "My whole goddamn childhood."

I don't mention the hitting. Wally wouldn't know what to do with that anyway.

He mutters something under his breath—angry. Ashamed. Maybe both.

I let it go.

"The aneurysm—" he says finally, "it was sudden. There was no warning. No one caused it. *You* didn't cause it."

My jaw tightens. I stare through the windshield. At the halo of fog clinging to the glass.

"But I asked for it," I whisper. "That damn cheesecake. It was his birthday. I begged her to fix my mistake."

"And she would've done it again," Wally says, voice steady now. "A hundred times. That was her love language—showing up. Making something sweet. You didn't steal her, Kyle. You were her reason."

I shut my eyes, trying to breathe past the guilt.

I was just a kid. One request.

One cheesecake.

And she never came back.

Wally's voice drops low.

"She was gone, and your dad… he just didn't know how to live in that house without her. Didn't know how to be a father. And every time he looked at you, he saw the one person she loved more than him. He couldn't stand that. I don't think he even understood why."

That stuns the air from my lungs.

"He didn't hate you, Kyle. He just didn't know how to love what she left behind."

A long beat.

"I think I'm fucked up, Wally," I admit. "With people. With love. I want a wife and a family someday, but I don't let anyone in. I'm scared I'll turn into *him.*"

Silence again. Then, "Maybe it's time to forgive him," Wally says quietly. "Not for *his* sake—but for yours."

~~~

The truck engine hums low in the alley behind the restaurant. I step out, clipboard in hand, the morning sun just beginning to creep down the narrow passage.

"Hey, Darius. Can you help me with this truck?" I call down the hall before the door swings shut.

"Yes, Chef." No hesitation. No ego. Just action.

I watch him move. Efficient. Focused. I remember when I was him. Hungry, quiet, and invisible until I made myself matter. Standing outside Le Début, staring through the glass like it held a future.

My phone buzzes. I pull it out, thumb already expecting a supplier delay or another front of house scheduling change.

Cassie: Want to come see her today or tomorrow?

I freeze.

Darius is already hauling boxes off the truck and doesn't notice me standing there—leveled.

Cassie. After weeks of distance, all this silence—*she's letting me in.*

Kyle: Sure. I have errands to run today. I can stop by before service.
~~~

Cassie: See you then.

~~~

I scale the steps up to her house. To her perfect life. The perfect porch, with its perfect little chairs, table, and lamp. I bet they sit out here in the evenings—drink wine and wave to the neighbors.

Most people bring flowers and a cute outfit. I brought dumplings and a jar of chili jam.

I knock lightly. Because what the hell do you do when you're standing on the porch of a woman you might love, delivering dumplings like some grief-stricken Uber Eats driver?

The latch clicks and the door opens. "Kyle." Her eyes brighten.

A better reception than I deserve, especially after how I left her. Hot from a fight with Jack. Still burning when I walked away.

"Come in," she steps back and waves me in.

"Here," I say, handing her the bag. "Figured you might be going through withdrawals by now. Dumplings."

"Oh, hell yes. Thank you." She says, walking towards the kitchen. "Kyle, this is my mom, Anne."

And there she is—wiping down the counter. A snack-size version of Cassie. Same dark hair, same sharp features… just smaller.

"Oh, hi Kyle," she says, voice sweetened with the most adorable Southern drawl. "I've heard so much about you. Can I get you something to drink, honey?"

"I'm fine, thank you."

"Well, you want to see her?" Cassie asks.

"No, I just came to deliver dumplings. I'll be going now." I turn slightly, halfway toward the door.

"Smart ass." She grabs my arm. "Come on. She's sleeping." She waves a hand, "Well, she's always sleeping."

In the bassinet is the most adorable bundle of warm pink cheeks and tiny fists tucked tight against her face. Her little mouth puckers once. Then stills.

"God," I breathe.

Cassie leans over, brushing a hand across the blanket like she can't help but touch her. "Right? It's annoying how cute she is."
~~~

I nod slowly, eyes still on the baby.

"She looks just like you."

"I know," she whispers, then nudges my arm. "Poor Jack. Not a single feature yet."

My jaw tenses at the mention of his name, but I let it go. I'm not here to pick another fight. I'm here because I couldn't *not* be.

Cassie straightens up beside me, her shoulder brushing mine.

"She's named after your mom, isn't she?" I ask softly.

She glances over, surprised. "Yeah… how'd you—?"

I shrug. "Umm… you texted it to me the night she was born."

She slaps a hand to her forehead, groaning. She lifts her brows. "Good drugs."

"Cora Anne," she says quietly. "She's… everything."

I nod, eyes still on the baby. "Yeah. She really is."

"You wanna hold her?" Her eyes look to mine.

"Oh… I… I don't know. I've never…" I stammer.

"You won't break her, Kyle. I promise."

I glance around the room. "Where's Jack?" Wondering if he's about to walk in, ready to throw hands just for touching his kid.

She chuckles. "Work." She narrows her eyes. "Just for a few hours." She shrugs.

I sigh. "Okay."

She lifts Cora, who lets out a soft protest, wiggling against the snug wrap.

"Is this safe? It's giving me claustrophobia looking at her."

"Yes, Uncle Kyle. It's safe. And she loves it. Remember, she was jammed inside me for nine months."

She places her in my arms. A little chrysalis. She squirms once, and I can make out the shape of her tiny legs beneath the blanket.

"Wow."

"See? You're a natural," she says, touching Cora's cheek, settling her down. She knows her mom's touch.

I instinctively start to bounce.

"So, what has it been like?" I ask, not sure whether to look at Cassie or the baby.

She scoffs. "Well, other than being a human dairy farm," she gestures to her comically oversized breasts, which my eyes now absolutely cannot unsee, "and her deciding night is day? It's been amazing."

I laugh, low and from the chest, eyes back on Cora.

"That's a thing?"

"Oh yeah. She thinks three a.m. is jazz hour," Cassie mutters, reaching for her half-drunk coffee, most likely cold by now. "And Jack… well, he sleeps like a man who didn't just help push a watermelon out of a pinhole."

"Charming." I bounce again without thinking. "But damn, she smells good."

"It's that new baby scent. They come out with it, like some factory default setting. Lasts about four weeks, then it's just sour milk and overpriced organic lotion."

I glance over at her, biting back a grin. "You're so romantic."

Cassie shrugs. "Hormones. My days are numbered. When my mom leaves, I won't be showering or peeing alone for the foreseeable future."

"Jesus."

She smiles, softer now. "But I wouldn't trade it. Not for anything."

I nod slowly. My fingers tighten slightly over the baby's blanket. "Yeah," I say. "I can tell."

A silence settles, but it's not uncomfortable. Just something stretching between us. Something that used to buzz with possibility. Now it just hums, soft and steady, like static.

"I mean it when I say this," I add, voice low. "You're doing great. She's lucky to have you. You're going to be an amazing mom, Cass."

Cassie leans back against the arm of the couch and closes her eyes for a second. "You really think so?"

I look down at Cora. Her tiny fingers flex in her sleep like she's trying to hold the world already.

"Yeah. I do."

There's a stretch of silence. Then: "You ever want one?" she asks, cracking one eye open.

My breath catches.

"I think so," I admit. "Someday. When I'm not working 80-hour weeks. When I can trust myself to show up and… be there."

Cassie's expression softens. "You will, Kyle."

I swallow. Hard. And I nod, still bouncing.

Cora lets out a tiny sigh and settles deeper into my arms. And just like that—something quiet and deep rearranges inside me.

Cassie stands, stretches, and disappears down the hall.

I stay where I am, still bouncing, still holding Cora like she's a secret I'm not ready to give back. I glance down at my watch, and realize I need to get back to the restaurant.

When she returns, she's dragging a box behind her.

"What are you doing? What is this?"

"Swag delivery," she says, setting it at my feet. "You're out here in that gross-ass shirt from… what? Opening week?" She sneers. "Like we don't run one of the sexiest kitchens this side of San Francisco."

"It *used* to be sexy—until you pissed all over it." I chuckle softly, careful not to jostle Cora.

She purses her lips. "That's wrong."

I smirk. "This is vintage."

"It's pit-stained and tragic."

She peels back the lid. Inside—Sagi-Shi gear. Hats. Tees. A hoodie I'm already claiming. Then she pulls out something folded with more care. Pressed and crisp.

A new chef coat.

White and clean. Embroidered.

She hands it to me. "This is only for going into the dining room," she says, all mock-authority.

I unfold it.

For one flicker of a second, I expect to see *Executive Chef* stitched under my name. Like maybe this was it. Like maybe she was ready to let go.

But it just says:

Kyle Berkley

Chef de Cuisine – Sagi-Shi

The pang hits fast. And stupid. Because some buried, reckless part of me thought this might be it. That she was ready to step back. Choose a different chapter.

But she's still Exec. Still hers.

She watches me like she felt that flicker pass through me.

Then she says, softly, "You deserve a pristine one."

I nod, eyes still on the embroidery. "Thanks. It's beautiful."

"You're beautiful," she says, grinning.

"I meant the coat."

"I'm practicing my motherly compliments for when she yells, 'I'm so ugly' when she's twelve. Just go with it."

She smiles, but something in the room shifts again. Like we both know it was never just about a title.

Chapter 25

INK & IMPULSE

The buzz of the tattoo machine is something I instantly loved. Like therapy. Not the same therapy as Mira therapy, but the permanent kind. You could call it an addiction, like a drug. After that first rush, your first tattoo, you're already thinking about the next one.

I'm in Elijah's chair for what has to be the thirtieth time. Elijah, also on the growing list of unofficial neighborhood therapists, is the coolest dude I know. Wild travel stories. Shoots old-school 35mm. Loves his momma. And has the best damn hair I've ever seen on a man. Long, dark, and curly. I'm jealous.

"So," he says, eyes still on his iPad, Elvis shades on indoors, because of course they are. "Who is she? I didn't even know you were seeing anyone."

I let out a short laugh. "She's four."

Now he looks up. Slowly.

"Brah… did you—"

"No," I cut in, shaking my head. "It's Cassie's kid." I shrug.

He tilts his head, suspicion sharp. "You're getting your boss's kid's name tattooed on you, and you're sure she's not yours?"

"Yes, I'm sure. She's just a special kid."

He looks back down at his iPad, then up at me again, brow lifting.

"I swear," I laugh. "Come on. How long does it take to write *Cora*, dude?"

"Here. This script cool? You want it above your watch line, right?"

"Perfect."

The buzz. The ink. The finality of it.

I love this fucking tattoo. Maybe more than my flaming Nashville hot chicken drumstick that Ritchie and I share.

~~~

The wheels hum under me. My foot kicks, smooth and steady. Rocco's leash loops around my wrist, the dog pacing me like a pro—ears flopping, tongue out, *alive.*

It's been months since I carved pavement like this. Wind biting my cheeks. Sun coating my shoulders in gold. Since my body moved because it wanted to.

A small crowd watches from the pier railing. I pretend not to notice, but I'm hitting every old trick in the book—board flip, deep carve, a lazy nose manual just because.

This old dude still has it.

Rocco barks once from the grass, like he's cheering me on. I laugh, breathless, and drag my toe to brake.

I prop up my phone, hit record, and skate past—trucker hat backward, grinning like I'm nineteen again.

Rocco blurs through the shot in a flash.

"Get it, boy," I laugh.

We collapse in the grass. I pull the clip into a reel, something I haven't done in a long time. Text overlay: *Earning back my edge.*

I scroll for music. Blink-182, "What's My Age Again?"

Perfect. I hit post.

~~~

I'm cracking a beer and pulling my preserved tomato sauce from the pantry when *knock, knock, knock,* Collin walks in, dramatic as always.

"Hey, you decent?" he calls.

Rocco loses his damn mind. His whole body wags like it's glitching in five directions at once, nails skittering across the floor.

"Hello, friend," Collin grins, bending to scratch behind Rocco's ears.

Rocco launches at him like he's about to knock him flat.

"Okay, okay. Calm your tits, dude."

I laugh, lifting my beer. "That's what you get for skipping Sunday visits, asshole."

He manages to make it fully into the kitchen. "Sorry. It's what happens when you have a girlfriend like mine. She's slightly… tick-like. Cuddly. With the soul of a bounty hunter."

"Seriously?"

He shrugs. "Told her I was going to the store. Saw your car and ta-da. Here I am, bitch."

"And she believed you were going to the store in that?"

He looks down at himself, dead serious. "What? This is a normal store-run outfit."

He tugs at the lemon-yellow sweater vest, koi fish and all. Japan? eBay? A haunted estate sale? Who freaking knows.

"If you say so," I mutter, still stunned that he has a girlfriend.

The high-waisted mint-green cords are the cherry on top. I try very hard not to notice the moose-knuckle.

He raids my fridge without asking, cracks a beer, clinks it to mine.

And then he sees it.

"Bro."

"What?"

He points. "What the hell is that?"

I follow his gaze to my wrist. *Cora* in delicate script. Fresh black ink. Still shiny.

I shrug. "Oh. Yeah." I open the jar and pour it into the pot, waiting for my ration of shit.

"Oh my god. You are in it. Like, deep end. Does she know you inked her kid on you? Please fucking tell me she does." He takes a long pull of his beer.

"No." I pull a wooden spoon from the drawer. "Why would she need to know?"

He sighs. "Oh, Jesus Christ. You are either going to be uncle of the year or one creepy move closer to being on *Dateline*."

I stir the sauce and drop the pasta into a pot of salted boiling water.

"How is this creepy?" I lift my wrist.

His jaw drops.

"Jack's kid, Kyle. You tattooed Jack's kid's name on your body. I guarantee some serial killer out there has this exact vibe."

I stir the sauce, ignoring the way he's still staring at my wrist like it's a crime scene.

"You're insane," Collin finally says. "But, like, in a weirdly sweet, Hallmark-but-make-it-tattooed kind of way."

I snort. "Thanks, I guess."

He shrugs and takes another sip. "You know she's probably going to cry when she sees it."

I don't answer. At this point, I did it for me. I ink things that are important. Memories I never want to forget. Things that changed me. Dates. Places. Names.

He flops onto the barstool like he's planning to stay for dinner. "Also, I see you posted. Finally. It's been a hot minute since Chef Thirst Trap made an appearance."

I grin. "Seriously? Did you just come to bust my balls tonight?" I laugh, stirring, tasting, adjusting.

He holds up his phone like a trophy. "Oh, who's this hottie? Hello, *Mira*. She gave you three flames, Top Chef."

My breath stalls. It's my little secret. The one I've kept for years, even from my closest friends. I spilled it once on a drunken night with Ritchie, but he was too hammered to remember. Thankfully.

I don't know why we've kept each other quiet. I'm not ashamed of her. She's smart, successful, hot as hell. But people would judge. They'd want more for me. A relationship. A box to check. Something we never promised each other.

"This one's a smoke show," Collin says, scrolling. "Do you ever actually talk to any of these girls?"

I shrug. "Sometimes I answer their DMs."

"Huh." He side-eyes me. "You should reach out to this one. She's cute."

"Whatever," I mutter, nodding toward the stove as I strain the pasta. "You staying?"

"Nah. She'll smell your sauce on my breath and know I lied. Damn, my plan sucked."

The door slams behind him, and I sit at the counter, bowl in front of me, pasta soaked in sauce, phone in hand.

I scroll to her contact.

Kyle: Where are you?

Ping. Almost instant.

Mira: Dancing. Come meet us.

Us.

~~~

I'm back in the same dark club where I first laid eyes on her. The anticipation makes it feel dangerous. Electric.

The bass rolls through me before I even reach the bar. Dark corners. Red, swirling light. Sweat-slick rhythm in the air. Same place. Same buzz. Same woman.

I spot her the second I walk in. Center of the floor, like she's on the payroll. Tight leather pants. Black tank doing exactly what it was meant to do. Hair wild. Eyes closed. Moving slow, like the beat is wired straight into her bloodstream.

She hasn't seen me yet.

I slide onto a barstool in the shadows, hold two fingers up to the bartender. "Bourbon on the rocks, please."

I don't take my eyes off her.

She spins, dizzy and laughing. Her body coils into the next drop like she's riding a wave. She dances like someone who doesn't need an audience, and somehow it makes it worse that I am one.

Her eyes flick up and find me, and everything changes. The dance slows. Her hips keep the rhythm, but now it's deliberate. Now it's for me. A strip tease without the stripping. Seduction wrapped in confidence.

She trails a hand up her side, fingers skimming the hem of her shirt before pushing her hair back. Her smile is wicked. Knowing.

I sip my bourbon in my front-row seat. I have no idea how I'm supposed to keep it together.
~~~

Mira turns her back, rolls her hips once, twice, then throws a look over her shoulder that knocks the wind out of my lungs. She's showing me exactly what I remember. And exactly what I need to forget.

Am I doing it again? Turning comfort into a crutch. Turning a secret into a shield.

Did I just swap one woman for another because I'm still that scared little boy who doesn't know how to stay?

I drag a hand down my face and throw back the bourbon, hoping the burn will shut me up.

"Another," I tell the bartender.

When I look back, she's gone. She disappears into the crowd, and then I see her again.

But this time, she's not alone. A brunette presses in behind her. Hands low. Skimming hips. Palms flattening against Mira's stomach. Mira lets her. Leans back into it like it's easy.

Her eyes flick to me again. Still locked on mine.

The music swells. Mira reaches back, fingers slipping into the girl's hair, twisting gently to bare her neck. She turns, lips ghosting over skin. Soft. Slow. Deliberate.

My grip tightens around the glass. My zipper is not equipped for this kind of pressure.

Mira kisses her. Not a peck. Not a performance. A kiss with weight. With history. With heat.

And even as the girl turns fully toward her, hands roaming, Mira's eyes cut back to me. Watching me watch them. It's not a show. It's a test. And I'm failing. Badly.

The bourbon burns. My jaw ticks. My blood is lava.

She kisses her again, harder this time. A warning. A memory. A dare. This is who she is. This is who we were. We never played by the rules.

The crowd shifts. Mira whispers something in the brunette's ear, then turns and walks toward me. Every step is slow and measured, like she's savoring my reaction. Like she knows she's already wrecked me.

I'm her wounded prey, bleeding out on the sidelines, and she's here to finish it.

The girl follows one step behind, her gaze sliding to me like she's curious what makes me so special.

Mira stops in front of me. Close enough to smell the sweat and her perfume. Close enough to taste the danger.

"Hi, Kyle," she says. Low. Sweet. Laced with sin.

I clear my throat. "Mira."

She takes the empty glass from my hand and sets it on the bar without looking.

"This is Sloan," she says, turning just slightly. "She's a friend."

Sloan smiles with full lips and wide eyes. Confidence that reads fluent in chaos.

"Hi, Kyle," she purrs. "You're the reason for this girl's smile, I hear." She drags a finger slowly across Mira's bottom lip. Their mouths hover dangerously close.

Mira smirks. "He's the reason for a lot of things."

They're both watching me now. Like a decision's already been made.

I lean back on the stool, palms braced on my thighs, pulse thudding in my ears.

Mira leans in, hair brushing my cheek. "We're going to my place. You're coming with us."

Not a question. A command.

Sloan steps between my legs. Close. Too close. "Unless that's not something you're into… *Us.*"

I laugh. It comes out rough. "Oh, I'm into that."

And yet, internally, I'm on fire. From the outside, I probably look like a tattooed menace. The kind of guy who rides motorcycles and collects women like souvenirs. The truth is less impressive. The tattoos are just art. I've never driven a motorcycle in my life. And monogamy is very much my game.

I have a hard enough time keeping one woman happy with two hands and a mouth.

What the hell am I agreeing to?

Mira leans in again, eyes dark, voice brushing my ear. "Good." She grins. "You're not going to forget this."

~~~

The second the door shuts behind us, I'm on her.

Mira tastes like gin and power. She pushes back just as hungry, pinning me to the door with a smirk that says, *You thought you could handle this.*

Sloan slips past us like smoke, shedding her jacket, glancing over her shoulder once before disappearing down the hall.

"You sure?" Mira asks, breath hot against my jaw.

"No." I grip her hips. "But I don't give a damn."

She grins and pulls me back in. Tongue. Teeth. Hands. God, her hands. Every part of her moves like she knows exactly how to undo me, because she does. Five years of this secret dance. Now we're adding another step to it.

Her fingers slide under the hem of my shirt, nails grazing skin I'm not even pretending to flex. She yanks it up and over my head, tosses it somewhere I'll never find.

I walk her backward toward the bedroom, kissing her like I need to mark the moment. Like I need her to know this isn't some hazy, club-fueled mistake.

This is us.

Sloan's waiting. Leaning against the wall. Her gaze slides over me slowly, like she's reading instructions, and I'm the manual.

She moves to Mira first. Kisses her like she owns her. It's possessive. Hot. And I'm not gonna lie—I'm wrecked watching it mere inches from their lips.

But when Mira pulls back and turns those dark eyes on me, everything else fades.

"Come here, baby," she says.

I move like I'm tethered to her voice. Like my body doesn't recognize another command.

Sloan's hands slide to my chest, pushing me to the edge of the bed. Her lips trace my collarbone. Mira peels away what's left of me—my belt, my jeans, stripping me like she's unwrapping a secret. Then she presses me down.

They stand before me and undress each other. It's seductive and mesmerizing. All silent in their movement, laced with lips and heat.
~~~

Then, they are on me, moving in sync, like this isn't new. Like they've done this before. Together. With others. Maybe just with each other. I don't know. I don't ask.

Because right now, I am *not* thinking. I'm *feeling*. Every breath. Every drag of skin on skin. Every scrape of teeth, every shift of weight on the bed, every wicked sound Mira makes when I slide my hands over her hips and pull her down onto me.

She's not delicate. She rides me like she remembers everything—every night we stole, every touch that we never got to finish. Sloan's behind her, fingers tracing down Mira's spine, lips brushing her shoulder. She whispers something, and Mira lets out a low moan that makes me twitch inside her.

"Fuck," I breathe, biting my bottom lip. "You two are gonna kill me."

Mira grinds harder, leaning in close. "You die, I'll revive you. Then I'll ride you again."

My grip tightens. My thighs burn. She rolls her hips in these slow, devastating circles that make it impossible to hold on.

Sloan leans in and kisses me. It's brief and unexpected. A flicker of heat and curiosity. But all I see is Mira—head thrown back, nails digging in my shoulders, sweat glistening at the base of her throat.

This is chaos. Hunger. Everything I've tried to outrun. And I don't want to run anymore.

Sloan climbs onto the bed, one long leg extending as her arms slide around my neck.

"Touch me, Kyle. Touch me while you fuck her." She begs, kissing me deep.

My hand finds her. Heat. Need.

"Yes, just like that." She moans. Her forehead resting against mine.

Mira's body grinds against me, heat and motion overwhelming. I'm buried deep inside her, and my mind can't keep up.

I slide my fingers slowly into Sloan, my thumb tracing torturous circles over her clit. She gasps.

Mira reaches over and pulls Sloan's face toward her.

"God, he feels so good." She lifts herself, moving with purpose now, setting the pace.

"Yes. Fuck yes." Sloan whimpers into Mira's mouth as my fingers work her harder, deeper. She pulses against me, slick and shaking, close to unraveling.

Mira's rhythm quickens. Hips snapping now, riding the edge like she was built for it. One hand braces on my chest. The other reaches back, gripping Sloan's thigh, holding her between us.

"Don't stop," Sloan gasps, breath hitching. Her body's trembling. "Fuck, Kyle—don't you dare stop."

I don't. I couldn't if I tried. My fingers are soaked and cramping. My thighs burn. Mira's heat drags me under with every movement, every filthy word, every moan she lets slip past those parted lips.

"Look at you," Mira breathes, eyes locked to mine as she drives harder, chasing it. "Completely wrecked. You love this, don't you?"

I can't answer. My jaw's locked. My world narrows to her rhythm, and Sloan's fingers tangled my hair like she'll come apart if she doesn't let go.

Mira leans in, lips brushing mine. "You gonna come for me, baby?"

"Jesus," I choke, my body humming. "Mira—"

She reaches between us, slick fingers sliding down to rub where I disappear inside her. One touch. That's all it takes.

Everything snaps.

My orgasm slams through me like a freight train—hips jerking, hands seizing, breath torn from my chest. I spill into her, gutted, gone, barely conscious of the guttural sound I make as I come so hard I see fucking stars.

Mira's not far behind.

She cries out, nails raking down my chest as her body locks, shudders, then collapses forward onto me, sweat, heat, and skin.

Sloan's still grinding on my fingers, her head tipped back, riding the edge—until she goes rigid, mouth falling open on a silent scream as she shatters against my hand.

And then there's just the sound of breathing. The three of us undone. Tangled. Splayed across a bed that smells like sex and sin and something dangerously close to salvation.

My muscles ache in places I forgot existed. Mira's breath fans warm across my neck. She drapes her thigh over mine, claiming space. Sloan shifts, fingers grazing my stomach like she's checking if I'm still alive.

My heart's still pounding when Mira kisses my jaw. I kiss Sloan's temple. Then we just… breathe.

No one speaks. There's nothing to say.

Mira's hand finds mine next to my sweat-slicked thigh, fingers lacing tight. She knows. She knows this wasn't just sex.

I squeeze her hand. She doesn't look at me. She doesn't have to. She already knows.

My mind starts to catch up. Starts asking questions. *What the fuck just happened?* And… *Why do I already want it again?*

Chapter 26

THE RECKONING

I've stared at the produce spreadsheet for ten minutes and entered exactly two things: shishito peppers and shame.

Visions from last night won't stop creeping in. Mira's breath on my throat. Sloan's mouth on my collarbone. Mira's voice, whispering, *You're not going to forget this.* I didn't. I can't.

I type *shiso* into the order form and immediately delete it. We don't need it. I'm just blindly ordering shit.

A light tap on the door frame pulls me out of the spiral.

Darius leans in, tablet in hand. "If you're placing orders, we need leeks, Thai basil, and lotus root. Oh, and those baby daikon things you like to roast."

I nod, scribbling on the pad beside my keyboard. "Got it."

He lingers a beat. "Everything alright?"

"Yep. All good, Darius."

He doesn't believe me. He shouldn't.

By the time I make it out to the dining room, Nate is mid-conversation with my bartender, Daniel, at the bar. I don't hear a word they're saying, because that's when I feel it. A tug on my chef coat. Soft. Insistent. Familiar.

I turn.

There she is. Big dark eyes. Long brown hair. A grin that could power a small city.

"Uncle Kyle!" she squeals.

Before I can react, I'm lifting her. She wraps her arms around my neck like it's the most natural thing in the world, and just like that, my heart turns into a goddamn balloon animal.

Cassie's right behind her. "Cora, baby, don't interrupt when someone's in a conversation."

"He was…" Cora gets distracted by my neck tickles and giggles. "He's just talking to Daniel."

I nuzzle into her neck crease, making her screech.

"Stop, Uncle Kyle!"

Daniel chuckles and boops her nose. "Uncle Kyle and I were done anyway. He's all yours, kiddo."

He nods at me. "Did you need me?"

I shift Cora to my other hip. "Yeah. Can you have that bar order ready by end of day?"

"You got it," he says, heading off.

Cassie shoots me a look like I'm the problem. "You spoil her."

I shrug. "And?"

We walk through the dining room, Cassie talking menu notes and weekend ideas. I'm half listening, half holding Cora like she's a toddler instead of a gangly four-year-old with opinions and sticky jelly fingers.

"Kyle," Cassie says, pouring herself a coffee, nodding toward the floor, "you can put her down. She's not a baby."

"Nope." I grin, tightening my hold. "Never putting my princess down."

Cassie turns, mug in hand.

And that's when it happens. Her gaze drops to my wrist. She freezes.

Her voice goes flat. "What is that?"

I blink, confused, until she steps closer. Her fingers brush my wrist, tracing the fresh script, still shiny from healing.

Her voice drops. "Kyle… Jesus. That's real."

"Yeah," I say quietly. "It's real."

Cora wiggles in my arms, craning her neck. "What is it?" she asks.

My heart stops.

I don't know if this is the moment Cassie cries or rips her daughter from my arms and calls the cops.

"Your Uncle Kyle is very silly, Cora," Cassie says, unreadable over the rim of her coffee.

I have no idea how to take that. Sweet silly? Psychotic silly?

Cora, meanwhile, is still investigating. She cups my face in her sticky hands, smooshes my cheeks together, and stares at me.

"What is it?" she demands, dead serious.

I flick my eyes toward Cassie, heart hammering.

Did I fuck up?

She shrugs, raises her brows, and rolls her eyes. "Go ahead, you maniac."

I adjust my grip and lift my forearm in front of Cora.

"I got a new tattoo yesterday."

She studies my arm like it's a puzzle, eyes bouncing from ink to ink until she finds it. She squints, pressing her finger to each letter.

"C-O…" she mumbles, scrunching up her nose. "I don't know."

I smile. "Yeah, it's cursive. R-A. Cora."

Her eyes snap up to mine. A pause. Then she beams.

"Uncle Kyle, you got a Cora tattoo on your body?" she giggles.

"I did."

"Why?"

"Because I get tattoos about special things." I kiss her temple. "And you, Cora, you're special to me."

She traces the black script again. "Did it hurt?" she asks, suddenly quiet.

"Nope. Didn't hurt."

She wrinkles her nose, then giggles. "You're weird."

And that's that. In the mind of a four-year-old, my entire personality is summed up in two words.

"Do you have that list for the Asian market?" Cassie asks, casually sidestepping the fact that I permanently etched her kid's name onto my body.

"Yeah. It's in the office. You going now?"

She nods. "Yeah. While she's at dance."

I don't know how she does it. Juggling Cora, Jack, and this place like it's nothing. I can barely manage a job and a dog who naps for a living. I'm over here emotionally waterboarding myself after one night with two women, and she's out here in survival mode without complaint.

"I can send one of the guys, you know." I gesture toward the kitchen.

"It's fine. I don't like staying at the studio. The moms who do are annoying as hell." She lowers her voice. "Talking about what private school they've got little Sally on the waitlist for and where they're vacationing next."

She tucks a stray hair behind her ear and sighs. "I don't even know when I'm seeing Jack again. Or when I'm getting my next shower. If you saw how long my leg hair is right now, you'd gag."

"Hot," I deadpan, wincing.

"Seriously, put her down, Kyle. She's going to start expecting me to carry her around like a Cabbage Patch Kid."

I kiss the crown of Cora's head and lower her to the floor. She plops down immediately, fishing a Barbie out of her mom's bag and launching straight into her own little fantasy world.

"Actually, maybe you should take a vacation," I say. "Charleston. Visit your parents. Let someone else handle shit for once."

"Fat chance," she says flatly. "Let's go get that list. I don't have all day."

Cassie walks beside me, and I catch her glance drop to my wrist, right above where my fingers are laced with her daughter's.

"That is really freaking sweet, Kyle." Her eyes lift to mine, glassy.

"You think that's sweet?" I murmur. "Your name is on my—" I mouth *ass* and get exactly what I deserve: a punch to the arm.

"Of course you had to ruin a sweet moment," she says, shaking her head. Then she points at me. "Whatever you do, don't let Jack see that. Ninety degrees? Long sleeves. Get cozy with thick leather bands. I don't want to hear about it."

We reach the office. I step inside, snag the list off the desk, and hand it to her.

"Got it." I grin. "I won't make Jack mad. We're on such a good streak these days."

There's a moment of silence. Then we both laugh.

I don't think I've seen Jack in over a year. He barely sets foot in this place anymore. It's like they live separate lives.

~~~

Finally, a day off that isn't a Sunday, and I'm standing in line waiting for coffee.

I glance back through the front window to check on Rocco, loosely tethered to a bench outside. He's sprawled in the sun, panting, watching people pass like it's his job. Being a massive bulldog mix, no one's quite sure if he's sweet or a threat. His tail says yes. His big, grumpy face says, I could eat your arm off.

Little do they know, he's a gooey marshmallow.

I order an iced coffee. Black. No nonsense. The sweet barista has it ready in about four seconds, bypassing the eight middle-schoolers ahead of me waiting on their twelve-dollar, rainbow-dusted frappuccinos made with organic, grass-fed, noncommittal milk and three shots of artificial flavored bullshit.

I shake my head as I pop the straw through the lid.

I don't think I even knew what coffee tasted like until I was twenty. These kids are eleven, and they're juiced on caffeine like tiny investment bankers.

And that's when it hits me. I'm sounding like a grandpa in my own damn head.

As I'm untying Rocco, my phone buzzes in my back pocket. I pull it out, expecting… I don't know. A work text. A flirty Mira emoji. One of Collin's cursed memes.

What I don't expect is the name on the screen.

I stand there, staring at it longer than I should.

Whit. Not Dad. Not Father. Just… *Whit.*

It's been four years. After our last disaster of a dinner, he tried to reach out a couple of times. Short, one-sentence texts. Nothing else. I never responded. Never pushed. I remembered what Wally said.
~~~

I know I'm playing chicken with forgiveness. I know he's getting older. I know anything could happen.

Sometimes I think maybe that's how it should be. Just go. I don't need forgiveness to feel whole.

But here I am. Staring at his goddamn name like it might catch my phone on fire. My heart pounds against my ribs, like it's trying to claw its way out.

I sit on the bench. Rocco drops beside me, staring like I'm the biggest tease in the universe.

I rest my elbows on my knees and swipe the message open.

Whit: I hope you are well. I'm coming into town. I would like to see you, son.

Son.

Still burns. Even now. A word he never earned. Just like *Dad*.

My chest tightens. I need moral support. A lifeline. Wally. Ritchie. Or maybe I dive face-first into Mira and pretend none of this is happening.

Panic bubbles up, fast and messy.

I drain half my coffee before I realize I'm doing it. Still staring at the message. Still spiraling. Still not ready.

Finally, I peel my eyes off the screen and look across the street. The park is alive. A girl on rollerblades wipes out. Her friend nearly collapses laughing in the bushes. They both look high as hell. I smile despite myself.

People pass on bikes. A couple reads on a blanket beneath a tree. And then I see a dad and his kid, tossing a baseball. The kid's maybe five or six. Just learning. His throws are awkward. Wild. But the dad looks patient and kind. Like he gives a shit.

I glance down at my phone. Then at my wrist.

Cora.

Her name flashes back at me. Bright, permanent, and loud.

I want to give a shit. I *do* give a shit. I want a kid someday. A family. Something real. And if forgiveness is the gate, I don't want to be kept standing outside forever.

My fingers start moving before my brain can stop them.

Kyle: When?

Send.

When my phone pings, my heart nearly stops.

Whit: Next weekend. Friday through Monday. Hopefully you have some time for your Dad.

Dad.

Rage sparks before I finish reading. My fingers slam the screen, every word sharp with intention.

Kyle: I'm off Sunday. See you then… Dad.

Send.

Jesus Christ.

He won't hear the sarcasm screaming through that text.

But I meant it.

And I didn't.

And that's the fucking problem.

~~~

Rocco trots beside me like he knows I'm about to lose it, and he's activated full emotional support animal mode. I show up at Ritchie's without warning, not that I need to. He's the only person I know who's ever texted: *Fridge stocked. Feelings optional.*

He opens the door in a stained tank top, a spoon in one hand and a pint of something high-dollar and unapologetically fattening in the other. Rocco barrels inside like it's his second home, making a beeline for the water bowl without asking permission.

"You look like someone just told you oat milk has dairy," he says.

"I need a beer," I mutter, pushing past him.

"You need therapy, dude. We've gone over this like… ten times. But sure." He follows me toward the kitchen, digging into the container, shuffling along in his ridiculous Christmas slippers. "Beer's in the fridge, my emotionally repressed man-child."

I grab a bottle and twist the cap off hard. It clatters past the trash, and I collapse onto his couch.
~~~

He watches me like I'm about to blow and he's not sure whether to hug me or call Collin for backup.

"Okay. Who pissed in your espresso?"

I take a long pull before answering. "Whit texted me."

Ritchie freezes mid-spoonful. "Plastic Pop?"

"Yep."

"Did he offer you a hug or a horse-drawn carriage ride straight into generational trauma?"

I scoff. "He's coming to town. Wants to meet next weekend." I sit forward, the beer dangling between my knees, peeling the label from the bottle.

Ritchie twirls his spoon, mouth full. "Ah. That explains the storm-cloud energy and the 'I definitely just sent a text I'll regret' face."

He goes back to digging for more Phish Food.

I tilt my head. "How do you always know?"

"Because you're predictable. Like Nashville hot chicken, baby. Always promising chaos."

I look at him, deadpan. "He called himself Dad."

"Oooh shit. Whit, Whit, Whit." He shakes his head, "Coming in hot with the dirty right hook."

I grunt. "Pretty much."

Ritchie drops onto the couch beside me and offers the pint. "You want fudge fish or comfort? Because I've got both."

I glance at the melted mess and actually consider it. "Nah. Comfort for three hundred, please."

He leans back, staring at the ceiling. "You gonna go through with it?"

I shrug. "I said I would."

"Then go. See him. But don't do it for him." He points the spoon at me. "Do it for the kid version of you who deserved better."

I side-eye him. "Who the fuck are you?"

He shrugs. "Too many Instagram quotes. Maybe a self-help book."

I hate when he's right.

"You know," he adds, "I'm proud of you."

I glance over. "For what?"

"For not burying this in bourbon or boobs."

"Yet," I say, lifting my bottle. "This is my first trauma beer."

He grins. "Progress, not perfection, Kyle."

Then he checks his watch. "It is kind of pitiful, though. You're drinking at nine forty-five."

I scoff. "Oh shit." I point my beer at his pint. "Breakfast?"

He nods without shame. "Judgment-free zone. Drink up, Chucko."

He clinks his spoon against my bottle with a wink.

~~~

It's Sunday. 4:52 p.m. I check my watch. Scuffed leather band. Cheap face, but still ticking.

We agreed to five. Because if this goes badly, I want some day left to recover. To make it better.

Of course he picks a place in Jackson Square. Because nothing says father-son healing like a twenty-eight-dollar cocktail in a room full of men who think therapy is weak and tailored suits are armor.

I'm still in the car. It took me twenty minutes just to decide what shirt to wear.

Long sleeves hide the ink. It looks the part. It lets me be the son he imagines when he talks about me, if he talks about me at all. I'm probably nonexistent.

Short sleeves is being myself. It's honest. Lets him see exactly what he never tried to understand.

I pulled the long sleeve on. Took it off. Put it back on. Off again. Stared at myself like a damn teenager.

Finally, I said it out loud. "Fuck it."

Short sleeves.

Now I'm sitting at the bar, shoulders tight, forearms exposed. A roadmap of memory and meaning on display, wishing I had a long-sleeved shirt on.

Whit walks in like the room was built to hold his name. Charcoal blazer. Pressed shirt. No one would guess he's here to reconnect with the son he emotionally benched more than two decades ago.
~~~

He sees me and I stand.

His gaze sweeps the room, lands on me, and goes straight to the ink.

Of course it does.

No hug. No handshake. Just a slight tilt of his head.

"That's new," he says, eyes tracking my arms.

"Yeah," I reply. "A lot of things are."

He gestures toward the bar. "You said just a drink. Is this okay? Or would you prefer a table?"

I shake my head. "This is fine."

I'd rather not face him directly. Also, it's easier to stab someone under the bar if necessary. If I follow through this time.

The bartender steps in, setting napkins on the rich mahogany. "What can I get you, gentlemen?"

"A scotch. Neat." Whit commands without looking at the menu.

"I'll have a glass of Cabernet, please," I say, forcing a smile.

"You got it."

Whit sits, hands steepled, calm. Like this is a business meeting. His watch is pristine. No scratches. No stories.

Meanwhile, I'm vibrating. Nerves sparking. One wrong word and I might snap. He looks settled. I feel braced for impact.

The silence stretches until the bartender returns.

"Here you go." He sets the drinks down gently. "Would you like food menus tonight?"

Whit glances at me, hand opening slightly.

"I'm fine. Thanks," I say. I didn't come for a meal. I came for answers. Maybe peace. Who the fuck knows?

"No, thank you," Whit adds with a nod.

I take a sip. Try to breathe through it.

"Where's Caroline?" I ask, purely out of social obligation. I don't care. I'm grateful she's not here.

He takes a sip of his scotch and sucks his teeth. "She's on a girls' trip. In Italy."

I drag my wine glass by the stem, watching the burgundy swirl. It's the only thing in this room I trust.

"Kyle."

I don't look at him. Keep my eyes on the wine.

"Yes."

"I talked to Wally."

My chest tightens. I flick my eyes sideways. "Is something wrong with Wally?"

Because if Wally told him what I think he did, about that conversation, about the things I said out loud for the first time, there *will* be something wrong with him.

Whit raises a hand. "No. No. He's fine." He exhales, twisting his glass like it might offer guidance.

"He told me I needed to bury the hatchet with you. About some things."

"What exactly did he tell you?" I cut in.

"Ah… well…" He hesitates. "He didn't tell me anything. Exactly." He stammers.

My father doesn't stammer.

"He just said you'd called. That you sounded upset. That you were having a hard time."

I scoff. "A hard time?"

"Son," he says quietly. "Keep it down."

And just like that, my blood starts to boil. That word in his mouth feels stolen.

I grit my teeth. "I'm not having a hard time, Whit."

I set my glass down. Hard.

"I'm fucked up." I lean in, finger stopping inches from his chest, eyes locked. "*You* fucked me up."

His brows knit together. Confusion flickers across his face. He shrugs.

"I'm confused," he says, lowering his voice. Calm. Rehearsed. "How exactly did I do that, Kyle?"

He wants quiet. He wants control.

I face forward and take a long pull of my wine. When I set the glass down, I see her name. Black and permanent. Etched into my skin like a truth I can't outrun.

I breathe. Slow. Steady.

And then I hear Ritchie in my head. That ridiculous voice. That one perfect line.

Do it for the kid version of you that deserved better.

The words come quietly. Not furious. Just honest.

My eyes stay on the tattoo.

"I want to get married someday. Have a family." My voice barely holds. "And I'm fucking terrified I'll be like you."

I finish the wine. Push the glass away. Then I turn and really look at him.

He's staring at his half-finished scotch like it might speak for him. Speechless.

This moment used to haunt me. Confronting the demon. The springform pan. The blood on my hands. My entire world ending with the image of her taillights disappearing down the driveway, red fading to nothing.

He screamed it at me my whole childhood. Spit it like venom.

Now I get to say it back. Calm. Measured. A reckoning.

"Now," I say quietly, "look what you did."

I stand, shoulders squared, and walk out.

Chapter 27

A DOG & THE DREAM

I lace my sneakers slowly. Quietly. Rocco doesn't even lift his head from the oversized orthopedic bed in the corner.

"Wendy'll be here in a couple hours to take you out, my man," I say softly, brushing a hand over his back. "Here, buddy. Mr. Pickles will keep you company while I'm gone." I tuck the ragged toy under his paw.

Rocco shifts, exhales, but doesn't move otherwise.

His hips are shot. His bladder's unreliable. His naps are longer than my shifts used to be.

But he's still here. Still… mine.

I stand at the door. Keys in hand. I glance back.

I know it's coming. I just refuse to believe it.

I swallow hard, and a tear slips free, uninvited. I wipe at it, pressing my thumb into my cheek like I can erase it.

"I guess my dream of feeding my wife mushroom risotto barefoot," I whisper, "with a fat Rocco snoozing next to the stove, isn't going to happen." A beat. "Fuck."

The door clicks shut behind me. Soft and final.

~~~

The restaurant is alive. Moving. Demanding.

I step into it on muscle memory.

I slap the new prep list onto the clipboard, hands moving fast. Fast enough to outrun the image of Rocco's cloudy eyes. Fast enough to outrun the lump in my throat.
~~~

The new curry pork bao buns are flying out of the pass. Darius is in the weeds but still wearing that relentless optimism of his. The line needs another cook, and nobody in this damn town wants to work.

I thrive in the chaos now. It asks nothing of me emotionally. Except… Cassie isn't here. And that's new.

~~~

Time moves on. Another morning, another day of this place sucking time from me like a sponge.

My phone buzzes on the desk.

Cassie: Hey, I'm running fifteen minutes late. Sorry.

I almost chuckle. She's a tiny tornado. Breezing in and out, leaving messes she thinks are helpful, and letting me clean up the wreckage. But I'll play her game.

Kyle: No problem, Chef. Delivery truck is late as well.

I've got Darius and my new guy, Reggie. The place runs fine, but I keep her looped in. Make her feel like she still has a stake in this dream we built, even if her heart's somewhere else now.

The menu, the voice, the energy. It all pulses with my rhythm. Sagi-Shi has evolved, and people have noticed. The new Thai-inspired weekend tasting menu is fire. Literally. We had to replace the wall sconce by the grill after someone flambéed duck fat too close to the bamboo.

Knife's Edge Quarterly called me "a rogue talent with the soul of a monk and the hands of a sinner."

Mira texted to laugh at that one. I never responded. It's been over for more than a year.

Even Whit sent a short text. No subject line. Just: *Well done. – Dad.*

I actually replied with, *Thanks.*

Growth.

Cassie made me Executive Chef six months ago. Said it was to give her more time. To be present. Be a mom. Be a wife.
~~~

I took the reins, but she keeps showing up anyway. Lately, though, she's been different.

The back door slams, and she barrels into the office like a bat out of hell.

"Good morning. Sorry I'm late," she says, dumping her giant leather tote onto the chair in the corner.

This office is a disaster. Less workspace, more dumping ground. A glorified janitor's closet with mop heads and a lost-and-found box full of junk we're too nice to throw away.

"Want to go over this weekend's specials while we wait on the trucks?"

She glances at me, oversized sunglasses still on like she's playing Jackie O. "I need more coffee while we do this, but yes. Walk with me?"

We move through the quiet, dim dining room, pulling chairs down, prepping for the day. My mind buzzes with excitement over the new menu. Thai street food. Bold, loud, and unapologetic. And I'm doing it without her this weekend.

Cassie's quiet. Listening. Tweaking things here and there. Focused… but not fully present.

Then I see her eyes. Swollen. Red-rimmed. Shiny like glass.

She's been crying. Hard.

This isn't stress crying. This is something's-broken crying.

I try to play it off. Deflect. It's safer.

"Jesus, Cass. What happened to your face?" I say. "You look like you're having an allergy attack or something."

She waves it off. "Yeah, I don't feel great. After we're done, I might head out, if that's okay?"

We both know it's bullshit.

Nineteen years in, and we're still doing this dance.

I can hear Jack's voice in my head. Two nights ago, he was shouting outside the office about how her career hijacked their marriage. Like she didn't build this. Like she hadn't held this restaurant, their kid, and Jack's ego together with duct tape and overtime.

I can't say what I want to. I still can't make promises. Even Mira gave up trying. They all do.

But I *can* do something.

We head back to the office. She's staring blankly at the computer, phone in hand like she's waiting for someone to call and save her.

"Hey," I say. "You know you can take time off, right? You pay me the big bucks and gave me the Exec title to handle things six months ago."

She shrugs, the fight draining out of her. "Yeah. Where would I even go, Kyle? All my friends are here." She looks up and smiles, but it doesn't reach her eyes.

"Maybe somewhere with Jack and Cora?" I offer gently. "Just… know I've got your back here. Okay?"

The second I say Jack's name, she flinches.

My jaw tightens. *What the fuck did he do this time?*

The anger is old and familiar. I should be numb to this by now.

An hour later, I'm on the phone with my new mushroom purveyor, wheeling and dealing like a first-class fungi drug mule, when my phone buzzes.

Cassie: Since you brought it up, I think I'm going to take you up on that vacation. Can you live without me March 29 through April 5? It's also a work trip for the Food & Wine Festival in Charleston.

I smirk. Of course she's working on a vacation. She can't help herself.

Kyle: Done. I've already taken two weeks of vacation this year, and it's only March. You've had zero since Cora was born.

Cassie: Your point?

She still writes my paycheck.

Kyle: Yes, Chef.

~~~
~~~

It's Sunday, it's sunny, and I'm at Collin and Vicki's place for a cookout with friends.

Little did I know, I was blindly hired to man the grill and make the sides. *Become a chef*, they said. *You'll have lots of friends*, they said.

Bullshit. I'm basically their honorary kitchen boy at every gathering.

Collin claps a hand on my shoulder, grinning as he steals a carrot from the tray I'm slicing and fanning out.

"So," he says, "how's Executive Chef life treating you?"

I raise a brow and smirk. "Well, the pay's better than this unpaid gig I didn't know I was working on my day off."

"Dude," he whispers, leaning in. "Vicki was this close to cooking." He holds his fingers millimeters apart, eyes wide like he's describing a near-death experience.

"She asked me what temp I wanted my chicken cooked." He shudders, then straightens, slaps my back, and cranks his voice back to full volume as he steals a celery stick. "You're actually saving lives today, bro. You're a goddamn hero."

"Yeah. Hero, my ass." I point my knife at the tray of marinating chicken. "So… rare?" I chuckle under my breath.

"Really, though," he says, grabbing another carrot. "I miss your cooking. My wife is amazing, don't get me wrong. But this?" He gestures to the chaos on the island. The bowls. The herbs. The magic. "She can't do *this*."

"Well, what's wrong with your hands?" I slide the finished tray toward him, because he's insane if he thinks I'm serving too.

He laughs. "Oh, I'm just lazy as fuck. And watching you cook in my kitchen is like watching porn."

He takes the tray in one hand and slaps my ass with the other before strutting out to the porch like he just closed a deal.

I crack a beer and head out to light the grill. My phone rings.

Like Pavlov's dog, my heart skips when I see Cassie's smiling face light up the screen. It's a picture I stole off Facebook. Originally, her and Jack, but I cropped him out and zoomed in on her. That smile still gets me every time.

"Chef," I answer, balancing the phone on my shoulder as I turn the gas. "How are you? How's Charleston?"

"Everything's great. How are you? If I'm interrupting, call me back later."

The grill ignites with a low *whoosh*. Heat blooms, sharp and fast, echoing the one in my chest when I hear her voice. She sounds better. Lighter. Almost happy.

"No, you're good. I'm at a friend's, having a few beers, about to grill out. Or trying to get out of cooking. So, this is perfect timing." I laugh. "Everything okay?"

"It's great. I just wanted to catch up. Like I said, I was going to call."

"You're really into this vacation," I tease. "You said you'd call Monday. It's Sunday. That's a real vacation. Well done, Chef."

I take a swig of my beer and scrape off the charred remains of whatever Collin burned last time he touched this grill.

"Shit. I'm sorry," she says. "I'm calling you on your day off. I didn't even question why you were drinking beer and grilling on a Monday."

I laugh. "No worries. We're here now. What's going on?"

That's when she drops the bomb.

The one I used to fantasize about. The one I always imagined would come in a moment meant for me. Not like this. Not like a confession. Not like defeat.

"Jack and I are splitting up."

She just says it. Flat. Careful. Like she's been holding it in forever.

"Oh, shit."

I set my beer down. Drag a hand over my head, fingers grazing bare skin, searching for the right thing to say.

"It's okay. I'm okay, Kyle. If you noticed I was off my game lately… Well, now you know why. And—another thing."

Shit. There's more? How is she upright?

"That little something exciting I wanted to tell you about?"

"Oh yeah?"

"While I was here, I was offered a kind of celebrity chef gig. Back in San Francisco."

I hear the fire bloom in her voice.

"Holy shit. Like… on TV?"

"Yeah. Cookbooks. Cookware. All of it." A light laugh escapes her. "It's kind of bananas."

We talk logistics. The offer. The timeline. The plan. The grill goes cold while we talk, but it feels like old times. Like standing shoulder to shoulder at a counter cluttered with soy sauce-stained 3x5 cards, mapping out something we believed in.

Something about it lights me up in a way I didn't expect.

No Jack. Just Cassie.

Maybe—just maybe—this is my shot. A crack in the universe, barely wide enough to step through.

I drift.

"Hello? You there?"

I blink. "Yeah. I'm here." *I've always been here.*

"Sorry. I'm talking too much. Probably oversharing." Her voice softens. "I mean… it's been, what? Nineteen years?" Her voice softens.

"Nineteen." I laugh, awkward, deflecting. "Jesus. I need a life outside the kitchen. I'm in a ratty T-shirt and jeans, rocking a damn mohawk, and the only thing I'm responsible for is a dog. I should probably grow up. Find a good woman."

This is the part where she's supposed to say it.

Me, Kyle.

She doesn't. She just keeps talking. About the restaurant. About when she's coming home.

We hang up.

I lean against the deck railing, picking at the label on my beer bottle, staring out at nothing.

The sliding door opens behind me.

"Kyle, you haven't even started grilling the chicken yet?" Collin points at the cold grill.

I glance over. "No. You're out of gas."

He crouches, checks the tank. "Oh shit. I've got another. No worries." He straightens and slaps my arm. "You thought you were getting out of grilling?" He laughs. Then notices I'm not.

"Hey," he says. "You okay?"

I mumble, "Cassie and Jack are splitting."

"No fucking way." His eyes go wide.

Then he swipes a hand across my mohawk like he's erasing a whiteboard.

"Okay," he says. "It's showtime, Brah."

He steps back, hands on my shoulders, eyes locked. "That shit has to go. It was funny when you lost that bet, but it's time to rein it in." He gives me a small shake. "We gotta get you ready."

Chapter 28

PATCHWORK HEARTS

I unlock the door and push it open into a stillness that nearly knocks me over.

No greeting. No nails skittering across the floor. No huff of breath or wicked tail thump against the wall.

Just silence. The kind that echoes, bouncing the pain around my chest until it has nowhere to land.

Everything I look at—the leash by the door, the empty water bowl, the corner where the bed used to be—is haunted by good memories.

I can't move anything. Can't touch a goddamn thing. Like shifting one object would erase what's left of him. I know in my head he's gone, but my body hasn't caught up yet. I just can't let go.

And then… there he is.

Mr. Pickles.

Still sitting exactly where I left him. Head tilted. One eye missing. More stitch than fabric.

I crouch and lift him slowly. Carefully. Like he's holding the last heartbeat in the apartment. Tears come hot and fast, my mind playing an unfair reel of every woman in my life patching him up. Restuffing. Stitching life back into his ridiculous little body. They came and went.

But Rocco? Rocco was always here. Here to hold. Here to remind me I wasn't ever alone.

I press the plush toy to my chest and whisper, "Fuck." Then quieter, broken, "Where are the girls now… to patch up *my* heart?"

~~~

I took the rest of the week off work. I just couldn't go. Couldn't be productive. Couldn't smile. I can't even fucking breathe.

The leather couch has my body dented into it like a chalk outline at a crime scene.

My phone is face-down on the coffee table, buzzing like it's trying to get free. I stopped looking at it yesterday. I thought it would have died by now. I don't care. I don't want to care. I don't look. Hell, I don't even move.

I just stare at nothing on TV and Mr. Pickles who's sitting on the armrest like a sentry. My only company.

Then—*knock-knock-knock.*

Pause.

Knockknockknockknockknock.

Pause.

Knock. Knock.

"What the actual fuck?"

I drag myself off the couch, slog to the door, and fling it open.

Collin is in a hoodie that says *"Feelings are Gross"* and holding a six-pack and a plastic container. Ritchie is wearing sunglasses *inside*, an oversized pizza in hand, and chewing gum like it's got nutritional value and it's his last meal.

Together, they smile in sync. Collin throws up a peace sign. Ritchie says, "Surprise, bitch. Grief counseling's here, and we brought carbs."

I just blink.

Ritchie walks in first, pushing past me and muttering, "He's not wearing pants. This is worse than we thought."

Collin holds up the Tupperware container like it's a bomb. "Mac and cheese so cheesy it's a hate crime. You're welcome."

I shut the door behind them and groan, "I was fine."

"Lies," Collin says, flopping onto the couch with such force I heard a spring pop.
~~~

Ritchie sits backwards in a dining chair like he's about to host a TED Talk on heartbreak.

"I know you're devastated, so first we'll feed you. Then we'll reintroduce you to sunlight and clean underwear." He waves his hand back and forth. "Maybe in the other order, though." He shrugs.

I crack. Just a little. How are my best friends Ren and Stimpy in human form?

My voice rasps, "You two in the same room feels like an *Avengers* spin-off nobody asked for."

Collin raises his beer. "Damn right. We're the Mid-Life Crisis League."

Richie holds up a beer and grins. "I was thinking more like Wonder Twins Grief Counseling." And takes a sip.

Collin cracks open his beer like it's communion. "Alright, bro. Here's to the real ones."

"To Rocco," Ritchie says, leaning forward, clinking bottle to bottle. Then he pauses, glances over. "You want to say it?"

I shake my head, jaw tight. Can't. Not yet.

They don't push. Just sip in sync like two idiots from a sitcom that got canceled too soon.

Ritchie flips open the pizza box. "This pie cost thirty-eight dollars. It better suck the grief out of your pores."

"Is that fucking goat cheese?" I ask, peering at it like it insulted my entire Italian lineage.

"Collin's idea," Ritchie mutters.

"You said fancy," Collin shoots back. "And I quote: 'Get something elevated but comforting.' Like I'm your fuckin' pizza sommelier."

"I meant pepperoni with extra crust bubbles, not a charcuterie circle jerk."

I shake my head. "This is why no one lets you guys plan things."

They both shrug. Simultaneous. Synchronized. I suddenly hate them. And love them. And hate that I love them.

Ritchie tears into a slice like a barbarian. "You've got, like, three cups of dog food in that bowl in there," he thumbs toward the kitchen, talking around a mouthful.

"I filled his bowl. Out of habit." I say numbly, staring down at the slice on my plate, unsure whether it's grief or the choice of toppings that's made it inedible.

That hits. Blow after blow, they keep coming.

I press the heels of my hands to my eyes. No tears fall, but the sting is there. Ritchie says nothing. Just slides the mac and cheese and a fork toward me like a peace offering. Or an anchor.

Collin leans back, kicks his feet up, and says, "You know what's really fucked? You're still the most emotionally available one in this room."

I grunt. "Lowest bar ever."

"Like… ankle height," Ritchie adds, reaching over and stabbing at the mac and cheese.

We all go quiet.

On the TV, a car commercial pretends it's a movie trailer. Outside, someone's kid screams with joy or rage—impossible to tell. Inside, the scent of overpriced pizza with goat cheese fills the space where my dog used to live.

And for the first time all week, I actually eat something. And smile.

~~~

I get back to work, and aside from a few quiet "Sorry about Rocco, man," comments and the occasional back pats that linger too long, I'm back in my groove. Letting Sagi steal my focus. Letting it scrub my grief clean.

Cassie's barely in the kitchen these days. She floats through like a goddamn movie star—oversized sunglasses, phone glued to her hand, schedule too full for real sentences and deep kitchen talk. She still owns the lease. Still controls the money. But this menu? This rhythm? It's all mine.

She used to taste everything. Drag a finger through the sauce and tell me it needed more acid. Now she just says, "Looks great, Chef," and drifts off like we didn't build this place together from nothing.

Weird thing is—for someone going through a divorce and juggling single-parent life…
~~~

She's glowing. Smiling. Lighter.

Maybe life with Jack really was *that* miserable.

But as I stir the pot—literally and not—I keep asking myself the same damn question:

How long do I wait before I take a risk on her heart?

~~~

It's been a month since Cassie stepped into her new role as a TV star and cookbook juggernaut.

And guess who's been holding down the fort? I sit in the office, paperwork spilling across my desk like a crime scene. The invoices, the emails, the scheduling—*her part of the job*—is burying me. Slowly. Daily.

I'm shifting Darius into my CDC role, trying to make space for it all. Trying not to drown. But holy hell, this is a lot.

My phone pings.

Cassie: That reservation for the Fishbowl this weekend is mine. I have friends coming to town to celebrate an anniversary. FYI.

Kyle: Yours? As in you're dining with them or cooking for them?

Cassie: Dining with them.

Huh. I've never cooked for her. Not once, in all these years. Well, not like… *this.*

Kyle: No pressure.

Cassie: Stop it. It's just me and some friends.

"Just me and some friends." Cassie… now has *friends*. Outside this restaurant.

My chest goes hollow. Something feels different. *Off.*

~~~

I've never—*never ever*—seen her look like this.

Tight black dress. Heels made for fucking. And the look on her face? Says she *has been*—right up until this very moment.

Two days ago, she went over tonight's menu with me. Every detail, intricate and specific. Nervously twisting her hands as she talked about the steamed snapper balls wrapped in chrysanthemum petals. We don't break that recipe out for just anyone.

Now I know why. This is special. This is to impress.

So, I watch through the glass. As *he* pulls her chair out. As she tucks her hair behind her ear and smiles up at him like he hung the damn moon.

Goddamnit.

One month. I kept my mouth shut for one fucking month. And he walked through that sliver—the one I'd been waiting nineteen years for.

Nineteen fucking years.

And this guy—this Armani-suited, perfect-hair, Rolex-wearing, big-dick energy motherfucker—*steals her.*

Goddamnit.

She glances up and sees me through the glass. And smiles.

I'm right where she wants me. Right where I've always been. Her friend. Her constant. The one who promised to never leave. The one who *can't.*

So, I run my line. I actually cook this meal and each dish goes out like a goddamn love letter. We hold our breath, waiting for the reaction, waiting for the look—like we're chasing a Michelin star or a write-up in *Eater.*

"Damn, this is stressful," Darius mutters, wiping his brow as he turns back to the pass.

If he only knew.

Eventually, I make my way into the dining room in my crisp clean chef coat, ready to impress. I stand directly behind Cassie with my arm draped over her chair. Like I own the place. Like I belong there. I smile. I answer their questions. I charm the hell out of her friends like I'm hosting a cooking segment on her new show.

But I don't miss it.

The subtle slide of his hand to her thigh under the table. Her casual, practiced kiss to his cheek I clocked from the kitchen. The shortness in my own tone when they went to leave? Yeah, he caught that, too.

Fuck it.

I'm tired of waiting. Tired of the sidelines. Tired of feeling like the warm-up act on someone else's main stage.

Service ends. I'm in the office, staring blankly at the screen, thinking my my to-do list is so long it might actually be a cry for help.

Margaret walks in with the credit card slips.

"Here's front of the house and my bar," she says. "We crushed it tonight."

"Yeah." I glance up and take the stack. "Thanks."

She doesn't move. Instead, she hops up on the corner of my desk like she's decided to camp out for the night. Arms crossed. Eyes twinkling with gossip.

"So." she starts, "Cassie and Stephen? That feels… *fast.*"

I tighten my jaw. "Margaret, what Cassie does outside this place is none of my business." I shoot her a look. "And it sure as hell isn't yours."

Margaret lingers like she wants to say more. Then she leans in, voice conspiratorial.

"Are you sure? I looked him up. His last name's *Harlow*—he's a—"

"Margaret." I cut her off, sharper than I meant to. "Stop. Just… stop the gossip."

Her eyes widen, lips press into a thin line. She backs off, nods once, and slips out, leaving me alone with a name that suddenly feels like a punch to the gut.

Harlow.

Of course, it's something sleek and sharp. Like him.

Then, I reach for my phone, open Google, and type in his name.

Jesus Christ.

Chapter 29

910

Sitting at the desk, I stare at the schedule, then glance at my watch. It's Thursday, 2:47. I pick up my phone, thumb hovering over the screen before I type and hit send. I hate to do it, but I have no choice. I'm out of options.

Kyle: Call me. 910.

My exhale is long and hard as my leg twitches under the desk and I… *wait.*

It's our system. Our code. Not a full-blown 911 emergency, but close. The restaurant isn't on fire, but I need her to respond. Fast.

I'm staring blankly at the schedule, trying to play Tetris with the staff lineup, when her face flashes across my screen. Still, as pissed as I am, my heart does that stupid thing—aches with relief. And joy.

"Chef?" I answer, trying not to sound like I was waiting.

"Hey, Kyle. I got your message. What's going on?" she asks, calm as ever.

I toss my hat onto the desk and run a hand through my hair. "Reggie's wife went into labor—he's out. I'm seriously short-staffed. I can swing tonight, limping by with one of the new guys, but tomorrow, being Friday… Can you help? I hate asking, Cassie."

She laughs lightly. "Hey. Actually, I can. I have taping until four, then I can be there. That work?"

"Yeah. That's great. What about Cora?"

"All's good. It's summer, and she's sleeping over at a friend's most of the weekend. 910 diverted. Crisis downgraded." She chuckles.

"Thank God. I was stressed out. We're completely booked, I need hands, and we've got a Fish Bowl table tomorrow. You know how I hate being on display when I'm not at my best."

It's a lie. I don't rattle anymore. Not in the kitchen. I just… need her here. I need to know she's still in this with me.

"I can't believe Reggie's gonna be a dad," she says, softer now. A tone I know by heart.

My mind flashes back to that night fourteen years ago. The way she needed me. Held my hand through gritted teeth, heaving breaths, and sweat. I glance over at the leather chair she gripped tight, now piled high with a T-shirt order. What a shit show. What a gift.

I glance at my wrist. Cora's name. Gray now. Faded from the sun, but still my favorite.

"Yeah," I say quietly. "Can't believe he's gonna be a dad."

A pause.

"It's crazy," she whispers.

"See you tomorrow," I say.

Then she's gone. Again.

~~~

Cassie walks through the back door in a chef's coat that's more prop than uniform—pressed and pristine, like she just walked off a magazine shoot, not into a kitchen. Her hair's pulled into a sleek bun, not the chaotic twist she used to wrangle into place in the tiny 8x10 mirror above the mop sink.

She ties on an apron without a word and steps up beside me on the line.

"Where do you want me?"

My lap? My mouth? My face? Jesus. Now you finally ask?

"Sauté." I nod, gesturing to the space on the line where we used to work side by side.

I slide over the specials, our game plan scribbled on my legal pad. She squeezes in tight. God, she smells like citrus and heaven.

Our rhythm clicks back into place like muscle memory. Like
~~~

dancing with someone whose steps you never forgot. The kitchen hums. The flames crack, and our audience at the Fish Bowl table eats it up.

When it's over, I half expect her to bolt—but she doesn't. The doors lock. The music goes up. And Cassie comes smiling around the corner holding cold Kirins like it's a peace offering.

"Here, guys."

I pop mine and point my bottle at our new guy, Brandon. "Don't get used to this. It only happens when Chef graces us with her presence on the line."

She laughs. "Come on, we're celebrating. Cheers to Reggie's new baby."

Then she levels me a look. "Now play some tunes, Kyle. Let's get this bitch closed down."

I scroll through the playlist, then stop. There it is. Our old kitchen anthem from Le Début. Limp Bizkit. "Break Stuff."

I spin my hat backward and hit play.

"We're closing with violence," I smirk as the first beat drops.

Her laugh. Her arms in the air, beer in one hand, scrubbing the flattop like she's wiping the slate clean.

This. This is my Cassie.

The kitchen sparkles when we're done. It's never looked better. I round the corner into the hallway, and she's there, leaning against the wall.

"You don't have to stay," I say. "We've got it from here."

"I know. I'm good. Actually having fun. I don't have anywhere to be… for once." She smiles.

"It's just strange, seeing you here. And… you look *good.*" I smirk, lifting my beer in her direction like I need something to do with my hands.

She raises a brow. "What?"

"You've got, like, full makeup on. Your hair looks… good." I glance down. She sees it. The shift.

She grins, teasing. "Are you crushing on the celebrity chef, Kyle? Should I call my publicist?"

I lean against the wall, beer dangling in one hand, eyes on my shoes, heart pounding in my chest.

"I've been crushing on you long before you were a celebrity, Cassie."

She goes still. Then she reaches out, wrapping her fingers around my wrist.

I glance down at where she's holding me.

"I know I don't have a chance," I laugh softly. "I Googled Stephen." I exhale. "I just thought… maybe. Since you and Jack…"

"I'm sorry, Kyle," she whispers. "I… didn't know."

I scoff. "Come on, Cass. Would it have made a difference?"

She shakes her head slowly. "No, but—"

That's all I need to hear.

I let the words pour out. All of it. How I've always wanted more. How I just want to be near her. How I've spent nineteen years trying not to want what I wanted.

Silence.

Her face is a mix of shock and something softer—sad, maybe. Confused.

I lift her chin gently.

"Hey… don't let this be weird. I won't." I turn to leave, then pause. "But… if for some reason you ever decide you don't want a millionaire—or anyone else—and you want to give this guy a try…" I smile, gesturing to myself. "Just know I won't say no. I'd actually like it."

And then I walk away, leaving her speechless.

Soon after, she waves goodbye to us in the kitchen, and the slam of the door follows.

I can't believe I finally said it.

~~~

When I step out into the parking lot, her Mini Cooper's still parked in its spot. She's inside. A silhouette in the glow of her phone.

I walk up and tap the glass.

She jumps. "Fucking shit!"

She cracks the door.
~~~

"You okay?" I ask.

Her chin quivers, the tears begin to fall, and she crumbles beneath the weight of everything she's been holding together.

I crouch down, pull her legs gently out of the car, and press her against me.

"Shhh," I whisper. "It's gonna be okay."

She sobs into my chest, makeup smearing, nose running, parking lot gravel digging into my knees—but I don't let go.

"I'm just alone," she whispers. "My life is falling apart. You think I have it together, but I don't."

"You don't have to be anything but this," I say, blotting beneath her eyes with a napkin from her center console. "This is real."

"Kyle… I can't do this without you."

I press my lips to her forehead, and it kills me not to kiss her lips. "I'm not going anywhere," I promise. Again.

I knew it was coming.

She asks between sniffles, "Why did you tell me all that tonight, knowing I probably didn't feel the same way?"

I squeeze her hand. "Because I'd rather live with rejection than regrets." I smile gently. "And I'm okay. You'll be okay, too."

She nods, but I linger—just long enough to memorize the moment. The way she's crumpled in the driver's seat. The way her hand still holds mine like she doesn't want to let go.

But she does. And I walk away. Not angry. Not hopeful. Just... *free.*

~~~

I had every intention of going home, to let the noise of the night bleed out in my kitchen through an old recipe and nervous hands. Standing barefoot on cold tile, staring at nothing, finally not fighting the silence.

Instead, the neon hum drags me in. A low buzz. Muffled voices. Laughter that sounds too easy for how I feel.

I push the heavy wooden door open and step into the dark, into the noise, into something I didn't plan for.
~~~

Chapter 30

FALL FROM GRACE

The bar is too loud. Too crowded. Too full of people who still think everything ahead of them is possible as long as they've got a full drink.

The first person I see is a woman, brown hair tied loosely back. She's alone at the far end, fingers wrapped around a rocks glass, watching the room like she's studying it. Chef blacks. My kind.

Her eyes flick to me. Then back to her drink.

No recognition. No curiosity sharpened into expectation. And for some reason… that feels like relief.

I take a seat two stools down. Not next to her, but not far. Safe.

"What can I get you?" the bartender asks.

I glance up. "Just an IPA on tap." I nod toward the handles.

He nods and turns away.

"You look like someone who just lost a bet."

Her voice is low. Confident. The kind that's used to being listened to in a kitchen.

I glance sideways and smirk. "Something like that."

She finally turns toward me, resting her chin on her palm. "Let me guess. You either got dumped, quit your chef gig, or found out your dog's been cheating on you with another human."

She smiles and takes a slow sip of her drink.

I blink. "Wow. Okay. Two out of three."

Her brow lifts. "Seriously?"

"Well," I say, taking a pull of my beer, "no dog betrayal. But… he did die." I shrug lightly.

She presses a hand to her chest, a soft, reflexive gasp slipping out.

"And I didn't technically get dumped," I add. "I just let someone steamroll my heart for over two decades, and I finally cried mercy."

She goes still. It's not pity. Not performative sympathy. Just... real.

"I'm sorry," she says quietly, covering her mouth with her hand.

I nod. I can't believe I said that out loud. Why did I tell her? Like some bar-top confessional I didn't mean to step into.

She reaches across the space between us.

"Truce offering?" she says. "I'll keep my therapist instincts holstered for the rest of the night. Promise."

"And I'll tell fewer depressing stories," I chuckle.

It's the first time I've laughed with a stranger in longer than I can remember.

"I'm Kyle."

She takes my hand. Her grip is warm. Steady. Like she means it.

"Grace."

Of course it is.

Her eyes lock on mine. Her hand pauses mid-shake.

"Wait. You—" She tilts her head. "Are you Kyle Berkley? From Sagi-Shi?"

I smirk. "Uh... yeah?"

She drops her hand and presses her palm to the bar. "I just read that last write-up on you. Nice." She nods, approving.

I take a sip of my beer, heat crawling up my neck. "Thanks."

"Your owner—Chef Buckley? Cassie?" she says. "She tapes over at the studio with my exec, Noah."

She drains the last of her drink and lifts a finger for the bartender.

"Put that on my tab," I say before she can reach for her card.

She arches a brow. "Well, thank you."

"Anyhow," she says, waving a hand, "how long have you been working alongside her?"

I let out a breath and roll my eyes, clinking my glass to hers. "Two decades." I tap my chest. "Hence the heart-steamroll comment."

She sits up straighter. "Oh hell. You've been crushing on your boss that long?"

I nod, finish my beer, and slide the glass toward the bartender with a quiet ask for another.

She winces. "I'm sorry."

"It's okay," I say, and this time the smile sticks. "I'm actually… really good, Grace. Like—right this second."

She smiles back. Radiant.

"So," I say, leaning in, "tell me about your shittiest night of service. Full disaster mode." I grin. "Don't leave out a single curse word."

She groans, pressing a hand to her forehead like the memory physically hurts. "Oh hell. This night isn't long enough, Kyle."

I laugh, elbow settling on the bar. "I've got all night. And there's a twenty-four-hour diner down the street."

~~~

We walk in comfortable silence. The kind that doesn't need to be filled with words or nervous laughter. The kind that just… exists.

The sidewalk is slick with condensation, rainbow-laced halos wrapping around the mist-softened streetlights. Just the sound of our footsteps keeping time on the wet pavement. Not rushed. Not hesitant. Just there—meeting mine.

She brushes against me by accident. Barely. Just the backs of our hands, but it's enough to short-circuit my entire nervous system.

My heart starts pounding like it missed the cue and is now scrambling to catch up.

She doesn't say anything. Just glances sideways, and I catch the corner of her mouth twitching in my periphery.

Jesus Christ.

I feel sixteen. And alive.

We reach the diner—a narrow, chrome-edged miracle that smells like scorched coffee, griddle grease, and late-night regret.

She grins at the red vinyl booths. "Oh, hell yes."

We slide into one across from each other. The table is sticky in that familiar way that somehow comforts me more than it should.
~~~

The server—a woman who looks like she's worked here since the Clinton administration—slaps down two laminated menus. They're covered in more pictures than words, because pointing and grunting is easier at this hour—especially in certain blurry-minded states.

"I already know," Grace says, flipping her coffee cup right side up like she's not a rookie. "I've had the same order since I was nineteen. If I died mid-bite, I'd die a happy girl."

I lean back, arms crossed. "Alright then. Let's hear it."

The server lifts an unimpressed eyebrow, framed in the most electrifying thick blue eyeshadow I've ever seen—like it was applied in 1987 and reapplied ever since, layered on like spackle.

I try not to stare.

"So?" she deadpans, pen hovering over her pad.

"Double bacon cheeseburger," Grace says. "Over-easy egg on top. Extra pickles. Side of hash browns—not home fries." She lifts a finger. "The shredded ones."

She smiles at me.

God. That smile.

I blink. "That's my order."

She beams. "See? This was meant to be."

I grin. "Except no pickles."

I look up at Tammy Faye. "They don't taste right with the egg." I wince. "And black coffee that tastes like burnt motor oil, please."

Grace lifts her mug. "I want his pickles. And make that two on the coffee. Extra motor oil." She winks.

I try not to notice the pickle comment. But I do.

Medusa doesn't find our humor remotely funny. She snatches the menus from our hands and shuffles off in her orthopedic shoes, the scent of hairspray trailing in her wake.

We toast with chipped porcelain, and it's the best thing I've tasted in months.

As we wait, we lean back and do what all late-night diner saints do—we people-watch.

"See that guy?" Grace whispers, nodding toward the counter. A man sits alone—jeans, flannel, newspaper opened wide. Late forties. Quiet. Tired.

"Yeah?"

"He's a private investigator," she says, eyes narrowing. "Following… that guy." She tilts her head toward the corner, where a couple is going at it like they're auditioning for low-budget soft porn. His hand creeps up her shirt. Hers is buried under the table, firmly in no-man's-land. Their plate of fries and two milkshakes—now entirely liquid—sit abandoned like casualties of war.

I stifle a laugh. "What's his angle?"

"Do you even have to ask?" She smirks. "Cheating spouse. Double life. His wife, Tanya, is home waiting for photo evidence. They've been building the case for three weeks."

She takes a sip of her coffee, trying not to laugh.

"You just made that up."

"Obviously," she grins.

I nod toward a girl in glitter heels and tight white jeans, crying into a plate of crinkle fries. "She just found out she failed her final. And that her psychic was a fraud."

Grace leans in, eyes sparkling. "And that her psychic is also the woman dating her ex."

We're both laughing now—quiet, breathless, and way too comfortable for two people who met two hours and fifteen minutes ago.

For the first time in a long time, I don't feel like I'm performing. Or pretending. Or proving I'm enough. I just feel… *here*.

The food arrives, gloriously greasy, piled high, and completely obscene. We don't talk for a few minutes—just eat, occasionally looking up at each other with reverent nods like *yes*. This. Exactly this.

She wipes her mouth. "I swear diner chefs are the most underappreciated miracle workers in this industry."

I lean in. "They should be getting Michelin stars for cooking while hungover, understaffed, and dodging drunk couples trying to fuck in the bathroom."

We clink hash-brown-loaded forks in salute.

In the lull that follows, I look at her, and something shifts in my chest. Nothing dramatic. Nothing loud. Just a quiet easing. Like the noise finally dialed down. Like this was supposed to happen.

Right now. Right here.

Me. Her.

It doesn't feel exciting or terrifying or sharp around the edges. It doesn't feel accidental. It feels like… *home*.

~~~

We step out into the cool night air, the diner bell jingling softly behind us. The quiet hits harder than I expect.

There's no crowd. No music spilling from open windows. Just wet pavement, a car splashing through a puddle down the block, and the low neon hum overhead.

She pulls her jacket tighter and gives me a sleepy smile. "Thanks for dinner, Chef."

"Thanks for letting me tag along on your PI surveillance shift," I tease, sliding my hands into the back pockets of my chef pants, rocking on my heels.

She laughs, soft and easy. "Always room for a rookie."

We linger on the sidewalk. One beat. Then another.

My chest tightens. Not panic—clarity.

This is it. My life's Hail Mary. My mulligan. I've been here before—stood still, said nothing, watched a woman walk away and called it safer.

I'm not doing that again.

She starts to turn. "Well—"

"Grace?"

She stops. Turns back.

And I don't overthink it. I don't talk myself out of it. I just say it.

"I don't know why," I murmur, voice low, rough, "but I don't want you to go."

Her eyes widen—not alarmed. Just open.

"I'm not a clinger," I add quickly, shaking my head with a small laugh. "I just… can't walk away tonight and wonder what that was." I gesture back toward the diner. "You sat across from me and it felt like something in my life finally clicked back into place."

She presses her hand to her mouth. Her eyes soften.

"I don't want to go either, Kyle."
~~~

Something in me breaks—but not the old way. Not the quiet, swallowing-it-down way.

This time, I move. I step forward, slow enough to give her time to pull away. She doesn't.

My hands frame her jaw, thumbs brushing warm skin, the faint tremor there telling me everything I need to know. The brick at her back is cool, solid, anchoring us as the neon hums overhead. My forehead rests against hers for one breath—close enough to feel her exhale, close enough to smell coffee and rain and something unmistakably *her*.

Then I kiss her. And my body forgets how to behave.

When her lips part on instinct, soft and sure, the contact knocks the air out of me. My knees threaten to give way, like they've forgotten their job. She makes the smallest sound, barely a breath, and it vibrates through me like a fault line shifting. My hands flex through her hair, around the nape of her neck like they're holding on to the only solid thing left.

She grips the front of my jacket, pulling me closer, and the kiss deepens—not rushed, not polite. Hungry. Real. I taste coffee, salt, and something electric that settles low and heavy, lighting me up from the inside out.

For a second, the world tilts. Neon blurs. The street disappears. There is only her mouth, her breath, the way she fits against me like this was never new.

When we finally pull back, it's because we have to breathe.

"Shit," she whispers.

"Yeah," I murmur, forehead still resting against hers. "Same."

We stay like that a moment longer—under the neon, hearts racing, the world reordering itself.

It's only then I know.

Something just changed. For good.

Chapter 31

CINNAMON & NOISY SECRETS

There's something about the way Grace folds her napkin when she's done eating. The way she reaches under the table and rests her hand on my thigh. It makes me feel like I've finally made it. Like, *really* made it.

No promotion, no magazine spread, not even a packed dining room. Nothing compares to the way she makes me feel.

We're sitting around Wally and Becky's farmhouse table with the remnants of dinner spread across mismatched ceramic plates. Becky went all out: pot roast, fresh rolls, and her kick-ass roasted rosemary-garlic potatoes. Grace offered to bring dessert and showed up with a bourbon pecan tart that made Wally tear up. Swear to God.

Now we're in that post-dinner haze as Becky pours coffee. Wally kicks his feet up and tells stories that are about seventy percent true. Grace, *my* Grace, fits into the picture like she's always been here. Like she's part of what's left of this family.

I catch Wally watching us. That little glint in his eye, the one he gets when he's about to meddle like it's sport. Then he drops it like a winning touchdown in the goddamn playoffs, but he's the only one celebrating.

"You should introduce Grace to your dad, Kyle."

The clink of Becky's spoon hitting the sugar bowl is the only sound in the room for half a beat. She side-eyes Wally like he just ruined the entire night with that one comment.

I don't look at Grace. I smirk, shake my head, and try to ignore the knot tightening in my chest.

"Yeah. Be careful what you wish for." I cut Wally a warning glance.

He just shrugs and winks like he hasn't lobbed a live grenade onto the table.

Grace, ever the diplomat and completely unaware of what she's agreeing to, smiles gently and says, "I'd like that."

That's when I officially want to crawl under the table and live among the dust bunnies and fur from their cat, Barney.

"Mmm," I grunt, reaching for my coffee. "Let's not ruin dessert… or the rest of my life," I chuckle, raising a brow.

Becky stands, sensing the shift, and starts gathering plates. Grace rises to help, and in seconds, they're in the kitchen together, laughing softly, washing dishes like they've done it a hundred times.

Wally leans back, crosses his arms.

"You're not mad at me, are you?"

"I'm always mad at you," I mutter, smirking.

"You gonna stay mad at him your whole life, too?"

I let out a long sigh through my nose.

"I don't even think I'm mad anymore. It's more like… numb."

He sets his coffee on the table, tents his fingers, and looks directly at me.

"Kyle, I bring it up because I care. I also know what holding that kind of grudge does to a man. End it before something happens. Please?"

I glance toward the kitchen, at Grace smiling over suds and silverware. Then back to Wally.

"I said what I needed to say." My voice is low, steady. "The ball's been in his court for years. All he has to say is sorry, and the bastard can't even say that, Wally. He can't even say that."

Before, this conversation would've enraged me, sent me into a two-day tailspin. Now it doesn't. It's just facts.

"You've got something good here, son. Don't let an old ghost steal it from you," he says, arching a brow over his coffee.

I stare at the last bite of tart on my plate.

~~~

I wake to the feel of her fingers tracing my stomach in lazy, possessive circles. Like she's memorizing me all over again just because she can.

The sheet's kicked halfway down the bed. Her thigh is slung across my hip. She's not wearing a damn thing, and neither am I.

Outside, the sky's just starting to lighten. Inside, she's breathing against my neck like a slow fuse.

"Mornin', Chef," she murmurs, lips brushing my jaw, voice rough, low, smug.

I groan. "Jesus. You trying to kill me?"

I swear I just pulled out of her an hour ago. She's ten years younger, and her body's running tactical drills around my dick.

"Not yet."

She shifts across my body, slow and smooth, until she's straddling me. Her long brown hair falls around her face, fingers pressing into my chest like she owns the rights to it now. Because she does.

"You were talking in your sleep," she says, mouth hovering just above mine. "Kept saying 'yes.'"

I thread my fingers through her hair. "Dream version of me has excellent taste."

"Real version of you isn't so bad either." Her tongue darts out between her lips.

She grinds down once, just enough to make my breath hitch. Then again. She watches me like she's cataloging every twitch, every weakness, feeling me getting hard beneath her.

"You gonna do something about that?" she asks, voice silk and challenge.

I flip us before she can blink.

Her gasp is sharp and perfect.

"Oh, I plan to," I smirk against her lips.

I press her hands above her head, sliding down her body with my mouth and my hands. I trace slow, sensual circles over her nipples with my tongue, taking my time.

"Mmm, yes," she whispers. "That feels good."

I move lower, trailing kisses along her warm skin. Her fingers tangle in my hair, grip tightening as my palms press her thighs apart.
~~~

My tongue finds her, wet and sweet and tangy, and mine. All fucking mine.

Her body grinds against my mouth.

"Oh God," she moans, fingers curling into the sheets. "Right there."

My fingers slide inside her, finding her G spot as my tongue flicks her clit in the rhythm I know makes her come apart. She chases it—breathless, desperate—until her body finally breaks beneath me. I don't stop until she's completely ruined.

She's still shaking when I finally sink into her. She wraps her legs around me like she doesn't plan on letting go.

Ever.

It's slow and filthy. The kind of morning sex that feels like claiming. Like *you're mine* and *I'm not going anywhere.*

We move together like we've done this a hundred times. Like our bodies remember something we haven't put into words yet.

She comes again, quiet and clutching, mouthing my name like a secret. I follow, forehead pressed to hers, hips stuttering, breath caught against her mouth.

When it's over, I don't move. I don't want to. Her hands are in my hair. Her thighs are still trembling. And I think—this is it. This is the peace I've been chasing.

~ ~ ~

The smell of cinnamon and sugar hits first. Thick and sweet, clinging to the air like something holy. I'm used to savory smells in my kitchen, onion and garlic. But Grace, being a pastry chef, brings a whole new level of sweetness into my world.

She stands barefoot at the kitchen island, long brown hair twisted up in a loose knot, a few soft strands escaping around her face, rolling out dough like it's therapy. Her hips sway a little to the music, something old and crackling from the record player she insisted we haul home from a thrift store in Haight-Ashbury last weekend.

She's humming to something else. Not loudly. Just under her breath. I don't even know the song. It's got a rhythm like childhood, like vinyl and Sunday mornings and… "*Sweet Caroline…*"

My breath catches. Suddenly, it's Neil Diamond, and I'm ten years old watching my mother press down pasta dough. Flour on her hands. Her laugh loud and bright. That same hum. The same sway. The same everything.

My heart swells and stutters at the same time. It's like remembering something too beautiful to hold.

I lean back against the counter with my coffee and just watch her, lost in her own world at the island.

She looks over her shoulder and smiles. "What?"

"Nothing," I say, my voice thick. "You're just… you're so gorgeous, that's all." I shake my head slowly.

She tilts her head, eyes soft, then steps over and kisses me, warm and sweet, cinnamon and sugar still on her lips, holding her buttery hands up in the air.

I tuck a stray hair behind her ear. Sunlight catches the flour drifting through the air, backlighting her like a dream.

"You're a charmer in the morning," she teases. "Can you grab the pan for me?" She wiggles her fingers.

I nod, push off the counter, and crouch to open the lower cabinet.

Right side. Lower shelf.

I reach in without thinking.

CLANG. CLANG. CLANG.

The springform pan rockets out of the cabinet, slamming to the tile like a cymbal crashing through an empty concert hall. The sound hits hard, too loud, too sharp, echoing through parts of me I've learned to keep shut.

I don't move. I can't.

Grace laughs, light and easy, chasing it across the kitchen floor before crouching to pick it up.

"Damn," she says, fiddling with the loose latch. "This thing has seen some miles."

My body goes still. My breath disappears.

Grace freezes mid-movement and looks up at me. "Kyle?"

My coffee's still in my hand, my knuckles white around the mug.

That hum, that wonderful memory, vanishes. Something floods my chest, thick and sudden, crawling up into my throat until it's hard to breathe. In its place comes the nightmare. The smell of smoke. Her taillights. Her never walking back through the door. His never-ending blame. The guilt.

I slowly reach over and trace the metal rim. "Yeah," I whisper. "A lot of miles."

Her hand covers mine, still warm and faintly slick with butter. "Babe? Are you okay?"

I swallow hard.

"It's a pan," I scoff, trying for humor. "You shouldn't have childhood trauma over a pan, right?" My eyes find hers, now glassy, full of worry.

She sets the pan aside. "Mine was crayons." She gives a small grin, then taps the pan lightly. "Totally valid. Talk to me." Her brows knit.

She wipes her hands on a towel, then laces her fingers through mine. We sit at the counter like that, her body turned toward me, quietly listening. *Really* listening.

"I'm thirty-nine," I say with a quiet huff. "Let me give you the Cliff's Notes version of my childhood trauma. I was just a little kid." I scrub a hand down my face, then take her hand again, my thumbs moving slow and absent over her knuckles. "It was my dad's birthday. We wanted to surprise him with his favorite. My mom's Italian cheesecake." I close my eyes as the memory presses in.

"I forgot to set the timer. Burned it. She insisted on remaking it, but we were out of ricotta." I open my eyes and meet hers, my mouth twisting. "Fucking ricotta."

"Babe." She rubs slow, comforting circles up my arm.

I shake my head. "She left and never came home," I say softly. "It was an aneurysm. She hit a tree. Died instantly."

Grace gasps, covering her mouth. "Oh my God. Honey, I'm so sorry."

I turn to look at her. Really look at her.

"The icing on the cake is that Whit has blamed me my whole life."

"No." She shakes her head in disbelief. "Babe, you didn't cause that. You were just a kid."

"He hates me, Grace. He blames me." I nod toward the counter. "And this pan, that recipe," I add, pointing to the avocado-green box on the shelf, "and his fucking forgiveness… that's what's left standing between me and real happiness." I exhale, backtracking. "I mean, you make me happy."

She cups my face in her hands, warm and smelling faintly of butter and cinnamon, and looks straight into my eyes. "Then we deal with it. We make that cheesecake. And after that, we work toward the forgiveness." Her smile is soft and understanding, "We get you everything you deserve. All your happiness, Kyle."

I kiss her and breathe her in. "Cinnamon rolls today," I whisper, "but… someday."

I swallow. "I can't believe I told you. Ritchie, Collin, and Wally are the only ones who know that."

She sits up straighter. "Really?"

I nod. "Yeah. I just… trust you. With everything, Grace."

She doesn't put the pan back in the cabinet. Instead, she sets it on the shelf, right next to the avocado-green recipe box, like a trophy. Like it belongs there. Like it's not cursed or shameful. It's just… part of the story.

I stare at it for a long time after she slides the cinnamon rolls into the oven and walks out of the room.

Maybe it'll stay there now. Out in the open. Something I can't shove away anymore. Maybe every time I see it, it'll hurt a little less. Maybe it'll soften something in me I thought was too far gone.

Maybe forgiveness is possible. Maybe it's been waiting for me this whole time.

Maybe.

Chapter 32

UNPACKING PRIDE

There's a pile of laundry on her couch. Most of it's hers, but somehow a good chunk of it's become mine. My sweatshirts never seem to make it home.

We're both sitting cross-legged, eating Chinese takeout straight from the containers, drinking Pinot Grigio, and folding clothes like we've always done this, like this is just us now.

"You know you've had a toothbrush at my place for like… three months now, right?" she says, twirling lo mein around her chopsticks.

"It's a squatter toothbrush," I smirk.

"Pretty sure squatters don't bring their wok, their espresso machine, and commit to a whole case of IPA," she says, sliding a basket between us.

I smile.

"Maybe we should just make it official," she shrugs, taking a sip of her wine like it's nothing, then pulling a shirt from the pile without making eye contact.

I panic for half a second, but then I look at her, remember who just said this to me, and breathe easy.

"You really want to live with me?" I ask. "You've seen the kitchen. You've endured my sweaty night terrors. The… *pan.*" I wince.

She just looks at me, mid-towel fold, then drops it into her lap. She tilts her head.

"Yes. Because I know what's in the cabinet, and I still want to open it with you."

Then, as if that didn't just level my heart, she holds up one of my ratty old band shirts.

"This has holes in three major zones and smells like garlic confit. Want to keep it or set it on fire?"

I gape at her. "That's vintage, Grace. Show some respect."

She rolls her eyes and tosses it into the keep pile. I grab a pair of her underwear and fold it neatly in half.

They're lacy. Black. Deadly.

"These should probably come with a warning label."

She grins. "That's the thong I was wearing when you licked bourbon whipped cream off my stomach."

"Good times." I waggle my brows.

She laughs, then leans into my shoulder, warm, loose, and beautiful in that way she is when she's not trying to be anything.

That's when it hits me.

This isn't just a good night. Her move-in comment wasn't just a lighthearted whim. This is the life I want. Her scent on my clothes. Her laugh in my kitchen. Her underwear in my laundry pile.

I look at her, and it just… comes out.

"I love you, you know."

She freezes. Eyes wide. Mouth slightly open. Then she deadpans.

"Did you just 'I love you' me while folding my thong?"

I choke on a laugh.

"It was a strong thong. An emotional-support thong, maybe."

She stares at me for a second, and then her whole face softens. Just… melts. She sets the towel aside, shifts onto her knees, and kisses me like I just rewrote gravity.

"I love you too, Kyle."

We sit there in a pile of mismatched socks, old T-shirts, and future plans we haven't spoken out loud yet, and I don't think I've ever felt more certain of anything in my damn life.

I smile into her hair, her arms wrapped around my waist.

"Let's do it. Let's make it official. Your thongs. My underwear. A permanent toothbrush. The whole damn thing." I kiss the top of her head.

She looks up at me. "Move in here?"

I shake my head and smile. "Anywhere you are."

~~~

Between packing up my life, working obscene hours, and watching Cassie's roller-coaster of a life breeze in and out the door, I manage to keep full control of Sagi, minus one thing: the financials. That part? She keeps me in the dark.

Cassie's in her quarterly investor meeting for most of the morning, tied up in the office on a Zoom call before she barrels out, practically taking me out in the process.

"Oh shit, sorry." She grabs my arm, steadying herself.

"How did it go?" I nod toward the office. "We still in business?" I joke.

"It went fine," she grumbles, "except two of our investors are pulling out. Fortunately, we have the money to buy them out now, thank God." She runs a hand through her hair. "It's just going to eat into some of my working capital. I don't know. I need to talk to my accountant later today." She throws her hands in the air as she walks down the hall.

That's when I blurt it out, like I'm asking if we should run a special on those Asian sticky ribs she refuses to make ever again for some weird reason.

"I should invest in Sagi," I say.

She keeps walking until it finally registers what I said, then stops cold in the hallway. She turns, looking at me like I have three heads.

"What?"

"I'm serious right now, Cassie."

Shock washes over her face. "Okay." She gestures toward the office. "Let's go talk."

That's when I tell her everything. How Grace and I are moving in together. How I want more for my life. And, well… how I'm rich as fuck.

She sits in the leather chair, trying to pull her jaw off the floor, realizing I could've invested in Sagi all along. Realizing she shouldn't have listened to Jackoff all those years ago.

I shrug. "I just didn't need it. I like the way I live."
~~~

She emerges from her daze, reality finally hitting her. "Wait. You're a trust-fund kid? Vineyard lineage?" She blinks.

I nod. "Yeah. My grandparents were really wealthy and left me a fuck ton of money." I smirk. "Why? You second-guessing dating *Mr. I-Have-a-Private-Jet* now?" I laugh.

She narrows her eyes. "No."

"Well, talk to your dad and whoever. Tell me what you think," I say.

She nods. "I think I wouldn't want to be partners with anyone else, Kyle." She smiles. "I'm going to cry."

I go in for a hug. "You and your crying."

~~~

The music plays low, and the kitchen smells like garlic, broth, and what I imagine the first tier of heaven might be. I don't know how else to say it. It's midnight, I'm plating ramen after a long day at work, and my head is buzzing. I'm excited, nervous, and honestly not sure how to approach this subject. So I use my love language. Silky ramen and a broth that could soften any hardened heart.

Grace is curled on the couch, doom-scrolling, wine in hand, wearing one of my old skater hoodies with nothing but little panties underneath. The sleeves swallow her hands. The hem hits dangerously high on her thighs.

I try to focus on not burning the damn pork belly, but my stomach's been in knots since I told Cassie about the trust fund. The one thing Grace doesn't know.

I set the bowl in front of her, drop down beside her, and wait.

"This looks like sex in a bowl," she says, peering in.

"That's because it is," I smirk.

She takes a bite and moans. Actually *moans*. Then she eyes me suspiciously. "Okay. What's going on? You're cooking like you just cheated on me."

I laugh, short and nervous, because fuck if she doesn't already know me.

"I didn't cheat. But I did… withhold something. Something kind of big."
~~~

She stiffens and slides the bowl onto the coffee table.

"What kind of 'big' are we talking, Kyle?"

I stare at the steaming bowl, my pulse hammering in my ears, then meet her eyes.

"I have a trust fund. A really big one. It's from my grandparents, and it's been sitting there for years. Pretty much my entire life." I ramble.

Silence.

Her brows pinch together, confusion creasing her face as her mind bends around my words. Her eyes narrow slightly.

"How big?" she asks hesitantly, her voice low. Like she's afraid there's a lot more to this conversation. Like I've been hiding a body in a basement freezer.

"Big enough that I could've retired at twenty-five. Bought a house." I snort. "A culinary degree. I don't know. An island?" I shrug. "But I didn't. I never touched it."

Her expression shifts, processing what I just said while holding something back.

"Why? Why didn't you tell me?"

That lands hard. I feel it in my ribs.

"Because I hate where it comes from. It's my dad's side. Vineyard money. All that wealth and his control." I shake my head. "His control of me. I didn't want to be anything like him, so I lived like I was broke. It was my way of fighting back, I guess." A laugh escapes me. "God, it pissed him off."

"Kyle, I'm not mad that you have money. I'm… I'm hurt you didn't think you could tell me."

I nod. It's fair. More than fair.

"I didn't want to be that guy. The rich kid with a chip on his shoulder. But today, Cassie lost two investors. And I offered to step in. Not because I want to save her. But because I want more. For me." I look down at my hands, then whisper, "For *us*."

Her breath catches.

"Us?"

I take her hands and look into her big brown eyes. The ones that aren't looking at me like I'm a liar or something to pity, but like someone she can dream with. Build with.

"Yeah. I want to build something bigger. A future. Maybe even a restaurant someday, with you. A bakery. A bistro. Whatever you want. I don't know." I shrug. "But Sagi can be a great stepping stone. It could be ours."

She studies me for a long moment. Then something in her softens, and her shoulders drop.

"You're a pain in the ass sometimes, Kyle."

"I know. I annoy myself daily."

"But I love your pain-in-the-ass self." She shakes her head, laughing softly. "Even if you are secretly rich."

She pulls me in and kisses me, slow and deep and forgiving.

"Next time, just tell me sooner," she says quietly. "I want to know all of you. Even the parts you try to hide." Her thumb brushes softly along my jaw. "Because I'm not here for just the easy parts. I'm all in. So, be all in with me."

I exhale for the first time all night.

"Deal."

She points past me toward the kitchen. "And you're still doing the dishes, Mr. Moneybags. You made a major mess in there."

I hand her back her ramen.

"Here. It's made with love… and anxiety."

"Mmm." She smiles. "My favorite combination."

~~~

The last of the boxes sit half-open on the floor. Grace is at work, and the apartment is quiet in a way that feels… new. Settled. Like I might actually live here now.

It's ridiculous how much kitchenware we have between us. Pots, pans, sheet trays, five whisks, and enough cookbooks to open a wildly eclectic restaurant or start a major fire hazard.

I flip open one of the boxes and stop cold. Right there on top is the green recipe box. And Mr. Pickles.

Jesus Christ.

Thanks, Collin, for the emotional unpacking grenade.
~~~

I lean against the counter, just staring. Then I pick it up and open it slowly. The plastic hinge is barely holding on, worn thin from age and overuse.

And there it is, sitting front and center. Chewed and taped all to hell. Rocco's teeth marks, jagged along the edge of the card. The memory floods in. Me screaming at him. His tiny body trembling under the kitchen chair, ears pinned back, tail still wagging, desperately trying to make it better.

The instant forgiveness he gave me. No hesitation.

I trace the card with my finger. Down the ingredient list, bumping over tape, mending it all together.

Mom's Italian cheesecake. Lemon. Sugar. Vanilla bean. Ricotta.

Ricotta.

My throat begins to burn as the feelings bubble up, hot and heavy. I glance down to see Mr. Pickles glaring up at me with his one good eye from the box.

"Don't side-eye me, you little fuck."

A beat so silent it feels like a vacuum. Then I sigh, sliding my phone from my pocket, staring at a contact I haven't willingly touched in years. I type slowly, half in disbelief that my fingers are actually doing it. That my mind is letting it happen.

Kyle: How have you been?

I press send. I feel… sick. Is this what the first stage of forgiveness is supposed to feel like? Nausea?

Chapter 33

RUNNING ON REGRETS

There's a beat of silence, and I don't think I breathe for a full two minutes while I stare at the blue bubble like it's judging me.

Text sent. No reply.

The room doesn't echo, but it might as well. The quiet stretches long enough to feel like punishment. Punishment for the time I let lapse. For my pride. My anger.

Then, like a damn miracle—or a curse—I see it.

Ritchie. At the gym that day. Sweating through his AC/DC tee, wearing those hideous cutoff jean shorts, that stupid NO REGERTS trucker hat cocked sideways on his head. His comment when he caught me staring. *"It's not a typo. It's a lifestyle."*

The image hits so hard I bark out a laugh.

That's it. That's the mantra.

Fuck it.

I glance down at the empty stretch of my lower forearm. Just begging for a bad idea. I pull out my phone.

Kyle: It's been a minute. Wanna go see Elijah? Some matching ink?

I may wait an eternity for Whit's reply, but Ritchie's will come. Always does.

Ritchie: Sounds therapeutic.

God, I love this idiot. He doesn't ask what. Doesn't ask why.

He just says yes. And that's why he's not just my best friend—he's my chosen brother. And right now I need someone who doesn't flinch.

~~~

Elijah's machine hums like a wasp, steady and precise as it carves ink into Ritchie's shoulder.

Ritchie winces, craning to look, but Elijah's blocking his view. "You still not gonna tell me what it is, huh?"

I shrug, casually flipping through a book of flash tattoos like I don't already know exactly what I'm getting. "Just trust me."

Ritchie raises an eyebrow. "It's not like... matching dicks or anything, is it?"

I smirk. "Why? You scared mine'll be bigger?"

He deadpans. "Just wondering if mine's curving right and yours is going left. Like an anatomical yin and yang."

I snort. "Close. It's a pussy."

Elijah's hand falters just slightly. He chokes on a laugh, pressing a gloved fist to his mouth like he's trying not to lose his shit.

I add, totally straight-faced, "Full-on eighties bush. Poof." I make a little puff-of-magic motion with my hands.

Ritchie barks out a laugh and hisses as Elijah hits a tender spot. "Fuck, man. I should've brought lube," he says, glancing back at Elijah.

Elijah, still smirking, says, "Ink's permanent, not erotic. Sit still. I'm trying to get all these pubes right."

Ritchie rolls his eyes, but he's grinning. Because this is how we do it. This is how we survive the heavy shit. Through banter, needles, and dumbass jokes. In a quiet room with buzzing machines and unspoken grief.

I lean against the counter and cross my arms. "I texted Whit today."

Ritchie snaps his glare up at me. Elijah's head lifts over Ritchie's bare shoulder. I can't see his eyes behind the dark glasses, but I can feel them on me. The machine idles in his hand midair, its buzz dropping to a low hum.
~~~

They shrug in tandem.

"I just asked how he's been."

"…and?" Ritchie asks, too loudly.

"Jesus. Nothing. He still hasn't responded."

Elijah exhales and goes back to tattooing.

Ritchie nods. "Ahh. So that explains why we're at therapy." He makes air quotes with one hand. "Gotcha."

I don't answer. I just stare at the stencil Elijah left on the counter, out of Ritchie's view.

NO REGERTS.

It's a joke. It's a lie. It's matching. And it's about to be mine.

I glance down at my arm, at the blank space still waiting.

Ritchie glances down at his own arm and grins. "Hell yeah. Put it somewhere you'll see it every day. Make it count."

Maybe that's the thing. I already am.

~~~

My phone pings and my heart ticks up like a goddamn bomb.

For a second—just one—I think maybe it's him. That Whit finally decided to acknowledge the fact that I exist.

But it's Grace.

I'm disappointed. Then I'm pissed. Not at her—at him.

Grace: On my way home. I'm stopping to pick up wine. Do we need anything else?

She's cheerful. Warm. Thoughtful. Everything I should be grateful for—and it's pissing me off.

I stare at the screen a second too long, then text her back.

Kyle: No. I'm good.

A lie. Another fucking lie.

I walk to the kitchen and pop her dinner into the microwave to keep it warm. Then I head to the bathroom.

The shower doesn't help. I stay in too long, letting the steam peel something off me I wasn't ready to lose. My skin feels raw. My head feels worse.
~~~

I lift my arm in the mirror and look at what I did. The tattoo is dark, the crisp lines a sharp contrast to the surrounding art faded by time. My arm throbs from the hot water.

NO REGERTS.

What a joke. I don't even know what I'm trying to say anymore. I don't know what I believe.

I wrap a towel around my waist, grab my toothbrush, and try not to think about the fact that she's walking into a kitchen that smells like my Nonna's vodka sauce—and into a man who doesn't know how to let her love him properly.

I stare at myself in the mirror while I brush my teeth.

Say nothing, Kyle. Because what do you say to someone who wants to help when you've only ever known how to carry your own shit?

It's not about her. It's not even about the tattoo. It's just… I don't know how to do this.

It's not looking in the mirror that scares me. It's what happens when she looks past it.

I come out to find her sitting at the bar counter in her chef whites, hair pulled back, hovering over her bowl of pasta.

"Oh my God, babe, this is so good," she moans.

I nod and smile, reaching into the upper cabinet for a wine glass.

"How was work?" I ask, pouring a glass of cabernet and leaning against the counter.

She shrugs, stabbing at the cavatelli. "It was good. Sold out of all my truffles."

She sucks the sauce off her fork slowly. Normally, I'd find that shit seductive—her plump lips wrapping around the glimmering silver, eyes fluttering shut like the sauce just made her come in her panties. But tonight? Nothing. I'm just numb. Wrung out like a soaked rag left in the sun.

"You okay?" she asks, head tilting.

Her voice snaps me out of it.

"Oh. Yeah. I'm fine. Sorry."

"I brought you something that might give you a little pep in your step. Goes well with that wine." She waves her fork at me in tiny circles.

"What?"

"I made an olive oil pavlova. I brought it home for you. It's in the fridge." She gestures casually, not even looking up.

I open the fridge and pull out a clear to-go container.

"Roasted strawberry balsamic compote, basil chantilly, and black pepper honey drizzle. You're welcome."

She smiles and goes back to eating like she didn't just say something that belongs in the Louvre.

"You're too good to me. I don't deserve this," I say flatly.

She looks up from her dinner. "Um, sir? You made me homemade pasta and sauce on your day off. I'm pretty sure you had a hundred other things you wanted to do." She glances at the stack of boxes still sitting next to the island. "Like… unpack those?" She chuckles.

"I started," I mutter, taking a long pull of wine. "Got a little sidetracked."

"Seriously. Something's wrong, and you're not talking to me."

"It's my shit, Grace. Just let me handle it, okay?" I snap before I can stop myself, turning to put the dessert back in the fridge and slamming the door harder than it needs to.

Her voice cuts sharp behind me. "Whoa. What the hell was that?"

"What?" I turn.

"The back of your arm." She squints, pointing. "I've memorized your tattoos. Let me see that, Kyle. That's new."

"It's nothing." I pull away.

Her voice cracks. "Kyle… I wish you'd just talk to me. We're a team."

Her eyes brim with tears.

Team. I don't know why, but it enrages me. I'm disappointing her.

Jesus Christ. What a fucking joke.

I was supposed to have a team once. When she died, it was supposed to be me and him against the world. But Whit bailed, and it's been me versus everything ever since. Teams don't exist. They're a fairytale for people who don't know what it's like to bleed out on the kitchen floor of your own life.

I slam the towel down on the counter. The sound cracks through the apartment like a gunshot.

"You don't get it, Grace!" My voice is sharp, louder than I've ever been with her—and I hate myself for it even as it keeps spilling out.

She steps back, startled, eyes wide.

"You think you want all of me? You don't." My chest heaves. "I'm fucked up. I've been fucked up my whole damn life, and nobody wants that. Not really." I slam my hand on the counter.

She flinches but doesn't move. Just looks at me like I'm worth fighting for, and that somehow makes it worse. Why does she stay? I'm not worth it.

"Kyle…" she whispers. A single tear slips down her cheek.

"I texted him," I snap. "I finally reached out after all these years. And guess what?" My laugh comes out hollow. Mean. "He doesn't give a shit. Just like he didn't give a shit when he left. Just like he didn't give a shit when she died." I pace, dragging a hand through my hair like I could claw the feeling out of my skull.

"So forgive me if I don't feel like playing happy fucking couple tonight, Grace. Forgive me if I don't know how to do this *team* thing you keep talking about." I shake my head. "I've never had a goddamn team."

She steps forward, voice quiet but firm. "Kyle…" She reaches for my arm.

I feel the sting. The tattoo. The stupid mistake. The regret.

"No." I pull my arm away, already retreating, already slamming every window and door inside me shut. "I can't do this with you right now."

The words slice my own throat as I grab my shoes and hoodie.

The scrape of Grace's chair across the floor cuts through me like a shiv to the ribs, but it still doesn't stop me. I slam the apartment door hard enough to rattle the frame and storm into the night.

San Francisco hills eat me alive. Every incline burns, my breath ragged, but I don't stop. I need pain to feel like penance. I need the cold air to bite harder than my thoughts do.

And fuck, I think about Rocco. That big idiot with his gangly legs, yanking me up these same streets like he believed there'd be something better around the corner. He believed in me even when I was a mess. Even when I screamed and scared him. He forgave me instantly. Every time. Tail wagging, no hesitation.

I stop under a streetlight, chest heaving, head tipped back toward the fog-thick sky. I've been running my whole damn life. Why am I still so good at leaving?

"What am I doing?" My voice comes out hoarse and bitter. I know damn well there's nothing out here for me. I have no home but the one I just stormed out of. No team except the one woman who keeps showing up for me. And I left her scared and alone.

By the time I climb the last hill back to the apartment, my legs are jelly. My anger has burned down to something ugly and small. I stand there, sweatshirt damp with fog and sweat, my hand hovering over the doorknob.

I half expect it to be locked. Half expect her to make me beg. Fuck, she should, after the way I treated her. My shit should be piled on this sidewalk.

I knock once. My forehead drops against the door in defeat.

Please forgive me.

My heart free-falls when I swear I hear footsteps. Then… nothing.

The silence stretches, each second chewing a hole through my ribs.

Jesus, what if she doesn't open it? What if I finally did it—burned it all down before I even learned how to build something worth keeping?

I knock again.

Then, finally, the deadbolt clicks. The door creaks open. She's barefoot, her eyes wet but steady. There's no anger, just that quiet strength I don't deserve.

She looks me over once, then meets my eyes. "You done running?"

Jesus Christ. That wrecks me more than anything else tonight. Because I really want to be.

"Baby… I'm—"

"I know," she says, soft but certain, taking my hand and gently pulling me inside.

The door clicks shut behind me, sealing out the fog, the noise, the part of me that thought running would fix anything. Her thumb brushes slow circles over my knuckles. It grounds me, and it feels like taking my first real breath in hours.

We don't speak as we cross the living room. She doesn't demand apologies or explanations. She just leads me to the couch, curls into me like we're something unbreakable, and whispers against my chest, "You don't have to know *how* to stay, Kyle. You just have to *want* to."

God, I do. I want it more than anything. For the first time in my life, wanting might be enough.

I kiss the top of her head, breathing her in like maybe she can glue the pieces of me back together just by being close.

"I tried so hard today, you know?" My voice is low, wrecked. "To be strong. Brave… all that shit. I reached out like you said. Like Wally wanted me to."

She sits up, tucking one leg under her, and looks at me—really looks at me. No judgment, no pity, just steady and patient in a way that makes my throat burn as I try to choke down tears. I take a shaky breath, drag a hand through my hair.

"When he didn't return my text, I thought some good ole brotherhood tat bonding would fix it." I huff out a humorless laugh. "And all it did was sting. Now I've got regrets… but it's misspelled, inked permanently on my body just so I never forget what a dumbass I am to think my father could ever be there for me."

She reaches for my arm then, fingertips brushing over the fresh lines of the tattoo, tender as a prayer.

"Kyle…" she whispers, her eyes shining.

And for the first time all day, I let her see the cracks instead of trying to plaster over them. I kiss her softly, finding solitude on her lips.

Grace takes a slow breath. She looks down at our hands, her fingers threading through mine, grounding me.

"You know why I bake?" she asks, her voice so soft it nearly gets lost in the quiet.

I shake my head.

"Because it was the only thing in my house that didn't hurt." Her eyes stay on mine, unblinking, like she's afraid if she looks away, I'll bolt.

"After the war in Croatia… after my dad came back all twisted and wrong… it was all noise and breaking things and a house that didn't feel safe. But my grandmother's kitchen? That was love and safety. It was warm bread and sugar on my fingers and someone reminding me that even when the world's a mess, you can still make something sweet out of it."

She squeezes my hand tighter, a tear rolling down her cheek, but her voice is steady.

"You think I don't get what it's like to be scared of teams, Kyle? My whole life, I thought love was a grenade waiting to go off. But you…" She pulls in a shaky breath, leans her forehead to mine. "You're my quiet kitchen. My safe place. And I'm not letting you fight this shit alone. Not ever."

And that's it. That's when my chest caves in and all the dry timber finally sparks—not anger this time, but with love, pure and terrifying.

I press my forehead harder against hers, my voice breaking on the truth I've been choking on for years.

"Then don't let go, Grace. Please… don't ever let go."

~~~

We're tangled up in bed, wrapped in the kind of quiet that feels like a blanket of safety stretching between us. Her fingers drift lazily down my arm, over old ink and scars, until they pause on the fresh lines.

"No regerts," she whispers, a tiny smile in her voice as she traces each letter.

The skin still stings under her touch, but it's different now.
~~~

Earlier, it burned like shame. Now… it's something else. Warm, alive. Like maybe it was never about Whit, or pain, or mistakes burned into my skin.

Because lying here with her, I know the truth. I don't have a single fucking regret. Not one.

Chapter 34

ACROSS THE TABLE

I'm balancing my coffee in one hand, climbing out of the car, and reading her text at the same time.

Grace: Good morning, hot stuff. Try not to set the place on fire with your smokin' hot ass. Xo

A slow grin spreads across my face. One of those stupid, can't-wipe-it-off smiles I'd normally mock another guy for having. I pocket my phone, and for a second, the world feels right. Like I was handed something good and didn't immediately screw it up.

God, she's wrecking me. Saving me too. A woman who can handle every jagged part of me, still drags me into bed every damn night, and somehow thinks I'm worth texting like this before breakfast.

I'm in my office most of the morning, running inventory reports, answering emails, and tightening prep sheets ahead of the weekend rush. Through the glass, I watch Noah working with Benjamin, our new hire from Charleston. He staged with us last fall. Sharp, driven, and hungry.

I lean back in my chair and watch their rhythm, remembering how it felt to be that age, that desperate to prove myself at Le Début.

Come on, Noah. Show him. Don't do it for him.

I head out onto the line, tasting as I go. A vindaloo that needs more acid. A ramen broth I tell Reggie needs another hour to deepen. I move quietly, tightening screws, setting the tone.

Noah's off to the side, arms crossed, trying not to laugh when he waves me over.

Benjamin's bent over a Cambro of green papaya soaking in something that smells like a salt lick pretending to be brine.

Noah flicks his eyes at the container.

I dip a spoon, taste, and feel my left eyelid twitch.

"Son," I say slowly, setting the spoon down like it might combust, "that brine could strip paint."

I swipe my tongue across my teeth. "Jesus, kid. You just burned my taste buds."

Benjamin freezes. "Shit, Chef, I—"

"This isn't a Charleston shrimp boil," I cut in. "Let the papaya taste like papaya. Not the bottom of the Gulf."

He hesitates a beat too long. "It's actually the harbor, sir." His shoulders dip as he adds, quieter, "Charleston sits on a harbor."

I deadpan.

He swallows. "Sorry, sir… Chef."

I slide the lime juice and chili jar toward him. "Try again." Then clap his shoulder.

Noah barks out a laugh and earns himself a glare.

Benjamin bites his lip, but the spark's still there. The kind that survives getting your ass handed to you.

He'll make it if he keeps showing up.

"I'll be in my office," I tell Noah.

"We'll be right here," he says. "Turning the *harbor* into som tam."

I'm just starting to feel good again. That text from Grace, the chaos of the kitchen, busting Benjamin's little nineteen-year-old balls—it's almost like last week never happened.

Then my phone buzzes on the desk. I glance at it, expecting Grace again. Something filthy, hopefully. Maybe a hint about dessert later, smeared somewhere nobody gets to see but me.

But it's not her.

Whit: I'm doing well. Thanks for asking.

That's it. Six words. Six goddamn words after years of silence. After a week of me tearing myself apart.

And this? This is what I get?

I'm doing well. Thanks for asking.

A thank-you like we're strangers in a grocery store. Like he's holding a door open out of courtesy instead of holding my entire broken childhood in his hands.

How do I even respond? There isn't even a follow-up question.

A week. It took a fucking week for him to answer me.

I drop the phone on the desk and fold forward, burying my head in my hands.

I hear Grace like she's right here, her hands cradling my face. *I'm not letting you fight this shit alone. Not ever.*

"We are a team. We are a team," I whisper, like a mantra. Like if I say it enough, I might actually believe it.

I pick up the phone again and text her. My fingers shake with anger and frustration.

Kyle: He responded. "I'm doing well. Thanks for asking."

Kyle: Tell me how to react. Please.

My thumb hovers, like there's a right answer hiding in the screen. Like she can translate this garbage into something human.

The phone buzzes in my hand, and it feels like a lifeline tossed into open water.

Grace: Breathe. It's okay. Ask him if he'll be in town anytime soon. Start a conversation. Ask questions, Kyle. I love you.

And just like that, the floor stops tilting. Not because it's fixed. Not because Whit is suddenly worth the pain. But because she still thinks I am.

I start typing.

Kyle: Glad to hear you're well.

I stare at it. It feels weak. Like small talk in line at the DMV.

Not like a son who's been choking on silence for over a decade.

Delete.

> Kyle: Been a long time. Thought maybe you'd want to talk?

My jaw tightens. God, I sound twelve. Waiting for him to show up to a ballgame he never came to.

Delete.

> Kyle: One week? That's how long it took you to get back to me? You know how long it took me to send that text, you motherfucker?

My heart pounds. For a second, it feels good. Right. Like striking a match to all the dry rot in my chest.

But I already know what comes next. Silence. Nothing. That black hole he's always been.

My hands shake as I delete it. Every keystroke a small surrender.

I drop the phone on the desk and lean back in my chair, my eyes burning. Maybe Grace was wrong. Maybe some fights you're meant to fight alone.

The phone sits on the desk like it's taunting me. Every version of the text I didn't send buzzes through my head, static I can't shut off. My fingers dig into my hair, pulling just enough to sting.

"Uh… Chef?"

I snap my head up. Benjamin's in the doorway, holding a pan against his chest like he's about to offer a sacrifice with Noah smirking behind him. His apron's smeared with chili paste. The wide-eyed look tells me he saw more than I wanted him to.

"What?" My tone comes out sharper than I mean.

He flinches. "Sorry, sir… it's just… Noah said you should taste this before we move forward. Said it's uh… a teachable moment?"

I drag a hand down my face and stand. The chef mask slides into place—the one that keeps all the shit locked down where no one can touch it.

"Alright, rookie," I mutter, grabbing the spoon from his hand. "Let's see what crime you've committed."

He half-smiles, nervous. It's the first human thing I've felt in ten minutes. It's not healing, just a distraction. And right now, that's enough.

I dip the spoon and brace myself. One taste and my face puckers like I licked a nine-volt battery.

I cough once and glare at him. "What in the unholy hell is this?"

"Green curry?" he says, sheepish. "Noah had me test one for staff meal."

"No, son. This is a war crime." I shove the container toward Noah, already doubled over laughing. "This is cilantro's evil twin choking on a lime wedge. What'd you do?"

Benjamin shrugs. "I thought it needed more brightness."

"This isn't bright. This is staring directly into the sun and losing your retinas."

Noah wheezes. "It's… aggressive, Chef."

I rub my temples. "Rule one—if your food could strip varnish off a church pew, you've gone too far." I slide the coconut milk and fish sauce over. "Try again. And taste before you send my kitchen into the afterlife."

Benjamin nods hard, cheeks red, but the spark's still there. He dumps the nuclear curry and starts over while Noah leans on the prep table, grinning.

"That wasn't curry," Noah adds. "That was trauma in a pan."

Benjamin groans. "Jesus, man."

I choke out a laugh despite myself. Noah notices and piles on.

"Chef, new menu item? *Benjamin's Bowel-Cleansing Curry*. Complimentary therapy included."

"Y'all are brutal," Benjamin mutters.

Finally, I let my grin slip. "Welcome to the team, Harbor Boy. Sink or swim."

I turn to Noah. "Teach him. No more hazing—and no more fucking with my food costs."

"Yes, Chef."

I'm still grinning when I get back to my office. It hurts my face. The banter, the noise, the normal—it's the first real laugh I've had all week.

I set my legal pad down, reach for my cold coffee—and my phone lights up.

There it is.

For a second my heart stutters. I'd forgotten. Forgotten that ten minutes ago I was ready to torch whatever this is with Whit.

Whit: I'm sorry it took me so long to respond. I honestly didn't know what to say. Can we please get together and talk?

My throat tightens, a burn crawling up fast. Six words last time. Now this. Still not much—but somehow everything.

It's not an apology that fixes years of silence. But it's a start.

I stare at *I'm sorry.* I've never heard those words from him. Not once. I know it doesn't undo anything. But it cracks something open. Like a window in the room I've been suffocating in for years.

I wait for the other shoe. Silence. A take-back.

My hands shake so badly I set the phone down and breathe. Grace's voice cuts through. *Ask questions, Kyle. I love you.* For once, I don't overthink it. I pick the phone back up.

Kyle: Yeah. Name a time and place.

Whit: Sunday? Brunch?

Brunch. Like we're normal. Like twenty years didn't happen.

My chest feels too small for everything in it—rage, hope, grief, love that never got a chance to be anything but painful.

Grace again. *We're a team.*

For the first time since I hit send, I don't feel like that scared kid anymore. I'm still shaking—but my hands aren't empty.

Kyle: Sounds good. I'll pick a place. Do you mind if I bring someone?

The dots move. My heart matches their rhythm. I picture Grace beside me, her hand in mine, where fists used to clench.

Whit: There's someone? I can't wait to meet them, son.

Son.

I let it slide. Because this time, I'm not walking in alone.

I've got Grace. I've got a teammate. And I think that's enough to face whatever comes next.

~~~

We're parked outside the restaurant, Grace's hand on my knee, her thumb tracing slow circles like she knows I'm one breath away from restarting the car and peeling out of the parking lot.

My phone buzzes. Of course, it's Ritchie. He must've seen the Bat signal.

Ritchie: I need the pics. Don't let me down, dude.

I smirk, a quiet huff of a laugh slipping out before I type.

Kyle: I'm not snapping pictures of how much plastic surgery they've had mid-apps.

Ritchie: Okay. During the drink order then. I don't care. Fuck. I'll just come up there and see for myself.

Kyle: I'll cut you if you show up.

Ritchie: Worth it.

I snort, shaking my head, my thumb hovering before I type.

Kyle: You're ridiculous.

Ritchie: And yet you love me. Hey... no regerts!

I laugh, shut the conversation down, and glance over to see Grace arching a brow from the passenger seat.

"Can we go in now?" she asks. "You done playing with Ritchie?"

I shrug, pocketing my phone. "Never."

My grin fades as I stare at the grand entrance of the restaurant. Laughing with Ritchie is easy. Facing Whit? That's a whole different battlefield.

The second we step inside, the smell of garlic hits me, and my stomach twists. It knows this isn't about food. Grace's hand stays
~~~

laced with mine—a lifeline I didn't realize I needed this badly—keeping me from splintering apart before we even reach the table.

My feet feel heavy. Concrete-heavy, as we follow the hostess toward a corner booth.

Whit is older. Grayer. Still carrying himself like the world owes him reverence. Like he's still the man who could tell me to wait on the porch, disappear for hours, and know I'd still be standing there when he finally decided to show back up.

And beside him is Caroline.

Hell.

I should pull my phone out for Ritchie now and get his money shot over with. Except knowing Caroline, she'd tilt her chin, puff those injected lips, and pose like a washed-up centerfold angling for a desperate comeback spread in *Vanity Fail.* She'd eat it up like caviar and compliments.

She's got that same high-gloss Barbie sheen I remember—only turned up a few thousand watts. Fresh highlights. Skin stretched and sculpted into something that doesn't belong to a woman in her late-forties. Glittering nails wrapped around her wine glass like she's starring in her own perfume ad. Eight years older than me. Married to my father longer than I can stand to think about.

Whit stands, smiling like this is just Sunday brunch.

"Kyle," he says, voice warm and practiced, like there's nothing fractured between us. "Glad you made it."

Caroline's lips curve into a perfect, fake, too-white smile. "Kyle," she purrs, giving me that once-over like I'm still eighteen, still the kid she married into like a bad inheritance. "And this must be Grace, right?"

Grace's hand tightens around mine—just enough to keep me grounded, to keep me from spitting out everything burning at the back of my throat.

"Yeah," I manage, my voice rough. "Grace, this is… Caroline." Then, "And this is Whit."

I don't choke on the word *father*, but damn if it wouldn't taste sour coming out.

Caroline laughs—tinkly and fake, like champagne poured over broken glass.

"Well, it's nice to meet you, Grace." Her eyes cut back to me, sharp beneath the smile. "It's been a while, Kyle. So nice to get together as a family again."

My jaw locks hard enough to crack a tooth. *Family?* Sure. That's what we're calling this now.

Grace slides into the booth beside me, her hand a soft anchor at my back. She murmurs low, just for me, "Breathe, babe. I've got you."

And for the first time since I walked in, I actually do. I breathe.

Whit clears his throat, unfolding his napkin with all the ceremony of a man about to knight someone. "So," he says, as if we're catching up over a casual beer instead of years of silence, "how's work? Still… cooking?"

Cooking. Like I'm running a neighborhood bake sale.

"Yeah," I say, jaw working once. "Still cooking. Executive Chef at Sagi now."

What I want to say is, *I'm not just cooking anymore, Whit. I built something worth bleeding for. I'm about to buy in. I'm pulling real weight.*

But the words lodge in my throat. Because if I say them, he'll just nod like he taught me everything I know. Like my whole life has been a warm-up act for his approval. So, I swallow it down with my water and let the silence stretch.

Whit nods politely, like he's skimming a résumé he doesn't quite believe. "That's… good. You always had talent." He says it the way you'd say a dog always had a nice bark.

Before I can answer, Caroline leans toward Grace, voice honeyed and lethal. "Oh, that Asian fusion place?" She gestures vaguely in my direction with glittering nails. "Kyle was always… creative. Never much for stability, though. Bless his heart."

Grace's hand tightens on my thigh under the table. A warning—or maybe a lifeline—because the heat climbs my neck fast enough to blister paint.

I keep my voice even as I lift my water glass. "Yeah, well, turns out you don't need *stability* to build a Fortune 500 company."

I take a slow drink, meet Caroline's gaze over the rim, and let a razor of a smile edge in. "Right, Whit?"

Whit clears his throat again, eyes flicking between us. This isn't going the way he pictured.

Grace squeezes my thigh once more, subtle, and whispers, "Easy, babe." She knows I'm two heartbeats from flipping the table.

"So," Whit says quickly, "how long have you two been seeing each other?"

Grace smiles and looks at me. "Five months?"

"Yeah," I say. "We moved in together."

Caroline props her chin on her palm. "Making it official, I hope?"

Does she ever stop? *Jesus.*

"It's been five months. I just basically learned how she likes her coffee." I narrow my eyes.

Grace giggles softly, running her thumb over my knuckles like she knows I'm seconds from saying something that'll turn this brunch into a headline. "Don't let him fool you," she says sweetly, looking straight at Caroline. "He's got my coffee order memorized down to the last sugar crystal. And he brings it to me in bed every morning."

Caroline's perfect brows twitch—just enough to let me know I scored a point.

I can't stop the smug grin tugging at my mouth. "See? That's commitment right there. Real official."

Whit chuckles like this is a warm family moment, but my teeth grind hard enough to spark. Grace keeps her hand on mine, and just like that, I decide I can make it through this meal without flipping anything over… yet.

We're on autopilot—polite words, fake laughs, a minefield I've learned to cross without blowing my own legs off. Grace's hand stays on my thigh the whole time, the thin thread keeping me from unraveling completely.

Outside, the sunlight feels different. Lighter. Like I'm finally standing on my own two feet.

I lace my fingers with hers and take a breath that doesn't hurt.

"Well," Whit says, almost hesitant, "this was nice. Maybe we can do it again sometime?"

For the first time, I see it—worry. A look that doesn't belong on his face.

I nod slowly. "Yeah." I exhale. "Yeah… I'd like that."

I take his outstretched hand. Not forgiveness. But a truce.

In the car, the doors shut and my body hums—every nerve buzzing to a frequency I've never known.

"I'm proud of you," Grace whispers, breaking the static.

I turn to her, cradling her face in my hand. "Now I know what it means to be a team." My thumb traces her cheekbone. "God, I love you. You are my Grace."

She presses her forehead to mine. "No, Kyle. You're mine."

I let out a shaky laugh. "Screw it. Maybe she's right. Maybe we should make it official."

Grace leans back, brows knitting. "What?"

My hands find hers, restless. "Marry me, Grace. I love you, and I don't want to waste another second not being yours." My mouth quirks. "First time I said that, I was holding your thong fresh out of the dryer. Guess I don't need props this time."

She laughs through the tears filling her eyes, and my heart feels too big for my chest.

"I know it's not candles and champagne," I murmur, kissing her knuckles, "but it's me. And it's forever—if you'll have me."

She shakes her head, smiling like I'm unhinged. "Kyle Berkley… only you could turn a half-ass car proposal into the second-most romantic thing you've ever said to me."

I grin. "Second-most?"

She smirks. "Nothing tops that laundry-day confession."

"So?" I ask softly.

She tilts her head, thumbs brushing my jaw, voice trembling and laughing all at once. "I will most definitely marry you."

I'm across the console before the tear even falls, kissing her like I'm sealing a deal I never thought I'd get.

She laughs into my mouth, pushing at my chest. "Babe—babe."

"Yeah?" I murmur, chasing her lips.

She cups my face, breathless, wicked grin firmly in place. "You're gonna have to pretend this didn't happen and ask my dad for permission first." She laughs, dark and delighted. "You think Whit's a tyrant? Wait until you meet Ivan Novak."

Chapter 35

JOY COMES IN THE MORNING

Morning light spills across the sheets, turning her skin to gold, like honey. My hand is already under the covers, tracing over her ass and down her thigh, then back up, slow enough to make her whimper into the pillow.

"Kyle," she breathes, voice raspy from sleep and last night's kisses, "coffee first…"

"Nope," I growl against her neck, hips pressing forward. "You taste better than coffee." I breathe her in—sleep-warm skin, clean sheets, and the faint, addictive proof that I'm still everywhere.

She twists under me, laughing low, breath hitching when my teeth scrape her shoulder. Her hands reach back, clutching my hair, pulling me closer like she's already forgotten what she asked for.

"Babe…"

"Yeah?" My lips drag along her jaw, my grin filthy.

"You keep doing that," she gasps, arching against me, "and you're never making it to work."

"Perfect," I murmur, flipping her onto her back, already lost in the sound she makes when I slide between her thighs.

"Damn, look who's ready," she teases, wrapping her hand around my hard cock, stroking me slowly.

My eyes close, head dropping to her chest. "Fuck, your hand feels good," I whisper.

"You know what would feel better?"

"Hmmm?"

"My mouth."

My breath punches out, rough and shaky, her lips curving wickedly under mine.

"Grace…" I groan, already half gone, already imagining her mouth wrapped around me.

She pushes at my chest until I'm flat on my back, crawling over me, hair a mess, eyes dark and locked on mine. My hips jerk up like I've got no control left.

"Work's overrated," she whispers, kissing her way down my stomach, teeth nipping lightly. "But this?" Her hand wraps around me again, slow and perfect. "This is mandatory."

Whatever sound tears from my throat as her hot, wet lips swirl over the head of my throbbing dick could wake the neighbors, but she doesn't stop. Doesn't give me a second to think.

And I don't care if I'm late. Don't care if the whole damn world burns outside this apartment, as long as I keep this. Keep her. Right here.

~~~

I'm leaning against the counter, crisp uniform on, waiting for the coffee to finish brewing. The apartment still smells like Grace—organic shampoo, sex, and everything good I spent half my life convincing myself I didn't deserve. But now? Now I'm starting to wonder if I was wrong about that.

My phone pings. New message.

Whit: I had a nice time yesterday. We really like Grace. She's a beautiful person.

I stare at it for a second, thumb hovering like I don't know how to do this father-son thing without someone bleeding at the end of it. Then I type before I can think myself out of it.

Kyle: Yeah… she's incredible.

Damn, I want to tell him I proposed. But part of me feels like
~~~

he'll suck the joy right off the bone. My fingers hover again. Once again, I just do it.

Kyle: I asked her to marry me.

The dots appear, disappear, then reappear before his reply comes through.

Whit: You did good, son. I'm happy for you.

Whit: Did you give her a ring?

I swallow hard.

Jesus.

My dad just said *I did good*? The world might actually tilt off its axis today. But of course, my mind shifts to him probably wondering if what I gave her was good enough. Big enough.

Kyle: Not yet. We're going to shop for one together.

Whit: I've been holding on to your mother's ring for you. If you want it. I know how much you loved her, Kyle.

For a second, I just stare at the screen. My throat's tight, my vision doing this stupid blur thing I can't blink away.

This is it. The part in every Hallmark movie where the soundtrack swells, the estranged dad stands at the end of the drive, and the broken son gets handed back a piece of the love he lost years ago. Except it's not some actor in a fake snowstorm on TV.

It's me.

Me, standing in my kitchen. Fresh coffee brewed. The smell of shampoo still clinging to my damp hair. Morning sex still humming in my veins. And my dad just handed me my mom's love through a damn text message.

That's when I feel something shift. It's nothing seismic. No earth cracking open beneath my feet like I half expected. Just a quiet weight lifting off my chest. A calm settling into my bones I didn't know I'd been missing.

For the first time, I honestly think I can stop fighting every good thing that tries to stay.

Maybe I believe I deserve this. All of it.

Grace bounces into the kitchen, hair up, grinning like she's got a secret and a day off to burn.

"How am I supposed to keep our little secret a secret?" She holds up her bare hand, wiggling her fingers with a laugh. "Guess it's pretty easy when you haven't put a ring on it yet."

I'm still staring at my phone, lost in the weight of what just happened, until her hand waves in front of my face.

"Babe? You okay?" she sings. "Hellooo… is anybody in there?"

And just like that, I remember where I am. Who I'm with. And why the hell I said yes to forever.

"I'm sorry." I lean in for a kiss, trying to focus on her instead of the swirl in my head. "Just distracted." I shake it off and hold up my phone. "It was Whit. He texted to say he had a nice time yesterday." I lift a brow, tip my head. "He really likes you."

She bobs her head, smug as hell. "I mean… what's not to like?"

She turns in her tight little black leggings, pouring coffee into her travel mug completely oblivious that she's killing me.

"Yeah, don't wear that around my father," I murmur against the shell of her ear, caging her in against the counter. "He likes them young, you know."

"Oh, I only want one Berkley," she purrs, pressing her perfect ass back into me. "And this one has his dick hard against me right now."

"God," I groan, hands braced on either side of her hips, "you're making it very hard for me to go to work."

She wiggles against me deliberately. "Oh yeah?" she teases, biting the tip of her finger, tongue darting out just enough to make my blood boil.

I grab her wrist, slide it down to where I'm already painfully hard. "Yeah," I rasp, half a plea.

She pulls her hand away, cruel and grinning, then spins to face me. "I hope you have a great day at work." She kisses me quick and wicked. "I gotta go. The girls are waiting on me."

She slips past me, tossing her bag over her shoulder, coffee in hand. She looks back with that devil's smile, pointing blatantly at the problem straining in my chef pants.

"See you tonight," she calls, eyes glinting as she twirls a finger once, slow and smug. "I'll take care of *that* then."

~~~

I'm at work, and I'm… smiling.

Not the usual polite, *yeah, life's fine* kind of smile. No. This is a *holy-hell, did he just win the lottery or get laid this morning* kind of grin. The kind that makes people stare like they're trying to solve a mystery.

"You okay, Chef?" Reggie asks, scanning the line. The flames are mesmerizing, and I'm caught somewhere deep in my head.

"Oh… yeah. I'm cool, man. I'm… cool. You?" I stammer.

He laughs, covering his mouth with his fist. "What?"

Darius stops mid-call and just stares at me, grinning so big I swear his face is gonna crack, teeth gleaming through the pass.

"What?" I splay my hands, an uncontrollable grin stretching across my face.

Good God, I don't know if I've ever felt this kind of joy. Sure, I've had happiness. Infatuation. Working beside Cassie all those years. But that was a big fucking secret I jammed down deep like a curse, nothing that breathed life into me.

I had Rocco. That big goof brought me laughs and companionship like no other, sure. But he never gave me *this*. This soul-melting, I-can't-breathe-without-you kind of joy. And he damn sure didn't suck my dick like Grace did this morning. I swear to God, I entered the pearly gates and shook hands with my ancestors at 6:30 a.m. sharp.

Darius snorts, shaking his head. "Chef lookin' like he just saw Jesus… and He was handing out hot cinnamon rolls."

The whole line busts up, and I just keep grinning like an idiot, because hell… they're not wrong.

I'm halfway down the line, pretending I'm not still catching stray looks from Darius and Reggie when Noah strolls in from prep,
~~~

clipboard tucked under one arm. He slows, clocks the stupid smiles plastered across their faces, then looks at me.

"What'd I miss?" he asks, way too casual to be innocent.

Darius can barely breathe, laughing so hard. "Chef over there lookin' like he saw the light of the Lord Himself."

Noah blinks once, glances at me, then smirks like the devil incarnate. "Ohhh," he drawls. "So *that's* what afterglow looks like on a chef who usually smells like garlic and rage."

He snorts so loud it echoes off the hood vent.

"Jesus," I mutter, rubbing a hand over my face, already knowing I'm doomed.

But Noah's not done. "Don't worry, boys," he says, flipping a page on his clipboard. "HR says if Chef keeps smiling like that, we're all entitled to ask for the Grace Package at the next benefits renewal."

The entire line loses it. Darius bends over the pass, wheezing. Reggie drops his tongs, tears streaming down his face. I just stand there, grinning like a man who is absolutely not winning this war.

Which is funny, considering I am HR.

"Yeah, laugh it up," I say, backing toward my office, pointing a warning finger at Darius. "I know where you keep your knives, Soup Head."

"Yeah, yeah," Darius fires back, still grinning. "Just make sure you bring her around again, huh? Place could use more good juju."

As I pass prep, Benjamin looks up from what can only be described as a mushroom massacre, a mountain of shiitakes spilling across his board.

"You doin' alright, Harbor Boy?" I nod at him.

He chuckles, pointing his knife toward the line. "Hey, Chef... how'd Darius get the nickname Soup Head?"

I glance at Darius, then back at Ben, my grin spreading slow. "You've seen the size of his head? Thing's the size of a stock pot."

Benjamin snorts, nearly dropping his knife, and I keep walking, still grinning like a damn fool all the way to my office.

I shut the door behind me, lean against it for a beat, and just... breathe. The smile won't leave my face, but now it's tangled up with nerves twisting in my gut.

My phone weighs a ton in my palm, screen lit, waiting on me to screw this up. That last message from him—his offer of Mom's ring—still sits there unanswered. Texting would be easy. Safe. But this feels too personal, too big for a bubble of words on a screen. And safe never got me anywhere good with Whit.

So, for once in my life, I take a breath, take a chance… and hit call.

He answers on the third ring, gruff but not unfriendly. "Kyle."

"Hey." I clear my throat, my voice suddenly too big for my tiny office. "Uh… got a minute?"

"Sure. Everything alright?"

"Yeah. Yeah, it's…" I drag a hand over my face. Jesus. I can lead a kitchen brigade blindfolded, but this? "It's Grace."

There's a pause. A small chuckle, like he already knows where this is going.

"She okay?"

"Yeah. She is. It's… about what you asked me this morning. The ring. I thought about it."

Whit doesn't speak for a second, and I can feel the weight of his breath on the other end of the line.

"Well," he says finally, voice softer than I expect, "I think your mom would like her, Kyle. If that helps."

That lands harder than it should, but in a good way. I let out a laugh, low and shaky.

"Yeah. Uh… I think so too." My throat tightens. "She actually reminds me of her. What I remember, at least." My voice cracks.

"I can see that."

A beat.

"You want it?" he asks.

My chest aches just hearing that. "Yeah. I… I'd like that. I think Grace would, too."

There's a stretch of silence where I imagine him staring at the ring. Remembering her wearing it. Remembering he once had a good thing, too.

Finally, he says, rough and real, "This is a good thing, Kyle. I'll bring it to you tomorrow."

I swallow hard, nodding even though he can't see me.

"Thanks, Whit." My voice cracks on the last word, but I don't care.

"Proud of you, son," he says, quietly.

Then the line clicks dead, leaving me alone in my office, phone pressed to my ear, heart pounding. My mom's love passed down in a promise I never thought I'd make. And a civil conversation with my father I never thought was possible.

~~~

It's less than twenty-four hours later, but Whit's standing there, hands shoved deep in his jacket pockets, looking about as awkward as I feel in the parking lot of some random coffee shop.

"Hey," I say, my voice rough.

"Hey." He clears his throat, tips his chin toward the café. "You wanna go in?"

I glance at my watch like I've got a million better things to do. "Yeah… I've got a minute before work."

Like this isn't one of the biggest moments of my life. The transfer of my mother's ring. A legacy of love from a man who's actually trying to rebuild what we lost. And I'm out here treating it like a sketchy Craigslist deal—half expecting him to pop the trunk and ask if I brought cash.

We sit across from each other, steaming coffee clutched in our hands like security blankets. In the awkward silence, he pulls something from his jacket pocket. A small black velvet box, worn soft around the edges like it's been handled a thousand times.

"Here," he says. "Before either of us overthinks it."

I take it, my fingers shaking as I reach for it. For a second, I swear I see her hands instead of mine—the way she held a wine glass, or threaded her fingers through my hair during bedtime rituals when I was a kid. My chest burns, almost trembles at the sight of it.

When I look up, Whit's watching me, eyes brighter than I expect.

"She'd be proud of you, Kyle." His lips pull inward, catching on a quiet quiver. "You've done well, son."
~~~

I can only nod as I open the box.

There it is—simple, classic. A round diamond set low in a worn platinum band. The kind of ring that doesn't scream for attention, but carries decades of love in every scratch and shine. It looks like something that's weathered anniversaries, storms, makeups, and make-believes. Something real.

My thumb brushes the cool metal once before I snap the lid shut, holding it like it might vanish if I don't.

"Thanks, Whit. Really."

He gives me one of those curt nods that passes for a hug between us, mutters something about traffic, about needing to get on the road. Then he taps the table twice and walks out.

I stay there for a long minute, alone, holding that tiny velvet box like it's the most important thing I've ever been trusted with. Other than Grace's heart.

Chapter 36

EARNED

My leg is bouncing under the sticky bar top like it's trying to launch itself to freedom. I'm waiting, nursing a beer, when Ritchie slams down onto the stool beside me as if he's auditioning for WWE and snarls, "I'm quitting. I hate it there."

I barely glance up. "Morning, sunshine."

"Don't." He jabs a finger at me like I personally caused his trauma. "Don't *morning sunshine* me. I'm underpaid, overworked, and about two seconds from quitting food entirely and opening a vape shop."

I chuckle. "*Hi, Kyle.*"

He shoots me a fake one-second smile before turning to the bartender. "Can I get an IPA? Draft. Anything. Thanks." Then he turns back to me, flat. "Hi, Kyle."

I grin over my beer. "What now?"

"I've got more experience and more years than all those stupid fucks," he gripes. "Cheap bastards." He shakes his head, takes the beer from the bartender. "Thanks."

"Just come work for me, fucker," I say, throwing up a hand.

"Nope. You don't fuck where you eat."

I squint at him, half questioning life choices, half questioning English. "Pretty sure it's *shit* where you eat."

"That too," he sighs, already halfway through his beer.

Before I can argue further, the door swings open and in glides Collin, radiating sunshine and smelling like some exotic redwood forest. He claps his hands to announce himself before sliding onto the stool next to me.

I'm suddenly flanked by what feels like something out of one of Grace's romance novels. Grumpy meets Sunshine bullshit.

"What's up, my bitches?"

"Wrong bar for that energy," I mutter.

"Every bar needs my energy, Kyle," he says, smirking.

He leans against the counter and tells the bartender, dead serious, "I'll have a glass of your best Pinot. Something with an oaky finish."

The bartender just stares. No blink. No soul. Finally, in a deep gravelly tone, "You're at Lizzy's, Collin."

"Fine," he grumbles. "Stella?"

He gets a single upward nod in response.

Collin spins toward us like this place is the Four Seasons. "So. What is the reason for the mandatory meeting?"

I take an exaggerated, long pull of my beer.

Ritchie slumps lower on his stool. "Oh, please… the suspense is killing me. Spit it out, Berkley."

"Shit! You have ass cancer," Collin blurts before I can speak, slapping a hand on my shoulder like a grief counselor in training. "It's okay, man. You can come live with me and Vick. We'll start a GoFundMe. Maybe make matching T-shirts?"

I just stare at him. "What the hell is wrong with you people?"

I smooth Collin's blazer collar without missing a beat. "No cancer." I shake my head. "Sorry. No arts-and-crafts night making shirts, man."

I lean back in my chair, dragging out the silence just long enough to make them sweat.

"I'm getting married."

Ritchie blinks. Collin gasps like I just announced free Beyoncé tickets. The bartender finally stops wiping the counter, sensing incoming chaos.

"BULLSHIT!" Ritchie slaps the bar so hard my beer rattles. "You? Mr. *Commitment Is a Scam*? Mr. *I'm Married to the Grind*? The hell did I miss?"

Collin's already fanning himself with a cardboard bar coaster like he's about to faint.

"Married? Married? To who? Grace? Where and when?" He starts chugging his beer like it's the next best thing to breathing into a paper bag. "You better not have proposed in a Taco Bell parking lot, Kyle. I have standards for you."

Ritchie jabs a finger at me. "She got you on a dare, didn't she? Like, *bet you can't tame this emotionally constipated fry cook*."

"Chef," I correct, pointing my bottle at him.

"Whatever, Gordon Ramsay-lite."

Collin's eyes go wide, deadly serious. "Oh my God. She's pregnant." He throws his hands up, proud as hell like he just solved the *Dateline* mystery in the first five minutes. "This is even better. We need a baby up in this bitch."

He's already halfway to texting someone, pounding away at his phone.

"Don't worry, guys, I'll handle the registry." He looks up, vibrating with excitement. "Ritchie, you're godfather. I'm getting us matching satin bomber jackets that say *God Squad*."

Ritchie perks up. "Oh hell yeah. Can mine say *Uncle Dick*? But I want leather. Satin is for pussies." He snorts. "I've been waiting my entire life to use that name." He nudges me, points at my wrist. "Duuude. I can get your baby's name tatted like you did with Cora's."

The bartender pours himself a shot, knocks it back, and mutters, "I don't get paid enough for this shit."

Ritchie's head falls back in relief. "Oh fuck, dude. You're gonna be a dad? You were so good with Rocco. I always—"

"Stop!" I laugh, barely able to breathe. "Nobody's pregnant. Nobody's dying. Nobody's wearing satin." I hold up a hand. "I just... love her."

There's a collective record scratch.

"...It's just fast," Ritchie says finally. "We just thought it was crazy she broke through your—" he gestures at me, "tough exterior so quick."

"Your hard candy outer shell," Collin adds.

Ritchie snorts. "Did you melt in her—"

"Enough," I protest, holding a hand up.

Collin's already swiping his phone again, "Pinterest board. We're saving this train wreck before it leaves the station. Where are we doing this deed?"

I sigh. "I don't know. I still have to ask her dad." I slide my empty bottle forward. "Supposedly, Ivan Novak is nothing compared to ol' Whit Berkley."

"Oh… fuck," Ritchie mutters.

Collin claps a hand on my shoulder, suddenly all business. "We got you." He nods fast, fired up like he's about to lead a SEAL Team rescue mission. "Nothing derails your happiness this time. This is your Golden Globe moment, man. Let's go get your girl."

"Good God, Collin," Ritchie mutters. "Do you have to be so dramatic?"

I snort. Understatement of the damn century.

"Is he like… a dick?" Ritchie asks. "We put on a little brotherly pressure? Take him out at the knees?" He says this low and gruff, like he's auditioning for a mob movie.

"Oh damn, maybe chill with the *Sopranos* reruns." I glare at him, but there's no heat in it. "We're not gonna pop a cap in Grace's dad's ass. He's just… Croatian. Ex-military. Kinda rough around the edges. Very protective of his only daughter." I laugh, shrugging. "But hey, according to Grace, the guy's got a killer accent, and we'll probably like him."

~~~

I'm standing on the Novak porch with a bottle of red wine in my hand, my palm slick with nerves, finally understanding stage fright.

Grace reaches for the door handle, squeezes my other hand once, and says quietly, "Just… let him talk first, okay?" Then she gives me a grin that doesn't quite hide the worry in her eyes and pulls me inside.

The house smells like roasted lamb, garlic, and something baked and buttery. Voices drift from the dining room—Croatian, fast and warm—but one voice cuts sharper than the rest, gravel and command wrapped together.

Ivan Novak.
~~~

Grace's grandmother appears first. Tiny, but fierce in her apron, she kisses Grace's cheeks like she's been gone a month instead of two days. She smiles up at me, pats my cheek, says something in Croatian I only halfway catch.

I nod like a fool. "Yes, ma'am," because that seems safe.

She laughs, big and warm, a sound that doesn't match her small frame, and waves me forward. "Come, come. We feed nerves here."

That's when I see the photograph.

A framed picture on the sideboard of a woman with Grace's same eyes, her arm wrapped around a younger Grace in a summer dress. A candle burns in front of it, soft and steady, like she's still part of dinner every Sunday.

My chest tightens. I don't even know this woman, but I know what losing her did to this family. It's in the way Grace's grandfather glances at the photo before bowing his head to greet me. It's in the way Grace squeezes my hand a little tighter as we walk past.

"She was amazing," Grace whispers through a smile.

Then Ivan steps into view.

He's broad. Taller than me. Older than I imagined. Hair cut close, steel-gray. He isn't smiling. His eyes flick to Grace, soften for half a second, then land on me like a scope locking in.

He wipes his hands on a dish towel, then extends his hand to me.

I take it with a smile.

Mistake.

He crushes my fingers like he's testing bone density. My knuckles scream mercy, and I'm one second from blurting my PIN number and the names of my childhood pets.

"Sir," I manage, teeth clenched.

"Hmm," Ivan says. Just that. Like a threat. Or a sentence. Or maybe just a note filed away in a mental cabinet labeled *Potential Dumbass Who Thinks He Can Have My Daughter.*

Grace grabs my belt loop like she's trying to save me from myself as I wheeze out, "Nice grip."

Ivan narrows his eyes, releases my hand, takes his seat at the table, and starts ladling soup like he didn't just try to end my cooking career by shattering my dominant hand.

I glance back at the photo, the candle throwing soft light over Grace's mom's smile, and it hits me. This is a family that loves like it's the only thing keeping them alive. And when they lose, it damn near kills them.

No wonder Grace scares the hell out of me.

She's crawled into every dark corner I didn't think could feel again, lit it up, made it hers. If I ever lost her, I don't think there'd be anything left of me to put back together.

The kitchen is a riot of warmth and noise. Grace's grandmother is a tiny storm, bustling between oven and counter, a dish towel slung over one shoulder like a badge of honor. The smell of roasted meat and garlicky potatoes is thick, chased by the sweet scent of buttery dough.

Before I can sit, she presses a tray of still-warm cookies into my hands like a weapon of mass hospitality.

"Kiflice," she says with a proud smile, tapping the powdered sugar dusting with her finger.

"Oh, *hvala*," I say, grinning like I know what the hell I'm doing.

Grace leans in, lips brushing my ear. "I hope you wore stretchy pants."

Ivan glares at me as he bites into a cookie, eyes dark as night. I swear they were blue when I got here. Hell, maybe green. Doesn't matter. They're black holes now, and I'm circling the drain with nothing but a tray of powdered sugar cookies between us as a shield.

Grace's grandmother glances over, catches my deer-in-headlights look, and mutters something sharp and melodic in Croatian, wagging a spoon in Ivan's direction.

Grace translates with a grin. "She says you can't yell at Kyle until you eat. It's tradition."

Ivan grunts like this is a grave injustice. "Fine. We eat first."

His eyes stay on me.

Grace's grandfather shuffles in from the other room, slippers scuffing the tile, carrying a bottle of what I assume is homemade rakija. He gives me a slow, squinty once-over, shrugs, and sets the bottle down with a thunk.

"He looks nervous," he announces in Croatian.

Grace translates, fighting a laugh. "English, please."

"Good," Ivan rumbles. "Means he knows what's at stake."

"Tata, please," Grace pleads softly to her dad.

Grandpa snorts, already pouring himself a shot. "What's at stake is the lamb, Ivan. Stop acting like you're the general again." He waves a dismissive hand and pops a cookie into his mouth. Powdered sugar explodes down his sweater vest like a crime scene. He glances down, shrugs, and keeps eating.

Grace's grandmother swats him with a dish towel, reclaiming the tray of cookies as she mutters a string of Croatian that has Grace snickering into her sleeve.

"She says," Grace whispers, "that you're the only one behaving, Kyle. And you've only been here three minutes."

I glance at Ivan, still glaring like he's already decided my fate, and mutter, "Guess I'm the favorite already."

Grace squeezes my knee under the table.

As we sit there, surrounded by people who've lost so much but still gather every week to eat, fight, and laugh, I start to understand how Grace loves. It's in her blood. Kneaded into every loaf of bread, every truffle she makes, every cookie baked in this house. A love that refuses to break, even when life does.

"Tata," Grace says sweetly, after Ivan has scowled through most of dinner like a man personally wronged by my existence. "Why don't you show Kyle your fruit trees?"

Ivan grunts. Doesn't look at me. Just stands, slow and deliberate, like a bear deciding whether to maul me or nap.

"Come, Kyle," he says finally, that accent making even *come* sound like a death sentence.

Grace kicks me under the table. "Go."

I gulp the last of my wine for courage and stand. Ivan's already at the sideboard, grabbing a tall, battered bottle of something that looks like it could clean a carburetor.

"Rakija," he says, handing it to me.

"Ah," I force a smile. "Liquid courage."

He does not laugh.

We step into the cool night air, backyard lit by string lights and moonlight. Rows of fruit trees line the fence, old and twisted, heavy with plums and figs. Ivan walks slowly, boots crunching gravel, hands clasped behind his back, slightly bent forward like an Eastern European Mr. Miyagi—only scarier.

He stops, gestures to the trees.

"These take patience," he says. "You plant. You water. You wait. Years before they give you anything worth having."

He picks a plum, turns it in his hand, then tosses it to me without warning. "But when they do, it is sweet. Worth all the work."

My heart hammers. This isn't a fruit lesson. It's a pop quiz on my intentions.

"My family's the same," I say. "Vineyard people. Napa. Nothing good grows fast. And if you don't nurture it every day, it dies on the vine."

Ivan studies me. Then he nods once. "Good."

He passes me the bottle.

It burns like fire and truth going down. Somehow, I think I just survived round one.

A breeze cools the sweat gathering on my neck. The trees stand silver in the moonlight. Beautiful and terrifying.

He stops beneath the largest tree, eyes on the branches above us. "Grace is everything I have left."

"Yes, sir." My voice cracks. Fantastic.

He turns, eyes sharp but no longer black. "I lost my wife. Lost friends in war. Spent years in bottle after." He exhales. "Only thing I did good was Grace. She has my wife's heart. Strong. Too strong for this world sometimes." He looks back up at the tree. "I have seen that pain once. I will not see her hurt again. Ever."

My chest aches. I take a breath that feels like stepping off a cliff. "Ivan?"

He flicks his eyes toward me, glassy and distant, like he's standing in two places at once.

"I can't promise the world won't throw hell at us," I say. "But I can promise I'll take it first. Anything that comes for her goes through me." I swallow.

"I love her. I want to marry her. I want to build a life with her—

one that keeps her smiling like she does in there." I gesture with the plum toward the house.

Ivan's silent. His jaw ticks. Fruit drops behind us, thudding to the ground like a warning shot.

Finally, he steps closer and grips my shoulder. Heavy. Solid.

"You hurt her," he says, low and lethal, "I hurt you worse."

I nod, throat tight. "Understood. Crystal clear."

Then his mouth twitches. Barely. A ghost of a smile.

From the porch, Grandpa's voice cuts through the night, thick with laughter and rakija.

"Kyle! Come drink with me! Ivan's looking where to bury you!"

Ivan exhales, mutters something in Croatian that sounds like *old fool*, and pats my shoulder.

"Welcome to family," he says quietly. "Hopefully she says yes."

My eyes drift back toward the house where Grace is laughing in the warm spill of light from the windows.

I finally breathe. The air tastes like relief, plums, and the faint tang of almost-dying.

~~~

We're driving home, the music so low it barely counts as background noise, just a hum beneath the sound of my own heartbeat. The night replays in my head like an Instagram reel on loop—her hand on my thigh, her mouth at my ear, the way Ivan looked at me like maybe, just maybe, I wasn't a total lost cause. The excitement of our future thrums in my chest, wild and unsteady, like a high school marching band pounding out a halftime show inside me.

I glance over at Grace. Her fingers trace the edge of my hand on the console like she still can't quite believe what happened either. And damn… I don't think I'll ever stop looking at her like this. Like she's the only thing that's ever made the chaos go quiet.

We coast slowly through Sausalito, headlights sweeping over one perfect bayfront house after another. Her fingers linger a beat longer, then drift from the console to my thigh, her thumb moving absently like she doesn't even realize she's doing it.

"Slow down," she says suddenly, leaning forward, eyes wide.
~~~

"That one." She points up at a weathered gray house perched just above the water, all big windows and a wraparound porch that looks like it was built for long nights and red wine.

"God, I know it's ridiculous," she adds quickly, already half-laughing. "But I love that one. That porch…" Her voice drifts, dreamy. "Imagining myself sitting out there on a cool evening, wrapped in a sweater, drinking wine, watching the fog roll in off the bay…"

She glances at me, cheeks flushed. "Sorry. Silly pipe dream. Totally impractical."

I swallow hard because I've stared at that same damn house before. Different life. Different girl. Same dream lodged under my ribs. Only this time it doesn't ache. This time, looking at Grace, it feels like maybe I could finally stop dreaming in *what ifs* and start building something real.

I slide my hand over hers, tugging it fully onto my leg, lacing our fingers, and giving a small squeeze.

"Not silly," I say quietly, eyes still on the house as it disappears in the rearview mirror. "That porch… yeah. I could see that."

What I don't say—what burns at the tip of my tongue—is *I could see that with you.* Always you.

We drive the last few minutes in a silence that hums with something electric, something inevitable.

Hawk Hill's turnout is empty when we pull in, the city spread below us like a field of stars. Fog curls around the bridge, soft and luminous in the moonlight.

She looks over at me. "What are we doing here?"

I kill the engine and toss my head toward the door. "Come on." I pass her my sweatshirt from the back seat.

She steps out, shivering in the breeze, tugging my hoodie tighter around her shoulders. "God, it's beautiful up here," she says, moving toward the edge of the overlook.

My heart slams against my ribs. The ring in my pocket feels like it weighs fifty pounds. My legs are jelly as I climb out, but I follow her anyway, every step a prayer I don't screw this up.

She deserves better than a laundry basket, *I love you,* and a front-seat, ringless proposal. She deserves a special moment. Something beautiful. Something under the stars.

She's staring out at the city, hair whipping wild in the breeze.

I say it low, my voice almost stolen by the wind. "Hey."

She turns, smiling. "Yeah?"

Damn it. Every smart thing I rehearsed is gone, blown clean out of my head by how much I love her. So, I just blurt it out—raw and unpolished, like the truth always is.

"I can't let another night go by without you knowing…" I pull the ring box from my pocket, flip it open slowly, and hold it like it's the most precious thing in the world besides her. "…that you're my forever."

My voice cracks, but I drop to one knee anyway, because this is the only way this should be done.

"Grace… will you marry me? Build all the stupid, impossible, sweater-and-wine-on-the-porch dreams with me? Because you're the only thing I know I can't live without."

For a heartbeat, she just stares at me—eyes wide, lips parted like she forgot how to breathe.

Then her hands fly to her mouth, tears spilling as she nods fast and wild. "Yes. God, yes!"

My hands shake as I slide the ring onto her finger, but when she drops to her knees to kiss me—laughing and crying all at once—it doesn't matter. The whole city could fall away beneath us and I wouldn't notice.

It's just us. The wind. And a promise that feels like the first unbreakable thing in my life.

I press my forehead to hers, my voice unsteady. "Told you. Not a pipe dream."

My vision blurs as I smile against her lips.

She laughs softly, trembling. "Guess not."

My chest feels wide open, like I can finally—finally—breathe.

~~~

The heater hums low as we sit back in the car, throwing soft warmth over the windows. Grace's hand rests in mine, her thumb brushing
~~~

over the new weight on her finger again and again, like she's afraid it might disappear if she stops touching it.

She lifts her hand toward the dash light, breath catching as the platinum glints, the diamond flashing under the lone streetlamp outside.

"Kyle…" Her voice is barely a whisper, wonder tangled through it. "This is… this is stunning. I thought we were going to shop for one?"

I grip the wheel harder than necessary. "Yeah. That was the plan." My mouth twists. "But I needed *this* one."

She turns toward me, brows knitting, still holding her hand up like the ring is a tiny universe she's just discovered. "Yours?"

I swallow hard. "My mom's." The words scrape out low and rough.

"I swore I'd never—hell, I thought I'd never even…" I trail off, staring at the bridge lights instead of her, because if I look at her, I'll break.

"After she died, I just figured… since Whit had it, it was gone."

My fingers find hers on my thigh, my thumb gliding over the band, the groove I know as well as my own name. The metal's warm from her skin, but all I feel are my mom's hands—the way the ring used to catch the lamplight when she tucked me in, brushing my cheek when she hugged me goodnight.

This ring was built around something I thought shouldn't be breakable.

But it was.

And yet… here I am, trying again.

"So, I told him I proposed," I say finally, taking a breath. "And he offered the ring."

I risk a glance at her. She's looking at me like I just handed her my heart and asked her to keep it safe.

"Kyle…" she whispers, tears glassing her eyes. Her other hand comes up to cradle mine, careful, reverent. "I don't even know what to say."

"You don't have to." My thumb traces the band again, a silent promise to both women who've worn it. "Just keep it. Wear it. Know it's more than a yes to me. It's everything I have. Everything I am." I smirk slightly. "Unless you want some store-bought thing. We can totally do that."

She slaps my hand. "Stop." Then softer, awed, "I love it. What a gift."

She leans across the console and kisses me hard, like I just anchored her to this new world. This new life.

We break apart breathless, foreheads pressed together, tears drying on our cheeks. The heater hums, the city lights blur outside the windshield, and for a moment it feels like the whole world is holding its breath with us.

I sigh, leaning back in my seat."Alright, babe… since we're officially engaged now, I feel like you need to know there's a fine-print clause in the fiancé contract."

She hiccups out a laugh, still blinking back tears. "God, Kyle… what clause?"

I run a hand down my face like a man barely holding it together, then gesture vaguely toward the road ahead. "The one that says after I survived dinner with your dad—which, for the record, felt like a twelve-hour stint in 'Nam—I'm legally entitled to one celebratory blowjob on the ride home."

Grace gasps and swats my chest, laughing so hard she's choking. "Kyle! You're unbelievable."

"Unbelievably brave," I correct, solemn as a war vet. "You weren't there, babe. He had the thousand-yard stare. Those long, quiet pauses before every question. I swear I saw my life flash before my eyes between the potatoes and the dinner rolls. I think I've got PTSD from dessert."

She's doubled over now, laughing so hard she's squeaking, and I can't stop grinning. My hand slides to the back of her neck, pulling her forehead gently to mine.

"What?" I ask, innocently. "You can't send a man into battle like that and not give him a medal at the end."

She groans, half mortified, half crying from laughing, and somehow it's the happiest sound I've ever heard.

The car goes quiet except for her hiccupping giggles. I lean back slowly, deadpan serious, and reach for my zipper.

Her gasp is instant. “You are *serious* right now.”

“Babe,” I say, solemn as a preacher, “after walking through the valley of side-eye to ask for your hand… after surviving sniper fire in the form of your father’s silence…” I tap the seat control, and the motor hums, reclining me inch by deliberate inch like I’m settling in for a very important rest. “…I think it’s only fair you decorate me with the highest honor a man can receive.”

Grace’s mouth drops open, her face going scarlet as she fights another laugh. She looks around, actually checking the windows for witnesses.

“Kyle, you are *insane*.”

I fold my arms behind my head, smirk slow and wicked.

“Insane?” I tilt my head. “No, sweetheart. I’m a decorated soldier of love. Now show some respect.”

Chapter 37

OUR FOREVER SHOT

The air still smells like last night—sweat, sex, her perfume clinging to my skin. Grace is tucked against my side, her hair a chaotic halo over my chest, and my fingers curl around a coffee mug that's already gone cold.

She yawns, stretching like a cat, the ring catching the light as she lifts her hand—and I swear my heart does a stupid little somersault every time I see it. Every damn time.

"How long have you been awake?" she asks, voice scratchy and cute as hell.

I kiss the top of her head. "Not long. Just made coffee. I got back in to watch you sleep like a creeper."

She slides up and steals my mug, takes a sip, then gags. "Eww… black."

I chuckle. "I'll go get your oat-milk sugar water." I climb out of bed.

She sits up, wrapping the blankets around herself, and the light spills over her like a quiet revelation. Not blinding. Not dramatic. Just enough to make something in me go still.

"Thank you, fiancé," she says, holding up her hand like a trophy.

I come back with her mug, hand it over, and climb in beside her again.

"Let's take a pic for our friends," she says. "Announce the news. Totally ridiculous. Get it over with." She snuggles into me.

"Alright," I say, already wary.

I grab my phone from the nightstand, lean back against the headboard, and snap a quick selfie. We look wrecked. Bed hair, puffy eyes, the kind of stupid happiness you can't fake.

I glance at the screen and grimace.

"Christ. I look like I crawled out of a ditch." I rake a hand through my hair like that might help.

Grace swats my chest, half laughing, half scolding. "Stop. No fixing your hair. No filters. Not pretending we're not sexed-up, stupidly in love, and slightly dehydrated from last night." She takes the phone, holds it up again, her free hand wrapped around her mug. Ring front and center. "This. This is us. Forever."

The shutter clicks, and I look at her—the woman who turned my whole damn life right-side up—and think, *yeah*. This is the one we send. This is the one that says everything.

She leans in to check the screen. "Ooh—make sure my boobs aren't showing. That would be awkward." She laughs into her coffee.

The moment hits me with a strange sense of déjà vu. Same messy bed. Same sunlight slicing through the blinds. But this time there's no weight in my chest, no emptiness waiting on the other side of goodbye. Just Grace. And the quiet certainty that this isn't an ending. It's a beginning we're stepping into together.

"Sweet," she says, already smiling at her phone. "Prepare for excitement overload."

Her thumbs start flying, grin widening as she disappears into whatever thread she's just unleashed us into.

~~~

My phone's blowing up like a grenade. Grace glances over from her laptop, eyebrow arched, smirking. She already knows it's not work.

I grab it off the counter, and sure enough, the group chat is on fire.

Collin: ANNOUNCEMENT TO THE MASSES – THE MAN IS OFFICIALLY WHIPPED.

Ritchie: Wait… Grace actually said yes? To YOU?
~~~

I chuckle, thumb flying.

Kyle: It's called love, dickheads. Try it sometime.

Collin: Love? Or a temporary lapse in her usual high standards? Asking for a friend.

Ritchie: Be honest, bro... is she pregnant? No judgment.

Kyle: Jesus. NO.

Collin: Sure? Her boobs looked kind of swollen in that pic. I swear I saw a nip.

I choke on my water mid-sip, coughing into my arm.

"What's so funny?" Grace asks, already laughing at my expression.

I shake my head, scrolling. "You don't even want to know."

Collin: Oh, just so you know, satin UNCLE DICK jackets are already on order. Matching. With patches.

Ritchie: Collin, I thought we agreed mine's leather? And YOU aren't UNCLE DICK.

Kyle: Muted. Forever muted.

Collin: You mute us, you die friendless. Remember that during your wedding toast.

Grace leans over my shoulder, reads, and absolutely loses it—laughing so hard she hiccups.

"Oh my God," she wheezes. "Please tell me you're letting them do the jackets?"

"Absolutely not."

"Absolutely yes," she says, already texting Collin back from my phone—traitor that she is.

Before I can snatch it away, another text pops up.

Unknown Number: *Don't screw this up.*

I freeze and point to it. "Please tell me this isn't who I think it is?"

She grins. "Oh yeah. Tata asked for your number this morning."

My face drops like butter on a hot skillet.

"He has my number?"

"Of course. I sent him the picture."

The thought of her dad—military-honed and terrifying—opening a photo of me half-naked, freshly fucked, grinning like an idiot in his daughter's bed… Jesus Christ. I'm surprised he hasn't shown up already to separate me from my lower half with a dull paring knife.

Grace just sips her green smoothie, eyes glinting with pure mischief. "Tata's got a way with words."

I'm pretty sure he's also got a tarp and a shovel.

I scrub a hand down my face, groaning. "I survived 'Nam last night for this. Can't a man enjoy his victory lap before you broadcast my crimes to the enemy?"

"Nope," she says, completely unbothered.

She tilts her head. "How come your work crew hasn't chimed in to congratulate you yet?"

I sigh, rubbing the back of my neck.

"Yeah… I can't send *that* picture, babe," I admit with a wince. "I'm the exec—"

She holds up a hand, grinning. "No, I get it. Eww. If Noah Foster ever sent me that kind of pic with Danielle, I'd vomit straight into my Chantilly cream."

Apparently, Tata was exempt from that rule.

I laugh, relieved.

"Let's take a new one," she says, stepping closer, smoothing her hand over my chest. "Freshly showered. Cute. Innocent. Fully clothed."

"Thank you," I exhale.

We take a new picture and off it goes. My phone lights up instantly, messages stacking one after another. I lean against the counter, scrolling, smiling like an idiot—already knowing this is what it feels like to be outed as happy.

Never thought I'd enjoy this so much: my phone lighting up like a Vegas slot machine. Somewhere along the way, Sagi-Shi stopped being just my gig and turned into my crew. My slightly deranged, soy-sauce-fueled, wildly inappropriate group chat family. And hell… I wouldn't trade 'em for anything.

Darius: No shit! That's why the big goofy grin! Congrats, man!

I smile. I really love this big dude. My right-hand man.

Marcus: Cheers! I'll have a bottle for you two behind the bar.

Reggie: It's about time, old man. Congrats!

Then my heart ticks up when I see her name. Not in the same way it used to, but like a long-lost friend coming in for a long-awaited hug. Someone you depend on. Every word of encouragement, every word of praise. Like a drug.

She broke free from the group text. This… this was private.

Cassie: Oh Kyle. My baby boy. I'm so freaking happy for you. I knew she was your Grace. I'm crying happy tears for you right now.

My eyes blur staring at the screen. All those years I pined for her—wishing, dying a little every day without her in my life. And now here I am, finally happy, and she's still cheering me on like she's been waiting for this ending as much as I have.

Kyle: First off, baby boy? I professed my love to you once. Isn't that some age-gap romance-novel kink? Eww. Second… thank you. Cass, I'm so fucking happy. She is my Grace.

I glance up. She's oblivious. Washing the morning dishes. Humming something happy. This woman turned my whole world right side up.

My phone buzzes in my hand again.

Cassie: So? When and where are we getting this party started?

Kyle: Well, homegirl is really excited, apparently.

I lean down and swipe at the touchpad on the laptop, waking up the screen. She's already started a wedding planning checklist, scrolling through possible venues.

Kyle: Spring? Maybe going back to my roots. A vineyard feels right. Feels like home.

Chapter 38

WORTH THE WAIT

The crisp spring day couldn't be more perfect. My bride couldn't be more stunning, gliding through the crowd like her silk gown was spun straight out of a dream.

My bride.

Even in my own head, the words sound ridiculous. After all this time, I finally tied the knot. I sip my wine and chuckle to myself. Just like this wine, good things take time. Totally worth the wait.

Footsteps approach behind me, quieter than most, but his presence is larger than anyone else's here. I don't have to look to know it's Whit.

He stops beside me, hands in his pockets, gaze fixed on the same stunning woman.

"She looks happy," he says after a beat.

"She is," I murmur. "We both are."

He nods. "That's good."

"Heard you took some ownership in the restaurant. That true?"

"Yeah," I say, glancing at him. "This month."

He shifts his weight like the next words are going to cost him something, but his voice stays steady. "That's no small thing. Owning something. Building it with your own hands."

I nod, unsure what to say.

"And her," he adds, eyes flicking back toward Grace. "She's a hell of a woman. Seems like you're building yourself a good life, Kyle."

I swallow hard. He doesn't say he's proud. He doesn't have to.

Then a hand slaps onto my shoulder, and he's gone.

"I can't believe you did it," Ritchie says, clinking his pint against my glass.

Then, like the universe refuses to let me have a serene moment, Collin materializes beside me, decked out in a paisley velour tux that could only have been tailored by Satan himself.

"What's up, my bitches?"

I glance sideways and swirl my wine.

"Wrong wedding for that energy, Collin."

"Why not? Otherwise, it's just sad people in fancy clothes pretending to like each other." He tips his mirrored aviators down at me like he's offering wisdom.

He shrugs, swiping a champagne flute off a passing tray, bowing like it's his personal butler service. "Ah, finally. The good stuff. Thank you, Jeeves." He straightens, takes a slow, exaggerated sip, then smacks his lips like he's judging a cooking show finale. "Mmm. Excellent tannins, lovely oaky finish. Is this a… 1986?"

Ritchie blinks. "Bro, that's not even how champagne works."

Collin ignores him completely, holding the glass up to the sunlight like it's a rare gem. "You wouldn't understand. Years of experience at a wine bar have honed this palate." He holds his hands up to his lips.

Whit strolls past, snorting. "Pretty sure your 'years of experience' were mostly you slamming half-price Merlot behind the bar after closing."

Collin tips his glass in Whit's direction, utterly unbothered. "Legends aren't born, Whit. They're… fermented," he calls.

He leans into me, whispering, "Damn, when did Whit get a sense of humor?"

I bend over laughing silently. "When he got the great big stick out his ass." I look around, making sure he didn't hear me.

Ritchie leans forward, nodding across at Collin's absurd tux. "That's… actually pretty dope. Didn't know that was an option."

Collin points at Ritchie's suit with mock disgust. "Yeah, thought that was… meh." A shrug. A scowl. "Took matters into my own hands."

Then he downs the entire flute in one gulp. "Good shit." He trades it for another as Jeeves walks past again.

I just stand there, casually sipping my wine, watching my wife glide through the crowd like sunlight on silk, and wonder how the hell these idiots made my guest list. Let alone be my best friends… my brothers I actually *chose*.

"Look at you," Cassie's voice cuts in from behind me, warm and familiar as her arm snakes around my waist, her head pressing into my chest. Stephen's right on her heels. "That ceremony? You had me in tears."

Before I can answer, Ritchie and Collin drift off toward the bar, already plotting their next round of chaos, leaving me blessedly free of having to explain their *questionable* wardrobe choices.

I groan, tipping my head back. "You're always in tears, Cass. What's new?"

Without letting her go, I reach out to Stephen, shaking his hand. "Stephen, how are you?"

"Great, Kyle. Not as good as you today, though." He gestures to my suit, smiling. "I don't think I've ever seen you out of your chef coat or a T-shirt before. Nice look."

Coming from a man who was probably born in an Armani suit and skipped his first car, taking a private jet to high school, I take it as a compliment.

"There you two are," Grace's voice floats in like a melody. Cassie squeals, pulling her into a hug like they've been friends forever. Watching them, my heart squeezes. I glance at Stephen, and he sees it too—Cassie's happiness is everything to him. The man's dragged her out of hell this past year. Jesus Christ, the stories… almost unbelievable. Worth a movie deal. At least a book.

"Where's Cora?" I ask.

Cassie sighs, rolling her eyes. "She wanted to be here. You're Uncle Kyle." She gestures to me and shrugs. "But Jack and Beth needed her elsewhere… don't get me started." Her lips twist apologetically. "Sorry."

"It's okay," Grace says softly, giving Cassie's wrist a reassuring squeeze just as Ivan walks up.

"Oh… Cassie, Stephen," she says, "this is my father, Ivan Novak."

Ivan lifts Cassie's hand and kisses the back of it as if he just stepped out of Casablanca.

"My pleasure, Cassie," he says smoothly.

"Oh… okay. Nice to meet you, Mr. Novak." Cassie blinks.

Stephen extends his hand. "Stephen Harlow, sir."

"Nice to meet you, Mr. Harlow," Ivan replies before shifting his gaze to me. There's a glare… then the faintest, almost imperceptible wink. My brows shoot up. Then his eyes soften as he turns to Grace.

"Dinner will be served in fifteen minutes, my love."

She smiles. "Thank you, Tata."

Cassie clutches her chest. "Aww, I want a Tata," she coos.

I choke on my wine, coughing hard enough to see stars. "Sorry," I rasp, smacking my chest. "Went down wrong."

"Sure it did," Stephen murmurs from beside me.

~~~

Dinner was… dinner. Grace and I both live and breathe this industry, but for our own wedding, we didn't have it in us. Sixty-five people, a perfect little tent in the vineyard, and not an ounce of energy left to obsess over courses and wine pairings. Caroline of all people begged and pleaded to take the reins, and we finally threw our hands up.

Noah Foster recommended a caterer who came with more Michelin stars than a constellation chart, and Caroline nearly cried when she got the booking confirmed. I think I remember someone saying there were seven courses? Or was it eight? Didn't matter. What mattered was dessert.

We had two.

Grace's request was a Croatian cake: layers of sponge soaked in rum, custard, chocolate glaze. It was something her grandmother used to make for every celebration back home. And my choice—Italian cheesecake. Not my mom's recipe. If I can't make it myself, I sure as hell wasn't going to let someone else do it. Still, I could enjoy similar flavors. And this one didn't come with the pain.
~~~

When I was a kid, dessert time came with long adult stories we were never allowed to interrupt, voices rising and falling like music while coffee mugs met saucers with soft little clinks. Forks scraped plates, sugar lingered on my lips, and I leaned back in my chair just listening, soaking it in.

This… this was what I lived for.

The after-dinner glow. The warmth of good food, good wine, and people you actually wanted to be stuck at a table with. Laughter that spilled over like the whiskey being passed around. Voices growing louder, more animated, hands flying in the air, mid-story, someone swearing they remembered it differently.

It reminded me of home. Of Sunday dinners where time didn't exist and dessert stretched on for hours because nobody wanted to leave the table. Tonight feels like that. Like my mom and grandparents are here somewhere, tucked among these guests, carrying on a tradition I thought was gone for good. I glance around the tent—Whit and Caroline sitting next to Ivan, who's toasting with a smile. *A goddamn smile.* Not the table I was shoved to at eighteen, lost in a sea of misfits. This time, it feels… different.

My gaze drifts back to Grace, to the way she lights up this whole damn tent just by being in it. This is my family now. It feels almost whole… but not quite. Like there's one last stitch missing, the final pull of the thread that would close an old wound for good.

Grace's grandparents are throwing back shots of rakija from a beat-up blue bottle at a table with Cassie and Stephen. My smile reaches all the way to my ears.

And then—*clink, clink, clink.*

Glasses start tapping in unison under the tent, candlelight catching on every crystal rim, pulling me out of my thoughts and right back here.

The toast is coming. *Holy hell.*

Collin pops up like he's on stage at the Comedy Cellar instead of under a tent full of our families. He clinks his knife against his champagne flute, loud as hell, nearly toppling a candle. He tugs Ritchie's arm up with him, like he's his trusty sidekick.

"Dude, come on… you're Uncle Dick."

Grace whispers into my ear, "Are you sure about this?"

I close my eyes and laugh silently. "Hell no. But I'm starting to think we could have charged a cover for it at the door."

"Alright, alright, people," he says, swaying like he's been waiting his entire life for his moment in the spotlight. "First off, shoutout to Whit for having some absolutely *kick-ass lineage.* Like, look at this place." He sweeps his arms wide toward the vineyard like he's presenting the freaking Sistine Chapel. "Who knew Kyle, a guy I once watched eat cold couch pizza for breakfast straight outta the box…" he pauses for effect, holding his hands up toward the tent like he's about to speak in tongues. "…came from THIS? God bless the vine. Truly."

The tent chuckles, glasses lift, and he's *just* getting warmed up. "And let's be real." He glances in our direction.

"Oh no," I mumble.

"Grace, you might have married above your weight class with Kyle here." He shakes his head, a grin tugging at his mouth. "But let's face it, it's the other way around. My boy lucked out so hard, it's borderline criminal."

Ritchie lifts his glass, beaming wide. "To Kyle and Grace."

The tent erupts—cheers, laughter, glasses raised high.

Collin glances at Ritchie, then taps his champagne flute again. "But seriously—tonight's about love. Family." He points a roaming finger out toward us, all serious now. "And finding that *one* person who makes you stop getting stupid haircuts… and keeps you from drawing all over your body every time you feel emotional. So, here's to Kyle and Grace—the only two people who could drag this misfit crew into a vineyard and somehow not get thrown out."

He raises his glass high, grinning like a madman as the tent erupts in laughter and cheers. Collin dips into a shallow bow like the applause is clearly meant for him.

~~~

We wander toward the far edge of the vineyard, the music and laughter thinning behind us, replaced by crickets and the soft rustle of leaves in the cool night air. Grace leans into me, her bare hand
~~~

brushing mine until I catch it, holding tight. I stop halfway down the slope just to look at her in the moonlight. Her dress flows softly around her legs, hair a little wild from dancing, cheeks flushed from wine and happiness.

I reach up, threading my fingers through her hair, and she tips her head into my palm like it's the most natural thing in the world. My chest feels too full, like I couldn't possibly hold all this—the day, her, and this incredible moment.

"Worth every insane minute," I murmur.

She smiles up at me, tired but radiant. "Even the part where Collin compared you to a human Etch-A-Sketch that ate couch pizza in front of everyone?"

I laugh quietly, pull her close, and press my forehead to hers. "Especially that part. Because it means they all know how hard I fought to get here, and how damn lucky I am to have made it."

She kisses me, soft and gentle, then looks into my eyes. "I cannot wait to get on that plane tomorrow and start our adventure."

"I know." I push her hair back behind her ear. "I can't wait to see where you come from, Mrs. Berkley."

"Mmm." She tilts her head, smiling. "That right there has a nice ring to it. I could never get tired of hearing you say it."

I lift her hand to my lips, pressing her rings against them and whispering, "I love you, Mrs. Grace Berkley."

The breeze carries laughter from the tent, glasses clinking in another distant toast, but here it's just us. Our world. Our new forever.

Chapter 39

MISE EN PLACE

"Kyle, oh my God. Taste this," she says, cutting off a piece with her fork and leaning forward to feed me. "This is a kremšnita. Mila used to make it every Sunday when I was little. This tastes almost identical, babe." Her voice softens on her grandmother's name.

I don't hesitate, letting her slide it past my lips, the pastry crumbling against my mouth, sweet cream melting on my tongue. Flakes of pastry and powdered sugar tumble down my black T-shirt, but I don't even care. Not one damn bit.

Because she's smiling like that—wide, unguarded, pure joy. I'd eat a thousand pastries, wear every single crumb, just to keep that look on her face.

"Mmm… that's good," I say, chasing it with a sip of coffee.

She takes another bite, eyes fluttering closed, savoring more than just the flavor. She looks like she's reliving her childhood through every salivary gland.

"I can already see I'll need a bigger wardrobe after this trip," I chuckle, swiping my napkin over my shirt.

She raises her brow, lifting her dainty espresso cup in mock salute. "Not if we keep walking these streets… and you keep doing what you did this morning." She winks, wicked and sweet all at once.

I smile, shake my head once, and refocus.

"So, where to next?" I rasp, dragging my mind anywhere but there.

Her long brown hair slips forward as she studies the map, finger tracing the paper, tongue darting out to wet her lip just enough to steal my attention completely.

"I was thinking we tackle the wall, then grab some lunch over here"—she circles a spot on the map with the tip of her delicate finger—"and then we've got that private boat ride to Lokrum Island at three, so we need to be back here."

She looks up, catching me staring intently. "Are you even listening?" she laughs softly, her eyes searching mine.

My chin's propped on my palm, leaning toward her like gravity itself is on her side. Love drunk doesn't even come close.

"No," I admit with a lazy grin, voice low. "I think I'd walk straight into the Adriatic if that's where your little tour led me right now."

She reaches over, fingers sliding through my hair, her smile undoing me right here on this sidewalk.

"Oh, poor baby. It's the Balkans," she teases, glancing around us. "It's magical. It does this to people."

I shake my head slowly, eyes locked on her like she's the only thing in this ancient city worth seeing. "No, sweetheart," I sigh, meaning every word. "It's you. Totally *you*."

As she folds the map and grabs my hand, I let her pull me to my feet, a crooked grin tugging at my lips.

"God help me," I murmur under my breath, just for me. "I'd follow you anywhere."

Later that morning, we weave through the narrow streets, sun climbing higher, and salt still clinging to our skin from the early terrace breeze. She pulls me into a shop spilling with linen and straw hats stacked high, running her fingers over everything, completely unaware I'm caught up just watching her move.

She plops a wide-brimmed hat on her head, tilts her chin at the mirror. "What do you think?"

I lean against the doorframe, letting my grin curl slow and wicked. "Oh, you know what that hat would look good with?"

She glances over, curiosity sparking. "What?"

I start to push off the frame.

She lifts a hand, stopping me cold, her smile saying everything. "You stay there. I know exactly what you're up to." She points.

She walks out a beat later, hat still perched on her head, eyes bright with intent. She steps in close, smooth and slow, laying her palm flat against my chest. Then, low enough that only I can hear it, her voice like honey and threat all in one, "I'll show you what this hat looks good with… later."

She slides past me with a subtle smirk and a sway that's pure retaliation, and yep, there go my knees. I'm grinning like an idiot because I know exactly what's coming—and I deserve it.

We duck into a few more shops, leaving me juggling bags of souvenirs and smiling like an idiot, high on the way she keeps pulling me forward through her world.

By the time we reach the harbor, the sun's high, turning the Adriatic into a sheet of living glass. The sea glows impossibly blue, light scattering across the water as we weave through rows of bobbing boats, her hand warm in mine, both of us flushed from the heat and the long climb along the walls.

We wander without urgency after that—down narrow streets, past open windows and bread-scented corners—letting the day unfold at her pace, tasting, stopping, laughing when we get turned around and don't bother correcting it.

Everywhere we went that day, she fed me pieces of her world—flavors from her childhood, stories from Mila's kitchen, Sunday mornings with her mom. Even the quiet mentions of her dad carried weight, shadows she didn't rush past. I held her hand through the light ones, brushed my thumb over her knuckles through the heavier moments, and felt something steady forming between us with every shared memory.

By the time we make it back, the city is cooling, the stone still warm beneath bare feet. We kick off our shoes, open the doors to let the evening in, and collapse together in that loose, boneless way that only comes after a full day well lived.

~~~

Dubrovnik is lit below—lamps and windows dotting the hillside like
~~~

constellations. The Adriatic breathes behind me, salt and warmth lingering in the air, and somewhere beneath us there's laughter, music, life carrying on gently without us.

Night has settled in as I stand at the balcony rail. The door opens behind me, spilling soft light across the stone. She steps into it, backlit in gold, wearing nothing but that hat.

"I promised later," she says, her voice honeyed and sure.

She crosses the threshold unhurried, the glow from inside fading as the night claims her. Moonlight settles over her skin as she steps onto the terrace, cool air and salt brushing against warmth.

"God, you're so beautiful," I say, my hand sliding into her hair.

She kisses me slow and deep. She tastes like sugar and wine. Like the whole day distilled into one perfect moment—and I know, with a quiet certainty, that I'll never get enough of her.

Her chestnut hair falls loose over her shoulder, her skin cool where it presses against mine, every inch of her sending a slow, steady warmth through me. My hands slide down her sides like I need to remember her again, even though I already know her by heart.

Grace tilts her head back when I kiss the hollow of her throat, a soft sound slipping from her lips—half sigh, half surrender. My breath catches, chest tight, because there's nothing casual about this. Not anymore. Not ever again.

The taste of her mouth, like sugar on my lips. The warmth of her hand, like silk wrapped around me.

"God," I whisper against her shoulder, sinking into her slow, and deliberate. "I swear, every time feels like the first."

She turns, the hazel flecks in her eyes catch flickers of moonlight over the ocean, and smiles that soft, devastating smile that ruins me completely. "That's because you love me different every time."

I press my forehead to hers, holding her face between my hands like she's the only thing keeping me steady. "No," I murmur, kissing her slow, deep, reverent. "I love you more every time."

Her fingers curl around the stone rail, her breath slowing as she leans into me, and for one long, perfect moment, the night belongs only to us.

~ ~ ~

The hiss of the wok's steady. Garlic and soy cut through the morning lull while I slice scallions one-handed, phone propped up against a bottle of yuzu. Cassie's face beams at me from the screen, hair piled in a messy bun, pen stuck between her teeth as she flips through a notebook.

"Okay, be honest," she says, muffled around the pen, "does Yujo sound too soft? I love it—it means friendship, but does it scream 'izakaya' or, like… 'yoga retreat with sake bombs and vegan options?" she says with air quotes.

I smirk, tossing the scallions into the pan with a sharp sizzle. "Cass, you could name it Dumpster Fire and people would still line up." I reach for the sesame oil and add a swirl to the pan.

She laughs, flipping me off through the camera. "Not helpful, Berkley."

"Fine," I say, pulling the pan off heat and wiping my hands on my towel. "Yujo's perfect. It's you. It's what you've been trying to build since day one." I smile at her. "Hey, feels like that day when we came up with Sagi-Shi, remember? Back when we thought we knew what the hell we were doing. You have the same look." I point to her. "I see it. Go with it and stop overthinking."

Her grin softens. "Yeah, yeah, okay."

I glance at the screen again, at her stacks of notes and the fire in her eyes, and there it is—that gut-punch pride. We survived hell, we built something real, and now she's out there chasing the next big thing… only on a smaller scale this time.

"Hey," she moves closer to the camera. "Why are *you* cooking?" she asks.

"I'm messing with a recipe." I nod once. "I've been gone for two weeks. I needed to busy my hands. Mind your own business."

She raises a brow. "Your hands weren't busy enough on your honeymoon?" she says and throws her head back, laughing.

I mock her dumb laugh in silence just as I get an incoming call from fellow chef friend, Simon Moss.

"Hey, I need to take this call."

"Fine, talk later." And just like that, she's gone.

I switch over and put the phone to my ear.

"Chef Moss, how are you?" I answer.

"Kyle, I hear congratulations are in order for two major events? Married *and* Owner?" he asks, pride in his voice.

"Yeah, that's the word on the street," I laugh, leaning against the counter.

"Well, I have something else that may be of interest."

A beat.

"Okay. What is that, Simon?" I ask, every instinct telling me I should probably brace myself.

"Have you ever been to Alaska?"

Chapter 40

THE WAIT OF WATER

The kitchen smells like roasted garlic and butter, chicken sizzling in the pan while rain taps softly against the window. Grace is perched on the counter in nothing but one of my old Alice In Chains T-shirts and a pair of black boy shorts, wine glass dangling from her fingers as she watches me pace like a caged animal, hands flying while I spit words like they might escape me otherwise.

"Babe, listen to this," I say, tongs gesturing wildly. "Top chefs. The best of the best. Flying into this tiny Alaskan town that's on its knees and building something that matters. Not just food, but community. A real shot at changing lives."

Grace tips her head back, laughing, eyes sparkling. "Kyle… we just got home from Croatia. My suitcase is still half-zipped. How long would you even be gone?"

"Three, four weeks tops," I answer without hesitation, crossing the room to cup her face with garlic-scented hands, like I'm selling her on my heartbeat.

"Babe, this is everything I've ever wanted to do. The country's top chefs are coming together to save a town. To… I don't know. Start a dream."

She snorts, unable to stop smiling. "Oh my God, Kyle. You sound like you're reading the back of a rom-com DVD. Only thing missing is the love story."

I grin and press my forehead to hers. "Nah," I murmur, taking her hand and placing it over my chest, where my heart's trying to kick its way out. "That's right here."

"Oh, good God. You've become such a sappy romantic it's almost nauseating," she teases, her voice low.

I set the tongs down, my hands sliding under her shirt, heat coiling low in my gut as I feel her muscles tighten beneath my palms. I brush my lips over hers, featherlight.

"Does this make you nauseous?" I whisper, my tone turning wicked.

She barely breathes, the glass clinking softly on the counter as she sets it aside. "No."

My hands gather fabric, dragging it higher until her breasts are bare to me, nipples peaked and begging. I roll my thumbs over them, watch her tremble, hear that tiny, irresistible gasp.

"How about now?" I murmur before drawing one into my mouth, her body arching, hips pressing forward.

"Oh God, Kyle."

She threads her fingers into my hair, tugging just enough to light me up, her breath hot against my cheek.

"You play dirty," she whispers.

I let her slip free with a wet pop, dragging kisses up the line of her throat, tasting wine and warm vanilla on her skin.

The tongs clatter to the floor, forgotten. My hands grip her thighs, pulling her forward on the counter until she's flush against me, legs spreading like she's been waiting for this since Croatia.

"Three to four weeks, huh?" she breathes, her voice shaky now, nothing teasing about it. "You'd really leave me that long?"

I hook my fingers in the waistband of her boy shorts, tugging them down slowly, my gaze locked on hers. "Baby, I'd fly you out there in a heartbeat if you wanted. Hell, I'd cook you breakfast in a snowstorm, build you a damn cabin with my bare hands if it meant you were close."

Her laugh comes out breathless, turning into a soft moan as my fingers trace between her thighs, finding her heat, how ready she is.

"God, Kyle…"

I don't give her a chance to say more. I kiss her deep and slow until she's arching off the counter, her hands clawing at my shirt. My free hand slips lower, finding her slick and waiting, and her raspy moan hits me like gasoline on a match.

"Three weeks," I murmur against her lips, sliding a finger inside, curling it just right. "Four, tops. But right now?" I pause, forehead pressed to hers. "You've got me, baby. All of me."

"Show me," she whispers, wrecked, her head falling back.

"You like that?" I growl, dropping to my knees on the kitchen tile, hooking her legs over my shoulders like I'm about to make a new religion out of her.

Her breath catches, a shaky laugh spilling free. "God help me, I love you," she says, fingers tangling in my hair as the rest of the world disappears.

The storm batters the glass, wind howling, chicken burning on the stove. I stay anchored on my knees, holding her like this moment matters because it does. Because this is us, right here, before anything shifts, before the world asks us for more than we're ready to give.

~~~

The rain's light but steady—enough to turn the morning sky into a low gray blur as I jog the last few steps from my car to the back entrance, coffee gripped tight, hoodie damp across my back. I shoulder open the door with a grunt, and the familiar aroma and clang of Sagi-Shi's kitchen swallows me whole.

"Hey Joe," I call out, stomping off the wet as I peel off my sweatshirt and hang it on the hook.

He glances back from the dish pit, hands buried in suds. "Morning, Chef."

The place is already humming.

Steam. Heat. The rich aroma of miso broth simmering low on the back burner, mingling with the sharp bite of fried garlic.

Reggie's elbow-deep in prep, slicing green onions with surgical precision, muttering Biggie under his breath—*"It was all a dream…"*—like it's a prayer, a pulse, a reminder of how far he's come. Every cut hits the board in rhythm, like the beat's wired into his bones.
~~~

Darius is up front, checking over the morning delivery, barking notes to the driver as he lifts the lid on a crate of tuna.

I hang back for a second, just watching. He's taken the reins beautifully. Tough, but kind. He knows product. He knows negotiation, and he shakes hands like a man who means it.

I pause near my office door, letting it all settle in my chest. This isn't just a restaurant. It's a machine we built from the bones up—every clatter, every hiss, every knife tap against the board is part of the rhythm I know better than my own heartbeat.

The broth bubbles. The deliveries pile up, and just like that, it's showtime… even with nine hours till open.

"Morning, boss," Darius calls without looking up, walking by with a clipboard piled high with orders, notes, and receipts.

"Morning," I reply, pushing the office door open, wiping a palm over the wet fringe of hair on my forehead. I sip my coffee. Still hot. Small miracles.

I make the rounds—checking ticket times, peeking into the walk-in, glancing over the ops board for the week. Nothing's on fire. Reggie's already fixed the fridge seal that was leaking before I left on my honeymoon. Darius has managed to rotate the staff schedule without anyone walking out.

It's calm. Controlled. And it hits me—I'm not the guy sweating on the line anymore. *Shit.* He doesn't even exist. I'm the guy steering the whole damn ship.

Later that afternoon, I pull Darius aside near the back prep sink, where Benjamin's busy prepping mountains of cabbage, and bobbing his head to some melodic beat beneath his AirPods.

"You think you can pinch hit for me again?" I ask.

He narrows his eyes. "Well, I *did* run it while you were off honeymooning through a spice market." He smirks. "I didn't burn the bitch down."

"Yeah, and you crushed it," I say, meaning every word. "I've got an opportunity. Three, maybe four weeks max. Alaska. It's… big."

His brow rises. "Like, *big* big?"

"Like, top chefs flown into some small-town rebuild-the-community kind of big. Feels insane. But also… right."

Darius just nods, wiping his hands on a towel slung over his shoulder. "You give me the keys, I'll keep the engine running."

I clap him on the shoulder, something loosening in my chest. "That's what I needed to hear."

~~~

An hour later, I'm sitting in my office, door cracked open, and I can hear the rain coming down harder every time the back door opens and shuts.

I look at the time. 4:45. Grace should be getting off work soon.

I reach for my phone, which is buried under a mountain of paperwork.

> Kyle: Be careful driving home babe. The weather is shit. Love you.

Then, my phone lights up with an incoming call—Simon Moss.

I answer on the first ring.

"You calling to tell me it's a scam?" I ask, leaning back in my weathered leather chair.

Simon laughs, low and wry. "Only if gourmet halibut and rustic charm are a con."

"You got logistics?"

"Flights and lodging's covered. Lodging's rustic, but solid. She's paying well."

I sit up straighter, elbows braced on my desk. "Anyone else locked in?"

"Oh yeah." He starts rattling off names. "I've recruited half of New York—Ophelia's sous, Garrett Wolf, two from La Belle Helene—Paula Nolan and Zachary Branch—and Rebecca Smith out of Estela."

I let out a low whistle. "That's a hell of a lineup."

I don't know the East Coast chefs as well, only recognize two of the names, but it still sounds impressive as hell. That scene's always felt like another country to me. Different techniques sometimes. Different rhythm.

"You in?" he asks.
~~~

I glance around, aprons, mop heads, food orders clipped to the corkboard. This place is mine. It's home. It's comfortable. But that storm outside is getting louder. And maybe it's time I step into something that scares the shit out of me again.

I grin. "Fuck it. I'm in."

"Sweet."

I exhale.

"If there's anyone you want to bring, I've got room in the budget for one more."

"I'll think on it. We're tight with staff right now."

"I hear you, man. I'll send over the details."

"Thanks, Simon."

I hang up.

Damn. Alaska.

My phone pings.

Grace: Looks like this storm's gonna be a big one. You be careful too. Love you. xo

There's a knock at my door.

"Chef? There's someone up front asking for you," Marci calls, peeking her head in.

"Me?" I look up from my phone, hands splayed. "Wine purveyor? Customer pissed about bad fish? Be specific."

She shrugs like she's got better things to do. "Uhh… a girl? She's soaked. Says she wants a job."

I blink. "Stacy's the one who handles front-of-house hires."

"Don't know where she is," Marci replies, full eye roll. "She asked for *you,* so I came and got *you.* Should I go find Stacy then?"

Her tone says she absolutely won't.

I check my watch and blow out a breath. "Who the hell shows up looking for a job right before dinner service?" I stand, already annoyed, wiping my hands down my thighs. "No, I'll take care of it."

She was right. A soaking wet girl was standing in my bar, blotting herself with a dish towel.

"Hi, can I help you?" I ask.

She turns quickly, long caramel strands stuck to her damp porcelain shoulders. Her jeans are soaked, plastered to her body—dark navy in the front, pale in the back, like the storm painted her in passing.

She smiles, sheepish, swiping the towel down her arms one last time before offering a hand.

"I'm so sorry. There was a break in the rain when I was crossing the lot, and then… " she mimics an explosion with her hands. "Monsoon."

I nod toward the towel. "Need another?"

She shakes her head. "No, I'm good. Thanks."

"So, you're here for a job?" I ask, brow furrowing. "You cook?" Nobody usually asks for me unless they're headed to the back of house.

She dips her chin, shy. "Yeah. Sorry. I just… I wanted to speak to you directly. I didn't mean to… "

"What can I do for you…?" I prompt, gesturing.

"Edie," she says. "I'm Edie Sanders."

"Nice to meet you, Edie. What can I do for you?"

She glances around. The dining room's starting to fill—couples sliding into booths, Marcus greeting a pair at the candlelit bar.

She leans in slightly, her voice low. "Is there somewhere we can talk? Privately? Just a few minutes?"

I blink. "What?"

She nods, earnest. Rain is still clinging to her lashes.

"…Okay," I say, motioning for her to follow me.

We weave past the line, the prep tables, and all the curious eyes. Darius catches my movement and mouths *what the fuck?* with his arms outstretched like I've just marched a drenched, runaway debutante into our sacred kitchen dojo.

I push the office door open and nod toward the cracked leather chair in the corner. Pretty sure no one's sat in it since Cassie tried to give birth in it.

"Sorry, it's a mess," I mutter, nudging a box of Sagi-Shi T-shirts out of the way with my foot before leaning back against my desk.

"Thanks." She sits, gripping the armrests like she needs them to anchor her in place.

I cross my arms and ankles, trying to project calm. "So… this is as private as you're gonna get me, Edie."

She looks up. Big brown eyes. Wide and worried. Then she reaches into her bag and pulls out a photo—creased, worn, soft at the corners, and holds it tight in her hand.

In a voice barely louder than the rain outside, she asks, "Do you remember Macy? Macy Sanders?"

Her eyes lift to meet mine. My stomach drops. My heart skips. I blink down at the photo in her hand and feel the air shift.

"Yeah." My voice is rough. "I worked with her… God, almost twenty years ago. We dated. For a minute."

She hands me the photo. Me and Macy. Tangled in sheets, grinning like idiots. Young, messy, and goddamn beautiful.

"Yeah," I breathe. "Damn."

I blink, still staring at it. That was a lifetime ago. *Shit.* Someone else's life.

"Where'd you get this, Edie?" I ask, confused. "Is she okay? Where is she?"

She closes her eyes for a beat, breathes in deep. When she opens them again, they're glassy but steady.

"She was my mom." A tear slips free, but she's still smiling. "And no… she's not okay. She passed away."

I press a hand to my mouth. "Oh my God." I shake my head. "I'm so sorry. Macy was…" I trail off, eyes flicking to the photo again. "She was something special."

"She gave it to me," Edie says, placing her hand gently over mine, over the photo. "Before she died."

"What?" I whisper.

She squeezes. "Kyle," she says quietly. "You're my dad."

~~~

The rain hasn't stopped. It's gone from steady to relentless—like the sky's trying to drown the whole damn city.

I'm standing at the sink, scrubbing a plate that doesn't need
~~~

scrubbing, watching the water sheet down the window like it's trying to hide me from myself.

Behind me, Grace laughs at something on TV as she folds laundry on the couch, pretending not to notice I haven't said more than twelve words since I walked through the door.

She does, though. Of course she does.

"Work okay?" she asks softly.

I nod without turning around. "Yeah. It was fine. Thanks."

More silence. More scrubbing.

I feel her eyes on my back before I hear the sound of fabric stop. Then, gentle footsteps behind me. My heart's thrumming in my chest. *Don't touch me.* I'm not holding it together. I'm just holding on. And one touch from her might be the thing that breaks me completely.

"Kyle," she says, voice low. "You're a thousand miles away."

I brace my hands on the edge of the sink. My shoulders ache from the tension I've been carrying since Edie walked into the restaurant and blew a hole through my past. Through my goddamn *present*.

"I'm just tired," I lie.

She says nothing. Just lays a hand on my back, and somehow it's heavier than everything I've been carrying.

I grip the sink harder.

"Shower's yours if you want it," she says, quiet, almost like she's testing how far gone I am.

I just nod. That's all I've got.

She waits another second. Then I hear her footsteps retreat down the hallway, the soft creak of our bedroom door, and the hush of her disappearing into routine.

I stay in the kitchen. Still. Staring blankly at nothing until my eyes burn. Like if I just keep holding the sink, I won't fly apart. Like I'm not standing dead center in the life I've always wanted with a grenade in my pocket and no fucking clue how to disarm it.

I want to be the man who walks down that hall and tells her everything, but I don't.

Because I don't know what everything *is* yet. And because deep down, I think I'm afraid she'll look at me differently. Not because I have a daughter, but because I didn't know. Because I *missed it.* I don't even know how to *want* to be a father—when I haven't stopped being pissed at mine.

I shut the lights off. The house creaks around me. The storm keeps pouring down. And for the first time since I put that ring on her finger, I don't crawl into bed beside her.

I just sit on the couch and stare out into the night and listen to my heart break into a thousand pieces.

I'm angry at Macy—for taking all these years from me. For not telling me. For keeping her secret even when she knew her time was running out.

And then I'm angry at myself. For not chasing her down relentlessly after that night.

For not calling. For letting her go without a word because I thought it was easier that way.

The storm outside hammers the windows. The one inside me? It's biblical. Flood-worthy.

I press my palms against my face and grit my teeth, willing myself to hold it together—but I can't. Not this time. Because I don't know what to *do* with this. I don't know how to be a father. I don't even know how to forgive mine.

I should go to Grace. I should wrap myself around her and tell her everything.

Why can't I do that? *Why?*

Because I don't deserve her comfort.

Because I don't know how to show up now.

So, I stay right here. On this couch. In the home I built with her. While the storm pounds, relentless and unforgiving. Just like the guilt that won't let me sleep.

Chapter 41

NINETEEN

The rain hasn't stopped. Not last night. Not now. Not in my aching chest.

It's 4:02 a.m., and I'm still on the couch—hood up, arms folded tight, like if I hold still long enough, I might not come apart.

The kitchen is dark, lit only by the glow of the microwave clock. Outside, the storm rages on. A steady drumbeat of judgment.

Then I hear her. Soft footsteps along the hardwood. The sound of my undoing.

I glance over my shoulder.

Grace stands in the doorway, her oversized sweatshirt slipping off one perfect shoulder, eyes heavy with sleep—and something deeper. Worry. Confusion. Fear.

She crosses her arms. Not angry. Not yet. Just trying. Trying like hell.

"Kyle?" Her voice is scratchy and small. "Baby… please. Come to bed."

I glance away, my eyes dropping to the floor. I can't look at her. "I'm not tired."

"That's not the point." She takes another step closer, barefoot and vulnerable. "I don't care if you sleep. I just… I just want you with me."

I should go to her. God, I want to. But I can't. The weight in my chest is a fucking cinderblock—dragging me down, breathless, to the bottom of the ocean.

"Babe," I say quietly, "can we talk about it later?"

A beat. That's all it takes. The worry flashes into frustration—fast and sharp. Her voice hardens.

"Fuck, Kyle."

She turns and walks away.

The slam of the bedroom door hits like a gunshot, rattling the frame. My heart shatters as it echoes down the hallway.

The silence that follows is a monster. Gnawing. Gaping. Patient.

I barely move, but when I do, the couch groans beneath me. The rain keeps falling.

And for the first time in our marriage, I let her go back to bed mad. And alone.

~~~

We move through the house like strangers. Toothbrushes. Coffee. Shifting past each other in the closet like coworkers in a walk-in cooler.

No words. Just glares and quiet dares—*you go first.*

Grace's stare cuts. Not cruel. Just pleading. *Don't shut me out.*

But I already have. It started the second I walked through the door last night. Now? I don't know how to let her back in.

She grabs her keys. She doesn't slam the door this time.

That might be worse. Quieter. Colder. More deserved.

I stand there alone, soaked in the silence, until it's time to go.

~~~

The back door swings open on a gust of wind and that wet-pavement stench, and I shuffle in like someone who's just crawled out of a shipping container.

Still fucking raining. Still tired. Still clinging to my coffee like it's Wilson from *Castaway* and we barely survived a plane crash together.

My hoodie's damp. My chef pants are two wear-days past acceptable. My soul? That's debatable.

I don't even register her at first.

Then I look up—and there she is. Standing in front of the whiteboard, arms crossed, lips pressed into a thin line.

Her gaze snaps up like she's been waiting. For me. Hands on her hips, eyebrow already raised.

"Well," she says, dry as hell. "Look who finally washed up."

I freeze mid-sip.

Oh. Right. *Cassie.* She's in town. A fact I absolutely knew yesterday and completely forgot by this morning.

Shit.

I take a breath and lower my head, like maybe that'll hide the insurmountable shame and guilt racing through me. I walk toward her.

"Didn't realize you were going for the full post-apocalyptic survivor aesthetic," she says, eyeing my hoodie. "Nice look." A smirk. "We playing that old game again—homeless or hipster?"

I mutter something about not sleeping.

She doesn't bite.

She turns back to the board, taps it with her marker, studies the week's lineup like it's a war strategy. Then, casually, she says, "Go. Get in the office." She jerks her chin toward the door.

I walk past her like a kid headed to the principal's office. Her clunky red rain boots squeak behind me, loud and judgmental.

No, *How's Grace?* No, *You okay?* Just a surgical read of my entire existence and an emotional subpoena to comply.

I'm standing in the middle of the office when she shuts the door with a thud. Every sound today feels like sandpaper on raw nerves.

I glance down at my coffee. Not even sure if I'm drinking it or just holding it for comfort.

Wilson, man. You get me.

Cassie watches me for a beat, then says quietly, "Something's wrong." Her voice is soft. Open. Like arms reaching out.

I feel the warmth in her words—and then the gut punch of guilt. Because I didn't feel that from Grace last night. Because I didn't let myself.

"I'm fine," I mutter, still staring into the cup.

"Bullshit," she says.

My eyes snap to hers. No judgment. No anger. Just friendship and love.

And then it happens. Like a confession I didn't authorize.

I rub a hand over my face.

"I fucked up, Cass. I really fucked up."

I finally set my caffeinated support group on the desk and look at her.

Her brows knit. "What, Kyle?" Her voice drops, cautious. "What did you do?"

I drag in a breath. "Her name is Edie."

Cassie stiffens. Eyes narrowing. A long pause.

"She's… nineteen. Almost twenty." Her mouth drops open.

"Kyle." She takes a half-step back, like I've sprouted a second head. "You cheated? With a teenager?"

"No! Jesus, Cass, she's my daughter."

Another beat.

Her expression shifts—horror giving way to instant exhale.

"Oh." Then, under her breath, "Shit, Kyle… lead with that." She shakes her head, one hand braced on her hip. "It kind of softens the blow, you know?"

Her brows lift. "And… you didn't know?"

I shake my head slowly. "Yesterday. She found me."

"Kyle…" She tilts her head, trying to catch my gaze. "Honey, that's not fucking up. That's… that's a miracle. You have a human." She rubs my shoulder.

I almost snort. *I have a human.* Only Cassie would have that locked and loaded at a time like this.

"Cass, I don't know what the fuck I'm doing." I shake my head, unraveling like a threadbare sweater. "I haven't told Grace. Now we're fighting. I don't know what to tell her. I don't know *how* to tell her. My relationship with my dad? Jesus." I throw my hands up. "I know she wants a baby, but this is going to—" I trail off, breath hitching.

"Kyle, hey." She squeezes my shoulder. "Take a breath. She's going to be okay," Cassie says. "Grace is the most understanding woman I know. She's patient. She's kind—"

I cut her a sideways look. "Are you doing that movie scene? The one with the shit pie?"

She laughs, loud and sudden. "Fucker. I'm a teen mom.

Consoling people in emotional crises is literally my full-time profession. Let me have my Oscar moment." She smooths her palms down the front of her shirt like she's pressing an invisible gown, then refocuses. Serious face back on.

"She's going to love whatever shit pie you throw at her, Kyle. Because you're her husband. And you don't get to lock her out."

I sigh and hang my head. She's right. Of course she's right.

"Come here." She pulls me into a hug. One I didn't even realize I needed until I'm in it.

Why do I always fight this kind of comfort?

"Thank you," I murmur into her hair.

"Anytime."

I pull back. She pats my chest like she's resetting my heartbeat.

"Now," she says, gesturing toward the hallway, "can you please explain what the hell Darius is doing with the special rotations out there?" She giggles.

I nod, start to follow her out—then stop, fingers catching her sleeve.

"Hey, Cass?"

She turns, one eyebrow raised. "Yeah?"

I swallow, thumbing over my shoulder. "That was… incredible friend shit back there. Thank you."

She smiles. The kind that reaches all the way to her eyes.

"Anytime, Kyle." Then, softer—so soft it breaks me. "Just remember, she's *your* Grace."

~~~

I'm heading out for the night. Heading home to face Grace.

My new position as executive chef and owner doesn't stay for the show anymore. It's spreadsheets. Numbers. Making sure the dream we built stays built.

I peek into the kitchen to wave goodnight.

The line is alive—burners flaring, voices sharp, everything moving fast but calm.

And then, right in the middle of it, time slows.

Noah's firing the black cod. Miso glaze hissing. Skin crisping
~~~

just right. But on the next burner, a yuzu-soy beurre blanc is bubbling too hard, foaming up the sides. One more second and that sauce is toast.

And Noah? The idiot's turned around, yelling something to grill. Not even looking.

Then I spot Benjamin walking past with a hot pan in his hand. His eyes are already on the danger.

"Hot behind," he calls.

He switches hands mid-stride, reaches out, clicks the flame down, gives the sauce a quick whisk, slides the pan to safety. Keeps walking. Doesn't even look back.

When Noah turns around, he's completely oblivious. Keeps cooking like he's on *Master fucking Chef*, while Benjamin disappears toward the dish pit, then prep, then slips in as a second set of hands on garde.

But I notice.

And something lands in my chest so hard it nearly knocks the wind out of me.

He's nineteen.

The same age I was when I did this shit at Le Début. The same tunnel vision. Same instincts. Same quiet burn. Same need to be better.

Holy shit. Benjamin is me.

...And I'm taking him to Alaska.

Chapter 42

THE STORM WITHIN

The bottle of wine sits between two glasses. A 2013 Oregon pinot. I read the label again, like the vintage is going to fix everything.

It's a good bottle. A good year. Not too flashy. Not too subtle. Something that says *I remember you like this.*

There's a candle burning near the edge of the counter—sage and orange. The one she loves. The one she says makes her insides feel clean.

Just the other night, she was right here—perched on this counter, my arms bracing her legs, her head tipped back—my hands and mouth on her like she was the only thing in the world worth worshiping.

I hope she remembers that tonight.

The wax has already pooled near the edge. She's not here yet.

I adjust one of the glasses. Wipe a phantom fingerprint from the stem. Rehearse opening lines in my head like this is a first date.

Hey.

Can we talk?

I'm sorry.

I should've told you.

I didn't know how.

Or maybe I should lighten it.

At least we're saving on diaper costs.

Jesus.

I drop my face into my hands. What the fuck am I doing?

Her keys jingle softly in the lock. The door opens slowly, like she's bracing for something on the other side.

My heart hammers against my ribs. I can't swallow.

"Kyle?" she says. My name on her voice feels like a pressure valve releasing.

"Yeah, babe," I say, rounding the corner.

Our eyes meet.

She presses a hand to her chest. "Oh God…" Tears well instantly. "I was so scared I was going to come home and you were—"

"Shhh." I pull her into me, tight. Her body trembles against mine as she cries.

I kiss the crown of her head. "I'm so sorry. I'm so fucking sorry."

Her face lifts, eyes wet and searching. "What happened? What is it?"

I kiss her once, take her things, and set them in the entryway. "Come on." I nod toward the kitchen. "I got wine."

Her eyes catch the candle. "Oh shit. You lit the candle. Did you kill someone? Because if you need me to help you bury a body, you should've at least made a charcuterie board."

She smirks through the tears, wiping her face with the sleeve of her chef coat.

"No. No bodies." I pour her a glass. "I mean, the night's still young. Could be mine." I hand her the wine and lift my own. "I love you."

She smiles, soft and shaky. "I love you too."

We clink glasses. She takes a sip, eyes still on me.

"No lie… you are slightly scaring me." She gestures to the candle, the wine, the empty room. "Please just tell me what's happening, so I can stop wanting to puke." She pauses, then adds lightly, "At least I don't have to worry about you telling me you're pregnant."

She laughs.

I don't.

I swirl the glass by the stem, watching the burgundy spin. *Swish. Swish. Swish.*

The motion fuels the words. I tell her about Macy. About the surprise visit from her daughter. About Macy's death two years ago. And Edie—Edie is my daughter.

Swish. Swish. Swish.

Until her hands cover mine, stopping the motion.

I look down and realize there are tears on the counter.

Mine. Hers. Both.

I look up to see her hazel eyes swimming. "Why didn't you think you could tell me?" she asks, curling her fingers tighter around mine.

I let out a short, bitter scoff. "You'd have to get inside my fucked-up brain to get that answer."

Her thumb brushes my knuckles, but I can't hold her gaze for long.

"I was scared," I admit. "Mad. Confused." I glance at our tightly woven hands, then force my eyes back to hers. "Still am."

She nods slowly. "Okay… but you told me now."

I take a breath. "That's… exactly what Cassie said today."

Her head jerks up. "What?"

"That's what Cassie said," I repeat, softer this time. Like maybe that will soften the blow.

It doesn't.

Her eyes flash. "You talked to Cassie before you talked to me?"

"It wasn't—"

She yanks her hands from mine, wine tipping, chair scraping loud across the hardwood. "Don't tell me what it wasn't, Kyle. It was. You trusted her before you trusted me."

"I didn't trust her—"

"Bullshit!" she snaps. "We've been married three weeks and the first person you unload this on is not your wife?" Her voice rises, the rain outside pounding harder like it's keeping score. "Do you have any idea what that feels like?"

"I didn't want to dump it on you before I could even—"

"That's exactly the problem," she cuts in. "You don't want to *dump it on me*. You don't let me carry anything with you."

"That's not fair."

She laughs without humor. "It's exactly fair. You do this every time something big happens—you go inside yourself, lock the door, and throw away the key. You think you're protecting me, but all you're doing is shutting me out."

"That's not what this is, Grace."

"It's exactly what this is." Her voice drops, but the words hit harder than any shout. "And you know who else did that? Your dad."

I flinch.

"And you hated him for it."

"That's not the same," I snap.

"It is." She shakes her head. "And until you face that—or forgive him—you're going to keep doing this. To me. To everyone." She paces, hands flying. "Oh my God—just pass it down to your daughter. Make it some generational trauma while you're at it, Kyle."

The words land like a slap.

And I have nothing. No defense. No answer.

She grabs her coat and keys. "I can't do this right now."

"Grace—no. Don't you dare—"

The front door slams, rattling the frame. Her taillights bleed red into the sheets of rain until they vanish. I stand there, frozen, listening to the rain pound the windows.

And I'm a little kid again. Face pressed to cold glass. Heart hammering wild in my chest. Sirens in the distance. Fists pounding on the door.

My father's crying—sounds I didn't know he could make.

Then I'm back in the dark. Screaming for someone to hear me. That's where I learned to stay quiet.

The rain is so loud it feels like it's inside the house. Inside my chest.

I take one step back from the window and the floor tilts. My knees hit the floor. Hard. I brace my hands on the floor, shaking. My breath comes ragged, like I've been running for miles.

Images fire through my head—grainy, silent.

My mom and me, flour on our hands, laughing at the counter.

Rocco cowering under the chair when I scolded him. The shame.

Ritchie and Collin on my couch, beers and pizza boxes.

Grace under that neon light the night we met.

Rocco's ears flapping in the wind on the skateboard.

Holding Cora for the first time.

Joy floods in.

Kissing Grace under the archway.

Sunset on the terrace.

Then—taillights. Wet pavement.

Fear crashes back.

Oh my God. Oh my God.

I squeeze my eyes shut and fold forward until my forehead hits the floor. Tears spill hot and heavy over my inked arms.

"I'm sorry, Grace," I shout into the hardwood. "God, I'm so fucking sorry."

My fists pound uselessly against the floor, swallowed by the roar outside.

The storm takes it all.

~~~

I'm leaning against the wall, sitting on the cold floor, memorizing the pattern of the wood grain beneath my fingers. The ridges and grooves catch at my skin, over and over, until I know every inch by heart. A thousand passes until time just… disappears.

The phone is in my other hand, heavy and useless. I've called. Texted. Nothing. The screen stays black, and every minute she doesn't answer feels like another nail driven into my ribs.

My eyes burn. My chest feels like it's been carved out with a dull boning knife—messy, uneven, the kind of cut you can't fix.

I don't know how long I've been here. Long enough for the storm to lose its rage. The rain has slowed to a soft patter, the kind that makes you think maybe the world will let you breathe again.

Headlights sweep across the room. A door shuts. *Her door.*

I'm on my feet before I even register it.

The lock clicks—and there she is. Damp hair clinging to flushed cheeks, eyes rimmed red. She drops her bag and comes at me fast, arms wrapping around my neck like she's afraid I'll vanish.

Her fingers bury in my hair, nails digging just enough to anchor me.
~~~

Her breath catches against my ear. "You're the only fight I want to keep losing," she whispers, her voice splintering.

My hands fist in the back of her coat, pulling her in until there's no space. No air. Just us.

Her tears are hot against my skin, and I don't know if they're hers or mine.

~~~

Summer turns to fall. Mornings colder. Nights creeping in earlier. Grace and I… we've found our footing again. Not perfect—sometimes stumbling like a couple of milk-drunk toddlers—but we're back on our feet. Team Berkley.

The airport bar smells like used luggage, fryer oil, and stale beer, but the bourbon's good enough. Benjamin's next to me, Coke in hand, jittery as hell, and snapping photos for Instagram like we're on some kind of press tour.

"I'll be right back, Chef. Gotta hit the bathroom."

I snag his sleeve before he can bolt. "Hey, Ben… you can call me Kyle when it's just me and you, okay?"

He laughs, a little shy. "Yes, sir." He can't help himself. He's Southern. That *sir* is stitched into his DNA.

I watch him weave into the crowd, all energy and potential. The tail-end of nineteen.

My age when I thought I had everything figured out—right before life grabbed me by the collar and dragged me into the fire. I grew up so goddamn fast, I skipped being a kid altogether. Truth is, I never learned how to be one.

Grace is pregnant.

We announced it at Cassie's fiftieth in Charlotte—champagne flutes raised, Cassie in tears, hugs long enough for the ice to melt in our glasses. Grace has been glowing ever since. Not just the pregnancy glow people talk about, but something deeper. Warmer. She laughs more. Touches me more. Sometimes I catch her looking at me like she's picturing a future neither of us could've imagined a year ago.

And for me… it's a second chance. A shot at being there for
~~~

what I missed with Edie. The first heartbeat. The first kick. The first time we hold them. I can't get back those years with my daughter—but I can be here for this. For us.

I think about what I want for our kid. What I want for Edie. Stability. A home without doors locked from the inside. A life where love is never in question.

And sitting here, it hits me—my head has finally caught up to what my heart's been trying to tell me for years.

My eyes drift back to Benjamin's Coke. Too young for a drink. Already walking the fine line of this industry. I don't want it to chew him up before he's lived. I don't want him to skip the years he can't get back. Not like I did.

And maybe that's why the truth finally sticks.

If I want to give them something better, I have to stop carrying this shit around. I have to stop letting it run me. I have to forgive. I take a slow sip of my bourbon, set the glass down, and pull my phone from my pocket.

"Whit." the cursor blinks.

Before life moves any further, I know one thing. I have to do this. I stare at the message once more, then hit send.

Chapter 43

EMOTIONAL BAGGAGE

The captain's voice crackles over the intercom, smooth and calm in that way that makes you wonder if pilots take voice-over classes in their downtime.

"Folks, we're about twenty-five minutes out of Anchorage. Weather's clear and brisk—forty-two degrees. If you're on the right side of the aircraft, you've got a perfect view of the stunning Denali range."

Benjamin's head swivels so fast I'm half-worried he's going to strain something, phone already up, snapping photos like he's on assignment for *National Geographic*.

I glance past him out the window. The peaks stretch forever—jagged, snow-dusted, cutting into a sky so blue it almost hurts to look at. The fall light is sharper here, edging toward winter. Clean. Almost metallic. I swear I can feel the cold pressing through the glass, waiting for us.

"Thank you for flying with us today," the pilot adds. "Flight attendants, prepare for landing."

I turn my phone over in my hand. Airplane mode. Silent. Still.

Benjamin grins at me like a little kid on Christmas morning, eyes wide.

I wish I could match his excitement.

~~~

The shuttle smells faintly of cedar, coffee, and cheap cologne. The
~~~

windows are cracked open just enough to let in crisp air, the kind that hits like a deep inhale after too many hours breathing recycled plane oxygen.

Benjamin's beside me in the back, face pressed to the glass, phone in hand, thumb scrolling.

"Soleil… de… Mee-noo-it?" He glances up from his search at me. "That means 'midnight sun.'"

I bite back a smile. "Soleil de Minuit," I say, letting the French roll clean and easy off my tongue.

Brian, our driver, catches my eye in the rearview mirror and grins. "Nice. Haven't heard it said like that in a while. You speak French?"

"French culinary trained," I say with a shrug.

Benjamin's eyebrows shoot up like I've just pulled a rabbit out of my toque blanche. "Damn, Chef. Didn't know you had that in your back pocket."

Brian laughs. "Midnight sun's my favorite time of year. Solstice festival, whole town's out. Live music, fire pits, food trucks, beer. You'd love it. Everything smells like woodsmoke and salmon."

I lean back as the road curves, the view opening wide. Snow-dusted peaks slice into a blue sky, the water below glinting like hammered silver. It's the kind of sight that makes you forget for a second that the rest of the world exists at all.

"Holy shit," Benjamin breathes.

Yeah. Holy shit.

Brian eases the shuttle to a stop in front of a low, modern building faced in black wood, steel, and glass. It sits neat on a postcard-perfect main street, mountains standing guard at the end of the block.

Big gold letters gleam above the door. *Soleil de Minuit.*

"All right, gentlemen," Brian says, popping the door. "Welcome to the Sourdough State—Alaska. As chefs, you can appreciate that one. Pretty cool history behind the name."

The cold air grabs my lungs the second I step out, sharp and merciless. When we push through the heavy wooden door, the noise hits: pans clanging, voices humming, butter and garlic drifting from the open kitchen.

Inside is organized chaos. Chefs in black aprons move with clockwork precision, stations already set, pans snapping with heat. Simon stands at the center of it, sleeves rolled, calling orders like he's been here for years instead of hours. Like it's his kitchen.

"Sorry we're late to the party," I say, stepping in.

He spots us instantly. "Hey, man. Great to see you again." His grin is all teeth as he strides over, draping an arm across my shoulder like we're old college buddies.

"Everyone," he calls, "this is Kyle Berkley from Sagi-Shi in San Francisco."

Hands lift. "Hi, Kyle," a chorus answers.

"Ophelia Crane," she says, stepping in for my hand, every bit as graceful as she is stunning.

I've read the articles. I've followed her career on social media like the professional stalker I am. But in person… I'm speechless.

"Thank you for coming and doing this with us, Kyle."

I nod, still catching up.

She moves on to Benjamin, who looks just as star-struck.

I give a quick wave to the room. "Nice to meet everyone."

Gesturing to Ben standing shyly beside me, I add, "This is Benjamin. He's new to our team. My protégé." I clasp his shoulder, rocking him a little off his axis like a proud dad. "Originally from Charleston, South Carolina. Don't let his baby face fool you. He's got mad skills."

Benjamin blushes. "Nice to meet y'all," he says sheepishly, that warm Southern drawl wrapping around every word.

Simon yanks an apron from a hook and tosses it to Benjamin. "Suit up, rookie. You're on veg prep."

Benjamin catches it, startled but grinning. "Uh… yes, Chef."

Simon claps me on the shoulder, steering me toward the pass. "Man, I know you've got a lot going on with the new marriage, Sagi, but I'm glad you're here. This is gonna be fucking great, Kyle."

I stop him with a half-smile. "Oh, more news. Grace is pregnant."

His eyes go wide. "Oh… no shit! Congratulations, man. Being a dad—it's the best thing you'll ever do."

Something about the way he says it lodges in my chest, heavy and unshakable. I can almost feel the weight of that unfinished conversation waiting in my phone.

Don't go there, Kyle. Not here. Not yet.

I roll my shoulders, stretch my neck, like I can physically shake it loose. The smell of searing salmon and garlic, the hiss of butter hitting a hot pan, pulls me back into the moment.

Simon's already moving, handing me a towel and an apron, pointing me toward a station.

"Come on, man, let's cook."

The restaurant is French. The menu is French-Alaskan fusion—clean, strategic, built on locally sourced produce and proteins.

Absolutely brilliant.

I'm mesmerized listening to Ophelia talk, her voice alive with plans to help another restaurant in town—teaching their cook new recipes, updating his skills. She's even reopening a local salmon factory to create more jobs. The fire in her eyes is almost palpable.

Benjamin sidles up beside me with a sample menu, finger trailing down the page.

"Look, Chef. She's using reindeer sausage in this cassoulet. All locally sourced beans. That's such a good idea."

I turn to him, honestly shocked. "You know what a cassoulet is?"

He smirks. "Yeah. I brushed up on my French cuisine when I found out I was coming here. Didn't want to look like a complete tool."

This is the same kid who probably spent the last month watching instructional videos on truffle microplaning like they were OnlyFans clips. I know this kid—because I see *me*.

~~~

Brian eases the shuttle up a long gravel drive, tires crunching under the weight of our gear. The view opens in slow motion, like a curtain lifting on some epic movie scene.

Pastures stretch out on both sides, fenced with weathered wood
~~~

that looks sturdy and lived-in, dotted with horses straight out of a Ralph Lauren ad. Beyond them, mountains rise dark against the fading light, snowcaps catching the last smear of gold from the sun.

Once again, Benjamin's got his phone up, snapping like a tourist. "Holy shit, Chef," he mutters.

Holy shit is right.

"I'll never get over this place," Paula, one of the chef's whispers, peering out the window over my shoulder.

Brian pulls us around to a sprawling timber-frame house with a wraparound porch, windows placed like they were designed for maximum eyegasm views. He throws it in park, kills the engine.

"Welcome to Bradshaw Acres."

Inside, the first thing I see is him. *Well… fuck.*

This guy's a presence. Big everything. Like GQ meets Paul Bunyan. Broad shoulders, easy stance, forearms that say he could split firewood with his bare hands and still have enough left in him to prep a delicate slab of salmon for the grill.

He's at the counter, knife gliding in steady, precise strokes across the fish. Then he looks up, meets my eyes with that quick, assessing glance men like him have. Protective. Measuring. Deciding if you're worth the time. But there's kindness there, too, under the weight of it.

"There's beer and random drinks on the deck, wine in here," he says to everyone passing through, pointing with his knife toward the laughter spilling in from outside. "Make yourselves at home."

Then his focus shifts back to me, and he reaches across the counter. His handshake is exactly what I expected—firm, warm… and holy crap, huge. His hand swallows mine.

"I was late and didn't get a chance to meet you. I'm Kyle."

He nods. "Oh, right. San Francisco. Cannon Bradshaw." He releases my hand, takes a long pull from his beer.

I tuck my hands into my pockets, nod toward the wall of glass framing the mountains. "This place is incredible. Those all your horses out there?"

"Yeah, mostly. A few boarders. It's my family's ranch."

Ophelia slips in beside him, snakes an arm around his waist, pressing her head into him like she's found her favorite place. He pulls her close without missing a beat.

I nod, suddenly aware of my own edges. I eye the cooler on the deck. "Very cool. Well, thanks for having us, man."

I head outside where the air's cooler and cedar smoke drifts up from somewhere below. Everyone's gathered in loose clusters, silhouetted against the mountains.

Conversation's light—mostly chef talk. What our restaurants are doing, how we can't find good staff. The usual.

Off to the side, Benjamin's deep in conversation with a strawberry-blonde girl—fifteen, maybe sixteen—who's hanging on every word, eyes tracking his hands like a cat chasing a laser pointer.

I glance back through the glass. Cannon's watching them like a hawk. Yeah… that's his daughter.

Oh, fuck.

I take my beer to the far end of the deck where it's quiet. Where I can breathe. Leaning against the rail, I think about everything I missed with Edie—the teen angst, the slammed doors, the awkward car rides. Now it's stilted lunches and a stranger's questions.

I look up. Stars spill across the sky like diamonds scattered over black velvet. I pull out my phone and snap a picture, snowcapped mountains framing it perfectly.

Instead of something generic, I type something real. Something… *fatherly.*

> Kyle: I think she's up there. Actually, I know she is. Thinking of you.

I hesitate, thumb hovering. My heart kicks hard against my ribs. Then I press send.

When I glance back toward the deck, Benjamin's still there—animated, smiling, making her laugh. He has no idea Cannon's probably mapping out how to bury his body if he steps out of line. But it hits me—the kid's doing it right. Connecting. Listening.

I don't just want to be here for Edie. I want to be someone she wants to be around. Someone worth listening to.

Just as I head inside for dinner, my phone vibrates in my pocket.

Edie: Uncool for making me cry on a date. But thank you, that was beautiful. I wish I was there. But I'm glad she is.

I read it twice, just to make sure I didn't imagine it. My shoulders loosen, something in my chest uncoiling.

Maybe I'm not too late.

~~~

Dinner's over, the clink of silverware replaced by the low hum of voices inside. I'm back on the deck, leaning against the rail, cold air biting at my cheeks.

My phone's still warm in my pocket from where I slid it earlier—the message from Whit still needling at me, the one that got my blood boiling before the flight. The door creaks open behind me, spilling light and warmth onto the boards.

"You hiding out here, or just claiming the last bit of peace?" Ophelia's voice floats out, amused but easy.

I glance over my shoulder. She steps out, pulling her sweater tighter, long brown hair catching the glow from inside.

I clear my throat, aiming for casual. "Is it that obvious?" I take a pull from my beer, try to smile.

She moves to stand beside me at the railing, both of us facing the dark stretch of land, the mountains reduced to shadow.

"No," she says. "You almost pulled it off."

I nod, a soft chuckle slipping out.

Her eyes flick sideways, studying me in that quiet way people do when they already know you're holding something back.

"You okay?" she asks, gentle.

"Yeah." I offer a faint smile, and nod. "Just a long day. Travel, new kitchen, big week ahead." I chase the lie with another swallow of beer and let the silence settle under the blanket of stars. I gesture toward the landscape. "You've built something cool here. Feels good."

She nods. "I hope so."

I lift my bottle toward the door. "I should probably head back in before Simon roasts me in front of your boyfriend."

She tips her head back and laughs. "Nah. He's too busy talking
~~~

about himself. He did tell me you're a great chef… and that you used to be fun."

I laugh, shaking my head. "Yeah. Back then I had worse hair and fewer regrets."

I tip my empty bottle toward her and head inside, letting the noise swallow me—anything to drown out the weight of that one message still waiting on my phone.

~~~

The lodge is quiet except for the low hum of the mini-fridge and the occasional pop from the baseboard heat. I sit on the edge of the bed, still in my jeans, elbows braced on my knees, my phone heavy in my hands.

The screen glows back at me—our thread. Just a few lines, but it carries the whole goddamn weight of my life.

Whit: For what? I didn't know I did anything wrong.

That's it. That's the reply. Years of silence and damage, dressed up as distance and denial, and wrapped up in nine fucked-up words.

The bane of my existence in nine words. No admission. No recognition. Not even a half-assed "sorry if I hurt you."

My chest caves in, static rushing my head. Forgive him for what, exactly? For being absent? For pushing me aside like I was a kitchen mistake he could scrape into the trash? For pretending my mother's death didn't wreck us both?

I scroll up, rereading my own words—how careful I'd been, how much space they took up inside me before I hit send at the airport. And he… just didn't see it. Or wouldn't.

Kyle: I'm letting it go, Whit. I forgive you.

Part of me wonders if I imagined it all wrong. If maybe I'm just… fucked up.

Then the memory hits—his hand slicing across my face, the sharp heat blooming under my eye. The wedding. Writing me off at eighteen with nothing but a trust fund and a fuck-off before he and Caroline left for their lifelong world tour.
~~~

Yeah. I didn't imagine that.

I swipe the phone closed and toss it onto the pillow like it burned me. My jaw aches from clenching. For a long beat, I just sit there, staring at the floorboards, breathing like I've run ten miles in snow boots.

I need air. No. I need… *her*.

I grab the phone again, thumb hovering over the FaceTime icon before I can second-guess it.

She answers on the second ring—hair up, no makeup, wrapped in one of my old sweatshirts. She's curled on the couch, warm light spilling behind her, like gravity pulling me back where I belong.

"Hey, babe," she says softly, a smile trying to find its way onto her face.

The tightness in my chest cracks. "Hey. You feeling okay? Still nauseous?"

She shakes her head. "No. Just tired today. I'm fine. I'm more worried about you." Her eyes narrow slightly. "Stop deflecting."

I rub a hand over my face, trying to find words that don't feel like jagged glass in my throat. "My dad texted back."

Her expression stills. "And?"

I let out a bitter laugh that feels too loud for the quiet room. "And… apparently he didn't know he did anything wrong."

Grace's eyes flash with a mix of anger and hurt that isn't even for herself. "Kyle…"

"I don't know what to do with that," I admit, voice low. "It's like… have I just been imagining it all these years? Or is he really that blind?"

She leans closer to the camera, her voice steady. "You didn't imagine it."

Her words settle heavy but true in my chest. For a second, I just look at her—my wife, my lifeline—and feel like maybe I can breathe again. Like maybe I can push this elephant off my chest.

"I'm trying," I say quietly. "For you. For the baby. For Edie."

Her mouth curves, soft and sure. "For you too, Kyle. This is for you."

I nod.

I'm not all the way there yet. But with her looking at me like that, I think maybe I could be.

Chapter 44

BOOTCAMP & BAR TABS

I'm halfway through my first cup of coffee when Simon decides we're filming a Top Chef bootcamp no one consented to. The new hires line the perimeter of the kitchen like they're waiting for roll call in a military mess hall. Each has a cutting board, knife, onion, carrot, and celery stalk lined up in front of them.

Simon paces like a battle general, hands clasped behind his back. "If you don't know—and I really hope you do—this is a mirepoix," he booms. "We want an even, fine chop. You have one minute." He checks his watch. "Go!"

The room erupts in staccato chaos—steel on wood, blades thudding like a hostage situation sponsored by Henckels, relentless and loud.

I make a slow pass behind them with Paula, arms crossed, scanning for our ringers.

"Oh my god," she snickers.

Ophelia catches my eye for a second, and that's all it takes. We both crack. This is ridiculous.

Benjamin's at the far end, knife flashing quick, shoulders loose, like he's been waiting his whole life to show off. Across from him, a guy grips his knife like a pencil, and I'm 90% sure he just diced his own thumb.

"TIME!" Simon barks. Knives hit boards and hands shoot up like we're on an episode of *Chopped.*

I look away to keep from laughing. They're taking him way too seriously, and Simon's eating it up—stalking behind the line, inspecting mounds of chopped vegetables like he's waiting to hand out kindergarten gold stars. Two recruits get quietly redirected to prep duty with Zach, faces grim like they're walking to their own executions. The rest survive round one, the knife skills test.

The noise ramps back up, but it's the good kind—stories traded, side-by-side prep work, that contagious kitchen energy that makes you want to get your hands dirty. Ophelia ducks out for a meeting with Cannon, and the kitchen barely notices before the rhythm takes over again.

Paula drifts toward the cooler, and I end up shoulder-to-shoulder with Kevin at the herb station. He's one of those guys who's clearly been in kitchens long enough to have stories—forearms like rolling pins, faded Celtic tats peeking out from under his sleeves with the red hair to match, and a grin that says he's either about to hand you wisdom or talk shit.

"Hell of a first day," he says, chopping parsley at a dizzying speed.

"Simon's got a flair for the dramatic," I say, nodding toward where he's holding court with Zach's two greenest recruits—narrating basic sauté skills like a damn war story. Zach's parked off to the side with a bowl of French onion soup, looking like a man who just got the night off.

Kevin chuckles. "Yeah, I've worked with his type. Good chefs, but they could turn peeling potatoes into a scene straight out of *Braveheart*."

I laugh, stripping oregano. "Where'd you work before?"

He scrapes the parsley off his knife into a bowl, tone shifting. "Seattle. Marrow & Moss. Upscale gastropub in Ballard. You heard of it?"

"Nope." I shake my head. "What brought you here?"

He shoots me a look, then grins. "What do you think?"

"Ahhh." I chuckle.

He starts in on more herbs, eyes down, still smiling. "Came for a fly-fishing trip. She worked at the salmon factory before it closed." He jerks his knife toward the back door like I should automatically know where the place is. "Hooked her instead of the fish. No chef gigs here, so we've been bouncing between odd jobs." He cuts me a smile. "Feels good to be back in a kitchen again."

I clap him on the back. "Chef's lucky to have you, Kevin."

I tilt my chin toward Benjamin at the far end, deep in conversation with little miss strawberry-blonde, who's leaning on the counter like she's settling in for the night.

When the hell did she sneak in?

Kevin follows my gaze and smirks. "Kid's got talent. Needs seasoning. And maybe someone to tell him when he's about to step in something he can't un-step in." He scoffs lightly. "Her dad's Cannon Bradshaw, you know."

I grin. "Yeah… noted."

By then, the kitchen's winding down. Cutting boards get stacked, the last pots hit the drying rack, and someone kills the playlist. Simon's leaning on the counter with a deli quart of bourbon like he just won it in battle, shooting the shit with Zach. Coats get pulled from hooks, and conversations shift to where people are headed next for dinner, as if this town actually has options.

That's when Cannon and Ophelia walk in the front door. At the same time, Benjamin and Francis drift out from the back, still talking, still smiling, like they've got all the time in the world.

Cannon's eyes hit the scene and it's like watching a bear catch scent of something it doesn't like. His jaw locks so tight I can practically hear enamel grinding.

"Francis Eliza," he says, low and sharp. I swear the entire crew's assholes puckered at once.

Francis freezes, then pastes on a bright, too-innocent smile. "Oh… hi. Hi, Dad. How was the meeting?"

Benjamin looks like he's about two seconds from bolting for the door, or at least in need of a fresh pair of chef pants.

Kevin leans into my ear, voice low. "Oooh shit. I watched this dude decimate every soul in Doc's one night over some chick."

I bite back a laugh. Poor Benjamin's not old enough for a legal bar tab, but too old to be grounded.

Cannon's glare lingers long enough to suck the air out of the room, then he jerks his head toward the door.

"Francis. Now."

Francis huffs, hands flailing, muttering something about not being a kid as she storms past him. Benjamin tries to melt into the wall on his way out, practically speed-walking past Cannon and Ophelia, mumbling something polite. Smart kid.

Kevin coughs "Dead man walking," into the crook of his arm.

The crew scatters fast—jackets zipped, knife rolls stowed. Nobody wants to get caught in the fallout. I end up trailing Benjamin out the front door, across the gravel lot toward the motel.

We cross the street toward the lodge. Behind us, Francis's voice cuts through the night—sharp, teenage angst sharpened on her dad's patience. Her hands flash in the glow of the restaurant lights, punctuating every word like sparks off a fuse.

Benjamin glances over his shoulder, winces, then huffs out a laugh. "Damn, that girl's got balls."

I shake my head. "She's also got you in deep shit. How old is she?"

He throws up a hand before I can say another word. "I know what you're gonna say. She's fifteen," he huffs. "I'm not an idiot. And we're just friends, Chef."

"Kyle," I correct.

He lets out a short breath, shaking his head. "We're just friends, *Kyle*. She's cool. You know she rides barrel horses competitively?"

Across the street, Francis is still laying into Cannon like she's trying to win a courtroom trial before curfew.

I glance back at Benjamin. Poor kid's toast, and he doesn't even know it yet.

We stop in front of our side-by-side motel rooms, breath puffing white in the cold. For a second, I forget he isn't a kid. At nineteen, I was sneaking into bars with a fake ID, pounding cheap-ass beers after shifts with Ritchie, thinking I was untouchable. Living with Collin, straddling that thin line between manhood and childhood. Benjamin's got this wide-eyed innocence I almost want to protect.

"You gonna join us at The Rusted Cupboard, then Doc's?" I ask.

He shakes his head, fumbling with the clunky motel keychain. "Nah. I think I'm gonna order a pizza and just chill with a movie. Is that lame?"

I chuckle. "No. Not lame at all." I point at him. "Just don't call Brian and get a ride over to her house."

He freezes mid-unlock, then shoots me a startled look as the door clicks open. "Are you serious? That man would rip my arms off and smile while he did it. End my cooking career before it even started."

~~~

The Rusted Cupboard is exactly what it sounds like—dingy carpet, mismatched chairs, a jukebox that hasn't worked since Sinatra was top dog, and a laminated menu that looks like it's survived three nuclear winters.

But it's not just a restaurant. It's a shrine to bad taxidermy. The more you look, the worse it gets. Dusty moose heads mounted crooked. A raccoon frozen mid-poker game. A badger with an expression like it sneezed itself to death. Two bloated bullfrogs locked in a fishing trip for eternity… why?

And then there's the pièce de resistance, an otter nailed to a slab of driftwood, grinning wide with a full set of dentures—human ones. Somebody thought they were being clever. They weren't.

Simon leans in and whispers, "I feel like he's auditioning for a toothpaste commercial."

He's not wrong. The teeth are too big. Too bright. Too *human.*

Then Simon strolls in like he's a regular, already grinning at the specials board hung crooked on the wall. "Chili, pot roast, and… salmon surprise? The surprise is salmonella, right?" He body checks me on his way to a booth.

Paula groans, tugging him toward our table, while Garrett mutters about keeping his expectations low enough to avoid food poisoning.

Then our server bounces over—tiny, wiry, with teeth like she
~~~

chews gravel for fun and a smile so bright you almost forget the dental situation.

"Well hiiii there, strangers!" She beams, plunking down paper-wrapped silverware and waters like we've just been seated at a Michelin-star restaurant. "I'm Ruby."

Simon's eyes go wide. I can practically hear the stand-up routine booting up in his brain.

"You look like a Simon," Ruby says, poking him in the shoulder like she's known him since kindergarten.

Simon gasps. "I *am* a Simon. Wait—are you a psychic waitress?"

"Oh God," I mutter low into my menu, grinning. "Don't encourage him."

Ruby cackles, clapping her hands together, and Simon's gone, grinning like he's just discovered his comedic soulmate.

"Really. How did you know?" he demands, eyes twinkling.

She throws her head back, laughing. "Wendy served you all last night." She points at him with her pen, narrowing her eyes. "She told me all about *you*."

Simon leans back dramatically, clutching his chest. "Betrayed. By *Wendy*."

Ruby smirks, hand on hip. "She said you were trouble. I like trouble."

She jots our orders on her pad, then winks and spins away, already calling out drink refills to another table.

We settle into conversation.

"Well, it's great to see Ophelia happy again. It was hard seeing her go through the last two years. Cannon seems like a great guy," Garrett says.

Paula nods, taking a long sip of her water. "He'll definitely protect her, that's for sure."

Across from me, Rebecca—the Estela chef who's been quiet all day, head down—finally cracks a smile. When the laughter fades, she fiddles with her water glass, then says, almost to herself, "I used to see Ophelia and her husband come into Estela sometimes. Patrick."

I glance at her, surprised. She keeps her eyes fixed on the glass, like that's where the memory lives.

"They were… sweet. Always sat at the bar. I'd catch them through the pass—her leaning in, laughing at something he said. They just… fit together. After he died, the whole place felt it. We only knew them as regulars, but… it mattered, you know? When I heard she was building something here, it just felt right to come."

Her voice trails off, and for a beat the weight lingers at the table.

Then the food lands, merciful and loud. Mine—a pile of gray pot roast drowned in gloppy, lump-heavy gravy, with carrots and potatoes that look boiled straight out of the Depression. The "salad" is mostly iceberg and despair.

Simon takes a bite of something fried, gags theatrically, then points at Ruby. "You and me, we're starting a comedy act. The Psychic and the Chef."

Ruby beams like he's just proposed marriage.

The whole table breaks into laughter again, the tension easing as the night folds around us—warm, ridiculous, and buzzing.

~~~

We pull the doors open to Doc's—the most local bar I've ever stepped into. The silence that drops when we walk in makes me wonder if we need membership cards, flannel, and probably a beard.

"What can I get you?" the bartender asks, flicking coasters down the bar like she's dealing us in for a game of blackjack.

"An IPA, please?" I nod toward the taps behind her. "Nice ink." I gesture at the full sleeves covering her arms.

"Ahh, thanks. I draw on myself when I'm bored." She slides the pint toward me and lifts one unruly brow. "We've got long-ass winters. I get *very* bored." She scoffs, eyes flicking down her arm before turning to Simon. "You, my dear? What's your poison?"

He laughs, thumbing toward the door. "I think that was dinner around the corner. Can I get a double Blanton's neat? Maybe it'll kill the alien bacteria currently colonizing my GI tract."

"Hey. Don't be shitting on our—" She cuts herself off mid-snap, mouth dropping open. "Wait." She points, eyes scanning all of us. "You're the Chefs, aren't you?" A grin spreads as she braces her hands on the bar.
~~~

"We are," Simon says, splaying his arms like the Messiah making his big comeback.

"Well damn. This round's on the house. Thanks for coming." She scans the crowd. "Where's my girl? Where's Ophelia?"

"She's on her way. She and Cannon," Garrett says.

"Did you say Ophelia and *Cannon* are coming?" a voice cuts in. It's Christian, the bar manager I briefly met earlier at the restaurant. Up close, the guy looks like he just walked out of a whiskey ad. Perfect black hair. Perfect white teeth. Perfectly annoying.

"Oh hey, man," I say, keeping it casual. "Yeah, they said they'd meet us here."

He taps the bar. "Can I get another, Helen?"

"Sure thing." She pours, slides it over. Their eyes catch for a second—quick, but heavy. Like a warning passing between them. Or a reminder.

Three beers and two games of very mediocre pool later, the air shifts.

I spot Cannon and Christian across the bar, squared up. Cannon's jaw flexes, broad shoulders crowding the space. Christian has a cool smile plastered on and doesn't back down an inch. The whole bar hushes, breath cinched tight.

My grip tightens on the pool cue, pulse spiking. I'm half-ready to smash it over somebody's back like I've been in a bar brawl before. I haven't, but if there ever was one, it'd be here. And yeah, I'd swing for my new tribe.

It's over before it even begins. Ophelia and Cannon leave, and the bar exhales back to life—pool balls cracking, pints clinking, laughter filling the air.

I chalk the tip of my cue.

"What was that about?" I ask Jeff, my new pool partner and the local fly-fishing guide I just booked a trip with.

He shakes his head, glare cutting straight to Christian. "That's been brewing a long time. That fucker needs to watch his back and stay away from Cannon."

I laugh, leaning in for my shot. "That's gonna be hard, since he's Ophelia's new bar manager."

I line it up, exhale, and miss by an inch. *Damn IPA.*

Jeff's head snaps toward me so fast I'm surprised it doesn't crack. He raises a fist to his mouth. "Bar manager? Oh, fuck." He laughs, then sobers. "That isn't good, Kyle. Not good."

He claps me on the shoulder, then runs the table and takes my twenty.

~~~

By the time we trudge back to the lodge, the night's got that quiet buzz to it—beer warmth and laughter still echoing in my chest. I kick the door shut with my heel, flop onto the bed and fish my phone out of my pocket.

Kyle: You'd die if you saw this place. Taxidermy raccoons playing poker. Simon tried to order salmon surprise. Pretty sure the surprise was salmonella.

Her bubble pops up almost instantly.

Grace: Please tell me you didn't eat it.

I laugh, head sinking into the pillow.

Kyle: Pot roast. Gray as morgue meat, but I'm alive. Simon's flirting with a waitress named Ruby. Paula wants to murder him. Cannon almost decked Ophelia's bar manager. Small-town drama's real.

There's a pause this time before her reply.

Grace: You sound happy, babe.

I stare at the words, the smile lingering even as the room tilts from the drinks.

Kyle: Yeah. I am.

The phone slips onto my chest, warmth spreading as the night settles around me.
~~~

Chapter 45

CATCH & RELEASE

I pull back the olive-green curtains in my dated motel room. Sunrise cuts a gold sliver across the sky, bouncing off the snow-dusted mountains in the distance. No matter how long I've been here, the view still knocks me flat.

6:48. At home it's 7:48, and she's getting ready for work.

I hit FaceTime.

She answers like she's been waiting, radiant even through the shitty motel Wi-Fi.

"Hey, honey," she says, voice tired.

"Hey, you. You sound wiped. Rough night?"

She sets the phone on the counter so I can see her body as she turns sideways, smoothing her hands over her small, round belly.

"I've got a new ailment. Heartburn." She smiles.

"Damn. Look at you. So damn beautiful."

She leans close again, swiping on makeup into the mirror. "I was thinking."

"Oh no." I grin, choking down bad coffee.

"Stop." She waves me off, then rests her chin on her palm. "Boy names. Roman, Nathan, Henry, or Johan."

I twist my mouth. "Are we talking family names, or did you just raid a baby-name list I'm about to roast?"

"You don't like any of them?"

"Roman?" I drop into a terrible accent. "Hear ye, hear ye! Sir Roman Berkley was born on the fortnight, weighing—"

Her deadpan cuts me off. "Asshole. Fine. No Roman."

"No Johan either. But Henry's solid." I pause, my smile softening. "Hard to believe I might actually have a little boy."

She rubs her bump, gaze dropping before lifting back to me. "You're going to be the best dad, Kyle."

Her voice tugs something deep inside me.

"You still heading out fly-fishing this morning?"

"Yeah." I flick my eyes to the clock on the nightstand. "He's picking me up in a few."

"Have fun. You can teach *Roman* someday," she teases.

"I'm shocked Whit didn't name me that. Very on brand for him."

She giggles. "Totally."

"Love you."

"Love you too. Hey, send me pictures of your prize-winning trouser trout."

I laugh. "Already did."

"Yeah, it's my screensaver." She winks before hanging up.

The screen goes black. I sit there with coffee in one hand, phone in the other, her words echoing.

You're going to be the best dad. Except there's always unfinished business sitting in this phone.

Whit. Edie. A thousand things unsaid.

I start somewhere. Anywhere.

Kyle: How'd it go with your second date with Drake the other night?

Her reply comes fast.

Edie: He ordered duck confit. I laughed so hard I snorted my water. He didn't call me back. Tragic.

I smirk.

Kyle: Maybe he didn't want to compete with another duck in the room.

Duck emojis flood the screen.

Edie: Why would you put that in my head? That's all I thought about. Low-key hilarious though. He was a jerk anyway.

Kyle: There's more fish in the sea. Possibly more waterfowl.

Edie: Pretty sure I inherited your humor. Dry as the Sahara.

My grin lingers. Then I type before I can chicken out.

Kyle: I just want to be a good dad. To Edie. To this baby. That's it. I want to wipe the slate clean.

My pulse hammers.

Send.

Silence.

By the time Jeff's headlights sweep across the lot, I've stuffed my phone deep in my pocket. I climb into the cab of his truck. The heater's blasting and the radio is playing on low.

"Morning," Jeff says.

"Morning."

Halfway down the gravel road, my phone pings.

Whit: You will.

One line. Once again, no apology. No weight lifted. Just… his cryptic bullshit.

My chest tightens.

"You good?" Jeff asks, eyes still on the road.

I force a laugh. "Yeah. Just my old man."

Jeff flicks me a sidelong glance. "Ah. So, you're *not* good." He steers one-handed, dry as hell. "Lucky for you, it's a fishing day. Water's therapy you can drink beer next to."

His truck crunches down a narrow dirt road, frost still weighing down the tall grass. Then the trees fall away, and there it is. The river stretches like a scar through the valley. Wide and glassy in places, broken into froth and rapids in others, the water catches the morning sun like liquid silver. A low mist curls over the surface, drifting lazy as smoke, wrapping around boulders big enough to swallow cars. Spruce and aspen lean in along the banks like they're eavesdropping, branches heavy with dew.

"Holy shit," I breathe, forehead pressed to the glass.

Jeff grins, one hand loose on the wheel. "Not bad, huh? Wait till you're standing in it. Cold enough to make you question every decision you've ever made. But she's got a way of cleaning your head out."

He parks, the engine ticking as it cools. I step out and the air bites clean and sharp, full of damp earth and smoky pine. The rush of water is constant. Steady. Like a heartbeat.

I shove my hands into my jacket pockets, staring at the river that feels more alive than most people I know. My phone presses heavy against my thigh, Whit's two words still echoing.

You will.

Standing on the bank, the river roaring low and steady beside us, I shift against the pull of the waders. They're heavy as hell, and the rubber bunches behind my knees. The rod feels awkward in my hand, too light and too long all at once, the line catching clumsily around my fingers.

"So, you said you've got a little experience fly-fishing? With your uncle?" Jeff asks, cinching his vest like he's suiting up for battle.

"Yeah. My Uncle Wally." I draw the line back, letting it whip forward across the grass, the motion tugging at memory. "He took me to Jackson Hole in my early twenties. Great trip. Long time ago, though." I laugh. "Pretty sure I've forgotten how to do this."

The line slaps down with all the grace of a drunk goose.

Jeff snorts. "Cast like you mean it, not like you're swatting a mosquito."

I reset my stance, laughing. "Hold on. It's been a minute."

"Don't worry." He nods toward the water, calm and cocky, like the river's a woman he knows well. "She's patient. But she'll still make an ass out of you if you come in too soft."

Jeff squints out over the current, scanning like he's reading a menu in bad lighting. "Alright, here's the deal. Late August, early September. Prime time. Silvers are running thick right now. Coho.

Strong, flashy, mean as hell. They'll fight you like Cannon and Christian over Ophelia." He winks.

He taps the water with the tip of his rod. "Chums and pinks are still straggling through, but they're like the cheap beer of salmon. You don't brag about 'em. You just... catch 'em anyway."

I laugh. "And that leaves...?"

"Trout and Dollies." He grins, tying a fly onto my line with his teeth. "Rainbows and Dolly Varden are stuffing themselves on salmon eggs like it's Thanksgiving dinner. Big, colorful, angry bastards. Hook into one of those and you're in for a wild ride, right up until he flashes a stripe, spits your hook, and laughs at you mid-air."

I smirk, shaking my head. "So basically, my options are mean drunks or gluttons?"

"Welcome to Alaska," Jeff says, deadpan. "Now cast like you mean it."

We wade in, the water pushing hard against my thighs. It's cold enough to steal the breath from my lungs if I let it. The river's alive and surging like it's got its own heartbeat under the surface. My waders feel heavy, boots sucking against the rocks with every shift of my weight.

Jeff stops a few feet away, rod tucked under his arm as he ties on a fly. "Alright. Lesson one. You're not stabbing the water. You're not swatting mosquitoes. You're painting a picture. Smooth. Back and forth. Let the rod do the work."

He casts, relaxed and easy, like the Bob Ross of fly-fishing.

I mimic his cast, but my wrist is all wrong, flicking too tight. The line snaps the air.

Jeff chuckles. "Jesus, Berkley. You trying to lasso a cow? Relax your grip."

I adjust. Exhale. Let the rod arc. The line sails a little truer this time, unfurling across the current before settling.

It feels good. Like the rhythm's buried in me somewhere, and I just have to dig it out.

"Better," Jeff says, already stripping line with a practiced hand. "This time of year, it's all silvers and fat trout. Salmon are the mean drunks. Trout are the gluttons. You'll like trying to catch both."

He grins, but I'm already tuning him out. The water hums and swirls around my legs. The line whispers through the air.

Back. Forward. Release. The world shrinks down to that rhythm. The cast and the pull. The steady tug of the current.

Forgiveness.

The word drops in, uninvited.

I think about Grace, her hand smoothing over her belly this morning. Her laugh when she said Roman. Her soft voice telling me I'll be a good dad.

I think about Edie, firing back duck emojis, admitting she's got my humor. That she got something from me even when I wasn't there to give it.

I think about Whit. The text, *You will.* Like he handed me a stone instead of an answer. Like he couldn't, or wouldn't, ever say the one thing I've needed from him my whole damn life.

My line snags in the current, jerking me back. I free it and cast again.

Water pressing in. Cold. Sharp. Honest.

Maybe forgiveness isn't about getting what you want. Not the apology. Not the clean slate. Maybe it's standing here anyway, line in hand, choosing not to let the weight drag you under.

Back. Forward. Release.

For once, it feels like I've got it right.

The line unfurls, lands clean, and drifts.

Maybe forgiveness is just this. Standing in the cold, letting the current carry what you can't. Choosing to unclench. To stop gripping so damn hard.

I'm almost lost in it when I see a flash of silver under the surface, darting toward the fly. My breath catches.

"Come on," I mutter, pulse thudding. "Take it. Just… take the bait. You know you want to."

The line snaps tight.

Ziiiing.

My whole arm jolts, and suddenly I'm not just fishing anymore. I'm hanging on for dear life.

"Fish on!" Jeff hollers from downriver, already grinning like a proud dad at Little League. "Keep the tip up, Kyle! Don't let him run you!"

The words hit harder than they should.

Don't let him run you.

It's not just the fish I'm fighting. It's every time I let Whit yank me around, every time I swallowed his silence like it was my fault.

I stumble, boots scraping slick rock, water surging higher against my legs as the line screams downstream. Panic and thrill tangle in my chest.

"Jesus," I mutter, clamping down, rod bending near double. I wasn't ready. Not even close. One second I was in my head. The next, chaos. Something wild is on the other end demanding I give it everything I've got.

The fish darts. I let the line sing, give him room, reel him back inch by inch. Every muscle's lit up, every nerve screaming. It's not graceful. I'm slipping, swearing, teeth clenched, but I'm still here. I'm still holding on.

Then—*splash.*

Silver and pink explode out of the water, twisting in the morning light. A Coho. Muscles thrashing. Beautiful and brutal. Mine, if I don't screw it up.

"Easy," Jeff calls, moving closer with the net. "Don't horse him. Just feel him."

I breathe. Steady the line. Let the rhythm come back.

Forgiveness. It's not about overpowering. It's about balance. Giving just enough. Taking just enough.

Jeff scoops. Water sprays. The fight's over. A gleaming salmon rests in the net.

I laugh. Loud. Raw. A little unhinged. My chest heaves. My hands shake.

Jeff grins. "Hell of a fish. And hell of a first catch, Kyle."

I bend down, staring at it. Slick. Shining. Stubborn as hell. The kind of thing that doesn't give itself easy. The kind you have to earn.

Maybe that's forgiveness too.

Hard-fought.

Messy.

~~~

Jeff's taillights fade down the gravel drive, red streaks swallowed by the dark line of trees. The last of the sky bruises purple and gold, that in-between hour where the river smell still clings to my clothes and the taste of beer lingers on my breath.

Headlights swing in from the opposite side as Brian's van rattles over the potholes and crunches into the lot. Tires spit gravel, and a door flings open.

Benjamin hops out before the van's fully stopped, hood half up like a kid sneaking in past curfew.

"Where'd you disappear to today?" I call, digging for my key.

He shifts, guilt written all over him. The kid's about as good at lying as he is at growing a full beard.

"Went out for the day." He fumbles with his key. No eye contact. "Horseback riding."

I narrow my eyes. "With who?"

He exhales, shoulders slumping, then looks at me. "It was just a trail ride."

"Ben…" I drag a hand down my face. "For fuck's sake."

He throws his hands up. "I swear, Kyle. It's not like that. We're just friends. Jesus. She's young, but I'm not stupid."

I take a step closer. "Cannon's going to fucking kill you. Does he know you were there? With her?"

He shakes his head fast. "No. He was at the restaurant, finishing stuff." He sucks in a breath. "Her grandmother knows we went riding." His voice softens. "Just chill. You're acting like you're my dad or something. Which I already have."

Then, quieter but firmer, "And I'm not a child."

That stops me.

He holds my gaze. For the first time, I see the steel under the eager puppy energy. Not me at his age. Not carrying the same weight. Not doomed to the same mistakes.

I press my lips together and exhale. "Yeah. You're right." A pause. "You're not me."

He nods once, relief flickering across his face, and unlocks his door.
~~~

I stay where I am, cold seeping through my jacket, my hand wrapped around the motel key. My thumb brushes my phone, still heavy with Whit's two words.

You will.

Maybe forgiveness is just this. Catch and release.

I caught something today. Felt it thrash and pull, thought if I loosened my grip I'd lose everything. My arms shook. My hands burned.

But I let it go. Watched the silver flash vanish into the current, free to swim upstream.

Benjamin isn't me.

Edie won't have the father I had.

Grace won't raise a child in the shadow of my ghosts.

I tighten my grip on the key and slide it into the lock.

Grace is right. I'm going to be a good dad.

~~~

"How was fishing?" she asks.

The phone is propped on the kitchen counter, and for a second, I almost feel like I'm sitting at the island with her, watching her shift back and forth in pajama shorts and a tank. Her belly is rounder now. Curves different. Gorgeous. Sexier than ever.

"It was good. I actually caught three."

Her eyes widen. "Really? Salmon?"

"Yeah. One Coho, two Dolly Varden."

"Damn. Look at you." She grins, eyes warm.

I chuckle. "How was your day? You're off tomorrow, right?"

"Yes, thank God." She backs away so I can see all of her, smoothing a hand over her belly. Then she spins, tugging at the back of her shorts. "So, this is hilarious. Your kid is stealing all the fabric up front."

She hikes the waistband higher, gathering what's left and wedging it tight between her cheeks. "Which means I spend the whole damn day walking around like this." She turns, her perfect ass filling my screen.
~~~

I bark out a laugh, my body responding even as I try to keep it together. Damn, she's killing me. Her skin. Her warmth.

"I think it's time for maternity clothes," she says, laughing.

"God, I miss you," I say quietly.

Her expression softens as she leans closer. "One more week."

"One more week." I press a finger to my lips, then touch it to the screen. "I love you."

She matches my finger. "I love you too, Kyle."

I slip my phone into my pocket, the screen still warm against my palm.

One more week. The words taste like hope and torture all at once.

Doc's is quiet when I push through the door. The kind of quiet that hums. A ZZ Top lookalike strums an acoustic in the corner, neon buzzes faintly overhead, and the wood-paneled walls soak up decades of stories. The place smells like beer and stale cigarettes, comfort and regret.

Helen glances up from behind the bar and smirks. "Well, if it isn't our visiting hotshot. You look like a man who either had a good day or a near-death experience."

"Both," I say, sliding onto a stool. "Caught three fish. Almost lost my ass to the river."

She doesn't ask. She just sets a pint in front of me with a knowing chuckle. "That's Alaska for you. Gives you something worth holding onto, then tries to drown you with it."

I take a sip, turning the glass slowly, watching the amber catch the light. Her words land deeper than she knows.

Helen props a hip against the bar, eyes flicking to the ink trailing down my arms now that my jacket's off. "Damn. You're a roadmap. Pain, good times, bad decisions. All right there in technicolor." She taps my arm. "That one's got a story."

I glance down. "Bourbon and hot chicken. Not my best friend's finest night."

She bursts out laughing. "I don't even want to know. But I kind of do."

"Tattoos are forever," I say, tipping my glass. "The burn the next morning isn't."

She shakes her head, still smiling. "Good friends like that… you don't let go of them."

She walks away, and I'm left staring at the blank skin on the inside of my arm.

For a second, I'm back at the river. Line screaming. Fish thrashing. My hands burning as I hold on.

"Keep him or release him?" Jeff asked after snapping the picture. I couldn't tell who was breathing harder—me or the fish.

I remember staring down at him, deep red flashing against my hand. His body swelled beneath my grip, gills opening and closing as he fought for air.

"Let him go," I said.

I did. I eased him back into the water. For a second, he stayed there, heavy and alive against my palms. Then the current took him, and he was gone.

I clear my throat and lean toward the bar. "Hey, Helen?"

She looks up. "Yeah?"

"Who's your tattoo artist?"

Chapter 46

LIGHTS OUT

The boards creak as I step out onto Cannon's back porch. Benjamin's already out there, leaning against the rail, the mountain ridges blurred, like the world can't decide if it's day or night.

I lean against the rail next to him, "I didn't mean to… " I start.

He waves me off. "It's fine. I get it." He scrubs his chin like he's trying to will a beard into existence. "This baby face, everyone wants to parent me. Dammit. Why can't I grow facial hair?"

I huff out a laugh, pulling two beers from the cooler next to me. "Seriously though, you've got talent. You're a good guy." I shake my head. "I'm sorry."

His eyes flick to mine, searching, then he nods.

I twist the caps off and hand him one, clinking it to his.

"I'm just glad Thor didn't rip your arms off," I laugh, turning to glance through the window where Cannon's moving around the kitchen.

Benjamin snorts. "Dude, don't say that. Our plane doesn't leave till tomorrow morning."

Before I can answer, a shadow sweeps across the porch. We both look up just as a massive bald eagle cuts across the twilight sky, wings stretched wide, catching the last burn of the sun.

The screen door creaks, and Cannon and Ophelia step out, their voices trailing quiet behind them. All four of us stand there, watching in silence as the bird disappears out over the pasture.

"Not a bad curtain call," Benjamin murmurs.

Cannon lifts his bottle in a lazy salute. "Alaska's good like that."

~~~

The flight feels like it takes years. By the time we touch down, my leg's bouncing so hard the guy next to me looks ready to call a flight attendant.

"You need to pee?" Benjamin leans in and whispers.

"No. I'm just ready to be home."

And then there she is. Standing just past security, belly round, cheeks flushed, hair a little wild like she ran her hands through it a dozen times like she does when she's excited.

They call it pregnancy glow. I call it the hottest damn thing I've ever seen.

She grins, and my chest cracks so wide I half expect my heart to spill onto the airport floor.

We barely make it through baggage claim before my hand is on the small of her back, steering her toward the parking garage. Neither of us talks much. No need. It's all there in the heat between us, in the way she keeps glancing up like she's just as wrecked.

By the time the front door clicks shut behind us, I've already got my mouth on hers.

I press her back against the door, hands cupping the swell of her belly, reverent and starving all at once.

"Jesus, Grace," I rasp against her throat. "You're… God, you're beautiful."

She laughs breathlessly, fumbling at my buttons like she can't get them undone fast enough. I huff a laugh against her mouth, wrestling with her top in return, hands clumsy as hell as I try to work around the curve of her belly. We're all urgency, fingers slipping, hips shifting like neither of us can wait another second.

"You're only saying that because I look like a big, beautiful planet."

I shake my head, kissing her hard, then softer. "No. I'm saying it because it's true. Because you're carrying our whole damn universe right here." My palm slides over her belly, and she shivers.
~~~

Her kiss deepens. She rips the last buttons so fast they skitter across the floor.

"Damn, baby." I chuckle against her lips.

She mutters something about hormones and me being impossible, then drags me toward the bedroom. I don't argue.

We tumble onto the bed, kissing like I've been starved, until she plants a hand on my chest. Her eyes are sharp, even with her lips swollen.

She slides her hand down over my cock, hard and straining against my boxer briefs. I'm seconds from losing it, but the look in her eyes stops me cold.

Not words—just raw, desperate need.

And it nearly undoes me.

I slide down, kissing every inch of her as I go. Her thighs tremble when I spread them, and then I'm gone—devouring, worshiping, making her gasp. Her fingers tangle hard in my hair, clutching like she's drowning as she chases the edge. Her voice breaks, curses spilling out as she moves wildly against my mouth.

The heat of her, the taste of her on my tongue—God, I've missed this. I've craved her.

When she comes, I hold her steady, stay with her until she's shaking. Then she's pulling me back up.

I drag my mouth up her belly, her breasts, the hollow of her throat, and finally kiss her again. She's still trembling when tears spill suddenly from the corners of her eyes.

"Why are you crying?" I thumb them away.

She pulls back just enough to whisper, desperate, "Don't you dare stop. I'm just crying because you're stupid hot right now… and that orgasm about ruined me."

I blink, thrown. Then laugh, rough and breathless. "…Okay. Terrifying and flattering all at once."

Her laugh hitches into another kiss, wetter, needier, and then I line up, ready to sink into her.

Except—the belly presses between us. I pause.

She snorts, breathless. "Yeah, that's not happening. Unless you want to high-five your kid mid-thrust."

I groan into her neck. "Jesus Christ."

We shuffle, clumsy as hell, her swatting me like it's my first time. Pillows, laughter, a few muttered curses, and finally, we find the angle.

I'm inside her, buried deep, and the world tilts. My forehead drops to her shoulder. "Christ. I'm not gonna last. You feel incredible."

We move together, messy and breathless, laughter turning into moans. My hand grips her hip, fingers splayed over her belly.

Then, the kick. Sharp and sudden.

I freeze. "Grace—"

She laughs, clutching me tighter. "Relax. He's clueless. Or cheering you on."

"Do not say that while I'm inside you." I mutter. "Is this okay? I'm not hurting him, am I?"

"No. He—or *she*—is fine." She reaches back, threading her fingers through my hair, "Don't stop.

That's it, I lose myself. Drowning in her, in *us*, in the fire we keep building together, no matter what.

She breaks first, body clenching around me, and I'm right there with her, groaning into her neck like I've been starved my whole damn life.

We collapse in a sweaty heap, both laughing and breathless.

She smirks, hair plastered to her temples. "Congrats. You still got it."

I kiss her belly, whispering, "You and this kid are my whole world."

Her hand slides into my hair, soft for a heartbeat. Then she leans back with that wicked grin.

"So… what are we making for dinner?"

~~~

The door opens, lighter than I remember, and the familiarity settles in when it shuts with a loud thud behind me.

Joe turns sharply from the dish pit. "Welcome back, Chef."

"Thanks, Joe."
~~~

I've never had a dishwasher so committed or happy. This dude needs a promotion, a raise, or both.

Darius rounds the corner just as I'm about to duck into my office.

"Well, well. Look who decided to grace us with his presence. Thought Alaska swallowed you whole, man." He fist-bumps me.

"Nope. Thanks for holding it down. You did great. I appreciate it."

He nods. "Ahh, well, I'm excited for my vacation, brother." He points his clipboard at me. "Payback's a bitch."

I laugh, clapping him on the shoulder. "Fair enough. You've earned it."

I hang my jacket in the office, then head back out just to feel the kitchen under my feet again. The line isn't firing yet. Prep trays stacked high. Knives working steady.

That's when I catch Benjamin's voice, loose with excitement, drifting from prep as he sets up his station.

"...Francis doesn't even flinch, man. Cannon's horse is massive, and she rides like she was born in the saddle. Smart, too. Wants to be an equine vet like her grandfather. She just... gets after life all fearless and shit."

Noah chuckles. The steady chop of his knife doesn't slow. "Dude, you sound seriously into her."

Benjamin snorts, but there's a smile tucked under his voice. "Nah. But she's cool. She's just... different."

I step into view, clapping Noah on the shoulder like I never heard a thing.

"Looks like progress in here, boys."

Noah smirks. "Hey, Chef. Glad to have you back. Sounds like you guys had a great time, according to lover boy here."

Benjamin's eyes snap up to mine. His knife stills.

I chuckle. "Yeah, me and lover boy had a good time. I think we did that town a solid by going." I wink at him, then head up front to check in with Marcus.

I swear I feel Benjamin exhale from six feet away.

~~~

Cassie's face fades off the screen from our FaceTime, but her words stick. *You look really good. Like you're finally where you're supposed to be.*

I lean back in the chair and let it settle, then glance at the paperwork scattered across my desk. Usually I'd blow this off, dump it on Darius or Reggie. But tonight? I stay. Pen in hand. Listening.

The clatter of pans. The hiss of burners. The stand-in for my heartbeat for so damn long.

Every half hour I take a break, lean on the expo line in admiration. Reggie firing tickets. Darius steering this ship like the captain he was born to be. Benjamin is steady at grill. Servers in crisp black glide under dim lights, moving like a choreographed dance. The rhythm is alive. Sharp. And all ours.

Guests take that first bite, and I see it hit. Eyes rolling back. Joy written across their faces. Cassie knew what she was doing with this Fishbowl. It wasn't just for them. It was for us. To witness that first reaction. To know we put that look there.

For years I broke myself in kitchens like this. Bleeding for scraps. Sweating through double shifts. Praying somebody would hand me a blue apron with a leather strap and tell me I mattered.

Now? Jesus. I built this. *We* built this.

The sound doesn't gut me anymore. It fills me with pride, not hunger.

By the time the last pan hits the rack and the lights dim, the place smells like bleach and stainless steel cleaner. I finish the paperwork, push back from the desk, and stand there for one last listen.

The echoes wrap around me. My past. My present. My proof.

For the first time in my career, I'm not chasing something I'll never catch. This isn't just a restaurant. It's a home.

Joe pokes his head into the office. "I'm done here. You staying?"

I close the laptop, stack the papers. "No. All done here, Joe. I'm coming."

He arcs the mop across the tile as I pull my coat from the hook.

"You ever think about moving into the kitchen? Getting out of dish?"
~~~

He chuckles. “I don’t know. Maybe prep. That looks fun.”

I shake my head, half-smiling. The mystery of Joe. How can someone be this content, this happy, without clawing for more?

He dunks the mop one last time, wrings it dry, swipes the last few feet of floor as I push the back door open.

Joe grabs his coat from the table and grins. “Have a great night, Chef.”

I flick the lights off, and Sagi-Shi goes dark.

“You too, Joe.”

Chapter 47

PERMANENT INK

The next morning is quiet—too quiet. I'm still replaying last night at Sagi-Shi in my head, Cassie's words about how I look, how Alaska changed me. It feels like a lifetime ago and just yesterday all at once.

I'm at the counter pouring coffee into my mug when Grace gasps behind me.

"Babe?"

I turn, and my stomach drops to my knees. She's frozen in the middle of the kitchen, green shake lifted like a celebratory toast, standing in a puddle spreading across the tile. Her eyes are wide as saucers.

"Is this really what happens? Because… holy fuck, Kyle!"

Déjà vu slams into me—Cassie behind the glass at Sagi-Shi, water breaking mid-service, the whole restaurant stopping dead like a slow-motion horror film.

But this time it's not her. It's Grace. My Grace. My baby. And the world doesn't stop.

I smile and step forward, steady as I can manage. "Yeah, babe. This is what happens. I've got you."

"I need to clean this up. Oh my God." She stares down blankly at the floor.

I tilt her chin up. "I've got it. Come on. Let's get you cleaned up. I need to call your doctor."

Her brows knit together, her hand sliding to my cheek. "You are amazi—" Her face falters and she doubles over, one hand white-knuckling the counter, the other digging into my forearm.

"Oooh God… *Kyyle*. Jesus hell."

I rub her shoulder and kiss the top of her head. "Just breathe through it, Grace. You can do it."

When the contraction passes, she looks up at me, tears spilling. "Is it too late to change my mind? I don't want to do this." She shakes her head, frantic.

I chuckle, tucking a stray strand behind her ear. "Unfortunately, I think this little bugger wants out. You put up with my ass—you can do anything."

Overnight bags in hand, I call from the front door, "Come on, honey. We need to go. Your contractions are getting closer." She comes out of the bedroom freshly showered and dressed.

She paces, hands in her hair, muttering to herself. Then she stops dead and looks at me, serious as hell.

"Babe, it won't stop. I'm not ruining the seats in your new car. Get me a diaper."

I blink. "A what?"

"A diaper, Kyle. For the baby. I'll shove it in my leggings. Hurry!"

She stands there in the hallway, awkward as hell but deadly serious.

I choke on a laugh even as I sprint for the nursery. "Jesus Christ, Grace."

Sure enough, she jams it into her pants, grabs her bag, and off we go.

The beeping machines, the harsh fluorescent lights, the too-white, zero-thread-count sheets—it's all a blur. We're checked in, Grace already gripping the bed rails like she wants to tear them off, and I'm hovering with no idea what the hell to do with my hands.

Ice chips. I know ice chips.

The nurse comes in mid-contraction, bubbly as hell, like my wife isn't being split in half right in front of me.

"Hi Mrs. Berkley, I'm Nina. I'll be your labor and delivery nurse this evening. How are you doing?" she chirps, jotting something on the whiteboard before glancing at the monitor. "Oh, looks like you're having a pretty good one here."

My wife's face transforms into another woman's. I shit you not, the exorcist just manifested in this hospital room.

"Yeah… pretty fucking good," she spits.

I reach for her hand—clammy, shaking. She looks up at me, eyes wide and brimming with tears, and I've never seen her this afraid.

"This is too much. Make it stop. Make it fucking stop, Kyle."

Nina lays a hand over Grace's, calm as if she's seen this a thousand times. "Grace, Dr. Holland is here. We'll do our best to get you more comfortable, okay?"

Grace nods frantically. "Thank you. Thank you."

The contraction passes, and she collapses back against the pillow.

I hold out the Styrofoam cup, spoon piled high. "Ice chips?"

She throws up a hand. "No."

I set the cup down and lean in to kiss her forehead. "You're doing great," I whisper against her sweat-soaked hair.

"Am I?" she barks, then immediately bursts into tears. "I feel like I'm failing miserably. I forgot all my breathing exercises from that dumb class we took." She throws up her hands, then lets them drop onto the bed with a thud.

I sweep the damp hair back from her face. "Oh, babe. Me too. The next one, I'll help you. Let's do the rainbow one, okay?" I smile.

She nods, whimpering. "Can I have some ice chips?"

I chuckle, lifting the cup again. "Sure."

"Sorry I snapped at you."

"Seriously?" I feed her a spoonful. "Don't even. Nothing you say during this will ever be held against you."

Her lips twitch into a wicked grin as she crunches down on the ice.

"Oh, in that case…" She pauses, dramatic, eyes glinting. "I spent *waaay* too much on that patio set being delivered next week."

Grace's smile falters as another wave hits. She doubles over, clutching the rails, a guttural sound ripping from her throat.

"Rainbow," I coach, trying to sound steady. "In red… out yellow. In green… out—"

Her head snaps toward me, eyes blazing. "It's ROY G BIV, Kyle! ROY G BIV!"

I bite back a laugh even as she crushes my hand. "Right, right—orange, indigo, whatever… Just breathe with me, babe!"

She groans, half-growl, half-scream, and finally the wave ebbs. She collapses back, sweaty and trembling, glaring at me like I just committed a felony.

"You did it," I whisper, forehead to hers.

And then the door bursts open.

"Where's my baby?" Collin bellows, balloons slapping against the doorframe.

Ritchie stumbles in right behind him with two bags and a shit-eating grin. Both of them are wearing matching shirts—block letters across the chest reading, UNCLE DICK #1 and UNCLE DICK #2.

Grace squints at them through sweat and tears. "You've got to be fucking kidding me."

Nurse Nina slips in behind them, her eyebrows climbing into her hairline. "Well. This is… a lot."

They just beam, pointing to their shirts like Vanna White.

Nina clears her throat and turns back to Grace. "I'm going to check your cervix now, see what kind of progress we've made, okay?"

The guys don't move. They just stand there, grinning.

Grace barks, nearly feral. "That's code for she's about to shove her hand inside my vagina. Now GO!"

Collin and Ritchie trip over each other in their rush for the door, balloons squeaking and bouncing against the frame as they disappear into the hall.

~~~

Four hours later, the balloons are gone, the matching Uncle Dick shirts are gone, even the jokes have faded. What's left is the storm.

Contractions come like waves, one crashing into the next until I can't tell where one ends and the other begins. A hundred rainbows breathed through. Clouds I try to paint in her head to distract her.
~~~

Every ounce of strength wrung out of her body, somehow to only find more.

I've watched Grace fight before—fight me, fight for us, but never like this. Never like a woman willing to be split in half just to bring someone else into this crazy world.

I'm watching my wife, my partner, my hero do the impossible.

And then—our son.

The room explodes with motion. Nurses shouting numbers. Dr. Holland's calm voice. Monitors beeping. But all I see is him. Red and wrinkled, his tiny voice wailing, fists clenched like he's ready to take on the world.

My throat closes. My chest cracks. Tears blur my vision.

The nurse settles him on Grace's chest. She collapses back against the pillows, wrecked and sobbing, whispering his name over and over like she can't believe he's real.

And I'm just… gone. My hand on his tiny back, my lips pressed to her damp hair, whispering the only words I have.

"You did it. You both did it. I've got you."

Nina eventually lifts him from Grace's chest and carries him to the scale, her voice steady as she works. "Seven pounds, eleven ounces. Ooh… he's lucky."

I bite the inside of my cheek, fighting the tears.

No. I'm lucky.

When she swaddles him tight and turns to hand him to me, my hands actually shake. I've held knives sharper than thought, carried pans full of fire, walked through kitchens where one wrong step could cost a finger. But this?

This is weight I'll never be strong enough for.

He's so damn small. So warm. Breathing against me like the whole world is already too much.

My chest breaks wide open, but it just made room for how big my heart grew.

I stand beside Grace, her hand warm against my thigh.

"He's amazing," I whisper, looking down at her. "You did amazing, Grace."

I brush a finger over his little pink cheek. His skin is velvet, softer than anything I've ever known. His lips pucker for a moment, settling as if he already knows this is where he belongs.

"Welcome to the world, Henry Wallace Berkley." My voice breaks. "I'm your dad."

~~~

After a little rest, the guests start to trickle in.

I hold off Dumb and Dumber as long as possible. Family comes first—Wally and Becky, Ivan, and her grandmother, all hovering over Grace and Henry with soft smiles and damp eyes. Even Benjamin slips in, shocking me, looking awkward but proud as hell.

And then, finally, there's no holding them back.

The door bangs open like a sitcom entrance, and in they come—Uncle Dick #1 and Uncle Dick #2 in matching T-shirts, arms full of chaos.

"Your favorite uncles are here!" Collin announces, nearly taking out an IV pole with that damn bouquet of balloons.

Ritchie stumbles in behind him, lugging shopping bags like Santa Claus. "We brought gifts!"

Grace groans, covering her face. "Oh god. Not again."

Collin doesn't wait. He rips into the bags himself and holds the first prize up like it's the Stanley Cup: a pair of tiny brown leather driving shoes with brass buckles.

"Custom made. Italian. You're welcome." He flashes that too-white grin.

Before we can process that, he pulls out the kicker—a onesie in bold block letters: NO HABLA.

Grace peeks through her fingers, glaring. "Okay… that's funny. I was expecting worse."

I pinch the bridge of my nose, but I can't stop laughing. "Collin…"

"What?" he protests, deadly serious. "Practical. Fashionable. Bilingual. The kid's set for life."

Ritchie lifts a finger and tosses me a crumpled paper bag. "Sorry. I don't wrap."

I roll my eyes, but when I pull it out, I nearly lose it—a onesie
~~~

that reads STRAIGHT OUTTA THE CRIB, complete with sheer tattoo-print sleeves. My kid has full sleeves.

Holy shit. I low-key love this so much I want to jump up and down.

"You can say it," Ritchie grins. "I win. I fucking win."

I glare at him. "You can't use that language anymore. He's impressionable." I gesture at Henry.

"I'm Uncle Dick." He tugs on his shirt. "I know I'm impressionable. That's the point."

I slap a hand to my forehead.

Collin slides me an envelope.

"What's this?"

He smirks, gives me the upward nod. "Told you we're smart, too."

Ritchie punches my shoulder. "It's his 529. College fund."

I stare at them, shaking my head. "Guys. Seriously? Why? You know I've got a fuck-ton of money, right?"

Collin shrugs. "Yeah. I do okay too. We just wanted to be part of this." He gestures between all of us. "More than silly shirts."

"I'm totally tattooing Henry on my body, though," Ritchie adds. "FYI."

Just then, a soft knock at the door. Caramel strands catch the light. Big eyes lift to mine.

God.

She's the perfect combination of her mother and me. Absolutely stunning, just like Macy was. And I see me, too. My nose. My stupid cowlick.

I'm sorry.

My throat tightens.

"Hey, Edie." I wave her in.

"Is this okay timing?" she asks, eyes flicking around the room, shy.

"Yes. It's perfect. Come in," Grace says with a smile, one arm outstretched, the other cradling Henry.

"Edie," I say, gesturing toward the guys, "these are my friends Collin and Ritchie."

"It's so nice to finally meet you," Collin says.

"Wow." Ritchie shakes his head, taking her hand. "You're the spitting image of your mom."

Her breath hitches. "You knew my mom?"

He nods. "Yeah. I worked with her. With Kyle. She was sweet… and beautiful." He glances at me, then back to Edie. "You're in good hands with this guy. He's a good dude. A good dad."

He gives her hand a soft pat before letting go.

"It's nice to meet you guys," she says, then looks past me toward Grace and Henry, eyes wide. "So… is this him?"

Her smile nearly undoes me.

"We're gonna head out, man," Collin says, clapping me on the shoulder.

I nod, but my attention is already fixed on Edie—my daughter, taking her first step toward my son.

Her brother.

Behind me, there's a soft click, and then Grace is handing Henry over.

"Oh my gosh. He's perfect," Edie whispers, staring at him in awe.

I hover, watching her cradle him. "Right? He's stupid cute." I smooth the blanket around his face. "Look at the dimple on his chin."

"Aww…" she breathes.

Then her eyes trail—from Henry's dimpled chin to the ink on my arm. Her finger shifts, landing against my skin.

"Kyle?" she gasps. "What…?"

"Yeah." I turn my arm so she can see it fully—the silver and red Coho salmon, her name flowing across it in script. "I got it in Alaska. I hope that's okay."

Her eyes glisten. She nods, biting her lip. "Yeah. It's… really sweet."

I look at her. At Henry in her arms. At the ink on my skin.

The Coho I fought like hell to catch and release in Alaska—the moment I finally let go of everything I'd been carrying.

But this? Her. Them.

This is what I'll never release.

Edie's name etched across that fish, carved into me permanently. A reminder that forgiveness freed me—but love is what fills me.

Chapter 48

I'M IN

The sun is out, and the bay is glittering like a million tiny diamonds, and our deck in Sausalito is alive with noise. Glasses clink. Wally tops off wine, and Becky fusses at the outdoor kitchen like she's still hosting Sunday dinners back in Oregon. Grace's laugh carries across the yard as Henry gets passed around like a hot potato from one set of arms to another.

It's family. Loud and messy and perfect.

Inside, it's just me and Edie in the kitchen. The chaos hums through the open doors, but here it's quiet enough to hear the scrape of metal on glass and the soft clatter of measuring cups. She's perched up on the counter, barefoot and ankles crossed, champagne flute in hand, grinning at me like she can't quite believe we're doing this.

The avocado-green recipe box sits between us. The springform pan with the janky latch is already buttered. The air smells faintly of vanilla.

"This is it?" she teases, flipping the card between her fingers. "The famous cheesecake, huh?"

"This is it," I say, sliding the bowl toward her. My voice cracks, but I cover it with a smile.

She laughs, takes another sip of champagne.

"Come down from there. You're helping me." I empty my glass and reach for the bottle. "I need emotional support." I fill both our glasses again.

She hops down, grinning. “I know it’s my twenty-first today, but don’t get me wasted.”

“Impossible with that spread.” I smirk toward the deck. “Just keep eating.”

“So, you never made it again, huh?” she asks, eyeing the beat-up card.

“Nope. Not since his birthday.” I glance over my shoulder at Whit out on the deck, Henry tucked into his arms. “We need five eggs separated.”

She gets to work while I measure out sugar.

“What was her name?”

I pause, then let it out as I pour sugar into the bowl. “Gianna.” The name rolls off my tongue like it never left. Like *she* never left.

“That’s so pretty, Kyle.”

“Yeah. And she was beautiful. Just like your mom.” I lean against the counter, voice low. “She was really special to me, Edie. Both of them.”

She nods, tosses the shells into the sink, then looks back at me.

“Can I ask you something?” she glances over at me.

“Shoot.”

She twists the whisk handle nervously, eyes down before lifting them to mine. “Can I call you Dad?” Her hand shoots up, stammering. “I mean, if it’s not comfortable… I get it. It’s just, we both don’t have moms and I…”

I reach across the counter, covering her shaking hand with mine.

“Edie.” I wait until she meets my eyes. “I would love it. I would love for you to call me Dad.” My chest aches as I press my hand over my heart. “I’m honored to be your dad.”

And then—the arms. The hug from her tippy toes. The unexpected that undid me completely.

Finally, we untangle, wiping at our cheeks.

“I think I got your softy, emotional gene too,” she laughs.

“What? I’m not a softy.” I narrow my eyes.

“Whatever… *Dad.*” She snorts.

Dad.

The word hits me square in the chest, ricochets through every scar I've ever carried, and settles somewhere deep I didn't know was still empty.

She unknowingly scans the recipe card, clearing her throat. "Alright, we need sixteen ounces of ricotta cheese."

The word *ricotta* lands like a stone in my chest.

My mom, Gianna left for that one ingredient that day and never came back.

For years, I couldn't even look at it on a shelf without feeling hollow. But here, now—my daughter is reading it off a stained, dog chewed card, smiling at me, waiting for me to hand it to her like it's nothing more than cheese.

My throat tightens, but my hands are steady.

"I'll grab it," I tell her softly.

I can do this. With my *daughter* by my side.

We slide the cheesecake into the oven, side by side, and I reach to set the timer. My hand lingers a second too long.

The last time, I didn't set it.

It burned. She left.

Ricotta.

I swallow the lump in my throat as I press the button and hear the beep. The timer's set. The cheesecake is safe, and so am I.

Edie exhales like she knew, like she felt the weight of it too as we stare through the oven door.

"Happy birthday, Edie." I whisper, wrapping my arm across her shoulder.

She reaches forward and pours us each another glass, bubbles fizzing high. "Thanks, Dad." She smiles, clinking hers to mine and lifting her glass, eyes shining.

The word lands solid in my chest, anchoring me in a way nothing else ever has. My grown daughter. All those years I missed, all the moments I can't get back—gone. But what I have now? What's ahead? I'm so damn grateful.

Grateful for the chance to show up. To be here. To be hers.

We step out onto the deck, and for a second, I just… stop.

The bay is glowing gold, the sky bleeding into soft pinks and yellows, and the whole place hums with noise. Laughter spills over the rail, everyone is smiling, and music plays low under it all.

Good God, Becky and Grace went all out. Edie's twenty-first looks like a catered gala, only better. Platters stacked with bruschetta and olives, salads bursting with color, trays of antipasti, and bowls of fruit so bright they look photoshopped. Even the dessert table, a space for the cheesecake waiting for its spotlight, looks like something out of a *Martha Stewart's Living* magazine.

And all these people are here for her.

For my daughter.

For this, her new family.

My heart kicks hard in my chest, but it's not fear this time. It's joy, threaded through every sound, every smell, every damn detail of this messy, perfect life I somehow get to call mine.

"Come here, big boy." I reach for Henry, taking him from Grace. His gummy smile wide, his big gray eyes bright, and his sticky fingers tangled in her long hair.

"Go to Daddy." She passes him to me. "Lord, he's getting heavy."

"Yes, he is. My big boy." I twist him back and forth as he chews on his fist like it's the amuse-bouche before the main course.

"Careful, he'll puke on you. He just ate," Grace warns.

I grin down at Henry gnawing his hand. "Wouldn't be the first time."

And then I hear it—Cassie's laugh cutting through the crowd, warm and unmistakable.

I glance up just in time to see her weaving across the lawn, holding hands with shy little Jonah and Stephen at her side, his hand resting on the back of the girl I used to hold just like this. Dark hair flowing down her back. Those big brown eyes. The first child who ever weaseled her way into my heart with a single look, a single smile.

Cora.

The sight of her damn near unravels me. So grown. So gorgeous.

Cassie spots me and grins wide, practically racing the rest of the way. She drops an oversized pink gift bag at her feet, her hands already reaching out, fingers wiggling. "Well, look at you. Domestic bliss looks good on you. Give him to me."

I hand Henry over, and he squeals in delight—drool stringing between us like a translucent thread.

Stephen shakes my hand, then ruffles Henry's blond fuzz. "Not bad, man. Not bad at all."

"Thanks. I can cook and make babies." I raise a brow. "Supposedly, women dig that stuff."

Cora squishes Henry's fat leg as Cassie nuzzles his neck, making him coo louder and drool straight into her hair.

"He's getting so big, Uncle Kyle," Cora beams, and my chest squeezes tight. I love that she hasn't grown out of calling me that.

I glance down at Jonah, gripping Stephen's hand in a death grip, peeking shyly from behind his leg.

I crouch down. "Hey, Jonah. Remember me? I'm Kyle." I smile. "Thanks for coming to our party, buddy."

"Hey, Jonah," Cora chimes in, stepping in to save him. "Want to come say hi to Edie? Get some fruit?" She holds out her hand.

"Okay." He slips his hand into hers, and off they go.

Stephen rakes a hand through his hair and exhales. "My Velcro kid."

"Hey," I tap his shoulder, "we've got the 'kid we didn't know we had' in common." I nod toward Edie with Cora and Jonah.

He tips his head back. "Ahh. Are there meetings for that? A support group? Do we drink at them? At least talk about whiskey?"

Cassie laughs, bouncing Henry on her hip. "Stephen, that's you at the restaurant, babe. Should we start calling it your support group now?"

"They made it!" Grace exclaims, hugging everyone.

"Thank you for my party favor." Cassie smiles down at Henry.

"Oh, you'll be bringing him back at three a.m.—trust me."

Grace grins, tickling his cheek.

Cassie pulls a face. "Actually, how about right now?" She starts to hand him back to me. "He's rank, dude."

I lift him from her arms, his smile wide. "How do you smile when your pants are full of shit? That feel good, buddy? All warm and squishy?" I shake my head. "You're nasty."

I head through the house. Henry is warm against my chest, drool soaking through my shirt. I pause in the kitchen and crouch to peek through the oven window. The cheesecake is steady, timer ticking down. No smoke this time.

Emotions twist inside me, pride and sadness tangled together.

Mom, you see this?

In the nursery, I lay Henry down to change him. My voice jumps up an octave, almost boyish.

"Ewww… you are gross, my man." I grin as I clean him up, fastening a fresh diaper. "You're a lady killer out there, yes you are. They're eating you up." I kiss his belly and he kicks, cooing with delight.

I'm snapping his outfit closed and wiping my hands on a burp cloth when I hear shuffling behind me.

It's Whit, leaning in the doorway.

For a moment, we just stand there, Henry gnawing his toes, grinning with his brand-new pants.

"You're such a good dad," Whit says, finally.

I let out a long sigh as I pick Henry up. "Thanks," I manage.

His eyes stay fixed on Henry. "Better than me. That boy's lucky."

The words gut me. I nod, pressing a kiss to Henry's head. "No. I'm lucky. Both my kids… and Grace. They're my world. Nothing else matters. They changed me."

Whit swallows, eyes glistening. "She's proud, Kyle. I know she is."

The timer blares from the kitchen, splitting the air.

"Here." I hold Henry out to him. "Can you take him back out? I need to get the cheesecake."

He hesitates, then he pulls Henry into his arms. Whit's always been a wall of a man, power radiating off him, but with Henry nestled there, he looks almost fragile. Like this tiny boy has undone everything iron in him.

We walk out into the kitchen, Whit cradling Henry against his chest. He stops short just as I pull the cheesecake from the oven and set it on the cooling rack in the center of the island.

My hands grip the counter as I just… *stare.*

It's perfect. Golden. Smooth. Not a single crack.

Gianna's Italian cheesecake. The one unfinished thing, sitting whole and real in front of me.

For a second I can't breathe, thinking, I finally did it.

When I lift my head, I see Whit watching me.

No words. Just silence between us. But it's enough. The last thread between us, stitched closed.

And then—Edie breezes in, her voice bright and oblivious. "Uncle Dick #1 just got here. He has a girl with him. I always thought he was gay." She reaches for another bottle of champagne like she didn't just toss a glitter grenade into the room.

She stops mid-step, eyes widening at the counter. "Oh, sweet! It's done."

She hurries over, leaning across the island, grinning at the impossible.

I glance back, but Whit is gone.

"Yeah," I whisper, looking at the cheesecake, then at her. "We did good."

By the time Edie and I step back onto the deck, the sun's slipping low, the bay burnished gold. The long table is crowded—platters raided, glasses filled and refilled, laughter bouncing like the waves below.

Becky and Grace really did it. Bowls scraped nearly clean, stacks of empty wine bottles lined up like trophies. Ritchie's booming laugh carries from the far end where he's holding court with his mystery date, Uncle Dick shirt stretched proudly across his chest. Edie wasn't kidding—he looks smug as hell.

Henry's making the rounds again, being passed from lap to lap, drool and coos and gummy smiles melting every single person who touches him.

I take a seat. There's a plate in front of me that I don't even need because the fullness in my chest could feed me for a lifetime.

Henry goes down not long after dinner, full belly and worn out from being adored by half the crowd. The quiet feels strange without him, but then Grace emerges from the kitchen proudly carrying the cheesecake like it's a crown jewel.

Dessert hour.

Cups of coffee steam across the table, spoons clink against saucers, laughter softens into that loose, golden hum I've always loved.

And then Ivan stands, a glass of rakija raised high, the bottle glinting on the table in the setting sun.

He clears his throat, switching to Croatian. The words roll rich and proud, melodic in a way that makes even the kids quiet down.

Grace translates softly at my side, smiling. "He says happy twenty-first birthday, Edie. May your days be long, your family close, and your heart always full."

Glasses clink. Laughter rises again. And in the center of it all, Edie beams, cheeks flushed, cheesecake in front of her.

I mouth silently across the table, *Happy birthday, baby.*

She mouths back, *Thank you, Dad.*

Grace leans into me, her breath warm at my ear. "Did Edie just call you Dad?"

I nod, throat too tight for words.

Her hand finds my thigh under the table, squeezes once. Firm and certain.

The house has gone soft.

From the kitchen, I can hear Becky and Grace laughing as they wash dishes, glasses clinking as they stack them to dry. Edie's passed out in the guest room, her hair spilled across the pillow like she never outgrew being my kid. Ritchie and Ivan tried to keep pace with her, but rakija won. Not even Uncle Dick was a match for the birthday girl.

And me? I'm here. Standing over the crib in the dark. The only light is a soft glow from the nightlight. Henry's chest rises and falls in steady little waves, cheeks still flushed from the day, his tiny fist curled near his mouth.

Perfect.

A weight settles on my shoulder. Heavy. Familiar.

I don't need to turn to know.

Wally.

"So, Wallace, huh?" he whispers. "Not your dad or Ivan?"

"No." I glance at him, then back down at my son. "We wanted to name him after you because you never demanded anything back. You were always my constant. And that's what I want to be for Henry." I exhale. "His constant."

Wally swallows hard, nods once. His eyes glisten in the dim light, but he doesn't say another word. Just claps a hand on my shoulder and squeezes.

~~~

The deck is quiet now, the house settling behind us. Grace curls into my side, cozy sweater against my arm, the baby monitor glowing soft on the table between our half-empty wine glasses. The bay stretches out black and endless, city lights winking like a sea of stars. A cool breeze brushes past, and I pull her closer.

This is our dream. Not Rocco living to a hundred, but pretty damn close.

Once, I used to stand outside places like this, arms crossed over my knife roll, staring through the glass at people who belonged. Hungry. Hollow. Always on the outside.

But not anymore.

I'm not watching through the window, dreaming of my place, wondering about my worth. I'm here. Living *inside* the glow.

I'm home.
~~~

Acknowledgments

This book exists because you, the reader, kept asking for his story. You trusted me with your patience, your enthusiasm, and your hearts, with inbox messages that simply said, When is Kyle getting his book? You make the long hours worth it every single time. Thank you for believing he deserved it, and for turning every page.

I have never enjoyed being in a character's head as much as I did Kyle Berkley's. What a joy. What an honor.

To G—Thank you for listening, for driving, and for not judging when I write and don't shower for three days. Thank you for always reminding me why I write in the first place.

This book, and this dream, exist because you never let me give up. I dream, and you make it real.

Women often ask if the men I write about even exist in real life. Yes.

And he's mine.

To my alpha and beta readers (including Mom), thank you for your sharp eyes, honest feedback, and encouragement when the work got hard. It truly takes a village to finish a book, and I'm grateful for mine.

You make me laugh when I need it most. I live for the memes. I live for our friendship. You give me more material than you will ever know.

To my dream team—

Sarah Waterman (Editor): Girl. You. Get. Me. And thank you for it.

Lorna Reid (Formatting Designer): thank you for always untangling my mess, making it beautiful, and pulling me back from the edge when I go completely cuckoo for Cocoa Puffs. You are a rock.

To Libby: without you, my graphics would have no smoke and fire, and I'd have lost my mind. Thank you for everything.

Evgeniia Gurcheva (Cover Designer): the way you see my vision and bring it to life is pure magic. You are a joy to work with, every single time.

To my friends and family I disappeared on while writing this book—damn, you're patient. And I love you for it.

And finally, to Kyle, a character who grew up across these books and in my mind. I'm protective, and damn it, I'm proud.

Don't get too comfortable, my friend. We're not done yet.

Forever grateful, **Tempest Wick xo**

Loved the Story?

A quick review makes a world of difference.

Scan to leave a review on Goodreads

Your words matter. Thank you for keeping the fire going.

Want to stay in touch?

I love hearing from readers.
Facebook: Tempest Wick – Author
Instagram: @tempestwickromance
YouTube: www.youtube.com/@ChapterThreeAdventures

www.ingramcontent.com/pod-product-compliance
Lightning Source LLC
LaVergne TN
LVHW090548110826
845146LV00001B/65

* 9 7 9 8 2 1 8 9 1 0 5 1 8 *